FIRES OF EDEN

DAN SIMMONS

FIRES OF EDEN

G. P. PUTNAM'S SONS
NEW YORK

G. P. Putnam's Sons
Publishers Since 1838
200 Madison Avenue
New York, NY 10016

Book design by H. Roberts

Library of Congress Cataloging-in-Publication Data
Simmons, Dan.
     Fires of Eden / Dan Simmons.
         p.   cm.
     ISBN 0-399-13922-2
     I. Title.
   PS3569.I47292P45   1992
   813'.54—dc20   94-19464   CIP

Printed in the United States of America
1   2   3   4   5   6   7   8   9   10

This book is printed on acid-free paper.
∞

To Robert Bloch,
who taught us that horror is just one curious component
in the broader celebration of life, love, and laughter

ACKNOWLEDGMENTS

I would like to thank Tara Ann Forbis for her proofreading help and insightful comments. I would also like to thank the friendly people at the Mauna Kea Beach Resort, the Kona Village Resort, the Hotel Hana Maui, and the Hawaii Volcanoes National Park. Researching this book was rough work, but it was worth every sun-drenched, spray-splashed, rainbow-lit moment.

Sources that were helpful to me and that might be of interest to the reader seeking Hawaiian lore include: Mark Twain's twenty-five "Letters from the Sandwich Islands" (1866) for the *Sacramento Union,* later reworked in *Roughing It* (1872); Victorian traveler Isabella L. Bird's *Six Months Among the Palm Groves, Coral Reefs and Volcanoes of the Sandwich Islands* (1890); Pamela Frierson's fascinating *The Burning Island: A Journey Through Myth and History in Volcano Country, Hawai'i* (1991); *The Legends and Myths of Hawai'i* by His Hawaiian Majesty Kalakaua (1888); and *Myths and Legends of Hawaii: Ancient Lore Retold by W. D. Westervelt* (1913). There are many more wonderful books about Hawaii and the goddess Pele, but these books give the interested reader a good head start.

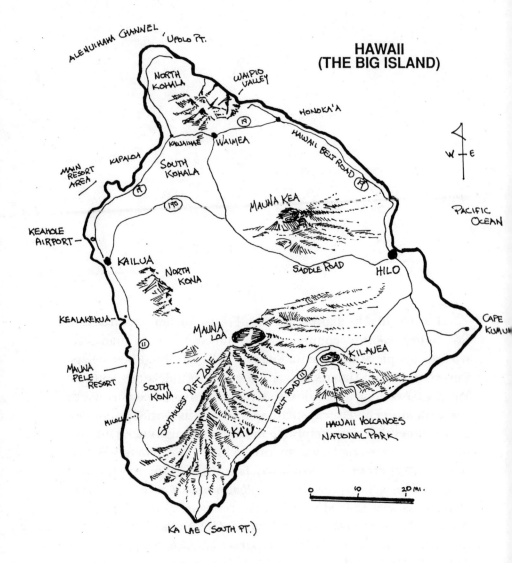

HAWAII
(THE BIG ISLAND)

ONE

E Pele e! The milky way turns.
E Pele e! The night changes.
E Pele e! The red glow is on the island.
E Pele e! The red dawn breaks.
E Pele e! Shadows are cast by the sunlight.
E Pele e! The sound of roaring is in your crater.
E Pele e! The uhi-uha is in your crater.
E Pele e! Awake, arise, return.
   —Hulihia ke au ("The current is turning")

At first only the wind is screaming.

The westerly wind has blown unimpeded across four thousand miles of empty ocean, encountering nothing but white-capped waves and the occasional off-course seagull before striking up against the black-lava cliffs and gargoyle-shaped lava boulders that line the almost empty southwest coast of the Big Island of Hawaii. But having reached this obstacle, the wind now screams and howls between black rocks, the sound of it all but drowning out the constant crash of surf against the cliffs and the rustling of agitated fronds in the artificial oasis of palm trees within the jumble of black lava.

There are two types of lava on these islands and their Hawaiian names describe them well: *pahoehoe* is usually older, always smoother, and has hardened to a smoothly billowed or mildly braided surface; *a'a* is new and jagged, its edges knife-sharp, its forms molded into grotesque towers and tumbled gargoyle figures. Along this stretch of South Kona coast, the *pahoehoe* runs in great, gray rivers from the volcanoes to the sea, but it is the sea cliffs and broad fields of *a'a* which guard the ninety-five miles of western coastline like tier upon tier of razor-edged warriors frozen into black stone.

And now the wind screams through these labyrinths of sharp stone, whistling through gaps in the pillars of *a'a* and howling through fissures of ancient gas vents and down the open throats of empty lava tubes. Night comes on as the wind rises. Twilight has crept from the coastal *a'a* fields all the way to the summit of Mauna Loa, two and a half miles above sea level. Most of the great shield volcano rises as a black mass blotting out sky to the north and west. Thirty miles away, above the darkening caldera, low clouds of volcanic ash gleam orange from unseen eruptions.

"So what then, Marty? You gonna take the stroke penalty or what?"

The three figures are barely distinguishable in the dying light, their voices almost lost to the shrieking wind. The Robert Trent Jones, Jr.–designed golf course is a narrow, sinuous path of grass fairways and carpet-smooth greens snaking its way through miles of tumbled, black *a'a*. The few palm trees along the fairways are swaying and rustling in the wind. The three men are the only ones on the course. It is full dark now, and the lights of the Mauna Pele Resort seem far away from the fifteenth fairway, where the three figures huddle to be heard over the sound of wind and surf. Each man has driven his own golf cart, and the three carts also seem huddled together from the howling wind.

"I tell you it's in them goddamn rocks," says Tommy Petressio. The orange volcano glow casts a florid light on the short man's bare arms and sunburned face. Petressio is wearing clashing yellow and red-plaid double-knit golf wear. A cap is pulled low over his sharp-featured face and he is chomping on a thick, unlit cigar.

"It ain't in the goddamn rocks," says Marty DeVries. He rubs his jowls and half a dozen rings scrape against stubble there.

"Well it's not on the fucking *grass*," whines Nick Agajanian. Nick has worn a lime-green shirt that strains against his massive belly, and the wide legs of his plaid shorts end six inches above his pale, knobby knees. He is wearing high black socks. "We'd see it if it was in the fucking *grass*," Nick adds. "And there ain't no fucking rough here, just this fucking grass and this fucking rock here that looks like petrified sheep shit."

"Where'd you ever see sheep shit?" says Tommy, turning in the gloom and leaning on his wood driver.

"I seen lots of things I don't usually talk about," whines Nick.

"Yeah," says Tommy, "you probably stepped in sheep shit when you was a kid out trying to fuck the sheep." He cups his hand and strikes a match, trying for the fifth time to light his cigar. The wind blows out the match in a second. "Shit."

"Shut up, you two," says Marty DeVries. "Look for my ball."

"Your ball's in the sheep-shit rock," says Tommy around his cigar. "And it was your fucking idea to come to this fucked-up resort." The three are all in their early fifties, are all sales managers from car dealerships in the Newark area and have taken their golf vacations together for years, sometimes bringing their wives along, sometimes bringing their current girlfriends, but most frequently just going with each other.

"Yeah," whines Nick, "what kind of place is this anyhow, what with all the empty rooms and the fucking volcano and everything?"

Marty steps into the edge of the endless *a'a* field, poking between the tall rocks with his 5-iron. "Whattaya talkin' about, why'd we come here?" he rasps. "This is the newest fucking resort in fucking Hawaii. It's Trumbo's big enchilada . . .."

"Yeah," laughs Tommy, "and look at all the good it's done for the Big T."

"Fuck that," says Marty DeVries. "Come help me find my ball." He steps between two black *a'a* boulders the size of upended Volkswagens. The soil there is mostly sand.

"Aww, nah," says Nick. "Take the fucking stroke penalty, Marty. It's gettin' *dark*. I can't see my fucking hand in front of my face." He shouts the last part to be heard over the wind and surf as Marty steps deeper into the rock maze. The fifteenth fairway runs along the cliffs south of the palm oasis that is the main part of the resort, and waves are crashing high not forty feet from where the men stand.

"Hey, there's like a trail in here that goes down toward the water," calls Marty DeVries. "I think I see my . . . no, shit, just some seagull feather or something."

"Come on out and take the fucking penalty," yells Tommy. "Nick and me ain't coming in there. Those rocks are as sharp as a motherfucker."

"Yeah," yells Nick Agajanian toward the tumble of black clinkers. Now even Marty's yellow golf cap has disappeared from sight.

"Stupid shit can't hear us," says Tommy.

"Stupid shit's gonna get us lost out here," whines Nick. The wind grabs at his cap and he scuttles across the fairway after it, finally running it down when it blows up against one of the golf carts.

Tommy Petressio makes a face. "You can't get lost on a fuck-ing *golf course*."

Nick returns, clutching his hat and a 6-iron. "You could sure as hell get lost in that"—he waves the handle of his club at the *a'a* field and the crashing surf—"in that sheep-shit rock."

Tommy tries to light his cigar again. The wind blows it out. "Shit."

"I ain't going in there," says Nick. "Probably break my fuck-ing leg."

"Probably get bit by a snake."

Nick takes a step back from the heaps of black cinders. "There aren't any snakes in Hawaii. Are there?"

Tommy makes a gesture. "Just them boa constrictors. And cobras . . . shitloads of cobras."

"Bullshit." Nick's voice is uncertain.

"Didn't you see them little weasel-like animals in the flowers this afternoon? What Marty said was mongeese?"

"Yeah?" Nick glances over his shoulder. The last of the twi-light has faded to night and stars are visible far out over the ocean. The lights of the resort seem very far away. The shoreline to the south is devoid of lights. The volcano glow is dim to the northwest. "So?"

"You know what a mongoose eats?"

"Berries and shit?"

Tommy shakes his head. "Snakes. Cobras, mostly."

"Get the fuck outta here," says Nick, but then stops himself. "Wait a minute. I think I seen something about that on cable. Those weasels . . ."

"Mongeese."

"Whatever. Them mongeese in India. Like, tourists pay to see them eat cobras on the street corners and shit."

Tommy nods judiciously. "The snake problem's so bad here that Trumbo and the other developers had to import the mongeese by the thousand. Otherwise, you wake up in your bed with a boa constrictor wrapped around your ankles and a cobra bitin' into your dick."

"You're so full of shit," says Nick, but he has taken a step toward his golf cart.

Tommy shakes his head and rams his cigar into his shirt pocket. "This is really stupid. It's too dark to finish. If we'd gone to Miami like we usually done, we'd be on a all-night lighted course. Instead we're out here in the middle of . . ." He waves his hand dismissively at the lava fields and black arc of volcano in the distance.

"Middle of fucking snake city," says Nick, settling into his cart and sheathing his 6-iron. "I say we say fuck it and drive back to the hotel and find a bar."

"I say right on," agrees Tommy, walking toward his own cart. "If Marty ain't back by morning, we'll think about tellin' somebody."

The screams start then.

Marty DeVries had followed what had appeared to be a path between the *a'a* boulders, a winding of sand and scrub grass between the heaps of clinkers. He was sure that his ball had come down this way and if he could just find it lying on the fucking sand, he could chip it out onto the fairway and save some face in this fucking game. Hell, even if it *wasn't* lying on the sand, he could set it there and chip it out. Hell, he didn't have to chip it at all, just rear back and let it fly . . . Nick and Tommy were too wussy to follow him down here, so all they'd see was this perfect chip shot come flying out of the lava shit and plop right onto the middle of the fairway, setting up an easy iron shot to the green. Marty used to have a pretty good arm when he pitched for Legion ball in Newark.

Hell, now that Marty thought about it, he didn't have to find the goddamn thing at all. He reached into his pocket and took out a Wilson Pro-Sport, the same number he'd been playing. Then he turned around to throw it out onto the course.

Which way was the fucking course?

The heaps of *a'a* cinders and heaped boulders had gotten him all mixed up. He could see stars overhead. The "path" that he had followed downhill wasn't so clear now—there were sand paths going every which way. Actually, the place was a goddamn maze.

"Hey!" shouted Marty. When Tommy or Nick answered, he'd pitch the ball in that direction.

No one answered.

"Hey, quit fuckin' around, you dipshits." Marty realized that he was closer to the sea cliffs here; the crash of surf was much louder. Those idiots probably couldn't hear him because of the stupid wind and the stupid waves crashing on the stupid rock. Marty wished they'd gone to Miami like they usually did. "Hey!" he shouted again, his voice sounding tiny even to himself. The heaps of cinder stone here rose twelve feet or higher, the black pumice lighted by that goddamn orange glow from the volcano. The travel agent had told Marty and them about the active volcano, but she'd said the thing was way the hell around the south side of the island, that there was no danger at all from it. She'd said that people were flocking to the Big Island because of the little eruption—that they showed up in droves every time there was any activity. She'd said that Hawaiian volcanoes never hurt anybody, they were just pretty fireworks.

So how come Trumbo's goddamn Mauna Pele resort is so goddamn empty, thought Marty, launching the thought in the direction of the travel agent. He hoped. "Hey!" he shouted again.

There was a sound to his left. Toward the sea cliffs. It sounded like a moan.

"Aw, you dumb shits," said Marty under his breath. One or both of the two clowns had come down into the sheep-shit lava to find him and had gotten hurt. Probably twisted an ankle or broken a leg. Marty hoped it was Nick; he preferred to play with Tommy and it would be a pain to spend the rest of the vacation waiting for Nick to duff his way out of sand traps.

The moan came again, so soft that the sound of it could be heard *beneath* the surf and wind noise.

"I'm coming," shouted Marty, and began picking his way down the slight incline between the lava heaps. He put the ball back in his pocket and used the 5-iron as a sort of walking stick.

It took longer than he thought it would. Whichever one of the idiots had come in here to get hurt, he'd really gotten lost. Marty only hoped he wouldn't have to carry the stupid shit out.

The moan came again, ending on a sort of sibilant sigh.

What if it ain't Nick or Tommy? he thought suddenly. The thought of dragging some poor schmuck he didn't know out of this rock did not appeal to Marty. He'd come to this fucking island to play golf, not be a Good Samaritan. If it was some goddamn local or something, he'd tell the guy to take it easy and head back to the hotel bar. The goddamn resort was almost empty, but they'd have somebody up there whose job it was to come out and get injured schmucks.

The hissing moan came again.

"Almost there," grunted Marty. He could feel the sea spray in the air now. The cliffs must be around here somewhere; low cliffs, only twenty feet or so to the water. He'd better watch it. The stars were out overhead. All he needed to make this stupid vacation a perfect fuck-up was to pitch headfirst off a cliff into the fucking Pacific Ocean. "Coming!" he wheezed as the moan came again. It was just around this heap of black rock.

Marty came into a slight opening in the *a'a* and stopped on the sand. There was a body lying there. It wasn't Nick or Tommy. And it was a *body*, not a live guy. Marty had seen dead bodies before, and this one was dead. Whoever'd been moaning, it wasn't this schmuck.

The form was almost naked, with only a short, wet cloth of some sort wrapped around its middle. Marty stepped closer and saw that it was a man—short, stocky, the calf muscles well defined as if he were a runner or something. It looked like he'd been lying around for some time: the skin was rubbery white, almost flaking with decomposition, and the guy's fingers looked like white grubs that would start wiggling back into the sand at any second. A couple of other ways that Marty could tell that the guy hadn't been the one to do the moaning: the man's long hair was matted with seaweed, his eyelids were up and one eye reflected starlight like glass while the other was completely gone, and there was a fucking baby crab or something crawling out of the guy's open mouth.

Marty fought off the surge of nausea and took a step closer, holding his 5-iron out ahead of him. He could smell the guy now, a sickeningly sweet mixture of ocean smell and rot. The waves must have washed him up this high, because the corpse was lying on some of those short, sharp lava rocks that looked like little stalactites or stalagmites or whatever the hell they were.

He touched the corpse with the head of his 5-iron and the body shifted slightly, rolling heavily as if sloshing with seawater.

"Jesus," whispered Marty. The corpse was some sort of hunchback dwarf. Unless his spine had been all smashed and twisted like this by being beat up against the rocks after he'd died, the guy'd had a hump like fucking Quasimodo.

And there was some crazy tattoo on the hump.

Marty leaned closer, bracing himself with his 5-iron, trying not to let the smell make him sick.

There was a wild tattoo on the hump all right—an image of a shark's mouth that spread across the wide bulge between the corpse's shoulder blades and disappeared under the arms. It was really weird, almost three-dimensional: whoever had done it had used jet-black ink for the open shark's mouth and had filled in the teeth with white.

Some native guy, thought Marty. He'd go back with Nick and Tommy, have a couple of Scotches, and then tell the hotel people that some native had fallen out of his outrigger or whatever. He'd tell them there was no hurry, that the guy wasn't going nowhere.

Marty stood up and prodded the hump with the head of his 5-iron, sliding the metal to the black ink of the mouth.

The head of the club slid into a cavity.

"Shit!" said Marty, and jerked his club back. Not fast enough—the shark's mouth snapped shut on the 5-iron. Marty could hear the clack of sharp teeth on graphite.

He made the mistake of wasting a precious few seconds tugging at his club—it had been a present from Shirley, his current squeeze—but then he realized what he was doing, felt himself losing the tug-of-war, and he let go of the handle of the 5-iron as if it were a hot poker and turned to run.

Marty had not taken three steps before movement in the rocks stopped him. "Tommy?" he whispered. "Nick?" Even as he spoke, he saw that it was not Tommy or Nick.

The shapes slid into the opening between the *a'a*.

I'm not gonna scream, thought Marty, feeling his courage leak away with the urine that ran down his pant leg. *I'm not gonna scream. This ain't real. It's some stupid joke like that time that Tommy had the hooker dress up like a cop at my birthday party. I ain't gonna scream.* He took a careful step back, his mouth open, breath rasping in his throat.

Shark's teeth clamped onto his ankle.

Marty began to scream.

Tommy and Nick have just reached the golf carts when the screams begin. Both men stop and listen. The wind noise is so loud, the surf sound so great, that the screams must be something to be heard over all that racket.

Tommy turns toward Nick. "Probably broke his fucking leg."

Nick is sitting in the golf cart, face pale now that it is shielded from the volcano glow. "Or a snake, maybe."

Tommy pulls the dead cigar from his pocket and clamps it between his teeth. "There ain't no snakes in Hawaii, dipshit. I was just kidding."

Nick fires him a glance.

Tommy sighs and begins walking toward the lava maze.

"Hey," says Nick. "You going in that sheep shit?"

Tommy stops just at the edge of the *a'a*. "What do you suggest—we leave him?"

Nick thinks a second. "Go for help, maybe?"

Tommy makes a face. "Yeah, and come back and not find him in the dark and have to fly home and tell Connie and Shirley that we left Marty out here to die? Uh-uh. Besides, the stupid shit's probably just got his foot stuck in a rock or something."

Nick nods but stays in the cart.

"Coming?" says Tommy. "Or you gonna stay there and let Marty think of you as prime pussy for the rest of your miserable life?"

Nick thinks a minute, nods to himself, and gets out of the cart. He starts walking toward the lava, then goes back to the cart, pulls out an iron, and crosses the dark grass to Tommy.

"What the shit's that for?"

"I dunno," says Nick. "Maybe somebody's in there." The screams from the lava field have stopped now.

"Yeah, Marty's in there."

"Somebody else, I mean," says Nick.

Tommy shakes his head in disgust. "Look, this is Hawaii, not Newark. Ain't nobody gonna be in there that we can't handle." He walks into the rocks, following the faint trail left by Marty's golf shoes in the white sand.

A moment later the screaming begins again. Two voices this time. There is no one on the fairway to hear it and the resort buildings are only distant lights occluded by agitated palm fronds. The wind whistles through the porous *a'a*. The rising surf explodes on the unseen shore.

In another minute or two the screaming stops and only the wind and surf fill the night with their banshee calls.

TWO

It was snowing in Central Park. From the fifty-second floor of his steel, glass, and stone condo tower, Byron Trumbo watched the snow partially obscure the branch-black skeletons of the trees in the Sheep Meadow far below and tried to remember the last time he had walked in the park. Years ago. Probably before he had made his first billion. Perhaps before he had made his first million. Yes—he remembered now—it was fourteen years ago, he had been twenty-four years old and new in the city, fresh and cocky from his S&L bonanza in Indianapolis and ready to take New York by storm. He remembered looking up at the towers looming above the Central Park trees and wondering which building he would have his offices in. Little did he guess on that long-ago spring day that he would build his own fifty-four-story skyscraper and occupy the top four floors with his complex of offices and penthouse residence.

Architectural critics called Trumbo's condo tower "that phallic monstrosity." Everyone else called it the Big T. Some had tried calling it Trumbo Tower, but the similarity to the name of Donald Trump's buildings had caused Byron Trumbo to quash that name quickly and for good. He loathed Donald Trump and avoided any association with the man. Besides, "the Big T" best described the look of Trumbo's high-rise condo with its overhanging top five floors, the glass-and-steel superstructure that Trumbo had imagined would look like the bridge of the world's tallest ship. And Big T had been Byron Trumbo's nickname since he was thirteen years old. Now Trumbo was pedaling his exercise bike in the corner of the T overhang, right where two floor-to-ceiling glass walls met at a sharp angle, so that it looked and felt as if he were on a small carpeted promontory fifty-two stories above Fifth Avenue and the park. Snow flew upward inches beyond the glass, rising on updrafts along the face of the building. It was snowing so heavily now that Trumbo could barely make out the dark ramparts of the Dakota on the west side of the park.

At the moment, he was not looking. He was on the headset phone, his head down, timing his comments into the small microphone between gasps for breath as he pedaled furiously. His cotton T-shirt was soaked across his thick chest and between his shoulder blades.

"What do you mean three more guests have disappeared?" he snapped.

"I mean three more guests have disappeared," came the voice of Stephen Ridell Carter, the manager of Trumbo's Mauna Pele Resort on the Big Island of Hawaii. Carter's voice sounded weary. It was 8:30 A.M. in New York, 3:30 in the morning in Hawaii.

"Fuck," said Trumbo. "How do you know they've disappeared? Maybe they're just off the grounds somewhere."

"They didn't check out," said Carter. "We have a man on the gate twenty-four hours a day."

"So maybe they're on the grounds but in someone else's whaddyacallit—*hale*. Those grass shack thingies. Ever think of that?"

There was a slight rasp of static that might have covered a sigh. "The three had gone out for a late game of golf, Mr. Trumbo. Right at twilight. When they didn't check back by ten P.M., our boys went out and found their golf carts on the fourteenth hole. Their clubs were still there as well—some in the carts, some strewn around in the boulder field near the cliffs."

"Fuck," repeated Byron Trumbo. He motioned Will Bryant closer and made a telephone gesture with his thumb and little finger. His executive assistant nodded and picked up a mobile extension. "The others didn't disappear near the golf course, did they?"

"No," said Carter tiredly. "The two California women last November were last seen on the jogging trail through the petroglyph field. The Myers family—both parents and their four-year-old daughter—were walking by the manta pool after dark. The cook, Palikapu, was walking home along the cliffs south of the golf course."

Will Bryant held up five splayed fingers on one hand and four digits on the hand holding the phone.

"Yeah, now we have nine," agreed Trumbo.

"Pardon me, Mr. T?" said Stephen Ridell Carter over the hiss of distance.

"Nothing," said Trumbo. "Listen, Steve, you've got to keep this out of the papers for a couple of days."

There was a noise that might have been an incredulous snort. "Keep it out of the papers? Mr. T, how can I do that? The reporters have contacts with the cops. The state police, local Kailua-Kona homicide cops, and Fletcher—that FBI guy—will be all over the place again. As soon as we report it in the morning."

"Don't report it," said Trumbo. He quit pedaling and took deep breaths. Below him, the clouds rolled up against the building.

There was a silence. Finally: "That would be against the law, Mr. Trumbo."

Byron Trumbo covered the microphone with his sweaty hand. He looked across at Will Bryant. "Who hired this pussy?"

"You did," said Will.

"I'm going to fire his ass, too," he said, and took his palm off the mike. "Steve, you listening to me?"

"Yes, sir."

"You know about the meeting with the Sato Group in San Francisco tomorrow?"

"Yes, sir."

"You know how much it means to me to unload this fucking white elephant before we lose half our capital propping it up?"

"Yes, Mr. T."

"And you know how fucking stupid Hiroshe Sato and his investors are?"

Carter said nothing.

"These boys lost half their money buying up L.A. in the eighties," said Trumbo, "and now they're ready to lose the other half buying up the Mauna Pele and other Hawaii losers in the nineties, Steve, but . . . Steve?"

"Yes, sir?"

"They may be stupid, but they're not deaf and blind. It's been three months since the last disappearance and maybe they think all that shit is past. They did arrest that Hawaiian separatist . . . what's his name?"

"Jimmy Kahekili," said Carter, "but he couldn't make bail and is still in jail in Hilo, so this couldn't possibly be his . . ."

"I don't give a shit," interrupted Trumbo, "as long as the Japs think that the killer is put away somewhere. Japs are chickenshit, Steve. Their tourists are afraid to go to L.A., afraid to go to Miami, afraid to come here to New York . . . shit, they're scared shitless of most of the U.S.A. But not Hawaii. I guess they think there are no guns on Hawaii, or since they own half of it, that it's not full of crazy Americans. Anyway, I want Sato and his group to think that Jimmy Kaheka-whatsis was the killer and that it's all over, *finito.* At least until we wrap up these negotiations. Three days, Steve. Maybe four. Is that too much to ask?"

There was silence.

"Steve?"

"Mr. Trumbo," came the tired voice, "you know how hard it's been to keep locals working here after the other disappearances. We have to bus people in all the way from Hilo, and now, with the volcano . . ."

"Hey," said Trumbo, "that volcano's supposed to fill the place, right? Isn't that what we said? So where are the fucking guests now that the volcano's doing its thing?"

". . . now that the volcano has cut Highway Eleven, we have to use temporary help from as far north as Waimea," continued Carter. "The boys that found the golf carts have already told their friends. Even if I break the law and don't report it, there's no way we can keep this a total secret. Besides, these missing men have families, friends . . .''

Trumbo gripped the handlebar of his exercise bike so hard that his heavy knuckles grew white. ''How long were these ass-holes . . . these guests . . . booked for, Steve?''

There was a pause. ''Seven days, sir.''

''And how long were they there before they disappeared?''

''Just this afternoon, sir . . . yesterday, I mean.''

''So no one expects them back for six days.''

''No, sir, but . . .''

''Give me three of those days, can you, Steve?''

Static hissed. ''Mr. Trumbo, I can't promise more than twenty-four hours. We could justify that as an internal check to make sure the men are actually missing, but beyond that . . . it's the FBI, sir. They're not happy with our help in the previous disap-pearances. And I think we . . .''

''Shut up a minute,'' said Trumbo. He clicked off the mike with a button on his belt-pac and turned to Bryant. ''Will?''

His assistant muted his own phone. ''I think he's right, Mr. T. The cops'll get it within a day or two anyway. If it looks like we're covering something up, well . . . it will be worse than ever.''

Byron Trumbo nodded and looked down at the park. Snow fell like black streamers of crepe across the meadows. The lake was a white shield. When he looked up, Trumbo was smiling slightly. ''What's the schedule for the next few days, Will?''

His assistant did not have to refer to his notes. ''The Sato Group will be landing in San Francisco late tonight. You're sched-uled to join them at our West Coast headquarters there tomorrow to start the negotiations. When it's done, if we agree, Sato wanted to take his investors to the Mauna Pele to play golf for a couple of days before heading back to Tokyo.''

Trumbo's grin widened. ''They haven't left Tokyo yet?''

Will glanced at his watch. ''No, sir.''

''Who's with them? Bobby?''

''Yes. Bobby Tanaka's our best man there—both in speaking Japanese and negotiating with Sato's kind of young billionaire.''

Trumbo nodded impatiently. ''OK, here's what we do. Get

Bobby on the phone and tell him that the meeting's been moved to the Mauna Pele. We'll do the negotiating there and let them play golf at the same time.''

Will adjusted his tie. Unlike his boss, who rarely wore suit or tie, Bryant was dressed in an Armani business suit. "I think I see . . ."

"Sure you do." Trumbo grinned. "Where's the one place we can control the news getting in? The resort itself."

Will Bryant hesitated. "The Japanese hate changes in their schedules . . ."

Trumbo hopped off the bike and strode across the expanse of carpet, grabbing a towel from a rack near his desk and mopping his forehead. "Fuck what they hate. Besides . . . hey . . . the volcano's acting up, right?"

"Both volcanoes, I think," said Will. "Evidently it's been decades since . . ."

"Yeah," interrupted Trumbo. "It may not happen again in our lifetime, isn't that what our volcano geek, Hastings, said?" He punched his microphone on line. "Steve, you still there, kid?"

"Yes, sir," said Stephen Ridell Carter, who was fifteen years older than Byron Trumbo.

"Listen, you get us twenty-four hours. Carry out an internal investigation, turn the place upside down, do whatever you need to do to make it look good. Then call the cops. But give us twenty-four solid hours before letting the shit hit the fan, OK?"

"Yes, sir." The voice was not happy.

"And brush off the Presidential Suite and my personal shack," said Trumbo. "I'll be there by tonight and the Sato Group should be arriving about the same time."

"*Here,* sir?" Carter's voice seemed to have slammed awake.

"Yeah, there, Steve, and if you want your one percent on this deal, not to mention your golden parachute, you'd better keep things as fucking clean and calm and normal as you can while we're there admiring the volcano and settling this deal. Then—as soon as our lawyers finish dotting the *i*'s, you can let the fucking axe murderers get the Japs as far as I'm concerned. But not until we're done with the deal, *comprende?*"

"Yes, sir," came the tight voice, "but you realize that there are only a couple of dozen guests here, Mr. Trumbo. The publicity's been so bad . . . I mean, the Sato people are bound to notice that there are five hundred some rooms and *hales* empty. I mean . . ."

"We'll tell them that we emptied the place out in their honor," said Trumbo. "We'll tell them that we couldn't pass up this chance to see the fucking volcano. I don't care what we tell them, as long as we get this fucking place sold. You do what you have to do to sit on it until we all get there, Steve."

"Yes, sir, but I think that . . ."

Trumbo clicked off. "Will, get the chopper on the roof in twenty minutes. Call the field and have the Gulfstream ready to go as soon as I'm there. Get Bobby on the horn and tell him his job depends on getting the Sato Group to change destinations and like it. Finally, call Maya . . . no, I'll call her . . . you call Bicki and tell her that I was called away for a couple of days. Don't tell her where. Send the other Gulfstream to pick her up and fly her to the Antigua house and tell her I'll join her as soon as I've finished with whatever you decide I'm supposed to be doing. And . . . shit, where's Cait?"

"Here in New York, sir. Visiting her lawyers."

Trumbo made a rude noise. He walked into the glass-and-marble bathroom behind his desk. The outer shower wall looked down on the park. He stripped out of his shorts and T-shirt and turned on the water. "Fuck her lawyers. Fuck her. Just make sure that she doesn't get wind of where I am or where Maya is, OK?"

Will nodded and followed his boss into the bathroom. "Mr. T, the volcano really is showing signs of life."

Trumbo poked his head and hairy shoulders out of the water. "What?"

"I said, the volcano really is doing strange things. Dr. Hastings says that seismic activity is the strongest along the southwest rift since the 1920s . . . perhaps the strongest in this century."

Trumbo shrugged and ducked his head under the water. "So?" he shouted. "I thought that the volcano acting up was supposed to bring us tourists up the ass, right?"

"Yes, but there's a problem with . . ."

Trumbo was not listening. "I'll talk to Hastings from the plane," he shouted, face in the water. "You call Bicki. Tell Jason to have my Hawaii bag ready in five minutes and let Briggs know that it'll just be him going. I don't want to spook the Japs with too much security."

"Is that wise . . ." began Will.

"Come on, Will, move," said Byron Trumbo. Still standing in the pounding spray, he raised his heavy hands to the water-beaded glass wall and looked down at the park. "We're going to sell that fucking white elephant to the dumbest bunch of Japs since the generals who advised Hirohito to bomb Pearl Harbor . . . and we're going to use that capital to start our comeback." He turned and looked through the spray at his assistant. Water flew like saliva from Trumbo's thick lips. "*Move,* Will."

Will Bryant moved.

THREE

What I have always longed for was the privilege of living forever away up on one of those mountains in the Sandwich Islands overlooking the sea.
—Mark Twain

Once, when asked why she refused to fly, Eleanor Perry's seventy-two-year-old Aunt Beanie—she was seventy-two when she was asked, she was ninety-six now and still living by herself—took out a book on the history of the slave trade and showed Eleanor a drawing of the slaves wedged in between "decks" that were no more than three feet high.

"See how they had to lie there, head to head, feet to feet, chained up and rolling in their own filth during the long passage?" Aunt Beanie had asked, pointing with a hand that even then had been bony and age-mottled with freckles: what Eleanor as a child had thought of as "Campbell's Soup hands."

That year, twenty-four years ago, having just turned twenty-one and only recently graduated from Oberlin—the same school where she now taught—Eleanor had looked at the diagram of the slave ship with the Africans stacked like cordwood, wrinkled her nose, and said, "I see it, Aunt Beanie. But what does it have to do with your refusing to fly down to Florida to see Uncle Leonard?"

Aunt Beanie had shaken her head. "Do you know why they laid those poor Negroes in there like so many hogsheads of molasses even if it meant half of them would die during the crossing?"

Eleanor had shaken her head, her nose wrinkling again at the word "Negroes." The term "politically correct" had not been coined when Eleanor graduated from Oberlin that year, in 1970, but, term or no term, it was still politically incorrect to say "Negroes," and while she knew that Aunt Beanie was perhaps the least prejudiced person she had ever known, the older woman's language betrayed the fact that she had been born before the century had begun. "Why did they lay the blacks in like so many barrels of molasses?"

"Money," said Aunt Beanie, withdrawing her bony hand and slapping the book shut. "Profit. If they crammed six hundred Africans in and three hundred died, it still paid them better than if they let four hundred ride like human beings and lost a hundred and fifty. Profit, pure and simple."

"I still don't see why . . ." began Eleanor, and then stopped. She saw the point. "Aunt Beanie, the planes aren't *that* crowded."

The older woman had not spoken, merely raised an eyebrow.

"Well, OK, they're crowded," Eleanor conceded, "but it only takes a *few hours* to get down to Florida by plane, and if you have Cousin Dick drive you it'll take two or three *days* . . . " She had stopped when she saw Aunt Beanie set her bony, Campbell's Soup hand on the slave-trade book as if to say, *Do you think they were in such a hurry to get where they were going?*

Now, twenty-four years later, Eleanor sat in the economy section of the stretch-747, squashed between two fat men in the center row of five seats, listening to the babble of the three hundred-plus people wedged in behind her. She craned over the high back of the seat ahead of her to see the flickering video of the heavily edited in-flight movie and realized that Aunt Beanie had been right again. *How we get there is usually as important as where we're going.*

But not this time.

Eleanor sighed, awkwardly bent to tug her briefcase out from under the seat in front of her, searched around in it until she found Aunt Kidder's small leather diary, and fumbled to turn on the overhead reading light. The fat man on her right snorted asthmatically in his sleep and laid a sweaty forearm on her armrest, making Eleanor shift slightly toward the fat man on her left. She opened Kidder's diary to the proper page without looking, so familiar was the journal to her fingers.

June 3, 1866, Aboard the *Boomerang*—

Still dubious about this unplanned trip to see the volcano on Hawaii and perhaps still more entranced with the prospect of a quiet week at Mr. and Mrs. Lyman's mission guest house in Honolulu, I nonetheless allowed myself to be convinced yesterday that this would be my life's only opportunity to see a "living volcano," and so this morning I found myself packed and boarded and waved farewell to by the majority of the delightful folk who have filled the previous two weeks with such frivolity and learning. Our "group" consists of the elder Miss Lyman, her nephew Thomas and nurse, Miss Adams, Master Gregory Wendt, the duller of the Smith twins I mentioned who attended the Honolulu dance all "got up" like linen-encrusted penguins, Miss Dryton from the orphanage, the Reverend Haymark (not the handsome young minister I mentioned in my earlier missive, but an older, heavier man of the cloth whose habit of taking snuff and sneezing violently at every opportunity would keep me in the solitude of my cabin were it not for the cockroaches), and an irritating young correspondent for a Sacramento paper which I have had the good fortune never to have read. The gentleman's name is Mr. Samuel Clemens, but it says something about the seriousness of his writing that he brags of having published under such "clever" *noms de plume* as "Thomas Jefferson Snodgrass."

Besides being vulgar and overly boisterous and terribly full of himself due to having been the only correspondent in the Sandwich Islands two weeks ago when the survivors of that ill-fated clipper ship, the *Hornet,* made landfall here, Mr. Clemens is somewhat ill-kempt and rather a braggart and a boor. He leavens his bad manners a bit with constant attempts at humor, but most of his witticisms droop as seriously as do his wilting mustaches. Today, as our intercoastal ship the *Boomerang* left Honolulu harbor while Mr. Clemens was describing to Mrs. Lyman and some of us the glories of his "scoop" on the forty-three-day ordeal on the open seas of the *Hornet's* survivors, I could not help but interpose some questions based upon some knowledge granted to me by the delightful Mrs. Allwyte, wife of the Reverend Patrick Allwyte, who volunteered her time at the hospital and who had confided in me when the tale of the *Hornet* was all the rage in Honolulu.

"Mr. Clemens," I interrupted ingenuously, adopting my pose as wide-eyed admirer, "you say that you interviewed Captain Mitchell and some of the other survivors?"

"Why, yes, Miss Stewart," said the red-haired correspondent. "It was my duty and professional pleasure to interrogate the hapless men."

"An obligation which may go far to further your career, Mr. Clemens," I suggested demurely.

The correspondent bit the end off a cigar and spat it over the railing as if he were in a saloon. He did not notice Mrs. Lyman's wince and I pretended not to. "Indeed, Miss Stewart," said the scribbler, "I will go so far as to suggest that it will make me about the best-known *honest* man on the West Coast." His smile, I confess, is boyish, although Mr. Clemens is all of thirty or thirty-one years old according to my informants . . . hardly a boy.

"Indeed, Mr. Clemens," I echoed, "how fortunate for you that you happened to visit the hospital just as Captain Mitchell and his men arrived . . ."

Here the correspondent puffed on his cigar and cleared his throat, obviously ill at ease.

"You *did* visit the hospital to carry out your interview, did you not, Mr. Clemens?"

The correspondent made a noise in his throat. "The interview was conducted at the hospital while the captain and his men convalesced, yes, Miss Stewart."

"But were *you* ever at the hospital, Mr. Clemens?" I asked, some of the demureness gone from my voice now.

"Ah . . . not . . . ah . . . personally," said the red-headed scribe. "I . . . ah . . . forwarded the questions through the agency of my friend, Mr. Anson Burlingame."

"But of course!" I cried. "Mr. Burlingame . . . our country's next minister to China! He was such a delight at the Mission Ball. But tell us, Mr. Clemens, how is it that a correspondent of your obvious talents and instincts would have used an intermediary in such an important story? Why not visit Captain Josiah Mitchell and his would-be cannibals in person for the interview?"

Something about my use of the phrase "would-be cannibals" seemed to inform Mr. Clemens that he was dealing with a person of some wit and he smiled slightly, although he was obviously still ill at ease as our little group looked on.

"I was . . . ah . . . indisposed, one would say, Miss Stewart."

"Not ill, I hope, Mr. Clemens," said I, knowing quite precisely the source of our newly famous correspondent's indisposition due to the good offices of the indispensable Mrs. Allwyte.

"No, not ill," said Mr. Clemens, his teeth showing through his mustaches now. "Merely indisposed due to far too much time spent on horseback the previous four days."

I covered my face with a fan like an ingenue at her first ball. "You mean . . ." I began.

"I mean saddle boils," said Mr. Clemens, his story of literary triumph quite derailed for the moment. "The size of silver dollars. It was a week before I could walk. It may be a lifetime before I board any four-legged creature as a passenger again. It is my fervent wish, Miss Stewart, that the natives of Oahu have some pagan ceremony wherein they offer up a creature of equine ancestry in one of their volcano rituals, and that the first nag they choose to throw into the fiery cauldron is the sway-backed creature who inflicted such misery upon me."

Mrs. Lyman, her nephew, Miss Adams, and the others did not quite know what to make of this confession. I fanned myself contentedly. "Well, thank heavens for Mr. Burlingame," I said. "Perhaps it would be only fair if he were to become the second most famous *honest* person on the West Coast."

Mr. Clemens drew deeply on his cigar. The breezes had picked up considerably once we were out at open sea between the islands. "It is Mr. Burlingame's happy destiny to be off to China, Miss Stewart."

"Indeed, Mr. Clemens," said I, "but we have not specified whose destinies have been formed by this event, only who has done the actual work to form them." And with that I went below for tea with Mrs. Lyman.

Eleanor Perry lowered the leather diary and found herself being stared at by the fat man on her left.

"Interesting book?" asked the man. His smile showed the insincere sincerity of someone in sales. He was in his late forties, a few years older than Eleanor.

"Quite interesting," said Eleanor, and closed Aunt Kidder's diary. She set it in her briefcase and kicked the briefcase into its cramped space under the seat in front of her. *Slave cargo.*

"Heading for Hawaii, huh?" said the salesman.

Since the flight was nonstop between San Francisco and the Keahole-Kona airport, Eleanor did not feel that the question deserved a reply.

"I'm from Evanston," said the salesman. "I think I saw you on the plane from Chicago to San Fran."

San Fran, thought Eleanor with a pall of resignation that was not unlike airsickness. "Yes," she said.

Undeterred, the salesman said, "I'm in sales. Microelectronics. Games mostly. Me and two other guys from the midwest division won the incentive bonus. I got four days at the Hyatt Regency Waikoloa. That's the resort where you get to swim with the dolphins. No kidding."

Eleanor nodded her appreciation of these facts.

"I'm not married," said the salesman. "Well, divorced, actually. That's the reason I'm going alone. The other guys—they won two tickets to a resort—but the company only gives out one ticket when the employee isn't married anymore." The heavy man gave a lame smile that was more sincere for its lameness. "Anyway, that's why I'm heading to Hawaii by myself."

Eleanor smiled her understanding and ignored the implied *Why are* you *heading to Hawaii by yourself?*

"You headed for one of the resorts?" asked the microelectronics man after a long silence.

"The Mauna Pele," said Eleanor. On the small screen five rows ahead of them, Tom Hanks was mouthing something with a boyish grin. People with earphones chuckled.

The salesman whistled. "The Mauna Pele. Wow. That's the most expensive super-resort on the west coast of the Big Island, isn't it? Ritzier than the Mauna Lani or Kona Village or the Mauna Kea.''

"I really don't know," said Eleanor. This was not quite true. When she had made the reservations through the travel agent in Oberlin, the woman had tried to convince her that the other resorts were just as nice and *much* cheaper. The agent had never mentioned the murders, but she had done her best to dissuade Eleanor from traveling to the Mauna Pele. When Eleanor had persisted, the rates the agent quoted were truly staggering.

"The Mauna Pele's like a new millionaires' playground, isn't it? I think it is," said the salesman. "I saw something about it on the TV. You must have a really good job to afford a vacation in a place like that." He smiled shrewdly. "Or be married to someone who's got a really good job."

"I teach," she said.

"Oh, yeah? What grade? You remind me of a third-grade teacher I had once."

"At Oberlin," said Eleanor.

"Is that like a high school?"

"A college," said Eleanor. "In Ohio."

"Interesting," said the salesman in a voice that was quickly losing interest. "You teach like one subject or something?"

"History," said Eleanor. "Mostly mid-eighteenth-century intellectual history. The Enlightenment, to be precise."

"Hmmm," said the salesman, obviously finding nothing to pursue there. He was frowning slightly. "The Mauna Pele, now ... that's the new resort. It's farther south than the others, isn't it?" He was obviously trying to remember what he had heard on the news recently about the Mauna Pele.

"Yes," said Eleanor, "it's farther down the South Kona Coast."

"Murders!" said the microelectronics man, snapping his finger. "There's been a bunch of murders there since it opened last fall. I seen something on *A Current Affair* about it."

Eleanor managed not to wince at the grammar. "I really don't know," she said, lifting the in-flight magazine out of its pocket.

"Sure! There's been a bunch of people killed or disappeared or something there. That's the resort that Byron Trumbo, the Big T, built. They arrested some crazy Hawaiian, didn't they?"

Eleanor smiled her lack of knowledge and studied a luggage ad. People around her chuckled as Tom Hanks shouted something silently at a young starlet.

"Gosh, I didn't know that anyone was going to that place after all of the . . ." began the salesman, but was interrupted by an announcement over the intercom and earphones.

"Ladies and gentlemen, this is your first officer speaking. We're about forty minutes northeast of the Big Island and just beginning our descent toward the Keahole-Kona airport, but . . . ah . . . we've just been advised by Honolulu Center that all traffic into Kona is being rerouted to Hilo on the east coast. The reason for this is probably the reason some of you folks are visitin' the Big Island at this time . . . namely, the activity of the two volcanoes there on the south end of the island, Mauna Loa and Kilauea. There's no danger . . . the eruptions aren't threatening any developed areas . . . but the prevailing winds are from the east this afternoon and those two volcanoes are spewing out a lot of airborne ash and crud. It sorta creates a smog layer from the fifteen-thousand-foot level right on down almost to the deck—no worse than home for you folks from the L.A. area—but FAA regulations won't allow us to fly through it even if there's no real danger.

"So, unless we hear that the wind's shifted or the volcanoes have ended their show for the evening, we'll be landing at Hilo International Airport right up on the east central part of the island. We're sorry about any inconvenience that this may cause you, and before we land, our flight attendants'll be giving you updates on contacting the United flight representatives at Hilo regarding hotel arrangements or alternate transport plans to the Kona Coast.

"Once again, sorry for any inconvenience this may cause to your travel plans, but we should be arriving right before dark, so all I can suggest is that we all settle back and hope we get a good view of Madame Pele's handiwork before we land at Hilo. I'll be talking to you later to keep you advised of the situation. *Mahalo.*"

Eleanor could hear the movie soundtrack muttering from earphones before the sound was drowned out by the soft but angry murmur of the passengers. The fat man on her right had awakened during the announcement and was cursing softly. The salesman on her left seemed less annoyed.

"What's *mahalo* mean?" he said.

"Thank you," said Eleanor.

The big man nodded. "Well, I'm sure the Hyatt's gonna get me over there tomorrow, if not tonight. What difference does a hundred miles or so make once you get to paradise, huh?"

Eleanor did not answer. She had tugged out her briefcase and pulled out the map of the Big Island she had bought at the college bookstore in Oberlin. There was only one real road around the island—it was labeled Highway 11 around the south end from Hilo, Highway 19 around the north—and it would be over a hundred miles either way to the Mauna Pele.

"*Merde,*" she said softly to herself.

The microelectronics man grinned and nodded. "Yeah, that's what I say. Don't sweat the small stuff. I mean, it's all Hawaii, right?"

The stretch-747 continued its descent.

FOUR

*. . . only seven of the thirty-two eruptions of
Mauna Loa since 1832 have occurred on the
Southwest Rift Zone, and only two of these have
impacted the project site.*
—Hawaiian Riviera Resort Final
Impact Statement, December, 1987

"What the hell do you mean we can't land at Kona?" Byron
Trumbo was furious. His $28 million Gulfstream 4 was twenty min-
utes ahead of Eleanor Perry's crowded 747 and descending south
of Maui, ready to begin its final turn along the west coast of the Big
Island. "What kind of shit is this? I helped pay for the improve-
ment of this fucking airport. And now they say they won't let us
land?"

The co-pilot nodded. He was leaning over the back of one of
the tan leather seats in the main cabin of the Gulfstream, watching
Trumbo pedal his exercise bike in front of one of the large circular windows. Rich evening light fell on Trumbo, who was wearing a
T-shirt, shorts, and his ever-present Converse All Star high-tops.

"So tell them we're landing," said Trumbo. He was panting
slightly, but the sound was almost lost under the background hum
of the Gulfstream's engines and the ventilators.

The co-pilot shook his head. "Can't do it, Mr. T. Honolulu
Center is waving us off. The ash cloud is pouring right over the
Kailua-Kona area and the Keahole airport. Regulations won't let
us . . ."

"*Fuck* regulations," said Byron Trumbo. "I want to be there

tonight before the Sato people land . . . *shit,* this means that the
Sato plane from Tokyo will probably be diverted too, right?"

"Right." The co-pilot smoothed his short hair back.

"We're going to land at Keahole-Kona," said Trumbo. "So is
Sato's plane. Inform the airport."

The co-pilot took a breath. "We could send the big chopper
from the resort to Hilo . . ."

"Piss on the big chopper," said Trumbo. "If Sato's people
land at Hilo and have to be choppered around the south side of
the island, they're going to think that the Mauna Pele's a hundred
miles away from everything."

"Well," said the co-pilot, "it *is* a hundred miles from . . ."

Trumbo quit pedaling. His stocky five-foot-eight frame was
rigid. "Will you get the fucking airport on the fucking phone or
do I have to?"

Will Bryant stepped forward with the phone in his hand. The
Gulfstream was rigged with a satellite communications system that
would make Air Force One jealous. "Mr. T, I have a better idea.
I've got the governor on the line."

Trumbo hesitated for only a second. "Good," he said, and
took the phone, waving the co-pilot back to the cockpit.

"Johnny," said Trumbo, "this is Byron Trumbo . . . Yeah,
yeah, I'm glad you enjoyed that, we'll do it again the next time
you're in New York . . . Yeah, listen, Johnny, I've got a little problem here . . . I'm calling from the Gulfstream . . . Yeah . . . Anyway,
we're on final approach to Keahole and suddenly there's some
bullshit about having to be diverted to Hilo . . ."

Will Bryant lounged on the taupe leather couch that ran
along the rear third of the main cabin and watched Trumbo roll
his eyes and tap on the table still set with the remains of dinner.
Melissa, the only cabin attendant, came forward from the galley
area and began clearing the table in preparation for landing.

"Yeah, yeah, I understand all that," interrupted Trumbo. He
dropped into the window seat and peered out the round window
as Mauna Kea came into view, the observatory domes on its summit gleaming as white as the snow there. "What *you* don't understand, Johnny, is that I'm meeting the Sato Group at the Mauna

Pele this evening, and if we get the fu . . . pardon me, Governor . . . if we get the runaround . . . Yeah, they're flying in about an hour from now . . . if we both get the runaround and are diverted to Hilo, then Sato and his boys are going to wonder just what kind of Mickey Mouse operation we're running out here . . . Uh-huh. Uh-huh." Trumbo rolled his eyes again. "No, Johnny, we're talking about *eight hundred million dollars* going into the area . . . Yeah . . . at least one more golf course, and it's almost certain that they'd want a whole shitload of condos to go with that . . . Yeah . . . that's exactly right . . . with golf memberships running a couple of hundred thousand bucks a shot in Japan, it's almost cheaper for them to buy the place and ship the golfers over here . . . Yeah."

Trumbo glanced up as they passed west of the Mauna Kea volcano and the tremendous ash plume of the Mauna Loa and Kilauea eruptions came into view. The cloud of gray ash and steam billowed out of the southernmost peak, flattened as the powerful trade winds struck it, and plumed westward for a hundred miles, obscuring the southwest coast in a pall of thick smog.

"Holy shit," said Trumbo. "No, Johnny, sorry . . . we just came around Mauna Kea and got a good look at all this volcano stuff . . . Yeah . . . impressive . . . but we've still got to land at Keahole and so does the Sato plane . . . Yeah, I *know* all about the FAA rules, but I also know that I put my money into donations for the Keahole airstrip rather than build my own as a favor to you and the boys. And I know that I'm bringing more money into this recession-struck island than anyone since Laurence Rockefeller in the sixties . . . Yeah . . . Yeah . . . well, I'm not asking for another tax break or something, Johnny, I'm just telling you that if we aren't allowed to land there tonight, then this deal will probably go down the crapper and we'll be selling off the Mauna Pele to the lowest bidder. Yep . . . the place'll look like fucking Royal Gardens . . . all overgrown by weeds and shit . . . the only residents will be the fucking marijuana growers."

Trumbo turned away from the window and listened for a minute. Finally he looked up at Will Bryant, grinned, and said into the phone, "Hey, thanks, Johnny . . . Yes . . . you bet I will . . . wait till the studio party we're going to throw when the new Schwarzenegger comes out . . . Yeah, thanks again."

Trumbo clicked the phone off and handed it to Will. "Go tell the boys in the cockpit that we have to circle for a few minutes, but they'll be getting clearance for Keahole-Kona as soon as the governor can get through to the dudes at Honolulu Center."

Bryant nodded and stooped to look out at the ash plume. "Do you think it's safe?"

Trumbo made a rude noise. "Tell me one fucking thing in life that's worth the effort that's *safe*," he said. He nodded at the phone. "Get me Hastings on the phone."

"He'd be on duty at the Volcano Observatory . . ."

"I don't give a shit if he's banging his old lady," said Trumbo, munching on some fruit from the compact refrigerator under the table. "Get Hastings."

The Gulfstream 4 circled ten miles off the Kohala Coast at 23,000 feet, staying north of the carpet of gray smoke and ash that billowed from Mauna Loa and spread west across the Pacific. The sun was low and particulates from the eruption turned the western sky into a riot of red and orange. The effect was unsettling, like watching a sunset through the smoke of a burning building.

Occasionally as the plane banked counterclockwise on the southern edge of its loop, Trumbo caught a glimpse of the eruption itself through the haze—a plume of orange flame rising 1,000 feet or more above the 13,677-foot summit—with more orange glows through the smoke hinting at the Kilauea eruptions farther to the south. Steam from where the Kilauea lava flow hit the ocean rose higher than the ash cloud itself, the white plumes reaching 30,000 feet.

"Jesus, every hotel on the island is booked solid for this show and we have five hundred some fucking empty rooms . . ."

Will Bryant came out of the cockpit. "Keahole tower called. We can land in about ten minutes. I've got Dr. Hastings . . ." He handed Trumbo the phone.

The billionaire set the phone in a speaker cradle built into the armrest of the chair. "I want you to hear this, Will . . . Dr. Hastings?"

"Yes, Mr. Trumbo?" The vulcanologist was old, the connection was static-ridden, and the voice sounded like a recording from some previous era.

"Dr. Hastings, I've got you on speaker. My executive assistant, Will Bryant, is here. We're on final approach to Keahole in the Gulfstream."

There was a moment of scratchy silence. "But I thought that Keahole Airport was . . ."

"It just opened up again. Doctor, I'm calling because we need some information about this current eruption."

"Yes, well, I will be very happy to discuss the events with you, Mr. Trumbo, as per our agreement, but I am afraid that at the moment we are very, very busy here and . . ."

"Yeah, I know, Doc . . . but look at your contract. The fact of it is, our consultancy agreement takes precedence over your work there at the Observatory. God knows we're paying you more than they are. If I wanted, I could order you over to the Mauna Pele and make you sit there and answer tourists' questions."

The speaker crackled with the doctor's silence.

"I don't want that, of course," continued Trumbo, voice soft. "I don't even like interrupting you there, what with all the neat volcano science you're probably doing with this eruption and all. Still, there's the little matter of the six-hundred-million-dollar resort we hired you to consult us on, and now we need some consultation."

"Yes, go ahead, Mr. Trumbo."

Trumbo grinned at Will. "OK, Doc, we need to know what's happening."

Something like a sigh came through the static. "Well, of course you are aware of the concurrent activity at Moku'aweoweo extending along the southwest rift and the increased flow at the O'o-Kupaianaha event . . ."

"Whoa, Doc, whoa," said Trumbo. "I thought it was Mauna Loa and Kilauea that were acting up. I don't even know where Moku-whatsis and O-o Crapola *are*."

This time the sigh was more audible. "Mr. Trumbo, it was all in my EIS report of August last year . . ."

"Tell me again, Dr. Hastings," said Byron Trumbo. His tone left no room for argument.

"The Kilauea eruption is irrelevant to your concerns. The O'o-Kupaianaha eruption now taking place is merely a more violent continuation of a lava flow that has been going on since 1987. It is true that there is increased activity at Pu'u O'o and Halemaumau, both part of Kilauea Volcano, but the lava flow there invariably runs to the southeast and can offer no threat to your resort complex. Moku'aweoweo, on the other hand, is the summit caldera of Mauna Loa," said Hastings, his scratchy voice taking on more timbre. "The current eruption began there three days ago. The actual lava flow and outgassing, of course, soon spread to numerous fissures and lava tubes along the southwest rift . . ."

"Wait," said Trumbo, leaning close to the window. "Is that the sort of curtain of fire I can see stretching down the slope from the big fountain?"

"Yes," said Hastings. "The current Mauna Loa eruption is following the same scenario as the 1975 and 1984 events—that is, the lava fountains begin at Moku'aweoweo near the summit and spread along the rift zones. The difference this time is that the fissures are spread along the southwest rift zone; in 1984 the activity was centered on the northeast rift zone . . ."

"Toward Hilo," said Will Bryant.

"Yes," said Hastings.

"But this time they're erupting southwest," said Trumbo. "Toward my resort."

"Yes."

"Does this mean six hundred million bucks' worth of my investment—not to mention me and the Japs who want to buy it—are going to be buried in lava in the next couple of days, Dr. Hastings?" asked Trumbo, his voice mild.

"Very unlikely," said the vulcanologist. "The current lava fountains extend along the rift down to about the seven-thousand-foot level . . ."

"Wait," said Trumbo, leaning against the window, "it looks like there's fire and lava almost to the sea down there."

"Most likely," came Hastings's dry response. "The 'curtain of fire,' as you put it, currently extends about thirty kilometers . . ."

"Twenty miles." Trumbo whistled.

"Yes," said Dr. Hastings, "but the lava flow is south of your resort, and should reach the ocean in the relatively uninhabited Ka'u desert area west of South Point."

"Is that for sure?" asked Trumbo. The Fasten Seatbelt sign was blinking above him. He ignored it.

"Nothing is for sure, Mr. Trumbo. But a simultaneous flow to the east *and* west of the rift zone is a low-order probability."

"A low-order probability," repeated Trumbo. "That's reassuring."

"Yes," said Dr. Hastings, evidently missing the sarcasm in Byron Trumbo's voice.

"Dr. Hastings," said Will Bryant, "in your paper of last August and in the EIS you did for us prior to the resort being built, didn't you say there was a greater chance of a tidal wave catastrophe than of lava incursion?"

"Oh, yes," said Hastings, his voice perking up with something like the pride of an author whose work has been read, "as I explained in the report, the proposed Mauna Pele Resort . . . well, I guess it is no longer 'proposed' . . . the resort you built is on the southwest flank of Mauna Loa and that flank extends far into the ocean. It is, actually, one of the steepest underwater slopes on the planet. This flank is what we call unbuttressed and is subject to major fault block slumps . . ."

"In other words," interrupted Trumbo, "the whole goddamn section of coast might just slide into the Pacific."

"Well," said Hastings slowly over the static, "yes. But that was not my point."

Trumbo rolled his eyes and sat back with a squeak of leather. The Gulfstream was descending steeply now, the engines changing pitch. Ash and smoke whipped by the round windows.

"What is your point, Doctor?" asked Trumbo.

"My point . . . the point in both papers I prepared for you . . . is that even a minor fault block slump and the related seismic activity such a slump creates can and will cause a tsunami . . ."

"A tidal wave," said Will.

"I know what a fucking tsunami is," snapped Trumbo.

"I beg your pardon?" came Hastings's voice.

"Nothing, Doc," said Trumbo. "Finish up. We'll be landing in a minute."

"Well, there is little else to say. In 1951, a six-point-five earthquake struck the area of coast where the Mauna Pele Resort now stands. There have been over a thousand seismic events plotted here since this new series of eruptions began four days ago. Fortunately, the events are small, but pressure seems to be building . . ."

"I think I've got it, Doc," interrupted Trumbo, fastening his seat belt as the Gulfstream hit turbulence in the ash cloud. "If the Mauna Pele isn't buried in lava, it's either gonna slump into the sea or be carried away by a tsunami. Thanks, Doc. We'll be in touch." He slapped the phone silent. The Gulfstream pitched and bucked. "Will," said Trumbo, "why does the FAA keep planes out of this kind of cloud?"

Bryant looked up from studying a contract. "There are stones and ash particles in the cloud that could clog up a jet's engines," he said.

Byron Trumbo grinned. "Now you tell me," he said softly. The view out the window was almost black. The Gulfstream yawed and bounced.

Will Bryant raised one eyebrow. There were times when he did not know if his boss was joking.

"Well, shit," laughed Trumbo. "It'd probably do us a favor if the plane crashes. Or the Japs' plane. If that dipshit Sato doesn't buy this place, we're going to wish that we were dead."

Will Bryant said nothing.

"Makes you wonder about people, doesn't it, Will?"

"How do you mean?"

Trumbo nodded toward the ash cloud flying past the window. "Thousands of people will pay premium prices to come see an eruption like this . . . risk tidal wave and being buried in lava to catch the show . . . but have some pissant murderer running around, a mere six people missing, and they stay away in droves. Weird, huh?"

"Nine people."

"What's that?" said Trumbo, turning from the window.

"Nine people have disappeared. Don't forget those three guys yesterday."

Trumbo made a noise and turned back to watch the cloud whip by. There was a sound against the fuselage as if children were throwing stones against a boiler.

The Gulfstream continued to descend.

FIVE

A male this, the female that
A male born in the time of black darkness
The female born in the time of groping
in the darkness.
—from the *Kumulipo,* a Hawaiian creation
chant composed about 1700 A.D.

Eleanor brushed aside the simplistic rental-car agency map and set her own highway map of the island on the counter. "What are you saying, that I can't get there from here?"

The thin blonde woman behind the counter shook her head. "No, no, it's just that you can't go the south way. The ash and lava flow have cut off Highway Eleven." The woman stabbed a bony finger at the single black ribbon that ran around the south end of the island. "Here, just beyond Volcanoes National Park."

"That's about . . . what?" said Eleanor. "Forty miles from here?"

"Yeah," the blonde woman said, wiping sweat from beneath her bangs. "But Highway Nineteen's open."

"The northern route," said Eleanor. "All the way up the coast, across to Waimea or Kamuela . . . which is it? I've seen the town listed both ways."

The woman shrugged. "The post office there says Kamuela. We all call it Waimea."

"Across the hills to Waimea," continued Eleanor, tracing the path with her finger, "down to the Kohala Coast, and then south to Kona . . ."

"Highway Nineteen becomes Highway Eleven there," said

the woman. The gum she was chewing smelled of tired spearmint.

"And then south to the Mauna Pele," finished Eleanor. "About a hundred and twenty miles?"

The woman behind the counter shrugged again. "Something like that. You sure you wanna drive it? It's almost dark. A lot of the other Kona Coast guests are bein' put up in hotels here in Hilo until the resorts can get vans over in the morning."

Eleanor rubbed her chin. "Yes, United offered that, but I'd prefer to get there tonight."

"It's almost dark," repeated the woman in a tone that let it be known that it was no skin off her nose if the *haole* wanted to go wandering around the Big Island in the dark.

"What about this road?" said Eleanor, her finger following a a curving black line that led out of Hilo and cut across the north central bulk of the island. "Saddle Road?"

The blonde woman shook her head so adamantly that her bangs flopped. "Uh-uh, can't use that."

"Why not?" Eleanor leaned on the counter. The row of car rental booths was outdoors, just across from the main terminal. The air was thick with humidity and fragrant with sea air and a thousand floral scents. As many times as Eleanor had been to the tropics, she always forgot that pleasant shock of heat, humidity, and *outdoorness* that assaulted one immediately upon stepping off the plane or out of the terminal. The terminal here at Hilo was small enough and open enough that the smells and sounds of Hawaii had enfolded her the second she had stepped off the jet port. Having only passed through Hawaii on her way somewhere more remote and exotic during her almost three decades of traveling, Eleanor had been shocked by the *Americanness* of it all.

"Why can't I take the Saddle Road?" repeated Eleanor. "It looks shorter than following Highway Nineteen all the way north."

The woman was still shaking her head. "You can't. It violates the rental agreement." She prodded at the forms Eleanor had just completed filling out.

"Why, isn't it paved?"

"Well . . . sort of . . . but you can't drive on it. It's too rough. Too remote. No services. Not even any houses. You break down, there's no way we can get to you."

Eleanor smiled. "I just rented a *Jeep*. At seventy dollars a day. Are you telling me that your Jeep is going to break down?"

The woman folded her arms. "You can't take the Saddle Road. It's not even *on* the map we gave you."

"I noticed," said Eleanor.

"It would violate the contract."

"I understand," said Eleanor.

"It's not a road we allow our vehicles on."

"I believe you," said Eleanor. She touched the contract and then pointed to the darkening sky. "Can I get the keys to the Jeep now? It's getting dark."

It took Eleanor almost half an hour to find where the Saddle Road left the suburbs of Hilo. Winding up through the last few houses and palm trees into the mountain scrub, she kept glancing in the mirror at the wall of clouds moving in from the east. It was raining hard just a mile offshore and headed her way.

She had lost fifteen minutes after checking out the open Jeep. It was a new Wrangler, fewer than twenty miles on the odometer, with an automatic transmission that Eleanor would have paid extra to do without, but there was no strap-down vinyl top tucked in the back or under the seat. Eleanor had rented four-wheel-drive vehicles on four continents, and even the most battered old open Rover or Toyota had some sort of foul-weather gear to lash over the roll bar.

"Oh, you mean the bikini top," said the blonde woman when Eleanor had driven back and waited for another client to finish his transaction.

"Whatever you call it. Usually they tie or Velcro on."

The woman nodded, obviously bored. "We don't include it anymore. Not with this new batch of vehicles. We take them out and store them."

Eleanor tried an old trick of counting to ten in Greek. It sometimes kept her from assaulting idiots. "Why is that?" she asked at last, her voice soft in a way that invariably made her students fidget with anxiety.

The woman chewed her gum. "People kept losin' them. Or losin' the little tie thingies."

Eleanor smiled and leaned closer. "Do you live in Hilo, miss?"

The gum popped and began its chew cycle again. "Sure."

"Do you know how much rain you get on this side of the island? How many inches per year?"

The woman shrugged.

"I don't live here," said Eleanor, "but I can tell you the annual rainfall. More than a hundred and fifty inches. Per year. Sometimes as much as two hundred inches just up the valley." She leaned even closer. "Now, are you going to rig my Jeep with some sort of cover, or do I have to drive the thing up those stairs and park it on the sidewalk here and wait for the reporters to show up while I'm talking long-distance to the president of your company?"

The "bikini top" rattled and flapped in the gale blowing in ahead of the storm as Eleanor drove up Waianuenue Avenue past Rainbow Falls and swung west on the Saddle Road, but she figured that the stupid strip of vinyl should keep her relatively dry unless she had to drive through a hurricane.

It was twilight as Eleanor flogged the Jeep up a series of curves past signs for Kaumana Caves and the Hilo Golf Course and into the realm of mountain shrubs. The road narrowed until it was barely wide enough for two vehicles, but she had encountered few cars and the pavement was fine here.

The rain caught her less than ten miles west of Hilo. Clever design by the Chrysler Jeep Division had ensured that the combination of upright windshield and flapping vinyl would channel the rainfall down the back of her neck and onto the inside of the windshield. The clunky wipers made swipes at clearing the outside of the glass, but Eleanor had to dig in her purse for a Kleenex to mop the inside. The rear compartment of the Jeep began to fill with rain within minutes, so Eleanor tossed her purse and duffel bag on the passenger seat to keep them dry. There was still a splendid sunset going on somewhere to the west, but the low clouds and rain here had brought on a premature nightfall.

Eleanor caught a last glimpse of the lights of Hilo in her mirror and then she was over the crest of a ridge and there was nothing visible except the bulk of the two volcanoes on either side of the narrow road and a tangle of low trees. There were no lights ahead, the road had no center stripe, and the effect was that of entering a tunnel of darkness. Eleanor tried the radio, found only static, and switched it off, humming contentedly to herself, keeping time with the *swwssshh-tk* of the wipers.

Suddenly the road entered a wider part of the valley between the two volcanoes—Mauna Kea to her right, Mauna Loa to her left—the clouds parted for a moment, and Eleanor caught a glimpse of a sunset gleam high on the icy flanks of Mauna Kea. Something metallic, perhaps one of the observatories, sent mirror flashes into the dark valley. But even more impressive was the orange-flame glow of the Mauna Loa eruption to her left. Previously hidden by clouds, the mass of the volcano was now revealed by the light of molten flames reflected on its own low ash plume. Eleanor had the fleeting impression that she was traveling down a hallway into a burning house, with heavy pillars to either side. To the west, the last of the fiery sunset mixed with volcano glow to ignite the clouds into a slow combustion of colors. Eleanor saw a double rainbow pacing the Jeep to her left, and despite the fact that she had read somewhere that the laws of optics do not allow one to catch up to a rainbow, she drove through it.

Then the rain came again and the sunset disappeared, the reflected light from the eruption on the other side of Mauna Loa receding to a sullen glow.

Eleanor began to understand why the car rental people were so apoplectic about the prospect of driving on the Saddle Road. The narrow road wound and dodged, as if trying to throw any pesky vehicles off its back. The trees in this valley were low and ugly but thick enough to block the view so that Eleanor had to slow for every curve in the endlessly curving road. Twice, battered cars passed the other way, and neither time were their headlights visible until seconds before the encounter. After fifteen or twenty

miles of this exhausting driving, Eleanor saw the only other road
on the entire stretch of highway: a small sign pointed to a narrow
lane running off to the right toward Mauna Kea State Park and
Mauna Kea itself. She knew from reading her map and guidebook
that this road dead-ended near the summit of the volcano some
fifteen miles and eight thousand feet higher, but it would have
been easy to take a wrong turn here and find that out the hard
way. Eleanor tried to imagine the dedication it took for the astronomers who lived and worked up there, gasping in the cold, thin air
of almost fourteen thousand feet, trying to take their photographs
and do their measurements before altitude sickness and its oxy-
gen-deficit stupidity forced them down for R&R. Eleanor had always thought that the academic environment on campus brought
on a similar enforced stupidity, but at least one could breathe
there.

Beyond the Mauna Kea turnoff, the road deteriorated. Signs,
half glimpsed in the orange-tinged gloom, announced that it was
illegal to stop by the roadside and warned of unexploded shells
lying about. Twice she caught sight of large armored vehicles
crashing and rending their way through underbrush to her left,
their weak headlights throwing beams as watery as lantern light.
Suddenly, Eleanor had to slam on the Jeep's brakes and sit, mouth
half open with shock, as four of these armored behemoths
crashed across the road ahead of her, their treads spewing up asphalt as if it were mud.

When they were gone, she pulled ahead slowly, peering from
left to right, hearing the damned monsters out there in the brush
but not able to see them. A sign appeared in the gloom, its redundant legend almost invisible in the rain: WARNING: MILITARY
VEHICLE CROSSING. Eleanor assumed this entire valley was
some sort of military reservation. She hoped that was the case; otherwise it appeared that the U.S. Army had declared war on Hawaii.

Eleanor drove on, mopping the inside of the windshield, her
back wet, her hair soaked, her canvas espadrilles soaking up water
from the two-inch puddle sloshing around between her seat and
the accelerator. Her eyes flicked from side to side like a fighter
pilot's, always ready for another convoy of tanks or stegosauruses

or whatever the hell had appeared or disappeared mere moments before.

Suddenly, just as she came around a twisting right-hand curve, the patched asphalt corrugated here to the point her fillings vibrated in her teeth, Eleanor had to swerve to miss a dark gray car half in the ditch and half on the road. A human form was on the road, looking under the left rear of the vehicle. Eleanor bit her lip and fought the oversized steering wheel as the Jeep threatened to skip sideways right into the underbrush on the left side of the road, and it took half a minute before she had the heavy thing under control and centered in the narrow strip of asphalt. She glanced in her rearview mirror, but the car and human form next to it were out of sight behind the low hill she had just passed over.

"Damn," muttered Eleanor, and brought the Jeep to a stop. The rain whipped in on the back of her neck.

The form she had seen back there had been short and stocky and it had not looked up when the Jeep passed. There had been no wave for help. But Eleanor had the retinal memory of a shapeless dress plastered to the stocky form.

The road was too narrow and the ditches too deep here to risk a U-turn, so Eleanor set the automatic selector to Reverse and backed over the rise, hoping that she would have at least a second's warning if headlights suddenly appeared.

There were no headlights. Eleanor backed the Jeep down the hill, wiping her glasses against the rain, and stopped next to the car in the ditch. It was some sort of cheap rental econobox. The left rear had been jacked up, but it looked as if the asphalt had buckled under the narrow jack, sliding the car deeper into the ditch. The person crouching near the rear of the car stood up.

"Miserable piece of shit," said a husky voice. "The spare's one of them little pissant undersized emergency jobs, supposed to get you to the next gas station. When the two-bit jack bit off the edge of the road there, the damned frame come down on the spare and ripped it all to shit."

"Are you all right?" asked Eleanor. She could see that it was a woman, short, moon-faced, her stringy hair plastered to her forehead and ears, the thin dress—what Eleanor's mother would have called a housedress—soaked through and seemingly painted over heavy thighs, bulging middle, and small breasts.

The woman sluiced her hair out of tiny eyes and squinted at Eleanor in the rain. "It's a rental and I'm going to leave it here. You headin' over to the west coast?"

"Yes," said Eleanor. "Want a ride?" Before she had finished the query, the woman had pulled open the rear door of the rental, tugged out two old suitcases, and tossed them into the back of the Jeep with no apparent concern for the pool of water there.

The woman hefted herself up onto the passenger seat, lifted Eleanor's purse and duffel, and said, "Mind if I set these back on my stuff?"

"No, fine."

"They'll get wet. But they'll get wet if I set 'em down here, too."

Eleanor nodded. "The back's fine." She was no Henry Higgins, but Eleanor prided herself on discerning dialect. This woman was not a native Hawaiian. She came from the Midwest; Eleanor guessed Illinois, although parts of Indiana or Ohio were possible.

She jammed the Jeep in gear and drove over the rise again. The rough road continued to wind through low trees. Reflected flames from Mauna Loa tinged everything with an eerie glow. "Car just run off the road?" asked Eleanor, hearing her own midwestern dialect kick in. It was a habit she allowed herself when off campus, her native accent having been eroded away during her years at Columbia and Harvard before returning to Oberlin.

The woman wiped her face with thick hands that were greasy from her work under the car. Eleanor noted the unself-consciousness of the act, more a man's motion than a woman's. "Didn't just run off the road," said the woman. "Some damn APC come out of the brush and almost hit me. I got a wheel off into that ditch and another wheel flat, but at least I avoided becomin' Desert Storm roadkill. Damn APC didn't even look back."

"What's an APC?" Eleanor used her wad of Kleenex to mop the inside of the windshield. The rain seemed to be letting up.

"Armored personnel carrier," said the woman. "They're

from the Pohakuloa Military Camp that we're passin' through. Boys out playing their games.''

Eleanor nodded. "Are you connected with the military?''

"Me?'' The woman laughed as unself-consciously as she had mopped her face. It was a deep, throaty sound—what Aunt Beanie referred to as "a whiskey laugh.''

"Hell no,'' said the woman, her voice still amused. "I don't have nothing to do with the Army except for two of my six boys who done time in the service.''

"Oh,'' said Eleanor, somewhat disappointed in her faulty speculation. It had seemed sensible that this no-nonsense woman was affiliated with the Army. "You knew what an APC was,'' she said, realizing as she said it how lame it sounded.

The woman laughed again. "Yeah, but don't everybody? Didn't you watch CNN during the Gulf War?''

"Not really,'' said Eleanor, her voice vibrating up and down the scale as they bounced over the washboard pavement. The road was rising.

Her passenger looked at her through the gloom and then seemed to shrug. "Well, my boy, Gary, was over there, so I guess I had me more reason than some to pay attention. And I admit it, after livin' through Vietnam and the Iran hostage thing, it wasn't too bad watching us kick somebody's butts other than our own.'' As if remembering something, the woman stuck out her hand.

Startled, Eleanor lifted her hand from the wheel to shake. She felt calluses on the other woman's palm.

"My name's Cordie Stumpf . . . that's S-T-U-M-P-F . . . and I'm much obliged that you stopped for me. I could've been out there for a long time, given how little traffic there is. Except for those goddamn APCs, of course, but I don't think I would've wanted to go where they're going.''

"Eleanor Perry,'' said Eleanor, retrieving her hand and fighting the Jeep around another hard turn. "You said you're headed for the west coast. Which part?''

"One of the fancy resorts,'' said Cordie Stumpf. She was rubbing her bare arms as if she were cold. Eleanor realized that it *was* cold at this altitude, in the dark, in the rain.

"Which one?" said Eleanor, turning on the heater. "I'll be going south to the Mauna Pele."

"Yeah," said Cordie.

Eleanor looked over inquisitively. It was hard to believe that this woman in her print housedress with her clunky old suitcases was headed for one of the most expensive resorts in Hawaii. *I should talk,* thought Eleanor. *I'll use up five years of savings in this one week of foolish adventure.*

"Yeah, that's the one I'm headed for," said Cordie. "Were you on the United flight that got sent over to Hilo?"

"Yes," said Eleanor. She had not noticed the other woman on the flight, but there were two hundred some bodies squashed between decks back there. Eleanor liked to think of herself as observant, but she would have had little reason to notice the woman except for her slightly out-of-place plainness.

"I was in first class," said Cordie, as if reading Eleanor's thoughts. "I guess you was in the back." There was no snobbishness in the comment.

Eleanor nodded again, smiling slightly. "I rarely get to fly first class."

Cordie laughed her whiskey-rich laugh again. "I never flew up front before. It's really a stupid waste of money. But my tickets was part of the prize."

"Prize?"

"Vacation with the Millionaires," said Cordie, and chuckled. "*People* magazine had that contest, remember?"

"I missed it," said Eleanor. She read *People* exactly once a year, during her annual visit to her gynecologist.

"So'd I," said Cordie. "But my boy Howie didn't. He sent my name in and I won. For Illinois, at least."

"For Illinois?" said Eleanor, thinking, *I knew it. Outside of Chicago somewhere. Downstate.*

"Yeah, the idea was that one lucky person from each state would win a week with the millionaires at this Mauna Pele place. It's Byron Trumbo's big brainstorm. He's the guy who built the place, according to *People*. So I was sorta Miss Illinois, only I haven't been a 'Miss' since 1965. Anyway, the funny part is that the contest people didn't want to tell me, but I'm the only one of the fifty winners who's actually coming now. All the rest said no and took the cash equivalent or are waitin' on it.''

"Why?" said Eleanor, although she could guess.

Cordie Stumpf cocked her head. "You ain't heard about the six people who disappeared at this new place? Some says that others have been killed but Trumbo's people are covering it up. It's been in the *Enquirer*. Headline was 'Billion-Dollar Resort Built on Ancient Hawaiian Burial Ground, Tourists Dyin' and Disappearin'.' ''

The road was straighter now, rising more steeply. The west slopes of both Mauna Kea and Mauna Loa were presences in the dark set far on either side of the road as the valley opened out. "I *have* read something about that," said Eleanor, feeling like a liar for the understatement. She had clipped everything she could find on the disappearances, including the absurd *National Enquirer* article. "Aren't you nervous about going there?" she said.

Cordie laughed softly. "Why, 'cause the hotel's built on an Indian burial ground and the ghosts are gettin' the tourists? Shoot, I seen that plot in that movie *Poltergeist* a bunch of years ago, and about a hundred movies like it. My boys used to rent those horror videos all the time."

Eleanor decided to change the subject. "You have six boys? How old?"

"The oldest's twenty-nine," said Cordie. "Gonna be thirty come September. The youngest is nineteen. How old're your kids?"

Usually Eleanor bridled at the presumption of people asking questions like that, assuming that she was married, but there was something about Cordie Stumpf that kept her from getting angry. It was the unself-consciousness of it, similar to her physical movements. Broad, gross almost, but coming across as nothing except what they were.

"No children," said Eleanor. "No husband."

"Not ever?" said Cordie.

"Not ever. I'm a teacher. It's kept me busy. And I like to travel."

"A teacher," said Cordie. She seemed to shift in her seat to look at Eleanor more carefully. The rain had stopped now and the wipers made a dry, scraping sound on the windshield. "I had some bad luck with teachers back when I was in school," said Cordie, "but my guess is that you're a college professor. History maybe?"

Eleanor nodded, surprised.

"What period you specialize in?" asked Cordie, the interest real and audible in her voice.

Eleanor was even more surprised. Usually people reacted the way the salesman on the plane had—dead eyes, slack gaze, the monotone of indifference.

"Actually my study and teaching has been about the intellectual history surrounding the Enlightenment," said Eleanor, her voice rising so that she could be heard over the Jeep's laboring engine and the whine and rumble of the oversized tires. "The eighteenth century," she added.

Amazingly, Cordie Stumpf was nodding. "You mean Voltaire, Diderot, Rousseau . . . those guys."

"Exactly," said Eleanor, reminding herself of what Aunt Beanie had taught her thirty years before—*Don't underestimate people.* "You've read . . . I mean, you know their writings?"

Cordie laughed more loudly than ever. "Me? Read Voltaire? Honey, it's everything I can do to take time to read *Jokes for the John* when I'm in the crapper." The woman turned her moon face toward the road ahead. "Uh-uh, Eleanor, I never read none of those guys. My second husband—Bert that was—he *wanted* to be educated and ordered the entire *Encyclopaedia Britannica* for the kids and all. He got this set of other books with it . . . the *Great Books.* Ever hear of it?"

"Yes," said Eleanor.

"It's like a set of important books for people who are worried that they ain't well educated. Anyway, each of the *Great Books* got a timeline in the whatchamacallits," continued Cordie. "The endpapers. Voltaire and all those guys. When they was born. When they died. I helped Howie do a term paper once using those endpapers."

Eleanor nodded. She remembered what else Aunt Beanie had said thirty years ago. *And don't overestimate people, either.*

Suddenly the Saddle Road crested and they were looking down on what had to be the beginning of the west coast of the Big Island of Hawaii. Volcano glow glinted on what might be the Pacific Ocean many miles to the west. Eleanor thought that she could see a few lights far to the north.

They came to a fork in the road. A sign pointing north read: WAIMEA.

"We want south," said Cordie Stumpf.

It was much warmer along the coast and the sky was clear. Eleanor realized how cold it had been high on the Saddle Road with the chilly trade winds at their backs and the rain blowing in on them. The air had become thicker and more gentle since they had followed Highway 190 down to the Waikoloa turnoff and then driven through the scattered lights of the first development they had seen, down to the coast highway. Here the sense of the tropics had returned, the salt-and-decay scent of the sea, the thick air that matted Eleanor's short hair, and the almost subliminal sound of surf under the tire and engine noise.

The coast road held little traffic this night, but even the occasional car was jarring after the emptiness of the Saddle Road. Eleanor had expected a much more settled area here, but except for the half-glimpsed lights of Waimea thirty miles earlier and the scattered homes of Waikoloa on the way to the coast, there seemed little enough. Mostly the headlight beams revealed the borders of great lava fields, sometimes softened by scrub trees. As they approached the resort areas, messages appeared in the lava— words and sentences spelled out in arrangements of white coral laid out on the black lava. Most of the messages were in the category of universal adolescent graffiti—DON AND LOVEY, PAULA LOVES MARK, TERRY SAYS HI!—but there was, Eleanor soon noticed, no obscenity, no vulgarities, almost as if the effort it took to find and lay out the dozens of white coral stones for each message eliminated the casual meanness of urban graffiti. Many of the messages were greetings—THE TAJEDAS WELCOME GLENN

AND MARCI, ALOHA TARA!, DAVID WELCOMES DAWN AND PATTI, MAHALO TO THE LAYMANS—and Eleanor soon found herself looking for her own name, half anticipating some greeting spelled out in coral.

The resorts were all but invisible, represented along the highway only by torchlit, guarded gates and roads heading seaward through black lava. Eleanor glanced at several of these entrances as they drove south: the Hyatt Regency Waikoloa, where the fat salesman would be sleeping tomorrow night, then the distant lights of the Royal Waikoloan, the Aston Bay Club, then a ten-mile stretch of empty road, then the torchlit entrance to Kona Village, the actual resort invisible across the lava fields, then another ten or fifteen miles in the dark before the sodium vapor lamps along the highway and brighter lights to seaward announced Keahole Airport.

"There's jets landing," said Cordie Stumpf.

Eleanor jumped, so lost in thought had she been. She had almost forgotten the other woman was along. "They must have opened it," Eleanor said, looking at the stars above. "The ash cloud must have stopped or moved south."

"Yeah," agreed Cordie, "or that jet's just carrying more important passengers than us. Rules get broke easier for powerful folks."

Eleanor frowned at the simplistic cynicism but said nothing. Several miles beyond the airport, the lights of Kailua-Kona glared to the west. Eleanor pulled into the town to top off the Jeep's tank and found only a single gas station open. She was shocked to see that there was no self-service. A sleepy attendant came out to pump the gas—and she was more shocked to notice that it was almost midnight. It had taken more than three hours to travel the eighty miles or so from Hilo.

"How far to the Mauna Pele?" she asked the overweight Hawaiian attendant. In her fatigued condition, Eleanor half expected the man to look up, drop the handle of the pump, and say something like, *You don't want to go* there, just like in an old Hammer horror movie.

Instead, the Hawaiian didn't even look up from his pumping as he said, "Twenty-two miles. That'll be seven fifty-five."

Beyond Kona the road grew more treacherous, the cliffs dropped off more precipitously to the sea, and the clouds occluded the stars once again.

"Jesus," Cordie said tiredly over the wind noise, "they don't make this place easy to get to."

"Perhaps we should have stayed in Hilo like the others," said Eleanor, speaking to stay awake. "And let them bring us over tomorrow." She glanced at her watch. "Today."

Cordie shook her head in the darkness. "Uh-uh. This prize was for seven days and six nights at the place startin' *tonight.* I'm not going to miss a whole night of my free vacation."

Eleanor smiled at this. The slopes rose more steeply to the east here, the bulk of Mauna Loa half sensed in the night. The slightest orange glow from the distant eruption remained visible through the lowering clouds. Except for a few homes and darkened commercial structures south of Kona, there seemed to be nothing but lava fields and cliffs along this stretch of road. Even the roadside messages spelled out in white coral rock were absent, making the *a'a* lava fields seem darker and sharper.

Eleanor had noted the odometer at the gas station, and at about eighteen miles the road left the sea cliffs and moved inland a mile or two, the black asphalt of the highway becoming almost inseparable from the black lava in the headlights except for the white stripes and reflectors, the sense of penetrating a stone wilderness stronger here.

"It sure doesn't look like the Midwest, does it?" Eleanor commented to her passenger, wanting to hear the sound of voices again more than anything else. Fatigue and tension from the long drive had given her a headache.

"Don't look like any part of Illinois I've been in," agreed Cordie Stumpf. "Nor Ohio neither. Your area around Oberlin's real pretty."

"You've been there?"

"The gentleman I was married to before the late Mr. Stumpf had some business there with the college. When he run off with the Las Vegas girl—Lester that is, Mr. Stumpf was too religious to even go to Las Vegas—I took over the Ohio business as part of my own and visited the college there in Oberlin."

"What business is that?" asked Eleanor. She had assumed that Mrs. Stumpf was "just" a housewife.

"Garbage," said Cordie. "Hey, there's something up there."

The "something" resolved itself into a gate, a stone wall, a guardhouse in the form of a thatched hut, all with half a dozen gas-fed torches illuminating them. The large copper letters on the stone wall—in a type set somewhere between that of *Jurassic Park* and *The Flintstones*—read: MAUNA PELE.

Eleanor found herself letting out a breath she had not noticed herself holding.

"Found it," said Cordie, sitting up straighter and pulling her lank hair back over large ears.

A sleepy-looking man in a security-guard uniform stepped out of the lighted booth as they pulled up. A thick chain ran from the guardhouse to the wall. *"Aloha,"* he said, looking surprised to see them. "Can I help you?"

"We have reservations at the Mauna Pele," said Eleanor, glancing at her watch. It was past 12:30 A.M.

The guard nodded and consulted a clipboard. "Your names, please."

Eleanor gave both their names and felt a second of strangeness, as if she and this odd woman—moon-faced, housedressed, red-fingered Mrs. Cordie Stumpf—were old friends and traveling companions. She put the sensation down to a mixture of déjà vu and pure fatigue. Eleanor loved to travel, but she never slept well the night before a trip.

"Yes, welcome to the Mauna Pele," said the guard. "We thought that the guests arriving tonight had all stayed in Hilo." He unclipped the chain and dropped it on the road. "Just follow this lane for about two miles. It's a little rough because of some construction traffic, but it gets better when you get closer to the Big Hale. Don't get off on any of the unpaved roads going through the lava . . . you'll just end up at a construction shack. You can just leave the Jeep under the porte cochere with the keys in it and they'll park it for you. OK?"

Cordie leaned over. "What's a Big Hale?"

The man smiled, his features flickering in and out of shadow in the torchlight. *"Hale* just means house. The Mauna Pele has more than two hundred little *hales*—like grass huts only a lot more comfortable—and the Big Hale is actually the seven-story main lodge where the conference center, dining areas, and shops are. There are about three hundred rooms there too."

"Thanks," said Eleanor. *"Mahalo."*

The man nodded and watched them drive on. In her rearview mirror, Eleanor saw him rehanging the chain.

"What's a porte cochere?" asked Cordie.

Since she was three years old, Eleanor had had an inordinate fear of asking what seemed to be a stupid question. Accordingly, she had begun looking up things in books at an early age to avoid showing her ignorance. She respected Cordie's ability to ask about things she did not understand.

"It's a covered section of an entrance," said Eleanor. "Usually it extends over the driveway. Useful here in the tropics."

Cordie nodded. "Like a carport only you can keep going."

The lane was in worse condition than the Saddle Road. The Jeep vibrated over patched asphalt, and Eleanor concentrated on moving ahead without skipping into the lava on either side. There were glimpses of earth-moving equipment parked off the main road and twice they saw steel shacks with fences and security lights.

"Pretty primitive approach to one of the most expensive resorts in the world," said Eleanor.

"How much does a room or *hale* cost . . . per night?" asked Cordie.

"Mmmm . . . I think mine is going to run about five hundred something per night," said Eleanor. "But that includes breakfast."

Cordie made a choking sound. "You'd think they could patch their road with them prices."

At 1.6 miles on the odometer, the road grew wider and smoother. Suddenly it divided into two lanes, a hedge of purple bougainvillea paralleled the drive, a carefully tended riot of tropical flowers and ferns filled the median, and gas-flame torches spaced only thirty feet apart lighted the way through the oasis of palms. Eleanor realized that the winding lane was passing through the darkened links of an elaborate golf course. Unseen sprinklers *tsk-tsked* at the Jeep as they passed and the air smelled of wet grass and dark loam. Electric lights became visible around the bend in the road.

A heavy woman in a *muumuu* came out under the porte cochere to greet them with *leis* and to lead them into the lobby. The Big Hale was part hotel and part giant grass hut with Disney-fake thatched roofs, with private *lanais* outside every room and waterfalls of flowering plants hanging down from each balcony as if the place were attempting to re-create the Hanging Gardens of Babylon.

Eleanor felt old as she got out of the Jeep. Her back hurt. Her head ached. The scent of the flowered *lei* came through the haze of fatigue like a distant shout. The lady in the *muumuu* had identified herself as Kalani and now Eleanor followed her and Cordie, the flowered *muumuu* and the soggy flowered housedress, up tile steps, into a beautiful tiled lobby with golden Buddhas flanking the entrance, across an atrium where birds slept in cages thirty feet tall, past a terrace overlooking the tops of palm trees, their rustling fronds catching torchlight, to the formalities of signing the register and imprinting her credit card—Cordie needed to give no credit card imprint, merely receive Kalani's congratulations, they were *so* excited to welcome one of the contest winners, "they" being Kalani and the dark-skinned little man who had appeared next to her behind the counter. Eleanor noticed that he wore a Hawaiian shirt and white pants and was smiling as broadly as Kalani had.

Then she was waving good-bye to Cordie, who was being escorted to an elevator—evidently contest winners stayed in the Big Hale—while the little man led her back to the terrace. Eleanor groggily realized that the Big Hale had to be built on a hillside: the first floor entrance on the porte cochere side was at least thirty feet off the ground on the ocean side. The porter led her down a staircase to a waiting electric cart which already had her duffel bag in the back.

"You are staying in Tahitian Hale twenty-nine?" asked the man. Eleanor looked at her key, but he had not really been asking a question. "Those *hales* are very nice. Very nice. Away from the noise of the Big Hale."

Eleanor glanced back at the Big Hale as they whirred away down a narrow asphalt lane between the palms. The main hotel was dark; only a few rooms showed even the hint of lights behind curtains. Torches sputtered in the night wind. She could not imagine that there were many people there this night or that the Big Hale could ever be noisy.

They whirred past lagoons, wound downhill through a garden that made her dizzy with its rich smells, across a bridge spanning a narrow lagoon, past a waterfall, across another bridge, around a small swimming pool, then in sight of a beach with white breakers crashing in with a flurry of phosphorescence, then back into a thicker stand of palm trees. Eleanor realized that there were little huts set back in these trees, the buildings raised six to ten feet above the level of the path they were humming along. Shielded electric lamps glowed inches from the ground, set deep in tropical foliage, but the torches set every few yards were not lighted here, perhaps they had been extinguished at some sane hour.

Eleanor felt with a strange certainty that the vast majority of these expensive *hales* were empty this night, that the Mauna Pele was mostly empty—Big Hale and little *hales*—all several thousand acres of it mostly empty except for its support staff and night workers back there in the island of light that was the main lobby and atrium and terrace. They whirred around another rock-lined lagoon, turned left onto a little path, and stopped in front of a thatch-roofed *hale* set ten feet up stone stairs.

"Tahitian twenty-nine," said her guide. "Very nice." He lifted her duffel out and bounded up the stairs, holding the door open for her.

Eleanor entered the *hale* as if in a dream. It was very neat—a porch, a small entry foyer, a narrow hall leading to an open bath area, a sitting area and sleeping area beyond, the queen-sized bed covered by a bright quilt of some island design, two lamps burning on either side of the comfortable-looking bed, windows on each side with louvered shutters half drawn, a high ceiling with latticework at the gables, at least two fans slowly turning. Eleanor could see a private *lanai* beyond shuttered French doors and could hear the recycling pump on her private hot tub there.

"Very nice," repeated her guide with the slightest hint of question in his voice.

"Very nice," said Eleanor.

The man smiled. "My name is Bobby. Please let me know if I or anyone else on the staff can make your stay more pleasant in any way. Breakfast is served on the terrace of the Big Hale and at the Shipwreck Lanai from seven to ten-thirty. It is all in here . . ." He tapped a thick sheaf of folders and service guides on her bedside table. "We do not have Do Not Disturb signs here, but when you wish to be left alone, just set this coconut on your front porch and no one will disturb you." He lifted a coconut with the volcano symbol of the Mauna Pele painted on its side. *"Aloha!"*

Tip, thought Eleanor through her fog of tiredness, and fumbled in her purse. She found only a ten, but when she turned around with it in her hand, Bobby was gone. She heard the whirr of the electric cart, but it was out of sight by the time she moved to the shuttered window.

Eleanor explored the *hale* for a few minutes, switching on and off lights in different areas, then made sure the accordion doors in back and the single door in front were locked. She sat on the bed, too tired to unpack or undress.

She was still sitting there, half dozing, dreaming of the Saddle Road and of huge metal beasts crashing around in the shrubs, when something or someone began to scream just outside her window.

SIX

*As I prepare for sleep, a rich voice rises out of the
still night, and, far as this ocean rock is toward
the ends of the earth, I recognize a familiar home
air. But the words seem somewhat out of joint:*
   "Waikiki lantoni oe Kaa hooly hooly wawhoo."
*Translated, that means "When we were marching
through Georgia."*
         —Mark Twain
         "Roughing It in the Sandwich Islands"

June 7, 1866, Hilo, Hawaii—

Our Mr. Clemens is becoming somewhat of an active
annoyance.

The two-day trip from Honolulu to the Island of Hawaii
might be generously described as one of life's least enjoyable
experiences. We were no sooner out to sea when the ship, the
Boomerang, an aging propeller of some 300 tons, began
wallowing and slewing its way from trough to swell and then from
swell to trough. Most of my fellow passengers had the good
grace to retire to their bunks to retch in comparative
privacy—although there was no privacy aboard that dreadful
ship, nor segregation of the sexes, for everyone—Hawaiian
native, Honolulu gentleman, British lady, Chinaman and *paniolo*
cowboy—was thrown together in the most promiscuous
circumstances, the stern "sleeping cabin" being merely an
extension of the crude saloon where one eats, drinks,
promenades, and plays cards.

After my previously recorded verbal victory over the

tiresome Mr. Clemens, I had taken myself down to my bunk in this abysmal cabin, but immediately upon entering the darkened confines of the long common room, I was confronted with two cockroaches on my appointed berth. While I have oft recorded how I detest and fear cockroaches more than grizzly bears or Rocky Mountain panthers, it needs to be added that these were no ordinary cockroaches. These monsters were the size of lobsters with red eyes and antennae on which one could have hung one's hat and parasol.

Besides the indelicate sounds of our more delicate passengers bringing up the celebratory luncheons they had enjoyed before departure at Honolulu, there were the snores of the indifferent sleepers who had stacked themselves like firewood around the periphery of this common room. I noticed that Mrs. Windwood was using a dozing gentleman's head for a footstool and later discovered that the gentleman in question was the Governor of Maui.

Keeping a careful eye on the cockroaches, which appeared to be plumping my pillow in preparation for a long nap of their own, I retreated to the upper deck once again and accepted the "berth" of a mattress near the transom. It seemed that Mr. Clemens also had planned to spend much of the voyage "out here where the air has only been breathed once" and so we were thrown upon each other for conversation once again. For several hours before exhaustion drove us to our respective "berths" on the deck, Mr. Clemens and I spoke of irrelevant and often irreverent things. I believe that the correspondent was surprised to find a lady who enjoyed banter and telling amusing anecdotes as much as did he. His youthful boorishness never quite departed, nor did his terrible habit of lighting up a cheap cigar without so much as a "by-your-leave," but having toured the Rocky Mountain wilderness and the Wild West between there and San Francisco, I was almost used to such a lack of manners. I do admit that the garrulous correspondent kept my mind and stomach off the pitching of the *Boomerang* and the possibility of being assassinated by cockroaches.

When I mentioned my disgust at the sight of these creatures,

Mr. Clemens agreed that they were "a fair share" of the reason he had come up on deck. "My resident cockroaches were as big as peach leaves," he said, "with long, quivering antennae and fiery, malignant eyes. They grated their teeth like tobacco worms and appeared dissatisfied about something."

I described the lobster-sized vermin who had laid claim to my pillow. "I tried to prod one with my parasol," I said, "but the smaller of the two cockroaches appropriated the instrument and used it as a sort of tent."

"It is best that you declined to do further battle," suggested Mr. Clemens. "I have it on good authority that these reptile-sized insects are in the habit of eating off a sleeping sailor's toenails down to the quick. This thought is what gave me an overwhelming hankering to come up and sleep in the rain."

And so it was in this vein of nonsense that we passed a good portion of that evening.

At five in the morning the ship put into Lahaina, the largest village on the green isle of Maui, and Mr. Clemens seemed very keen to go ashore. Unfortunately for both him and your interlocutor—welcoming as I would have a respite from his talkative presence—the captain of the *Boomerang* sent nothing ashore but longboats of mail and various provisions, receiving like in return, and Mr. Clemens had to stand at the rail, inhale the sandalwood scent of this southern isle, and regale me with stories of his visit to those green hills earlier in his three-month sojourn in the islands.

We departed Maui in early afternoon, and the channel between that isle and its larger sister to the south was a more restless bit of water than any we had encountered so far. The crossing itself took a mere six hours, but it must have seemed longer to the majority of our fellow travelers, some of whom were praying for death as deliverance from their *mal de mer* before we reached the coastal waters of Hawaii itself. Mr. Clemens continued to be unaffected by all of the tossing and rolling—the ship's, that is, he did seem somewhat put off by the tossing and rolling of the afflicted passengers—and when I commented about his resistance to such pitchings, he confided

in me that he had "served his time" as a riverboat pilot before
the War.

I asked him why he had traded such a profession for that of
correspondent. Mr. Clemens leaned on the railing, lighted
another of his detestable cigars, and said with a bit of glint in his
eye, "I hated to do it, Miss Stewart. Join the literary life, I mean.
I tried to find honest work, may Providence turn me into a
Methodist if I did not. I tried, and failed, and succumbed to the
temptation of making my living without having to work."

Not to be distracted by his childish badinage, I said, "But do
you miss piloting, Mr. Clemens?"

Instead of another awkward half-witticism, the red-haired
correspondent looked out over the ocean as if seeing something
quite removed from the scene before us. It was the first time I
had seen him serious. "I loved the profession of piloting as I
may never love another thing or another person," he said, his
voice and dialect less exaggerated than I had previously heard.
"My time on the river was as entirely free as I could imagine a
human being's life to be. I consulted no one, received commands
from no one, and was as unfettered as any soul could aspire to
be in this life."

Somewhat surprised by this serious answer, I said, "And was
your river as beautiful as this not-so-pacific ocean?"

Mr. Clemens took a moment to inhale his poisonous smoke.
"My early days on the river were as seductive as wandering
through the Louvre, Miss Stewart. There was unexpected beauty
everywhere. It took me, as the cowboy said upon finding a snake
in his boot, a bit unprepared. But as I became more proficient as
a pilot, that beauty faded."

"Due to familiarity?" I suggested.

"No," said Mr. Clemens, tossing the remains of his cigar
into the sea, "from my mastery of the language of the river."

I looked at him without understanding and rotated my
parasol.

The correspondent smiled that boyish smile again. "The
river was like a book, Miss Stewart. The face of the
water—traveling both upriver and down—was like some ancient
but recently discovered scroll written in a dead language. As I

learned that language—the language of treacherous floating logs and hidden bluff reefs and wooded shores memorized now not for their beauty but for their reminder to seek the safe channel—as this marvelous book surrendered its secrets to me, so too did the natural beauty of the river—its silences at sunrise, its hushed twilight stirrings—so too did all these recede, as if their beauty was bound by their mystery."

I admit that the gentleman's sudden transformation from boorish scribbler to frustrated poet made me silent for a moment. Perhaps Mr. Clemens noticed this, or was embarrassed by his flight of fancy, for he fished out another cigar and waved it like a wand. "At any rate, Miss Stewart, a riverboat might kill you—the boiler can blow, the hull be torn out in a second by one of those lovely bluff reefs—but it never makes the human body want to turn itself inside out the way this ocean-going raft has succeeded with our poor fellow passengers."

I left Mr. Clemens then and fell into an animated conversation with Thomas Lyman, Mr. Wendt, and the elderly Rev. Haymark about the "pros" and "antis" of missionaries and their effect on the islands. Mr. Wendt and Mr. Lyman held the currently fashionable views that the missionaries have been disastrous for the islands' economy, health, and autonomy, while the snuff-taking Reverend held the more traditional view that the natives had been baby-sacrificing heathens before his father and friends brought the Good News and civilization to them a generation ago. I admit that as the conversation followed its inescapable trajectory, I found myself wondering what irrelevancy Mr. Clemens might inject into the topic. But Mr. Clemens had claimed a mattress under a canvas awning and was sleeping away the hottest part of the tropical day.

We came in sight of Hawaii late in the afternoon, but clouds obscured all but the summits of two mighty volcanoes that appeared to gleam white with snow. The mere thought of snow in such latitudes was enough to make me giddy, and I decided at that moment to break my vows to all of my missionary friends in Honolulu who had made me swear that I would not attempt to reach the summit of Mauna Loa or its sister volcano.

*   *   *

It was already dark when we put in at Kawaihae on the northwest coast of Hawaii. Again there was the briefest exchange of mail and cargo and we set out again, steaming through the channel which separated Maui from the northernmost point of Hawaii. Here, although the skies were free of clouds and the stars brighter than I had ever seen them save for my excursions into the highest peaks of the Rocky Mountains, the sea was rougher than before, turning the common room below into a pitching repository of suffering humanity. There was no railside conversation with Mr. Clemens or any of the other passengers on this night; I gratefully accepted my "mattress" under the awning near the ventilator and spent much of the next seven hours hanging on to guy wires and brass brackets to keep from rolling bodily off the deck. Sometimes, when I slipped off to sleep and surrendered my grasp, the mattress *would* slide downhill toward the railing, only to slide back and deposit me in the place I began against the ventilator funnel as the ship rolled the opposite direction. I began to understand why they called the boat the *Boomerang.*

The sun rose in a glory of showers and rainbows and the sea calmed as if smoothed by an invisible hand. The northeast coast of Hawaii came into clear view, and it could not have been more different than the surprisingly brown and parched hills and black lava fields we had glimpsed of the northwest shore at dusk the night before. Here all was verdant—a thousand shades of green ranging from radiant emerald to the subtlest hues of muted celery—and the northern coast was a South Seas magic lantern show of dramatic cliffs, still perfectly green with vegetation although none of us could imagine how flora could thrive on such verticality, punctuated with sheer canyons opening to verdant valleys, decorated with the occasional small beach, gleaming white or black beneath the green cliff faces, and accentuated by a seemingly endless series of waterfalls that fell quite freely for a thousand feet and more from the jungles at the top of the unassailable bluffs to the rock pools and pounding spray beneath.

And everywhere along this impressive stretch of coastline

crashed the surf, sounding—the Reverend Haymark assured me—just like artillery in the recent war. In places the rolling combers exploded into cliffside caves and clefts, and everywhere they sent tall trailers of spray into the ferns that rioted along the grey rock faces.

For almost thirty miles or more along this north coast did we feast our eyes on this grandeur, seeing no sign of man's puny habitations save for a few native churches made of grass set in clearings near the cliff's edges, but ten miles or so from Hilo we caught glimpses of the first sugar plantations, their sweet fields an even more amazing green than the verdure our eyes had grown almost accustomed to, the white boiling houses and chimney stacks adding a pleasant contrast to all this mindless vegetable matter. And then there were more houses, more valleys, a profusion of grass shacks, more plantations, the bluffs and cliffs lining the coastline dropped until they reminded me of New England's more forgiving shore, and then we reached our destination at Hilo.

Even from the first moment of our entry into the crescent-shaped bay that served and protected this community, I could see that Hilo was the true paradise of the Pacific—the paradise that pretender-cities such as Honolulu could only gaze at with envy. Because of the wet climate and perfect growing conditions in air and soil, the city itself was more suggested than seen. Everywhere the tall coconut palms, candlenut trees, breadfruit trees, and a thousand other tropical blooms, ferns, and trailing vine hid all but the briefest glimpse of white wood or steeple from our direct view.

Here the sound of the surf was not artillery but more a soft chorus of children's voices, to which the entire canopy of greenery over the stately homes and grass huts alike seemed to sway in rhythm to Nature's music. It was as if our ship—so infected with illness and vermin during the two-day crossing—had transmogrified itself into a stately celestial vessel bearing its lucky pilgrims to this Eden-like anteroom to Paradise.

It was a sublime moment. It would have been a perfect moment—if Mr. Clemens had not scraped a Lucifer match along his boot sole, lit one of his unmentionable cigars, and said drily, "Those trees look sort of like a collection of feather-dusters struck by lightning, don't they?"

"Not in the least," I said as coldly as I could, still retaining the glow of sublimity that our entry had offered any truly sensitive soul.

"And those grass cabins—"continued Mr. Clemens, "look so furry that they might be made of bear skins, don't you think?"

I said nothing to this, hoping that my silence would act as reproof.

Oblivious to my disdain, the red-haired fool sent a cloud of exhaled cigar smoke between me and the view. "I don't see any skulls or skull-hunters," he said, "but it hasn't been that long since old Kamehameha and his boys were decorating these beaches with the heads of their victims and human sacrifices stuck on poles along the walls of their temples."

I opened my parasol and turned away, refusing to hear more of this offensive banter. But before I could retreat to the bow, where my real traveling companions were clustered, I heard the boorish correspondent mutter, as if to himself, "It's a darned shame—the damage that being saved and civilized does to a place. What a disappointment it means in terms of what a tourist gets to see."

SEVEN

When you're feelin' blue, here's what you gotta do,
Don't let 'em fool ya', just wiggle to the hula,
To the hula, giggle to the hula, to the hula,
To the hula, to the good ol' hula blues!
　　　　—Popular song of the 1930s

The morning dawned brisk and clear over the Mauna Pele Resort, sunlight crept around the south end of the volcano and threw thousands of palm fronds into green relief, while moderate winds moved the ash cloud far to the south and turned the sky over the resort into a bowl of perfect blue; the sea was calm, the surf seemed hardly more than a gentle curl onto the white-sand beach. Byron Trumbo didn't give a damn about any of it.

The Japanese had gotten in on time the night before, the airport opening again just long enough to land their jet an hour after Trumbo's, and the limo ride and brief reception at the Mauna Pele had gone according to plan. Mr. Hiroshe Sato and his entourage had been housed in the Big Hale Royal Suite, the penthouse complex only slightly less lavish than Trumbo's own Presidential Suite. Everyone in Sato's group had turned in shortly after arrival, claiming jet lag despite the fact that this was rarely a problem on the east-west leg of a trip. Because of the late hour, the resort had seemed normally quiet rather than unusually empty. Trumbo had set his security people three deep around the Royal Suite. When morning came, manager Stephen Ridell Carter reported that the three New Jersey car dealers had not been found, but at least no one else seemed to have disappeared overnight.

Byron Trumbo was still pissed.

"What's today's schedule?" he asked Will Bryant. "Our first meeting is over breakfast?"

"Check," said Bryant. "Our people meet their people on their breakfast terrace. You and Mr. Sato exchange pleasantries and gifts. You give the Tour. Then our people and their people work on the preliminary figures while you and Mr. Sato play golf."

Trumbo frowned over his coffee. "My people?" Everyone knew that Byron Trumbo did his own negotiating beyond the opening-bid stage. He and Sato had passed that weeks ago.

"I'm your people," said Will Bryant with a smile. He was wearing a gray, tropical-weight Perry Ellis suit. His long hair—Bryant's one affectation—was neatly tied back in a queue.

"We need to wrap this up in a day or so," said Trumbo, ignoring Will's comment. Trumbo was wearing what he always wore at the Mauna Pele—a bright Hawaiian shirt, faded shorts, and sneakers. He knew that young Sato would also be casual—golf clothes—while his seven or eight male aides would be sweating in gray suits. In this sort of situation, informality equaled power.

Will Bryant shook his head. "The negotiations are very sensitive . . ."

"They'll be a fucking sight *more* sensitive if one of Sato's people gets killed while we're talking," interrupted Trumbo. "We've got to wrap this up in a day or so, let Sato get his gutful of golf, and get them out of here while the ink's still wet on the paper. *Capisce?*"

"*Si,*" said Bryant. He shuffled papers, stacked them neatly, slid them into a folder, and set the folder in his calfskin briefcase. "Ready for the games to begin?"

Byron Trumbo grunted and got to his feet.

Eleanor awoke to a riot of birdsong. She sat up in a moment of confusion, then noticed the rich light through the shutters—light reflected off a thousand palm fronds—felt the thick, warm air against her skin, smelled the blossoms, and heard the soft murmur of the surf. "Mauna Pele," she whispered.

She remembered the screaming outside her window in the middle of the night. She had seen nothing through the shutters, so when the inhuman screams began again, she had looked around for something heavy—found only a complimentary umbrella in the closet near the door—taken a firm grip on that and unlocked the door. The screaming had been coming from the foliage along the path to her *hale*. Eleanor had waited almost a full minute before the peacock stepped onto the path, setting its feet as if they were sore, its feathers ruffling out and then folding again. It screamed a final time and waddled down the path out of sight.

"Welcome to paradise," Eleanor had said to herself. She had been around peacocks before—once camping in a field full of them in India—but their cries always demanded attention. She had never heard one calling at night.

Eleanor rose, showered—enjoying the scent of the shell-shaped soap—perfunctorily blow-dried her short hair, dressed in navy shorts, sandals, and a sleeveless white blouse, picked up the resort welcoming brochure and map from the nightstand, tossed it into her straw bag with Aunt Kidder's diary, and went out into the day.

The riot of flowering plants and soft sea breezes acted on her as such tropical places always did—making her wonder why she lived and worked in a part of the world where winter and darkness claimed so much of the year. The asphalt path meandered through a carefully tended jungle, *hales* rising on wooden stilts into the rustling palm fronds on either side of the path, while birds of bright plumage leapt and flew through the overhead canopy. Eleanor consulted the small resort map, checking her way as she encountered other paths, lagoons, wooden bridges, stone walkways, and well-tended dirt trails heading off into the artificial jungle. To her right, she caught glimpses of the lava fields that stretched for miles to the highway. The shield of Mauna Loa was visible to the northeast through the dancing fronds, its ash cloud only a watercolor slash of gray along the steep horizon line. To Eleanor's left, the ocean was a presence for all senses except sight: the sibilant wash of the surf, the scent of seawater and aquatic vegetation, the caress of the ocean breeze against her forehead and bare arms, and the faint taste of salt on her lips.

Eleanor turned left on the next path—a series of volcanic stepping stones winding through an explosion of flowers and palm trees—and walked past an empty pool onto the edge of the Mauna Pele beach. White sand curved away for half a mile to a rocky headland to her left and a long spit of sand and low lava to her right. She could see some of the more expensive *hales* rising near the water in both directions—large, Samoan-looking structures of polished redwood—and the seven-story Big Hale was visible through the cluster of palms along the main stretch of beach. Eleanor saw serious waves out beyond the entrance to the bay, their white curls smashing against rock and sand in geysers of spray, but within the protected curve of the lagoon the wave action became broad and slow, uncoiling onto the beach with an almost indolent sound.

There was no one on this perfect crescent of beach except two workers raking sand, one Hawaiian-shirted bartender in the open-sided grass hut bar near the pool, and Cordie Stumpf lying in the only beach chair, just short of the wash of lazy waves. Eleanor smiled. The other woman's swimsuit was a one-piece, flower-splashed thing that looked as if it had been purchased in the 1950s and worn for the first time today. Cordie's heavy arms and thighs were masses of white dough, and the woman's round face was already florid and sweaty from the morning sun. She wore no sunglasses and her small eyes squinted up as Eleanor approached across sand not quite hot enough to make her step lightly.

"Good morning," said Eleanor, smiling a greeting at Cordie and then looking out to where the smooth lagoon met the heavy breakers. "Beautiful day, isn't it?"

Cordie Stumpf grunted and shielded her eyes. "Do you believe that this place doesn't serve breakfast until six-thirty in the A.M.? How's a body to get a head start on a vacation day if you can't eat until six-thirty?"

"Mmmm," agreed Eleanor. She had left her watch in the *hale*, but it was not quite 7:30 when she started her walk. Eleanor rose early when she had early classes and on summer trips, but she was not really a morning person. Left to set her own schedule, she would work and write and read until two or three in the morning and sleep until nine. "Where did you finally find breakfast?"

Cordie gestured toward the Big Hale without turning to look at the rooftops rising above the palms. "They got an outside eating place there." She shielded her eyes and looked up at Eleanor. "You know, either everybody at this rich people's resort sleeps real late, or there ain't many people here."

Eleanor nodded. The sunlight and wave action filled her with a sense of buoyancy. She could not imagine anything terrible happening in such a place. Unconsciously, she shifted the strap of the straw bag on her shoulder, feeling Kidder's diary against her side. "I guess I'll head off to eat. Perhaps we'll see each other later."

"Yeah," said Cordie, her gaze on the lagoon once more.

Eleanor was just passing the thatched hut bar—the Shipwreck Bar she saw it was called, and then noticed the small sailing ship set on its side in the sand among the trees beyond the pool—when Cordie called out to her. "Hey, you didn't happen to hear nothing in the night, did you?"

Eleanor smiled. She imagined that Cordie Stumpf had never heard the cry of peacocks. She explained what she had heard and seen.

Cordie only nodded. "Yeah, but I didn't mean the birds. Something farther away." The woman hesitated a moment, hand raised over her squinting eyes, her neck creased into multiple folds. "Did you happen to see a dog?"

"A dog? No." Eleanor stood waiting. The bartender leaned on the polished counter of the bar and also waited.

"Okey-dokey," said Cordie Stumpf, and lay back on the reclined beach chair, closing her eyes again.

Eleanor waited a second more, glanced at the bartender, the two exchanged mental shrugs, and Eleanor went off in search of breakfast.

The breakfast meeting had gone about as planned on the Private Lanai overlooking the Sea Meadow, and after the meal Byron Trumbo took his guests on the Tour. The procession of golf carts rolled out of the private garage eight stories beneath the Presidential Suite, its order determined by protocol: Byron Trumbo and Hiroshe Sato rode alone in the first cart with Trumbo driving; the second cart was driven by Will Bryant with the elderly Masayoshi

Matsukawa, young Mr. Sato's principal adviser, alongside him in the front seat; in the rear seat of the second cart were Bobby Tanaka—Trumbo's Tokyo man—and young Inazo Ono, Sato's drinking pal and chief negotiator. The third golf cart was driven by Mauna Pele's manager, Stephen Ridell Carter—dressed as conservatively as the Japanese aides—with Dr. Tatsuro, Sato's personal physician, and Sato aides Seizaburo Sakurabayashi and Tsuneo "Sunny" Takahashi as passengers. The next three carts were filled with lawyers and golf cronies of the two principals. Following at a discreet distance were three more carts filled with Trumbo's and Sato's security details.

The golf carts rolled down the smooth asphalt path past the Whale Watching Lanai and through the Sea Meadow—a gradually sloping yard, putting-green smooth, bordered by flower beds and exotic plants. An artificial stream ran through the meadow, tumbled over lava rocks into pools and waterfalls, and ended in a grotto-bedecked lagoon that separated the beach area from the Big Hale area. Passing through a shield of coconut palms, they came out onto the Beach Walk Path.

"We pump more than twenty-two million gallons of seawater through these ponds and streams every day," Trumbo was saying. "Another fifteen million gallons to keep the lagoons fresh."

"It is recyclable?" inquired Hiroshe Sato.

Trumbo hesitated a second. He had heard—*It ii lecycraber?* Sato could speak almost unaccented English when he tried, but he rarely tried during negotiations.

"Sure it's recyclable," he said. "The hard part isn't the seawater ponds and streams, it's with the pools and koi ponds. We have three main pools for the guests, plus the swimming lagoon, plus the twenty-six private pools for the Luxury Hale guests on the Samoan Peninsula. And the carp ponds require the same quality water as the pools. All in all, it adds up to more than two million gallons of fresh water a day."

"Ahhhh," said young Mr. Sato, and smiled. And then, cryptically, "Koi. *Hai.*"

Trumbo swung the cart to the right, heading north along the Beach Walk, away from the Shipwreck Bar. "These are the manta pools. We have two-thousand-watt halogen floods underwater here. At night you can stand on that rock and reach out and touch the mantas we draw into the light.''

Sato grunted.

"This beach is now the finest one on the South Kona Coast,'' said Trumbo. "Probably on the entire west coast of the Big Island. It ought to be—we brought in more than eight thousand tons of white sand. The lagoon was original.''

Sato nodded, his chin deep in the folds in his neck. The young man's face was impassive; his black hair gleamed in the fierce sunlight.

The procession of carts hummed past dining pavilions, gardens, and lagoons into another line of coconut palms. Tall, stately *hales* rose on heavy legs. "This is the beginning of the Samoan Peninsula,'' said Trumbo. The carts passed down lanes of perfectly manicured tropical blooms, over wide bridges, and between lava boulders. "You see these are the largest of the two hundred some *hales* on the property. Ten people can sleep comfortably in each of these. The ones out here near the end of the peninsula each have their own pool and butler.''

"How much?'' said Sato.

"Excuse me?''

"How much per night?''

"Three thousand eight hundred per night for the Royal Samoan Bungalow,'' said Trumbo. "That doesn't include tips or meals.''

Sato smiled and Trumbo caught the impression that the Tokyo billionaire thought that this was a bargain.

Leaving the peninsula, the procession of carts hummed into a forest of palms and sea pines. "This is the closest of the three tennis centers. Each one has six Flexi-Pave courts. You can see the Sailing and Scuba Center off through the trees there—you can rent everything from kayaks and outrigger canoes to one of the Mauna Pele Classic Motor Launches—we have six—each one cost us three hundred and eighty thousand dollars. The Dive Center offers scuba lessons and excursions along the coast. In addition, we have parasailing, sailing, windsurfing, jet-boating—down the coast since the goddamn environmental regulations keep us from doing that in our own lagoon—sunset dinner excursions, surfing . . . all the usual shit.''

"Arr usuer shit," agreed Sato. The billionaire looked as if he were on the verge of dozing off behind his sunglasses.

Trumbo led the procession back past the Big Hale toward the lagoon.

"How big is the resort?" said Sato.

"Thirty-seven hundred acres," said Trumbo. He knew that Sato had all of the facts memorized from the prospectus. "That's counting the fourteen-acre petroglyph field." The golf carts meandered through the main *hale* section, around rock-lined lagoons where golden carp rose gaping to the surface. The carts encountered few pedestrians. Circling the beached schooner behind the Shipwreck Bar, they passed a twenty-meter pool where only a single family splashed and then wound through gardens of orchids. Trumbo noticed that Sato did not inquire why there were only a dozen or so people lounging on the beach or in the grassy shade under the hundred-foot coconut palms. Trumbo glanced at his watch; it was still early.

"How many rooms?" said Sato.

"Ahhh . . . two hundred twenty-six *hales*—bungalows—and another three hundred twenty-four rooms in the Big Hale. Some of our guests like to rough it. We get lots of movie stars and celebrities who just disappear into the *hales* for a week or two—Madonna was here last month. Norman Mailer and Ted Kennedy are regulars, as is Senator Harlen. They like the Samoan Bungalows and to be left alone. There's a painted coconut at each bungalow and if you set it on the steps, no one bothers you—not even to deliver mail. Others like room service and cable TV and direct dial phones and the in-room fax machines. We try to accommodate everyone's tastes."

Sato's lips were pursed as if he had swallowed something bitter. "Under six hundred rooms," he said softly. "Two golf courses. Eighteen tennis courts. Three main pools." *Three mine poors.*

Trumbo waited, but Sato said nothing else. Guessing at the

opinion being expressed, Trumbo said, "Yeah, we're heavy on space and guest services for the number of rooms. We're not trying to compete with the Hyatt Regency for population—I think they've got twelve hundred some rooms—or the Kona Village for quiet, or the Mauna Kea for old money—we're reaching all those target clients. Our concierge service is more efficient, our recreation more tailored to celebrity status than family fun, and our shopping more along Tokyo or Beverly Hills expectations. Our restaurants are better—we have five on the grounds, you know, plus room service in the Big Hale and catering to the Royal Samoan Bungalows—our courts are emptier and our golf courses are better designed."

"Golf," said Sato, pronouncing the *l* perfectly. His tone was almost wistful.

"Next stop after this," said Trumbo, and aimed the golf cart toward a boulder. Pulling a remote control device from his shirt pocket, he aimed it at the lava rock and thumbed the only button on it. A panel the size of a garage door slid up on the rock and the procession hummed down the asphalt path into a brightly lighted tunnel.

From her breakfast table on the Whale Watching Lanai, a large second-story dining area jutting out over the grass and gardens below like the bow of some oceanbound ship, Eleanor had watched the convoy of golf carts go by. All of the faces she glimpsed were Japanese and having seen such tour groups in most of the odd places in the world where she had wandered, Eleanor wondered if Japanese tourists were as cohesive in super-luxury resorts as they were among the more middle-class strata.

The *lanai* was large and pleasant; its windows were accordioned open and the scent of blossoms wafted in on every breeze. The floor was a dark, polished eucalyptus, the tables a light wood, the chairs expensive bamboo and wicker. Napkins were red linen and the water glasses were crystal. There was room for a couple of hundred people on the expansive deck, but Eleanor saw only a dozen or so there besides herself. All of the waitpersons were women, all Hawaiian, all of them moving gracefully in flowered *muumuus.* A light strain of classical music came from hidden speakers, but the real music was the susurration of palm fronds and the distant sound of surf.

Eleanor had perused the menu, making note of the specialties such as Portuguese bacon and French toast with coconut syrup, and then ordered an English muffin and coffee. The coffee was excellent—fresh-ground Kona—and Eleanor sat looking around as she sipped it.

She was the only solo diner on the *lanai*. This was not a new experience for her: for all of her adult life, Eleanor Perry had felt like a solitary mutant on a planet made up of cloned couples. Traveling, going to films or theater or ballet, eating out—even in postfeminist America, a woman on her own in a public place tended to be unusual. In many other countries of the world where Eleanor had traveled during her peripatetic summers, it was downright dangerous.

She did not care. Being the only single woman, the only solo person of either gender, on the *lanai* this morning seemed natural to her. For years she had brought books to read when dining out—indeed, Aunt Kidder's journal lay on the table at this moment—but at some point early on in her post-college life, Eleanor had realized that the book was a shield, a buffer against loneliness amidst all these happy families and couples around her. So she still read occasionally while eating—certainly that was one of the great benefits of remaining single, she thought—but she never leapt behind the book at the beginning of the meal. Eleanor Perry had become a restaurant voyeur, a veritable connoisseur of judging her fellow diners. She pitied the families and couples, so lost in their usual conversations that they failed to see the psychodrama going on in every restaurant and public place.

There was little psychodrama this morning in the Mauna Pele breakfast lanai. Only about six of the other tables were occupied—all near the open windows—and these were all couples. Eleanor appraised them at a glance: Americans except for the young Japanese couple and the gray-haired couple that might be German, expensive resortwear, the men with razor cuts and tans, the women with short, stylish hairdos and the less aggressive tans that were coming into vogue now that skin cancer was such a worry, the conversation soft or almost nonexistent as the men pored over copies of the *Wall Street Journal* and the women perused the day's activity sheet left on each table, or merely sat looking blank as they ate.

Eleanor looked out over the palm trees at the small bay and ocean beyond. Something large and gray suddenly broke the surface halfway to the horizon, a flipper caught the light, and a tall splash of water marked the place where the gigantic shape had disappeared as suddenly as it had emerged. Eleanor caught her breath and watched intently until she saw a spout of water about twenty yards from where the mammal had first appeared. The Whale Watching Lanai appeared to deserve its name.

She looked at the other patrons. No one seemed to have noticed. One woman three tables away was whining about how limited the shopping was here. She wanted to go back to Oahu. Her husband nodded, took a bite of toast, and continued to read the paper.

Eleanor sighed and lifted the single sheet of paper that listed the special activities that day at the Mauna Pele Resort. The printout was in cursive script on a heavy gray linen paper, looking as elegant as an invitation. There were the usual recreations one would expect at such a resort—none of which interested her—but two items caught her eye: At 9:30 A.M. there was an Art Tour led by Dr. Paul Kukali, Curator of Art and Archaeology at the Mauna Pele. At 1:00 P.M. there was a Petroglyph Walk, also led by Dr. Kukali. Eleanor smiled. Poor Dr. Kukali was going to be tired of her before this day was over.

Glancing at her watch, Eleanor smiled and nodded at the young waitress waiting to refill her coffee cup. Beyond the bay, the humpback whale hove into sight and slapped the water in what seemed to her to be—though Eleanor knew it was the worst sort of anthropomorphizing—a celebration of the beautiful day.

Trumbo led the procession down the long tunnel carved from black lava. Inset lights overhead provided pools of illumination.

"The problem with most of these damned resorts," Trumbo was saying to Hiroshe Sato, "is that most of the support services get in the way of the guests. Not here." He turned right at a broad intersection. White signs on the wall pointed the way. Another service cart passed, then a woman in hotel uniform on a bicycle. Large, round mirrors set high on the stone wall allowed riders and pedestrians to see around the corners.

"We've got all of the support stuff down here," continued Trumbo, gesturing at lighted offices as they passed. Windows looked out on the main corridor as if this were just another shopping mall. "The laundry here . . . at peak season, we do more laundry than any other place in Hawaii. There's twenty-six pounds of linen in every room and *hale*. Here . . . smell that? This is the bakery. Eight bakers on the staff. This place is humming all night . . . you should smell it about five A.M. OK, on our left here is the florist—we subcontract to a local garden, but somebody has to cut and arrange over ten thousand floral arrangements every week. Here's the office of our resident astronomer . . . ahh, here's the vulcanologist's office . . . Dr. Hastings is up at the volcano this week, but he'll be here to talk to us tomorrow morning . . . OK, our resident butcher, we get all our beef from Parker Ranch up by Waimea . . . *paniolo* country, those are Hawaiian cowboys . . . and here's the art and archaeology curator's office . . . Paul's a hell of a guy, he's native Hawaiian, Harvard-trained, and was our worst enemy when we were developing the Pele. So . . . what the hell . . . I hired him. I guess he figured the devil he knew, you know what I mean?"

Hiroshe Sato stared blankly at the American billionaire.

Trumbo turned left into another corridor. People looked out of doorways and lighted windows, nodding as they recognized the owner. He waved expansively, occasionally calling the workers by name. "Security here . . . Grounds and Maintenance . . . Water gets a special office . . . Ocean and Environmental Coordinator . . . Masseuse, we've got great masseuses here, Hiroshe . . . Wildlife Director, you may have noticed we've got birds and mongooses and other cute little critters coming out the ass . . . and here's Transportation . . ."

"How many?" said Sato.

"Hmmm? What's that?" asked Trumbo. Behind them, Will Bryant had laughed at something Mr. Matsukawa had said.

"How many employees?"

"Oh. Around twelve hundred," said Trumbo.

Sato lowered his chin to his chest. "Five hundred some rooms. Say average capacity of . . . eight hundred guests?"

Trumbo nodded. Sato was right on the number.

"You have one and one half employees for each guest." *Em-proyeez.*

"Yup," said Byron Trumbo. "But these are world-class guests. These are people who book suites at the Oriental when they're in Bangkok, who summer at the best private hotels in Switzerland. They *expect* the best service in the world. And they pay for it."

Sato half nodded.

Trumbo sighed and then turned up a ramp. A door opened automatically and they rolled out into brilliant sunlight, squinting. "But that's all detail, Hiroshe. Here's what we've come for this morning." The procession rolled through the shadow of tall coconut palms toward the low glass-and-cedar buildings surrounding the first tee.

"Ahhh," breathed Hiroshe Sato, his head coming up and the first smile of the day forming. "Golf."

EIGHT

The smoke bends over Kaliu.
I thought my lehuas were tabu.
The birds of fire are eating them up.
They are picking my lehuas
Until they are gone.
—Pele's sister Hi'iaka's chant on Pele's betrayal

June 14, 1866, Volcano of Kilauea—

Battered bones, aching muscles, and a fatigue so overwhelming as to be frightening, all forgo me from the added labor of writing this entry, but nothing can prevent me from recording the elation, thrill, majesty, and sheer, incommunicable terror of the last twenty-four hours. I write this by the light of Madame Pele's fiery handiwork.

I believe that I wrote earlier that Hilo seemed "the true paradise of the Pacific," and it is in terms of its blossomed streets, its quaint, white cottages, its exotic botany: *lauhala,* the pandanus, droops everywhere its funereal foliage and sends its aerial roots toward the wooden sidewalks as if preparing to join the other pedestrians on their evening sojourns, while banana plants hang their purple cones of undeveloped blossoms like proud medals, and each yard is festooned with gardenias, eucalyptus, guavas, bamboos, mangosteens, *kamani* trees, custard apples, coco-palms, and a veritable Garden of botanic delights. The missionaries who populate this particular terrestrial Garden offered me such attention in the way of social invitations that it was a full, frustrating week before I could begin my voyage to the volcano. For whatever reason, Mr. Clemens was similarly detained, so we began our adventure together.

I should mention here that the residents of Hilo, both native and transplanted, all ride regularly, each with the greatest skill and fervor I have ever witnessed, and all except the oldest of the ladies ride astride their mounts with perfect equanimity. Thus it was when I chose my mount—a handsome roan made up with an ornamented Mexican saddle and stirrups shielded with leathern flaps to protect my boots while riding through the brush—it was no surprise to see that I should be riding in the local manner. All of the horses chosen for this adventure had twenty feet or more of tethering rope wound about their necks, and the saddlebags were bulging with bread, bananas, and bottles of tea.

Our group for this outing included the younger and duller of the Smith twins, young Master Thomas McGuire (Mrs. Lyman's nephew), the corpulent Reverend Haymark, and our brash correspondent, Mr. Clemens. Master Wendt, who had first proposed this daring assault on Pele's realm, had taken ill and, from his sickbed, all but ordered the rest of us to go on without him.

I confess that I had widely contradictory feelings about Mr. Clemens's inclusion in our merry group: on one hand, his cynical presence threatened to reduce the spiritual dimension of what might be a transcendent experience; on the other hand, the Smith and McGuire boys were tiresome, totally incapable of either wit or the ordinary rigors of sustained conversation, and the asthmatic Reverend Haymark seemed interested only in Galatians and dinner. Thus it was that I greeted Mr. Clemens's expressive brow, untamed locks, and aggressive mustaches with something almost approaching relief.

Our guide, Hananui, who was dressed and garlanded most resplendently in the native style, wasted no time in introductions or explanations of the trip ahead, but spurred his horse and led us out of Hilo in a gallop. I then had the choice of either pretending to guide my horse or hanging on to the saddle horn with both hands and actually staying on the beast. I chose the latter.

We soon passed out of sight of the pretty little houses and trim little steeples, plunged through a jungle wild beyond anything in my experience, and continued climbing through this profusion along a hard track of black lava no more than twenty-four inches wide. Clinging to the saddle horn, the wide but soft-brimmed hat I had bought in Denver months earlier hanging around my throat by its drawstring, I could only watch for low branches and festooned trailers so that I would not be brushed off my horse, an obdurate creature I had thought was named "Leo," a name I later discovered as just a form of the Hawaiian for "horse"—*lio*. Passing out of this tropical forest, we soon moved through equally dense fields of cane, pausing about an hour's ride above Hilo as Hananui dispensed tin cups of cold tea to us.

After our tea party, we cantered out of the cane fields and final groves of trees onto the *pahoehoe*, or smooth lava, which continued on up the mountainside for as far as we could see. Such devastation—continuing on as it did for some twenty-three miles—would have been enough to make even this hardened traveler turn back, had it not been for the profusion of ferns and grasses which softened the black extrusion at every turn. As we climbed ever higher, the Pacific glowing far below and behind us in rich afternoon light, I easily identified a score of fern varieties, including the lovely *Microlepia tenuifolia*, the common Sadleria, the wirelike *Gleichenia hawaiiensis*, and the small-leaved *ohias (Metyrosideros polymorpha)* with their crimson blooms.

The human companionship was not of such a colorful variety. Here on the lava fields, the trail had widened and our party fell into sociable pairs. Hananui and the voluble Mr. Clemens led the way. Young Masters Thomas McGuire and Smith (the twins were never called by their Christian names since it was such a chore to tell them apart) followed, while the Reverend Haymark and I brought up the rear. The clergyman did not appear comfortable in a saddle, nor did the rather small horse under him appear comfortable with the clergyman's girth, and their combined lack of enthusiasm held back the pace more than if the other men had just been adjusting to my slower gait.

Mr. Wendt had told us that the trip was not an easy

one—more than thirty miles, most of it across the extensive lava fields, gaining some four thousand feet in elevation as we went—but I had not been prepared for my exhaustion late that afternoon when we reached what Hananui had called the "Half Way House," a term which had conjured images of comfortable chairs, hot tea, and warm scones, but which turned out to be a run-down grass hut. Even then, I might have collapsed in its shelter—a mild rain had come up and my hat was dripping from its soggy brim—but the "Half Way House" was quite securely locked.

Hananui was now visibly worried that we would not reach our objective before dark and, tying his horse by its tether, he went around to each of us and made sure that we had donned spurs—heavy, rusted Mexican instruments with rowels an inch and a half long. Upon Mr. Clemens's inquiry, Hananui admitted that there were at least five more hours of hard riding ahead of us with no place to rest or find water along the way.

Soon after leaving the Half Way House, I dropped behind, so exhausted were my limbs from their unaccustomed arrangement on this barrel-chested beast. I barely had the energy to keep spurring the tired animal on while clinging to the saddle horn. I found that if I turned my head to one side, the water from the now serious downpour would drip from my hat brim to the ground without soaking either my legs or the horse's neck.

I was surprised when I looked up to find Mr. Clemens riding alongside me. His solicitude, if that is what it was, irritated me, and I spurred "Leo" on to new heights of plodding indifference.

The correspondent was smoking one of his terrible cigars, the burning end just protected from the rain by the extra brim-width of the sombrero he was wearing. I noticed with something approaching envy that he also wore some sort of ankle-length waxed duster that—although it must be warm in such a climate—appeared to be repelling the rain with great effectiveness. My own skirts and layers of riding apparel must—I had estimated during the duller lengths of the Reverend's explications on Galatians—now weigh in the vicinity of a hundred pounds, so soaked were they by the evening's drizzle.

"Magnificent country, isn't it?" asked the former river pilot.

I agreed as noncommittally as I could.

"It was nice of the natives to perfume the air for us in this way, was it not?" he persisted. "And to choose this particular form of Sabbath light."

"Sabbath light?" I said. It was not a Sunday.

Mr. Clemens turned and nodded behind us, and for the first time in hours I swiveled in my saddle and looked to the east. It was raining where we were on this black-lava slope, but far out to sea the low sunlight ignited waves in a blinding gold and white. Other clouds and squalls cast their shadows on the sea, and these shadows moved like furtive animals seeking shelter from the general brilliance. To our left, where the low evening light passed through the valley between the Mauna Kea volcano and our own Mauna Loa, sunlight broke through clouds in streams and near-horizontal shafts, the light so golden that it seemed a solid thing, illuminating canopies of jungle so verdant that the green was not of this earth.

"Sort of makes you wonder why the heathens didn't surrender and convert to Christianity even before the first missionaries arrived, doesn't it?" drawled Mr. Clemens. He rode with the arrogant ease of someone who has spent much of his life in a saddle. The water dripped from his sombrero in rivulets.

I sat straighter, taking the reins in my left hand as if I were in charge of my horse's direction. "You are no friend of the church here, are you, Mr. Clemens?"

My uninvited companion smoked for a moment in what may have been meditative silence. "What church is that, Miss Stewart?"

"The Christian church, Mr. Clemens." I was soggy and sore, in no mood for what may have passed for banter in Missouri or California.

"Which Christian Church is that, Miss Stewart? Even here, the heathen have so many to choose from."

"You know very well what I mean, Mr. Clemens," I said. "Your remarks have shown a contempt for the efforts of these brave missionaries. And a contempt for the belief that has sent them so far from their comfortable homes."

After a moment, Mr. Clemens nodded slightly and touched the brim of his hat so that water drained away. "I knew a missionary lady once who was sent out here to the Sandwich Isles. Extraordinary thing, really. She was dispatched from St. Louis. Actually, I knew her sister . . . a more generous woman you would never want to meet . . . why, if you wanted something and that kind lady had it, you could have it in a minute. Have it and welcome."

The correspondent seemed lost in happy contemplation of this memory, so after a moment of no noise except for the rain pelting us and the clop of our horses' hooves, I said, "Well, what happened to her?"

Mr. Clemens turned his mustache and glowing cigar in my direction. "To whom?"

"To the *missionary*," I said with some exasperation. "To your friend's sister, the missionary who came here to the Sandwich Islands."

"Ahhh," said the correspondent, removing the cigar to flick ashes over the pommel of his saddle. "Well, they et her."

I admit that I blinked. "I beg your pardon?"

"They et her," said Mr. Clemens, the cigar firmly between his teeth again.

"The natives," I said, my voice small with shock. "The Hawaiians."

Mr. Clemens glanced at me with something that might have also been shock. "Of course the natives. Whom do you think I mean, Miss Stewart . . . the other missionaries?"

"How dreadful."

He nodded, obviously interested in his own tale now. "They said they were sorry. The natives, that is. When the poor lady's family sent for her things, the heathens said that they were dreadful sorry. They said that it was an accident. They said that it would not happen again."

I could only stare at him in the growing darkness. Our horses set their feet with care on the wet lava.

"An accident," I said, the scorn audible in my voice.

He shifted the cigar. "I agree, Miss Stewart. It was no

accident. Why, there's no such thing as an accident." He raised
one arm, his finger pointing skyward in the gloom. "It was Divine
Providence that caused my St. Louis lady-friend's sister to be
et . . . it is all part of the Cosmic Plan!"

I waited.

Mr. Clemens turned in my direction, twitched something
that may have been a smile under his mustache, and spurred his
horse ahead, swinging around the Reverend Haymark and the
two boys—now fallen into a sullen silence—to catch up to
Hananui again.

Ahead of us, beyond a screen of trees that were the first
grove we had seen in hours, the sky and earth burned red with a
glow more fierce than the reflected sunset that had already come
and passed. Puddles of water around us were transformed into
crimson pools, so that I admit that I had images of heathens
carrying out human sacrifice on the black rock and leaving
behind these puddles of blood.

I was looking at the volcano's glory. We were approaching
Madame Pele's fire.

To kill time before the art lecture, Eleanor walked the
grounds of the Mauna Pele. She was beginning to understand the
layout. East of the Big Hale were the gardens, a forest of palms,
one of the three tennis centers, and both of the eighteen-hole golf
courses, one curling away north toward the coast, the other south.
To the west of the Big Hale was the Sea Meadow, more gardens,
waterfalls, and lagoons, the Shipwreck Bar, the manta pool, and a
quarter mile of crescent beach. Walk south along the beach and
one would see the dense forest in which most of the *hales* were
situated—hers included. Walk north along the beach and follow
the long, rocky peninsula seaward, and one encountered the so-
called Samoan Bungalows—huge *hales* with their own pools and
yards. To the extreme east, south, and north were the lava fields—
heaps of *a'a* extending for miles. The bay and the beach, as well as
the sheltered sailing center on the north side of the peninsula,
were the only places where the sea could be approached: cliffs to
the north and south suffered the direct assault of the Pacific.

Eleanor had already located the petroglyph area—a jogging trail ran through the south boundary of lava field to the coast, just beyond the fairways of the southernmost golf course. A small plaque at the beginning of the trail explained that the designs on the rocks here had been painted by early Hawaiians and were being stringently protected by the Mauna Pele Resort. Other signs warned the joggers to stay on the trail and to return before dark, since the *a'a* fields were dangerous places, filled with crevices and collapsed lava tubes.

After a quick survey of the grounds, Eleanor returned to the Big Hale with twenty minutes to explore before the art tour was to begin. Passing the stairway to the Whale Watching Lanai and several fancier restaurants, closed during the day, she traversed a wide staircase to the Hale atrium. Eleanor realized at once that the Big Hale was a resort unto itself; guests could stay within the confines of this single building and feel that they had experienced an exotic vacation.

The exterior of the building was misleading: with a simulated thatched roof and wide overhang, its seven stories of terraces spilling with potted plants, the Big Hale fit into the "native hut" theme of the resort, but seen from the atrium or interior halls, the structure was elegant to the extreme. Built into a hillside, the Big Hale showed only five stories to someone approaching the east portico. Entering from the ocean side as Eleanor had, one passed shops and restaurants to step into a bamboo forest and follow a path through terraced grass hills past koi ponds and clusters of hanging orchids. The interior of the Big Hale was open to the sky, each ascending inside terrace stepped out a bit farther over the wooded atrium with vines and flowered plants hanging from planters. Eleanor thought that this was indeed what Babylon must have looked like.

The lobby was two stories up from the lower level, its tiled floors gleaming, gold Buddhas smiling at the entrance, all of it open to the trade winds that blew unimpeded from the eastern entrance steps across to the westward terrace above the Whale Watching Lanai. Eleanor could see a few hotel workers moving discreetly through the sunny corridors, but the primary impression was one of clean emptiness and silence broken only by the surf, the birds—inside and outside, since the atrium and lobby held a variety of huge cages in which cockatoos, macaws, parrots, and other exotic birds whistled and talked—and by the constant susurration of surf and fronds.

Eleanor had once had a long love affair with an architect, and now her eye appraised the expensive fittings, the polished brass, the gleaming cedar and beautifully carved mahogany, the dark ironwood moldings around windows and subtle marble framings around the elevators, and the traditional Japanese verandas and dimensions which somehow blended into a statement that was, incredibly, both post-modern and attractive. This structure avoided the Hyatt/Disney offensiveness without surrendering impact. Or at least that is how Eleanor imagined her former lover expressing it.

At this moment, she was thinking that she would like to have her hair done. Eleanor's hair was usually cut short—one friend had said that she looked like Amelia Earhart—but in the spring, she usually let it grow longer just for the purpose of having it cut wherever she traveled. Usually Eleanor's first act after settling into her hotel room was to leave the hotel of whatever city she had arrived in, and wander the streets until she found a place that cut women's hair: a beauty parlor, although Aunt Beanie had taught her to laugh at that phrase when she was five. There, receiving whatever terrible haircut was in vogue in that city, that country, Eleanor almost always broke through the barriers of language and culture to make contact with other women. After getting her hair done—and sometimes her nails—Eleanor was armed with enough information about the city to find the real restaurants, shop the real stores and marketplaces, see the real sights, and often ended up eating and traveling with some of the women she had met under hair dryers. She had suffered haircuts in Moscow and Barcelona, Reykjavik and Bangkok, Kyoto and Santiago, Havana and Istanbul . . . the hair always grew out and she would cut it after returning to campus in the fall. In the meantime, she was often mistaken for a local in the country she was visiting—buying clothes at the stores frequented by the women she met in the beauty parlors was usually the second item on her agenda—and this also helped break down barriers.

Now Eleanor wondered where the women who worked at the Mauna Pele had their hair done. Not here, certainly. The resort beauty salon might as well have been in Beverly Hills. Eleanor knew that the help were bused in from miles away along the Kona Coast, some from as far as Hilo.

She glanced at her watch. It was time for the art tour. The daily activity sheet had said only to meet near the Buddhas in the main lobby, but Eleanor saw no one else waiting. The Buddhas appeared to be made of gilt bronze and, upon closer inspection, were not Buddhas at all. Eleanor had spent enough time traveling the Pacific Rim to identify these as kneeling "Buddhist Disciples," their palms set together in prayer, their bodies thin under the gilded bronze–and–mirrored glass robes. She thought that they were probably from Thailand or Cambodia.

"Thailand," said a pleasant voice behind her. "Late eighteenth century."

Eleanor turned and saw a man about her height, perhaps a few years older, although his face had the unlined quality of people with Asian or Polynesian ancestry. His hair was cropped short but still showed a mat of curls, some graying. His eyes were large and expressive behind round Armani glasses. He was clean-shaven; his skin was the color of the richly tanned wood used in the interior moldings of the Big Hale. He wore a loose shirt of embossed navy silk, linen trousers, and sandals.

"Dr. Kukali?" said Eleanor, extending her hand.

His handshake was pleasant. "Paul Kukali," he said in the same rich baritone that had made her turn. "And you seem to be my entire art tour group today. May I ask your name?"

"Eleanor Perry," she said.

"Pleased to meet you, Ms. Perry."

"Since our group is so small, it will have to be Eleanor," she said, turning back to the figural sculpture and looking at its twin kneeling across the entrance. "And these disciples are marvelous."

Paul Kukali looked at her appraisingly. "Ah, you are aware of the use to which these were put. Did you notice that there are small differences in their appearance?''

Eleanor took a step back. "Now I do. Their noses are slightly different. Their robes vary slightly. They both have the long earlobes that mean royal birth . . .''

"Lakshana," said the art and archaeology curator.

"Yes, but this one's ears are just . . . *larger.''* Eleanor chuckled.

The curator stepped closer and set his hand on the gold leaf–and–black lacquer surface of the piece. "They're idealized portraits of the donors. One sees the same thing in Renaissance altarpieces in Europe. The donors could rarely resist seeing their own images displayed near the object of their worship.''

Eleanor looked around at the sculptures, carved tables, wall hangings, bowls, carved figures, and Buddhist altars visible in the lobby, the adjoining corridors, and the terraces above. "This place must be a veritable museum.''

"It *is* a museum," said Paul Kukali with a small smile. "Only I convinced Mr. Trumbo not to label anything with brass plaques or explanations. But scattered around the Big Hale and other buildings of the Mauna Pele is the finest collection of Asian and Pacific art in the state of Hawaii—our only competitor is the Mauna Kea up the coast, and that's because Laurence Rockefeller collected the art himself.''

"Why did you convince Mr. Trumbo not to label these treasures?" asked Eleanor. She had crossed the lobby to look at a red Japanese tansu that was at least five feet high and eight feet long.

"Well, my argument was that the guests should encounter the pieces not as if they were in a museum, but in the way they would if they were visiting at a friend's home and came across such marvelous things.''

"Nice," said Eleanor. Atop the tansu were two wooden votive tablets which she thought were Thai.

"Also," continued Paul Kukali, "leaving these things unlabeled would ensure that I kept my job here giving tours when I wasn't lecturing at the university in Hilo.''

Eleanor laughed. The curator made a gesture toward the main stairway. The tour began.

* * *

The Mauna Pele had two golf courses, the "easy" 6,825-yard, par-72 course laid out by Robert Trent Jones, Jr., and the newer, more difficult 7,321-yard, par-74 course designed by Bill Coore and Ben Crenshaw. Both courses had signature over-the-water holes and both resembled green landscape sculptures carved into the endless miles of lava rock. Byron Trumbo thought that Hiroshe Sato would enjoy the easier, southernmost Robert Trent Jones, Jr., course today and take on the ball-buster Coore-Crenshaw links tomorrow.

The first eight holes went well enough. The lead foursome would have been Trumbo, Sato, Inazo Ono, and Will Bryant—but, to Trumbo's endless irritation, Bryant refused to learn golf and had to stay with the golf carts while his boss played. Trumbo accepted Bobby Tanaka as their fourth, and although Tanaka played constantly in Japan as part of his role as liaison and negotiator, his game was uninspired at best. Sato, on the other hand, played a game almost as aggressive as Byron Trumbo's.

Trumbo knew that if the deal was to be settled with Sato, it might very well be settled here on the links. To that end, he kept his drives reined back a bit so that his ball ended up near Sato's more often than not. He had his usual Mauna Pele caddy, Gus Roo, and Sato was using a caddy he had flown in with him—an ancient old guy who looked as if he would be more at home in a peasant fishing village than a five-star resort.

The day remained clear and pleasant—temperature in the mid-80s but with almost no humidity, due to the ocean breeze—and Sato stayed within a stroke or two of Trumbo, who had the smaller handicap. Byron Trumbo was as fiercely competitive in golf as he was in everything else, but he would have been happy to lose repeatedly to this billionaire brat if it meant unloading the Pele. Meanwhile, the weather stayed perfect, the ash cloud stayed out of sight, no wall of lava came burbling down to bury the buyers, and Trumbo had hopes for a productive afternoon and then getting the whole thing settled.

Things started falling apart on the eighth hole. After he had putted in and was waiting for Sato to quit mumbling and putt, Will

Bryant beckoned him over to the cart. Will had been on the phone. "Bad news. Sherman called from Antigua. Bicki's on a tear. She threw a fit at Felix until he agreed to pick her up in the Gulfstream."

"Shit," muttered Trumbo. Sato putted—an easy six-footer—and missed it by ten inches. Trumbo shook his head and nodded his sympathy. "Where the hell is she headed?" he whispered to Bryant.

"Here."

"Here?"

"Here."

Trumbo gripped his putter hard enough to bend graphite. "Fuck. Who told her where I was?"

Will Bryant shrugged. "That's not the bad news."

Trumbo merely stared.

"Mrs. Trumbo and her lawyer left New York about four hours ago."

"Tell me they're not headed here," said Trumbo. Sato putted again, missed by two inches.

"They're headed here," said Will Bryant. "Evidently they're serious about putting a lien on the Mauna Pele. Koestler must have gotten wind of the sale."

Byron Trumbo had an image of the gray-haired, ponytailed divorce lawyer—once an advocate of Black Panthers and antiwar radicals, Myron Koestler was now usually a divorce lawyer to billionaires' wives—and tried to remember the phone number of the Mafia hit man he'd been introduced to once in Detroit. "Caitlin, Caitlin," he whispered to himself. "I'm going to have you killed, my dear darling girl."

"More," said Bryant.

Sato knelt, lining up his six-inch putt. Trumbo turned away before he screamed. "Maya?"

Will Bryant rubbed his chin with the phone and nodded.

"Headed here?" Trumbo tried to imagine the three women in his life being in the same place at the same time. He had tried before. He had no more success this time.

"Barry's not sure," said Will Bryant. "She went shopping at Barney's this afternoon and didn't come back."

Trumbo smiled. Maya had her own executive jet. "Find out," he said. "If she's headed here, tell the airport not to give her clearance. If she gets clearance, send Briggs over to the airport with a Stinger missile and shoot the plane down."

Will Bryant glanced over at the hulking security chief but said nothing.

"Aw, fuck," Byron Trumbo said sincerely.

"Yes," agreed his executive assistant.

Hiroshe Sato sank his putt. Trumbo applauded and smiled. "Have Briggs shoot down *all* their planes," he said to Will Bryant as he walked past. The party moved on to the ninth hole.

The art tour had been scheduled for one hour but it went on for almost ninety minutes before either Eleanor or Paul Kukali noticed the time. Wandering the seven floors of the Big Hale and the gardens outside, the curator had shown her exquisite Hawaiian bowls, five-foot-high New Guinea Ritual House masks, a fourteenth-century Kamakura Japanese Buddhist sculpture, Thai wood carvings from the Ayudhya period, a beautiful Indian Buddha from Nagapattinam hidden away under a banyan tree in the garden, "winged lion" bronzes guarding the entrance to the Presidential Suite upstairs, an amusing crouching goat carved in red-lacquered wood, and a dozen other treasures. Eleanor had rarely enjoyed an art discussion so much.

Also on their walk, she had discovered that Paul Kukali was a widower of six years, and he that Eleanor had never married, he had guessed that she was a professor but had been surprised at her specialty of the Enlightenment, they each had expressed a deep interest in Zen and found they had visited many of the same formal gardens in Japan, they discovered a mutual passion for Thai food and passionate dislike of campus politics, and found that they laughed at the same type of silly puns.

"I apologize for running over," said Paul as they finished the tour in the lobby. "It was the seated Buddha. I always get carried away when talking about the Buddha."

"Nonsense," said Eleanor. "I loved it. If you hadn't pointed it out, I never would have noticed the 'wheel of law' inscribed in his palm."

The curator smiled. "It was nice of you to leave a flower there. And correct."

Eleanor glanced at her watch. "Well . . . I'm almost embarrassed to mention it, but I'd planned to show up for your petroglyph tour. If I'm the only guest who shows, will the tour still go on?"

Paul smiled more broadly, showing perfect teeth. "If you're the only guest who shows, the tour may run late again." He looked at his own watch. "I have an idea. If you're interested, we could have lunch together on the *lanai* and go straight to the petroglyph field from there." He paused a second. "Damn. That sounded like a line, didn't it?"

"No," said Eleanor. "It sounded like an invitation. I accept."

There were fewer than a dozen people on the *lanai* for lunch, but one of them was Cordie Stumpf, wrapped in a flowered beach cover-up that matched her swimsuit. Cordie was sipping from a tall drink with several blossoms in it, and frowning at the menu as if it were written in a foreign language.

"Oh," said Eleanor, "there's someone you might enjoy meeting. Shall we see if she wants to join us?"

"By all means," said the curator with a grin, as if relieved by Eleanor's suggestion.

Cordie Stumpf squinted up at them. Her nose was sunburned. "Yeah, why don't you sit down with me? Hey, do you believe they serve *dolphin* here? I was just wonderin' if I should have a Flipper sandwich."

Things really fell apart for Byron Trumbo on the fourteenth hole.

His second drive put him onto the green while Sato was still chipping from the rough and then out of the sand trap. The Japanese billionaire's game had gone to shit. Both Bobby Tanaka and Inazo Ono were also having problems, so Trumbo just stood there on the edge of the green with Gus, his caddy, watching Sato get more and more pissed off. Trumbo wished he'd just sliced the goddamn ball into the lava fields and had done with it.

Finally Sato chipped onto the green and walked over to his

elderly caddy, who offered the young man a silk handkerchief with which to mop his now florid face. "Please putt in, Byron-san." *Preez purtt ih.*

"You're back, Hiroshe," said Trumbo with a friendly smile. Will Bryant had just informed him that Caitlin's plane was indeed headed for the Keahole-Kona airport and that she and her lawyer had made reservations at the Mauna Pele. Trumbo felt like throwing up, but *after* he bent his putter around a palm tree. "Please," he said, hand out in the universal *you first* gesture.

Sato shook his head with the first sign of petulance Trumbo had seen. "No, please, putt in while I contemplate whatever sins of mine have made me deserve this punishment."

Trumbo grunted and addressed the ball. He had about a ten-foot putt. Gus walked over to the flag, started to lift it, and then froze, looking at his shoes.

"Pull it, Gus."

"But Mr. T . . ." Gus's soft voice sounded strange.

"Pull it and get out of the way."

"But Mr. T . . ." The caddy was staring at the pin and his shoes as if he were frozen to the spot.

"Pull the fucking flag and get out of the fucking way," said Byron Trumbo in a command voice he rarely used.

Gus pulled the flag and moved back, his walk strange. Trumbo idly wondered if the little caddy was having a coronary and made a mental note not to send flowers if that was the case. The last thing Trumbo needed today was attitude, advice, or problems from his fucking caddy.

It took only a second for Trumbo to focus. He putted smoothly and watched it roll in. He looked up to get Sato's approving smile, but the other billionaire was whispering to Inazo Ono, who had managed to get his ball onto the edge of the green in four. *Fuck you,* thought Byron Trumbo, and walked over to retrieve his ball.

At first, when his fingers touched the other fingers in the cup, Byron Trumbo had no reaction at all. It was as if someone were underground, trying to shake hands with him, and the sensation was so weird that—except for the wild prickling on the back of his neck—he had no response at all but to freeze, still leaning over, arm extended to the hole.

Then Trumbo leaned forward and looked into the cup. His ball was there, just under the level of the green, perched delicately on the four upraised fingers and thumb of the dismembered right hand.

Still bending over, noticing peripherally that Sato and Ono were turning back to look and that Bobby Tanaka's last chip shot had brought him onto the green, Trumbo turned his head to look at Gus Roo. His caddy, still holding the flag, raised the other hand helplessly. For a Hawaiian, Gus's face was very pale. Trumbo noted that the base of the flag pin had been stained red.

Trumbo looked back at Sato and grinned, his own fingers still inches from the upraised fingers holding the ball. *What if the thing's alive down there and is going to come bursting up through the sod?*

"Nice putt, Byron-san," said Sato with little enthusiasm.

Trumbo smiled again, still frozen in his uncomfortable posture. He could see Will Bryant staring at him, obviously wondering what was wrong, perhaps concerned that his boss had thrown his back out.

Trumbo reached for the ball again, holding his breath at the thought that the severed hand might fight to keep the ball.

Straightening up, Trumbo tossed the ball, put it nonchalantly in his pocket, and said, "Who's for a drink?"

Sato and the others frowned. "Drink, Byron-san? We are at only fourteen hole."

Trumbo walked between them and the hole, shrugging expansively. "Hey, it's hot, we're working hard, I thought we might take a break for a few minutes and have a cold drink in the shade there." He pointed above the sand trap to where several palm trees rustled.

"I must putt," said Hiroshe Sato, obviously put off by his host's cavalier attitude toward golf.

Trumbo shook his head, still grinning stupidly. "It's a gimme, Hiroshe."

"A . . . gimme?"

"Sure," said Trumbo, throwing his hands up. "You'd make it anyway."

Sato's frown deepened. "I am twenty-eight feet from the hole, Byron-san."

"Yeah, but you're hot today, Hiroshe," said Trumbo. With his eyes and eyebrows he was beckoning Will Bryant over. The assistant walked out on the green, ignoring the Japanese guests' frowns at Bryant's walking shoes on the grass. Trumbo leaned close. "There's something in the cup," he hissed into Will's ear. "Get a fucking towel from Gus, get the fucking thing out of the fucking cup, and do it so Sato and the others don't see. Got it?"

Will Bryant looked at his boss, nodded slightly, and walked over to the caddy.

Trumbo went over to the billionaire and put his arm around the smaller man, feeling Sato flinch slightly as he did so. "Hiroshe, let me show you something." Trumbo led the party over to the parked carts, where he fumbled open Will's briefcase and pulled out the prospectus and site maps they had been referring to over breakfast. He smoothed out the map of the golf course on the backseat of the cart as if the paper held some huge surprise. Sato, Tanaka, and Ono were gathered around, as was Sato's old caddy, and Trumbo sensed them all staring at him as if he had lost his mind. *Maybe I have,* thought the billionaire, and stabbed a blunt finger down on the fourteenth hole. "I'm sorry, Hiroshe, but I've been thinking about this for the last few holes and just had to say something. Have you realized the potential for luxury condos if your people build here . . . and here . . . and here. I know you're considering the Pele for an exclusive golf club, two-hundred-thousand-dollar Tokyo memberships and all that . . ."

Sato stared at his host as if he were frothing at the mouth. That the Japanese wanted to close the Mauna Pele as a resort and plant condos for golfers was the subtext that was to remain unsaid by both sides in these negotiations. "Yes, but I must putt," said Hiroshe Sato, and started to turn back to the green.

Trumbo caught a glimpse of Will Bryant bent over the hole, towel gingerly extended. Gus Roo had sat on a lava boulder and was holding his head in his hands.

"Just consider this," said Trumbo, putting his arm around Sato and turning him back to the map. He could feel the Japanese tycoon's skin rippling in revulsion at the invasion of his person.

"I mean, bulldoze this area east of the links here . . . see? . . . put in trees and lagoons and all that shit we did to the west . . . and how much would it lease for, Hiroshe? Two million each?"

"Byron," said Bobby Tanaka. "I think we . . ."

"Shaddup," said Trumbo. Sato was looking at the map sadly, his body hunching away from Trumbo's hug. Trumbo glanced over his shoulder, saw Will Bryant moving into the *a'a* with the heavy towel.

"Hey," said Trumbo, "just something I had to get off my chest. OK, let's get back to the game." He glared at Tanaka. "Took you a while to get onto the green, didn't it?"

Inazo Ono was saying something to his boss. "I suggested that Mr. Sato putt next," he translated.

Trumbo nodded. He had heard the words for "foreigner," and "crazy." He didn't give a shit. From behind the palm trees and the lava boulders, there came the faintest of retching sounds.

Sato hunkered over his putter. Trumbo saw Will Bryant emerge from the rocks. No one else seemed to notice. Incredibly, Sato sank his twenty-eight-footer. Everyone applauded except Gus Roo, who still sat with his head in his hands.

On their way to the carts and the fifteenth hole, Bryant walked close to his boss and whispered, "I expect a bonus for this."

NINE

*. . . there existed in [Polynesian culture] a binary
world view whereby categories were set in
opposition to each other. The most common and
potent was the male-female dichotomy where
"male" qualities represented goodness, strength,
light, and "female" qualities were mostly weak,
dangerous, dark (but paradoxically also essential
as the givers of life).*
—William Ellis, *"Polynesian Researches"*

After lunch, Eleanor, Cordie, and Paul Kukali leisurely
toured the petroglyph field. The jogging track moved through the
a'a boulders like a smooth ribbon laid on a pebbly beach. To their
right were the ocean cliffs, to their left the palm trees and sprinklers and lushness of the southernmost of the two golf courses.
Eleanor could hear the occasional exclamations of golfers, but
other than that it was peaceful except for the wind and waves.

"When Trumbo and his consortium planned to develop this
area," Paul Kukali was saying, "we went to the state supreme court
to preserve these ancient Hawaiian fish ponds and petroglyphs."

"What fish ponds?" said Cordie, her head swiveling.

"Precisely," said the curator. "Before we could get a restrain-
ing order, his people had bulldozed the ponds. I threatened to
create an international stink if he destroyed the petroglyphs, so
these few acres were preserved . . . except for where the jogging
path cut through them, of course."

They stopped where a plaque pointed out a low rock with

small holes and a faded drawing of a male figure. "These are the petroglyph thingies?" said Cordie.

"Yes," said Paul.

"How old are they?" Cordie had crouched next to the rock, her heavy legs wide apart. She set a blunt hand on the rock.

"No one's sure," said Paul. "But these are amongst the oldest sites on the islands . . . probably dating back to about the time my Polynesian ancestors first landed here, perhaps fourteen hundred years ago."

Cordie whistled and touched the stone. "What are these little holes?"

Paul and Eleanor both crouched next to Cordie. "Those are *piko* holes," said the curator. "Umbilical cord holes. Tradition says that when the newborns lost that little stump of their umbilical cords, the cords were placed in these *piko* holes and covered with small stones. Families had to travel long distances with a child's *piko* in a gourd to deposit it here. We have only a sketchy idea why this place was thought to hold so much *mana*."

Cordie raised her thick eyebrows to question the word.

"*Mana* is spiritual power, isn't it?" said Eleanor.

Paul nodded. "Everything in the natural world was a matter of *mana* for the ancient Hawaiians," he said. "Some places, like this, seemed to be especially powerful."

Eleanor rose and walked to a rock where several painted figures filled the space between *piko* holes. She looked at one figure with bird feet, spiked hair, and a prominent penis.

Cordie stepped over. "This little guy's got a dick sorta like an arrow. Is that supposed to mean more *mana?*"

Paul Kukali laughed. "Probably. Everything the Hawaiians did or thought revolved around *mana* or *kapu*."

"Taboos?" said Eleanor.

Paul sat on the rock and laid his hand just above the male figure Cordie had admired. "*Kapus* were not just rules on what could or could not be done. For thousands of years, the Hawaiians were obsessed with *mana*—with this spiritual power that flowed from the earth and the gods and each other—and *kapu* helped keep the power where it belonged . . . helped to keep it from being stolen."

Cordie rubbed her nose. "They thought you could steal the power?"

The curator nodded. "To the point that when the *ali'i*—royalty—passed, commoners like you and me would have to lie on the ground and hide our faces. Even to allow our shadow to fall on them would be punishable by death. *Mana* was a rare commodity and the life of the village or people often depended upon it. Punishments were harsh."

Cordie looked out across the lava field. "So there was . . . like . . . human sacrifice going on here?"

Paul folded his arms. "Almost certainly. This area of the coast is rich in *heiaus*—old temples—where sacrifices were made. Even the great posts they set in the ground demanded the body of a slave in each hole."

"Yech," said Cordie.

"But there were other *heiaus* such as the Puuhonua O Honaunau just down the coast," said the curator. "The so-called City of Refuge where the weak could flee to be safe from such terror."

Eleanor stepped closer. "Wasn't there a *heiau* somewhere around here . . . on this bay perhaps . . . which tradition said was built in one night by the Marchers of the Night?"

Paul Kukali looked at her with some surprise. "Precisely," he said. "Exactly this place, although no sign of the actual *heiau* has been found. It was one of the reasons we tried to bring the environmental impact statement to court to put some teeth behind the preservation here."

"Marchers of the Night?" said Cordie.

The curator turned to the short woman and smiled. "Processions of the dead . . . *ali'i*, royalty, if you're to believe the tales . . . if you see them, you're generally believed to be in some trouble. One legend had it that the *heiau* at this spot was built on a single night in 1866 by the Marchers of the Night." He turned to Eleanor. "Where did you run across that tidbit?"

She hesitated only a second. "Mark Twain, I believe."

Paul nodded. "Ah, yes. I'd forgotten his letters from Hawaii. He was on the Big Island the summer the *heiau* was built by the walking dead, as I remember from some research I did. But I didn't think that particular letter was ever published . . . it's still in his papers, isn't it?"

Eleanor said nothing.

"Are you full-blooded Hawaiian?" asked Cordie, her curiosity as straightforward as a child's.

"Yes," said Paul Kukali. "There aren't that many of us, to be truthful. I read somewhere that a hundred and twenty thousand people on the islands claim Hawaiian blood, but ethnologists think that there are only a few hundred pure Hawaiians left." He paused a moment. "I think that's a good sign, don't you?"

"Diversity usually means strength," said Eleanor.

"Shall we see the rest of the petroglyph field?" he asked. "The golf course took a big part of it, but there are some good examples of a hawk-headed figure that *no one* has a theory about."

They strolled down the jogging path, chatting as they moved deeper into the *a'a* tumble.

Trumbo thought that the goddamned golf game was going to last indefinitely; he sent Gus back to the clubhouse, the caddy was so shaken. Gus's teenage nephew, Nicky Roo, caddied the last few holes for Trumbo, who was shaken enough himself to send Will Bryant ahead, for the last few holes, checking the remaining cups and sand traps for . . . anything.

"We have to report this," Bryant had whispered before humming off in his golf cart.

"Report what?" Trumbo had hissed back at him. "That we've got fucking severed hands lurking in our holes on our twelve-million-dollar golf course? Or that you tossed homicide evidence into the lava fields so that Hiroshe could putt? The local fuzz will love that."

Will Bryant did not flinch. "We'll have to report it."

"First you have to go back and *find* it," Trumbo had whispered, glancing over to where Sato and his cronies were cackling at something in Japanese. The last few holes had been very good for the duffer.

Bryant did flinch at the thought of that. "Now?"

"No, not now. First I want you to check out the next few

holes. I don't want Hiroshe or his pals having to par in past a fucking severed head or uncover somebody's foot when they blast out of a sand trap.''

Pale, his lips thin, Bryant nodded.

"Then I want you to find Stevie Carter and tell him that we think we found one of the New Jersey guys . . . part of him.'' Trumbo hesitated. "It was a *man's* hand, wasn't it?''

"Yes,'' said Bryant. "Right hand. Manicured nails.''

Trumbo shivered slightly. "For a second it didn't register, you know? It seemed natural that someone was handing me the ball when I bent over to pick it up.''

"We'll have to call the cops,'' whispered Bryant.

Byron Trumbo shook his head. "Not until this fucking deal is done.''

"Concealing evidence . . .''

"Will cost me a lot less in lawyers' fees to fight than keeping this goddamn resort will cost me. A lot rides on this, Will.''

Bryant hesitated only a second. "Yessir. What shall I tell Carter when he insists we call the cops?''

"Tell him that he promised me twenty-four hours and that the clock's still ticking,'' said Trumbo. He glanced over at the waiting businessmen. "Get going. Don't forget to check the bushes. Three guys are missing . . . there might be twenty or thirty little surprises like that waiting for us between here and the clubhouse. I don't want to lean over to putt in on the eighteenth and find some guy's dick lying between me and the cup.''

Bryant blinked. "Yeah. Got it.'' His cart hummed away.

Now, having a cool drink with Sato and Bobby Tanaka, Inazo Ono, Masayoshi Matsukawa, Dr. Tatsuro, Sunny Takahashi, and Seizaburo Sakurabayashi around the big, round table looking out over the Mauna Pele's prize-winning gardens, the "thatched'' roof of the Big Hale rising above coconut palms to the west, Trumbo allowed himself a sigh of relief.

The relief did not last long. Stephen Ridell Carter appeared at the table, still in a tan tropical suit, his gray hair as impeccable as always, but there was something frazzled and urgent about the manager's appearance.

Ordering him to silence with his eyes, Trumbo said, "Steve . . .
sit down, join us. We're just talking about Hiroshe's last five holes.
Dynamite game." Trumbo's look said, *One fucking word about the
news and you'll be managing a Super Eight motel in Ottumwa, Iowa.*

"May I have a word with you, Mr. Trumbo?"

Trumbo sighed again, the relief completely gone. "Now?"
He nodded toward his almost full drink, a chi-chi with fruit and an
umbrella floating in it.

"If you don't mind, sir." Carter's voice was on the edge of . . .
something. Panic perhaps. Insubordination, certainly.

Trumbo grunted, made his excuses to Sato, and joined the
manager. They walked from the clubhouse terrace to a point near
the tennis courts where they could not be overheard.

"Look, Carter," began Trumbo, "if you're insisting that we
call the cops now, I'm here to tell you that it ain't gonna happen.
There's too much riding on this fu . . ."

"It's not that," said Stephen Ridell Carter, his voice a sick
monotone. "Mr. Bryant brought me back to show me the hand,
but it wasn't there."

"Wasn't there?" said Trumbo.

"Wasn't there," said Carter.

"Fuck," Byron Trumbo said thoughtfully. "That *is* news.
Well, maybe the crabs or something . . ."

"No," interrupted the manager. "That's not the news."

Trumbo raised his heavy eyebrows and waited.

"The news is that Mr. Wills has gone missing."

"Who?"

"Mr. Wills . . . Conrad Wills . . . our staff astronomer."

"When?" said Trumbo.

"Sometime this morning. They saw him at breakfast. He did
not show up for the noon staff conference."

"Where?" said Trumbo.

"Almost surely in the catacombs . . ."

"The what?"

"Catacombs," repeated Stephen Ridell Carter. "It's what the
staff call the service tunnels."

"How do they know he disappeared down there?" asked
Trumbo.

"His office . . . well, I will just have to show you, Mr. Trumbo. Security Chief Dillon is down there now. It is terrible, terrible . . ."

Trumbo had the urge to either slap his hotel manager or pat him on the back before the man started blubbering. Trumbo did neither. "Well, we don't really *need* a staff astronomer over the next day or so, do we? I mean, it's not like there's going to be an eclipse tonight or something, is there?"

Stephen Ridell Carter stared, obviously aghast. Trumbo noticed for the first time that the man's gray hair was a toupee. *No wonder it always looked perfectly combed,* thought Trumbo.

"*Mr.* Trumbo," said the manager, his voice shocked.

For a second, the billionaire thought that Carter was responding in shock because he was staring at the man's wig, then he remembered his offhand comment. "Oh, don't get me wrong—we'll search for poor Mr. . . . ah?"

"Wills."

"Yeah. We'll have Dillon turn out all of the security looking for Mr. Wills, and we'll certainly tell the police tomorrow . . . or whenever we tell the police about all this . . . I just mean that, well, perhaps Wills thought he wasn't needed, because of the few guests and the low need for an astronomer and all."

"I hardly think . . ."

"But we don't *know,* do we?" said Trumbo, laying his hand heavily on the taller man's shoulder. He squeezed. "We just don't know. And until we do, it would be useless suicide to blow this deal just because of a few . . . irregularities."

"Irregularities," repeated the resort manager. His voice was much higher than usual and sounded almost drugged.

Trumbo squeezed his employee's shoulder hard enough to bring on a wince and then removed his hand. "Let's just let Security do its job while I do mine, all right, Steve? This is going to turn out all right. Trust me."

Carter looked as if he had swallowed something too large to choke down. "But the office . . ."

"Whose office, Steve?" Trumbo's voice was calming, almost lulling. This tone had worked with some of the most hysterical, high-strung women in America, he was thinking, it should work with this toupeed faggot.

"Mr. Wills's office."

"What about it, Steve?"

The manager took a breath and some strength came back to his voice. "You'll have to see it to understand, Mr. Trumbo."

The billionaire glanced at his Rolex. He did have some time. Sato and his people wanted a nap and lunch on their private *lanai* before the parties were to reassemble for the afternoon negotiations.

"All right, show me," he said, patting the manager's back in a friendly fashion.

Carter started to lead the way. "They don't want to be down there now, you know."

"Who?" said Trumbo, feeling like the conversation was starting over again. "Where?"

"The staff," said Carter. "Everyone who has their offices in the service tunnels or who has to travel there. They've never liked it, Mr. Trumbo. There have always been stories. Now, with this . . ."

"Fuck them," said Trumbo, tired of playing Mr. Nice Guy. "Tell them they only have to work down there if they want their paychecks."

"But Mr. Wills's office. It is too bizarre to tell you . . ."

"Don't tell me," said Trumbo, checking his watch again and almost shoving the thin manager ahead of him toward the catacombs. "Show me."

"What are those holes in the ground?" asked Cordie, pointing past the petroglyphs and *a'a* boulders to where a ragged tunnel was visible between the rocks.

"Lava tube," said Paul Kukali. He pointed toward the east. "They run all the way up the slope of Mauna Loa . . . twenty, twenty-five miles."

"No shit," said Cordie Stumpf.

"No shit," confirmed the art and archaeology curator.

"The lava tubes are a source of *mana,* aren't they?" said Eleanor.

Paul nodded. "*Po nui ho'olakolako.* 'The great night that supplies.' Legend says that the mouths of darkness are like the wombs of women, channels from which such power flows."

Cordie grunted as if amused by the thought. She clambered over rocks to teeter above the black pit.

"Careful," Paul said.

"It *is* a sort of tunnel," said Cordie, as if she had doubted the curator's explanation. "I can see where it curves away uphill. The walls are . . . whatchamacallit . . . they've got ridges."

"Striated by the lava as it cooled and receded," said Paul.

"Yeah." Cordie sounded thoughtful. "We could all walk upright in that thing. Would it be safe?"

Paul Kukali shrugged. "The hotel discourages it."

"Why?" said Cordie. "Bats?"

The curator shook his head. "No, most of our bats on the Big Island roost in trees. The resort is more afraid of someone falling. The lava tubes really are very extensive. One could get lost without much effort."

Cordie grunted again. "Maybe this is where all the missing guests have been goin'."

Paul Kukali stopped as if embarrassed by the sudden mention of the resort's troubles.

Eleanor watched him. "Haven't they arrested the person suspected of the kidnappings . . . murders . . . whatever they were?"

Paul nodded. "Jimmy Kahekili. But they'll have to release him soon."

"Why?" said Eleanor.

Paul looked at her, his face expressionless. "Because he's not guilty of anything. Or rather, he's just guilty of having a big mouth and being fanatical about the separatist movement."

Cordie picked her way back across the boulders and stepped down onto the jogging path. "What separatist movement?"

"A growing number of Hawaiians . . . native Hawaiians . . . want the United States government to return the islands to their former status as a sovereign nation," said Paul.

"Yeah?" said Cordie. "You mean it used to be a country? I always thought it was just an island with natives and grass shacks and all that before the sugar cane people showed up."

Eleanor winced a bit, but she noticed that Paul Kukali only smiled. "It had the natives and grass shacks," he said, "but until a January day in 1893, Hawaii also had its own government—a monarchy. Queen Liliuokalani was on the throne when the white planters and some U.S. Marines annexed the isles in an illegal invasion . . . and that was that. Not too long ago, President Clinton signed a paper apologizing for the seizure. That mollified some of the Hawaiians. But other people, like Jimmy Kahekili, want it all given back and the monarchy restored."

Cordie Stumpf snorted at such an idea. "That's like the Indians asking for Manhattan back, isn't it?"

Paul opened his hands. "Yes. If the demands are for total sovereignty on all the islands. No sensible person thinks that the U.S. will give back Waikiki and all the military bases. But some of us think that some sort of limited sovereignty is possible . . . rather like with the mainland Native Americans."

"A reservation?" said Eleanor.

The curator rubbed his chin. "Have you heard of Kahoolawe?"

"Ah, yes," said Eleanor.

"What?" said Cordie. Her sunglasses had white plastic rims and now they gleamed up at the two taller people. "What?"

Paul Kukali turned to her. "Kahoolawe is the Hawaiian island which no one goes to," he said. "It's only eleven miles long and six wide, but it was sacred in the mythology of the Hawaiians and still holds many *heiaus* and other archaeological treasures."

"I'll bite," said Cordie. "Why doesn't anyone go there?"

"One man—a white rancher—owned the island until 1941," said Paul. "The day after Pearl Harbor, the U.S. Navy took the entire island over as a bombing range and has been bombing and shelling it ever since."

Cordie Stumpf smiled, showing small teeth in her childlike smile. "So Hawaiians want *that* as a reservation?" she said. "A bombing range? I'd at least ask for the Mauna Pele Resort."

The curator grinned back. "So would I. But we're getting far off the subject."

"You mean who killed all the guests here?" said Cordie.

"No," said Paul, glancing at his watch. "They pay me to talk about the petroglyph field here. And our time's about up."

The three continued strolling along the asphalt path that

wound between black rock. They had not seen a single jogger all afternoon. "Tell us about Milu and the entrance to the Underworld," said Eleanor.

The curator paused and raised an eyebrow. "You know quite a bit of local lore."

"Not really," said Eleanor. "I think I read about the Underworld in that same piece about Mark Twain's visit here. The entrance is around here somewhere, isn't it?"

Before Paul Kukali could answer, Cordie snapped her fingers. "That's it then . . . we got the whole plot for why those people got disappeared. Hotel's built on an old Hawaiian burial ground. Not only that, it's the entrance to the . . . what did you call it . . . the Underworld. The old gods and ghosts and stuff got pissed and are haunting the place, dragging guests off for dinner in the tunnels. It'd make a good movie. Hell, I got me a friend who knows somebody who's married to a Hollywood producer. We could sell this to 'em."

Paul smiled. "Sorry, no special burial ground here. And the Underworld that Eleanor mentioned was supposed to have an entrance only near the seashore at the mouth of the Waipio Valley, and that's diagonally opposite us, all the way across the island. Hours from here."

"Well, shit," said Cordie, taking her sunglasses off and cleaning them on the tail of her flowered cover-up. "There goes that movie sale."

Eleanor paused. "Wasn't there a second entrance to Milu's Underworld? A back door? That would be on this coast, wouldn't it?"

"According to Mark Twain, perhaps," said the curator, his voice flat. "According to *our* people's mythology, there was only one entrance and that was sealed by Pele after a major battle with the dark gods. None of the demons or evil spirits . . . not even many of the ghosts . . . have bothered anyone since she closed that door. I guess it comes down to whom you believe . . . the Hawaiians who made up these tales, or Mark Twain, who visited here for a few weeks and heard them secondhand."

"I guess it does," said Eleanor. She looked at her own watch.

"It's almost three. We've kept you way beyond your duties, Paul. But it's been fun."

"Yeah," said Cordie. "It's been a real knee-slapping outing. I especially like the picture of the guy with the arrow-shaped weenie."

They had turned back toward the Big Hale, talking and pointing at some of the more picturesque petroglyphs along the way, when the huge black dog separated itself from the black boulders and stepped onto the jogging path. It was staring at them, tail wagging. In its jaws was a human hand.

TEN

I have seen Vesuvius since,
but it was a mere toy, a child's volcano,
a soup-kettle compared to this.
—Mark Twain, describing Kilauea

June 14, 1866, Volcano of Kilauea—

We arrived at Volcano House on the lip of the crater sometime before ten p.m. The approach had been quite spectacular with the blood-red glow of the active volcano illuminating low clouds until the crimson light fell on our entire party, making the horses' eyes shine with a ruby gleam and causing our exposed skin to look as if it had been flayed away. Half an hour before the Volcano House came into sight, the smell of sulphur drifted down on the breeze to us. I used a scarf to cover my face, but I noticed that Mr. Clemens seemed unperturbed by the stench. "Does the smell not bother you?" I asked. "It is not an unpleasant scent to a sinner," he replied. I ignored him for the rest of the approach.

I realized that I had been listening to the sound of the surf crashing on rock for some time, but that the ocean was thirty miles away. The noise must be the surge of lava and steam within the very rocks under our feet. As we grew closer, tall columns of vapor became visible like twisting pylons holding up the fiery cloud ceiling. Even though the horses had made this trip before, they rolled their eyes and stepped nervously as they approached the cauldron.

I had thought Volcano House to be a proper hotel, and it was not such a disappointment as the Half Way House. The caretaker of this unique establishment came out to meet us, and several native workers took charge of our exhausted horses. The caretaker wanted to show us to the only table in the dining room for a late supper, and then to our rooms, but as tired as we all were, all we had thoughts for was the volcano, and we went onto the veranda which hung quite literally over the crater mouth.

"Good Lord," said the Reverend Haymark as we approached the railing, and I believe that he spoke for all of us.

Kilauea Volcano is over nine miles in circumference and our little veranda hung out over an abyss at least a thousand feet to the surface of the dried lake beneath us. The caretaker pointed out a structure which he referred to as the "look-out house," a tiny building illuminated by the glow from the crater, and mentioned that it was three miles away around the lip of the volcano.

"It looks like a martin-box clinging to the eaves of a cathedral," said Mr. Clemens.

Between us and the look-out house, the volcano floor was a maze of fiery cracks, black lava geometries spouting geysers of lava, rivers of fire, and seething columns of vapor which rose to the bloody cloud which hung over the crater like a ceiling of red silk. I glanced at my companions' rapt faces and noticed their fiery countenances from the volcano light, their eyes glowing as red as the horses' had.

"A bit like half-cooked devils, aren't we?" said Mr. Clemens, smiling at me.

My first instinct was to ignore the correspondent's comments so as not to encourage further japes, but I found the excitement of the moment overruled that response. "Like fallen angels," I said. "Only not so handsome, I think, as Milton's cast."

Mr. Clemens laughed and looked back at the fiery spectacle. He had lighted another one of his atrocious cigars, and the smoke from it was as red as the other sulphurous vapors rising from the pit.

While the major parts of the great caldera showed pools and cracks and rivers of red-running lava, the great glow was from the permanent lake at the southernmost end of the crater—

Hale-mau-mau, or House of Everlasting Fire, which local mythology designated as the abode of the dreaded goddess Pele. Although all of three miles away across the lava bed of the pit, this lake threw up more fire and light than all the rest of the crater combined.

"I want to go there," said Mr. Clemens.

The others were shocked. "Tonight?" said the hotel caretaker, obviously appalled.

I watched the ember of the correspondent's cigar bob up and down. "Yes. Tonight. Now."

"Quite impossible," said the caretaker. "None of the usual guides will go down into the crater."

"Why not?" said Mr. Clemens.

The caretaker cleared his throat. "The lava is much more active after last week's eruption. There is a path, but it is hard to see in the dark—even by lantern light. If one were to get off the path, it would be quite likely that one would break through the crust of rotten lava and fall a thousand feet to one's death."

"Mmmm," said Mr. Clemens, removing the cigar. "I would think that eight hundred feet would answer for me."

"I beg your pardon," said the caretaker.

Mr. Clemens shook his head. "I would still like to go. Tonight. If you would be so kind as to lend me a lantern and point out the path . . ." He paused, looking at the rest of us. "Would anyone like to accompany me?"

"I think I'll get a good night's sleep and wait for daylight," said young Master McGuire.

"Good idea," said the Smith twin, obviously appalled at the thought of entering that cauldron this night.

Surprisingly, the Reverend Haymark mopped his face with a handkerchief and said, "I say, I've been there before, I'll go . . . and act as guide. I've been on the path in the daylight. I should be able to find it at night."

The caretaker began shaking his head and pointing out the dangers of wandering off the path, but Mr. Clemens merely grinned more broadly under his reddish mustache. "Wonderful," he said. Then, turning to me, "Miss Stewart, if we are not back by daybreak, please feel free to dispose of my hired horse as you see fit."

I sniffed. "You will have to make other arrangements for the disposal of your horse, Mr. Clemens," I said. "I plan to accompany you gentlemen."

"But . . . but . . . my dear lady," began Reverend Haymark, his red face growing even more florid.

I dismissed his objections with a curt bob of my chin. "Obviously if it is not folly for you gentlemen, it is not folly for a third member of the expedition. If it *is* folly . . . well, then, we shall all be fools together."

Mr. Clemens reinstalled his cigar and I watched the ember bob up and down. "Quite true, quite true. Miss Stewart will make a fine member of this Expedition of Fools."

The Reverend Haymark made blustering sounds, but could not find the words to express his misgivings. So, while the servants bustled to ready a late supper for Master McGuire and the sleepy Mr. Smith, Mr. Clemens, the wheezing minister, and I prepared ourselves for the midnight sojourn into the most spectacular few square miles on our surprising Earth.

Byron Trumbo and Stephen Ridell Carter were met by their respective security chiefs—Dillon for the Mauna Pele, Briggs for Trumbo—at the Big Hale entrance to the catacombs. The security men were a study in contrasts: Briggs, six feet four, bald, and massive; Dillon, a short, bearded man with impassive eyes and quick hands. Trumbo had hired both of them and used them for widely different purposes.

"You guys find anything?" said Trumbo.

Both men shook their heads, but Dillon said, "Mr. Trumbo, we've got a problem."

They walked down the ramp into the echoing tunnel. "I don't know why you say that," said Trumbo. "Unless you include dismembered guests and missing astronomers as a problem."

"No, I don't mean that," said Dillon. When Trumbo turned to glare at him, he went on. "I mean, yes, that's a problem, but what I mean is . . . well, that art curator, Kukali, and a couple of guests are up in the administration suite. They say they just saw a dog running around with a hand in its mouth.''

Trumbo stopped so abruptly that the other three men almost collided with him. "A dog? With a hand? Where?'' Pale faces peered at them from the windows of various offices and service installations along the underground concourse.

Dillon rubbed his beard and smiled slightly. The situation seemed to amuse him. ''Over on the jogging path, between the south golf course and the shoreline.''

"Damn,'' breathed Trumbo, lowering his voice so that the conversation would not carry down the echoing corridor. ''And you say three of them saw it?''

"Yep. Dr. Kukali and two of the . . .''

"Kukali's on the staff, isn't he?''

"Yeah, the art and archaeology curator. He's the . . .''

"He's the Hawaiian motherfucker who was going to sue us about the petroglyphs and fish ponds,'' finished the billionaire. "Shit. I hired him to get him to keep his mouth shut about all that. Now we've got to find a way to keep him quiet about this. Did you say that you have them up in the administrative suites?''

"I was going to bring them down here to my office,'' said Dillon, "but what with the problem with Mr. Wills . . .''

"Wills?'' said Trumbo, seemingly lost in thought. "Who's . . . oh, yeah, the astronomer. Steve, we'd better postpone the tour down here until after I speak to Kukali and the guests . . .''

The hotel manager shook his head and looked determined. "It's just another hundred yards, Mr. Trumbo. I really think you should see it. Then I'll go with you to deal with Mr. Kukali. The curator owes me a favor.''

Trumbo hissed through his teeth. "All right, show me the fucking office if it's so fucking important.''

The blinds were drawn on the small window. The sign above the door said DIRECTOR OF ASTRONOMY. Carter fumbled for a key on the chain. "It was locked when we came looking for Mr. Wills,'' said the hotel manager.

Trumbo nodded. He followed Carter into the small room. He was not prepared for what he found.

The room was small, no more than twelve feet by fifteen feet, there was no other door—not even a bathroom or closet—and most of the floor space was taken up with the desk, file cabinets, and a large telescope on a tripod. There were a few framed astronomy prints on the white walls. The only sign of disorder was the executive chair behind the desk, which had been tumbled on its side. That and an eight-foot crack in the wall behind the desk, a crevice that ran from floor to ceiling and opened onto darkness. And the blood.

"Jesus H. Christ," whispered Trumbo.

There was blood on the tumbled chair, blood on the white walls, blood across the desk, blood spattered on the papers on the desk, blood sprinkled randomly on the single guest chair opposite the desk, blood thrown in arterial sprays across the astronomy posters, and blood glimmering on the large telescope.

"Jesus H. Christ," Trumbo said again, and took a step back into the hallway. He looked up and down the dimly lighted tunnel and stepped back into the astronomer's office. "Have the others seen this?"

"No," said Carter. "Except for Ms. Windemere from Accounting, who came down looking for Mr. Wills because they had a lunch date. She was here when Mr. Dillon unlocked the door."

That fact sank in for Trumbo. "The door was *locked?* Something did this to Wills while he was in here behind locked doors?" He stared at the crack in the wall. It did not seem large enough for a man to squeeze through. "Where does that go? What caused it?"

"We don't know," said Dillon, stepping behind the desk, taking a flashlight from his coat pocket, and shining it into the crevice. The rough surface was slick with . . . something. "You know these grounds are honeycombed with old lava tubes. There might be one back there. The construction crews ran into dozens when they were excavating the service tunnels."

Trumbo took another step closer, making sure that he did not step in any of the blood on the floor. He tried not to touch the desk, the chair, anything. "Yeah, but what caused that? I didn't feel an earthquake." He turned to Stephen Ridell Carter. "Was there an earthquake?"

The director was very pale. He looked away from the spattered papers on Mr. Wills's desk and swallowed. "Ah . . . well . . . I called Dr. Hastings at the Volcano Observatory and he informed me that between eight A.M. and two P.M. there were more than twenty seismic events related to the eruptions, but none of them were felt here . . . not even by other people working in the catacombs . . . ah, service tunnel." Carter stared at the crack as if something might ooze out of it. "If this was caused by an earthquake, it was a very, very localized event."

"Evidently," said Trumbo. He looked at Dillon. "Why was the door locked?"

The security director reached down and lifted a magazine that lay with the various papers on the astronomer's desk. Blood had sprayed across the open pages, but Trumbo could see the color photograph of a naked woman lying on her back, legs spread. "Great," said Trumbo. "Our astronomer likes to jack off before lunch." He looked back at Carter. "Who's this Ms. Windemere from Accounting? Maybe she came in, found Wills going at it, got jealous, and chopped him up with a meat cleaver or something."

The manager only stared. Finally he said, "It seems rather unlikely, sir. Ms. Windemere *did* come to find Mr. Dillon when Mr. Wills failed to appear at lunchtime. And she did faint when she saw the condition of the room. She is still sedated in the infirmary."

"Good," said Trumbo. "How long can we keep her that way?"

"I beg your pardon, sir?" said Carter.

"We need to keep her quiet too. She can't go home. Send Dr. Scamahorn to see me. Maybe we can keep her sleeping for the next day or so."

Stephen Ridell Carter's expression conveyed his opinion of such a plan.

Trumbo looked around the room again and beckoned Briggs closer. "What could do this to a man?"

The hulking security chief shrugged. "Plenty of things, boss. You mentioned a meat cleaver. Plenty of arterial spray when someone gets going with one of those. Axe is good. Even a big knife or automatic weapon—say an Uzi or Mac-ten—would toss around a lot of blood. People always underestimate how much blood we carry around in us."

Trumbo nodded.

"There's a problem with that, though," said Dillon, his eyes quick and ferretlike beneath heavy brows.

"What's that?" said Trumbo.

"Meat cleaver, axe, knife, Uzi," said Dillon. "They all toss around blood, but they all leave bodies behind too. Or at least parts of bodies." He pointed to the empty room and held up his hands. "Unless our Mr. Wills was dragged through there . . ." He jerked a thumb toward the jagged crevice behind him.

"He would had to have been in pieces to get through there," said Briggs, his voice sounding professionally interested. He produced his own flashlight from a coat pocket, stepped up to the crack, and looked through. "It does look larger back there. Like a tunnel or something."

"Get some men down here with sledgehammers," ordered Trumbo. "Knock that wall down. Briggs, you and Dillon check out whatever's back there."

"Mr. Trumbo," said Stephen Ridell Carter in his shocked voice. "This is a crime scene. The police will be furious if we disturb it. It is, I believe, against the law to destroy evidence."

Trumbo rubbed his forehead. He had a miserable headache. "Steve, we don't know it's a crime scene. We don't know that Wills is dead. He may be in Kona at a topless bar for all we know. All I see is a trashed office and a possibly dangerous crack in the wall. We have to make sure that the wall is structurally sound. Dillon?"

"Yessir."

"I want you and Briggs to knock it down. Personally. We don't need any other people curious about this."

The small, bearded man frowned, but Briggs looked pleased at the thought of knocking down a wall.

Stephen Ridell Carter started to say something, but just then there was a knock at the door. Briggs opened it.

Will Bryant was there, looking worried. "Mr. T, can I have a minute?"

Trumbo stepped out into the corridor rather than invite his assistant in to view the carnage. The air was fresher in the tunnel.

"We've got a problem," said Bryant.

Trumbo smiled thinly. "Sato?"

"No, they're good. About finished with lunch. We'll begin the next session in about an hour."

"What then?" said Trumbo. "More body parts?"

Will Bryant shook his head. "Mrs. Trumbo's jet just landed. I've sent a limo to pick her and Koestler up. They reserved a suite here."

Trumbo said nothing. He was trying to imagine what kind of thing could have squeezed through that crack in the wall, dismembered a horny astronomer, and pulled the pieces of him out with it when it oozed away. He was wondering if the thing, whatever it was, could be enticed to snatch a New England–bred, cast-iron bitch named Caitlin Sommersby Trumbo.

"That's not really the problem," Bryant was saying.

Trumbo almost laughed. "No, Will? What *is* the problem?"

Will Bryant rarely showed nervousness, but now he smoothed back his long hair in a nervous sweep. "Maya Richardson's Gulfstream just radioed the tower. They'll be landing in two hours."

Trumbo leaned against the wall. The rough stone was cool and slightly sweaty under his cool and slightly sweaty palm. "That only leaves Bicki. I suppose she's parachuting in even as we speak."

"Deavers called from Lindbergh Field in San Diego," said his assistant. "Their plane refueled there about an hour ago. Their flight plan has an ETA in Kona at eight thirty-eight, local time."

Byron Trumbo nodded and said nothing. He was fighting down the urge to giggle. Carter, Dillon, and Briggs stepped out of the astronomy office, the manager locking the door behind him.

Trumbo set his hand on Will's shoulder. "Well, greet Caitlin and that blood-sucking motherfucker Koestler for me, would you, Will? Give them *leis,* kisses, fruit, the Ali'i Suite on the north end of the Big Hale, the whole nine yards. Tell her I'll come see her as soon as I talk to the art curator and a couple of guests about a dog and a missing hand.''

Bryant nodded his understanding. The cortege moved back down the dimly lighted corridor with purposeful strides.

Eleanor was tired of getting the runaround. Paul, Cordie, and she had asked to see the manager, who had not been available, so they had ended up talking to a bearded little homunculus of a security chief—Mr. Dillon—who had asked them to repeat their story to his assistant, an amiable black man named Fredrickson, while Mr. Dillon himself had run off somewhere. Paul Kukali was also becoming obviously bored with the repetition.

"Look," the art curator was saying, "we saw the dog. The dog had a human hand in its jaws. That's all we know. Shouldn't you be getting someone out there to find it . . . and the rest of the corpse?"

Mr. Fredrickson showed a white grin. "Yes, sir. Don't worry about that. But let's just go over this again. Which way did you say the dog ran off?"

"Into the lava on the ocean side of the jogging path," said Cordie Stumpf. She glanced at her cheap wristwatch. "And we've been telling this story for more than forty-five minutes. Time's up. I'm gonna get back to my vacation." Cordie stood up. Mr. Fredrickson stood up. Paul Kukali stood up.

At that moment, the door to the suite opened and Mr. Dillon returned with a short, aggressive-looking man wearing old shorts and a faded Hawaiian shirt. Eleanor recognized him at once from articles in *Time* and the *Wall Street Journal.*

"Paul!" said Trumbo, stepping forward quickly and pumping the curator's hand. "It's been too long since I've seen you."

Paul Kukali returned the handshake with much less enthusiasm than his employer was showing. "Mr. Trumbo, we saw . . ."

"I heard, I heard," said Trumbo, turning toward Cordie and Eleanor. "Terrible. And who are these lovely ladies?" He smiled broadly.

Cordie Stumpf shifted her weight slightly and folded her arms across her chest. "These lovely ladies are two thirds of the threesome that saw a dog running around your property with someone's hand in its jaws," she said. "And if you ask me, it's a hell of a way to run a resort."

Trumbo's grin stayed in place, but it began to resemble a rictus. "Yes, yes, so Mr. Dillon has told me." He turned back to the art curator. "Paul, you're certain it was a human hand? Sometimes a white crab looks very much like . . ."

Paul interrupted. "It was a hand. All of us saw it."

Trumbo nodded as if weighing new information. He turned back to the women. "Well, ladies, you have my personal apologies for this upsetting incident. We'll look into it, of course. And I apologize again for any upset or inconvenience this has caused you. We will, of course, pick up any charges for your scheduled stay here at the Mauna Pele, and if there is anything else we can do to make amends for this upsetting occurrence, please tell us and we will act upon it immediately . . . gratis, of course." He smiled again.

"That's it?" said Cordie.

"I beg your pardon?" said Trumbo through his smile.

"That's it? We tell you that a dog's runnin' around the resort with somebody's mitt in its mouth, and you comp us a room and shoo us off?"

Byron Trumbo sighed. "Ms. . . . ah?"

"Stumpf," said Cordie. "And it's Mrs."

"Mrs. Stumpf. Mr. Dillon and the others whom you've spoken to about this are quite bothered by it, of course, and we *will* find the dog and . . . whatever else there is to be found. But we believe that we know the cause of this . . . ah . . . unfortunate incident."

Paul, Cordie, and Eleanor waited. Mr. Fredrickson also seemed to be waiting.

"Sadly, there recently was a drowning accident down the coast a few miles," said Byron Trumbo. "A local gentleman fell overboard and drowned. Parts of his body were recovered, but . . . ah . . . the sharks had gotten to him, and the remains were not . . . ah . . . intact. It seems probable that this dog . . . which, by the way, must be a stray, there are no dogs at the Mauna Pele . . .

this stray dog must have found some of these remains along the coast and brought them here. We do deeply apologize for any trauma this has caused.''

Paul Kukali was frowning. ''Are you talking about the drowning of that Samoan boy from Milolii?''

Trumbo hesitated and looked at Dillon. The security chief nodded.

Paul Kukali shook his head. ''That was three weeks ago. And the boy's body was found miles north of here. The hand we saw today was a white man's hand.''

Security Chief Dillon made a rude noise. ''After a body's been in the water awhile . . .''

''I know,'' said Paul. ''But this hand wasn't white and bloated. You could see the tan. I don't think it had been in the water at all. It was a white man's hand . . .''

''I don't see any reason to disturb the ladies any more,'' said Trumbo, nodding in the direction of the two guests. ''I'm sure that Mrs. Stumpf and Mrs. . . . ah . . .''

''Perry,'' said Eleanor. ''Ms.''

''I'm sure that Mrs. Stumpf and Ms. Perry would prefer to get back to their holiday while we discuss this.'' Trumbo took two business cards from his billfold and scribbled on them. ''Ladies, if you would present these to Larry at the Shipwreck Bar, he will mix you my favorite drink . . . a secret mix . . . I call it Pele's Fire. All compliments of the Mauna Pele, of course.''

Cordie looked at the card and then looked up at the billionaire. ''This is all good stuff, Trumbo, but I got to tell you . . . I already had everything free. I won one of your Vacation with the Millionaires state contests. Illinois.''

''Ah, yes,'' said Byron Trumbo, smile still frozen in place. ''A beautiful state, Illinois. I know one of your senators very well.''

Cordie's head jerked up. ''Oh, yeah? Which one?''

''The senior senator,'' said the billionaire, as if knowing that this pale, chubby woman would not recognize the name. ''Senator Harlen.''

Cordie Stumpf laughed. ''I guess that makes two of us then,'' she said.

''I beg your pardon?'' said Trumbo.

"Never mind." Cordie looked at Eleanor. "You had enough of this nonsense?"

Eleanor nodded but hesitated a moment. She looked at the security chief and the owner. "We really did see this hand. It looked as if it had been cleanly severed . . . almost surgically. And Paul's right . . . it was the hand of a white man, the nails were manicured, and it didn't look as if it had been in the water."

Trumbo nodded tiredly, his smile fading. "Ms. Perry . . ."

Eleanor waited.

"I would take it as a personal favor if neither of you would mention this to the other guests. It would disturb their peace of mind for . . . no real reason. I assure you that we will get to the bottom of this."

"If we don't talk," said Cordie, "will you cut us in?"

Trumbo blinked at her. "I beg your pardon?"

"Let us know what you find out," said Cordie. "Keep us up-to-date on what you find."

"Of course," said Trumbo. He looked at the security chief. "Mr. Dillon, please make a note to keep Mrs. Stumpf and Ms. Perry abreast of any breaks in the investigation."

The hairy little man nodded, took a notebook and pen out of his jacket pocket, and ostentatiously made a note.

"I presume that the local police will want to speak to us," said Eleanor.

"Almost certainly," Trumbo said smoothly.

Eleanor hesitated. "I'm booked here until the end of the week," she said. "Your people know which *hale* I have."

"Thank you," purred Byron Trumbo. He turned to Cordie. "Is there anything else we can help you with, Mrs. Stumpf?"

Cordie had opened the door before Dillon or Fredrickson could open it for her. "Just say hi to Jimmy for me when you talk to him next."

"Jimmy?" Trumbo was smiling again.

"The senior senator," said Cordie. She and Eleanor went out together.

June 14, 1866, Volcano of Kilauea—
With the Reverend Haymark as our dubious guide, Mr.

Samuel Clemens and I prepared for our midnight descent into
the crater Kilauea.

I knew that the expedition was folly, but the fact that I was
committing folly had rarely dissuaded me from an adventure
before this. It did not do so now. Our preparations were modest:
the caretaker outfitted us with one lantern apiece, sturdy walking
sticks, and a canvas bag of bread and cheese and wine for a
"volcano picnic" once we reached the active lake of lava several
miles across the crater floor.

While neither Hananui nor any of the other locals would
serve as guides on this specific night—it seemed that another
cauldron on the crater floor was threatening to spill over—our
former guide did lead us to the "staircase"—a precipitous path
carved into a crevice along the crater wall halfway between the
Volcano House hotel and the thatched-hut Overlook House. The
Reverend Haymark attested that this was the way he had
descended during his previous expeditions, and with the portly
minister in the lead, myself in the middle, and our California
correspondent bringing up the rear, we picked our way down a
tortuous, thousand-foot lava-stone staircase to the crater floor. I
believe that the fact that it was so dark—the rock walls around us
lit only by the same ruddy volcano light that turned our hands
and faces red—was an advantage, the small circles of
illumination thrown by our swinging lanterns not showing us the
terrible fate that would be ours had we missed our step or made
a wrong turn.

Once down on the crater floor, it became obvious that while
the cooled lava surface had looked quite solid from our vantage
point above, it was actually comprised of thousands of chinks
and cracks and fissures, through which the red surface of the
still-molten lava beneath was quite visible. Reverend Haymark
cried that he remembered the path, and finding the smooth
section of lava ahead of him with his questing lantern, we set out
across the crater floor.

Although "cooled," the lava underfoot was still hot enough
to warm the soles of my feet through my sturdy boots. I could
not imagine the heat of the lava that even at that moment boiled

to our height and above in bubbling cauldrons only a few hundred feet to our right and left.

"It is, I believe, only a few hundred yards across this difficult space," cried the Reverend, and set off across the hot stone with some haste. I followed, my skirts billowing and reflecting the heat against my booted legs, the circle of my lantern light barely keeping up with the cleric's. Mr. Clemens hurried along behind, his cigar still in place, although it seemed rather redundant in this hellish pit. At least the stench of sulphur here masked the smell of his cigar.

It is impossible, even so short a time after experiencing this event, for me to adequately describe the wonders of a volcano in the midst of its activity. While it at first seemed that we were in a red-lit void, a rocky absence of texture or detail, we soon learned to adapt our eyes more to the fiery illumination around us than to the circumscribed range of our lanterns, and then the volcano floor became a fantastical place: terraces of black stone, lakes of flame, ridges, cliffs of fall, cones, rivers of molten fire, mountainsides of ash, great gobbets of leaping lava, sheer chasms filled with smoke and sulphurous fumes. Kilauea leapt and frolicked and breathed and gasped and spewed its fiery venom all about us, oblivious of us, as indifferent to our intrusion as some great Vulcan god would be to the timorous presence of three fleas in his fiery furnace.

And a fiery furnace it was. I believe that even Mr. Clemens realized the folly of our impulsive decision, for when the Reverend Haymark paused to check the trail and mop his sweating face, the correspondent called across the creak and cracking of cooling stone—"Are you sure you know the way?"

"It is easier in daylight," said the minister, his eyes looking wide and white in the awful light. "And with a guide."

The two of us must have shown our concern on our faces, for the cleric went quickly on, "But we soon will be across the worst part. And then it is mere hiking on stone."

As it turned out, there was a quarter mile more of "the worst part," and it required us to jump narrow chasms where lava flowed hundreds of feet below us. To think about the

consequences of not making each of these jumps would have
paralyzed me, so I set the thoughts aside and jumped. The heat
made my skirts smolder in the thick air. Once I fell into an
unseen hole and could feel the flames licking at my boots,
so—not waiting for the startled gentlemen to set down their
lanterns and fish me out—I set my hands against rock and pulled
myself to safety. Surprisingly, the stone under my hands was so
warm that my sturdy dog-skin gloves were burned almost
through, my hands blistered as if I had set them naked upon the
hissing surface.

I said nothing of this to the men, but lifted my lantern and
followed the Reverend in his halting, hopping progress across
the rough crater floor.

Our journey must have taken little more than an hour across
the crater of Kilauea, but because of the fiery light, the constant
danger, the need to always watch one's step where that step was
all but impossible to watch, the trip seemed endless. But then,
suddenly, without warning, we arrived at the lake of fire, the very
brink of Hale-mau-mau.

The words of common speech are quite useless. Those
words that come to mind—fountains, sprays, fire, jets,
explosions—simply do nothing to convey the total and
overwhelming other-worldness, the sheer power and terrifying
grandeur of what we saw.

The lake was some five hundred feet wide at its narrowest,
almost half a mile broad. Its shores consisted of perpendicular
walls of black lava—the same "cooled" material upon which I
now stood and which made my boots smoke from the
heat—none of which were less than fifty feet high, and some
more than two hundred feet, rising from the glowing lava like
some Black Cliffs of Dover from channels of sluggish flame.
Cones rose from the lake, from the shores of the lake, and each
emitted great gouts of steam and sulphurous fog, all tinted the
deepest reds and oranges from the churning lava itself. These
clouds of vapor rose to the crater rim—now a seemingly
inestimable distance above us—and to the fiery cap of clouds
hanging low above the crater.

But it was the lake of fire that caught my attention then and, I think, shall never release it.

Lava surged and fountained, rising on great waves against itself and the black cliffs which sought to contain it. Lava bubbled ahead of us—above us, for the surges sent combers crashing against the cones higher than our heads a hundred yards or less across the lake—and swirled in a thousand fiery vortexes that sent molten rock lapping against its containing shores. Directly ahead of us, eleven fountains of gory fire ejaculated this glowing effluvium into the air, and hence back into the lake of fire which had spawned it. Everywhere around us was the hiss and crackle of congealing rock, the whisper of steam venting from a thousand hidden crevices, the moan of expanding and contracting surfaces . . . and beneath all this, the constant heat-surge of this ocean of fire, this lake of raw creation which rolled and breathed at our very feet.

I turned toward the Reverend Haymark, but the cleric was staring with his jaw quite slack, his eyes glazed, muttering something to the effect, "I have never seen it at night . . . I have never seen it at night." Then I turned toward Mr. Clemens, as if daring the brash young correspondent to make light of this, but Mr. Clemens had thrown away his cigar and was staring, face rapt, expression one of something like religious awe. As if sensing my gaze, he turned in my direction—his reddish eyebrows and mustaches and curls made orange by the surging light—and he opened his mouth as if to speak, then said nothing.

I nodded and turned back to watch the spectacle with him.

For two hours or more we stood on the edge of Hale-mau-mau, Madame Pele's home, and watched as banks of cooling lava rose, now building ramps and islands into the lake of flame, now succumbing to the heat and roiling away as liquid rock once again, the waves lapping higher as the level of lava grew and the heat drove us back, now cooling as black rock curled into existence, creating new shores and shoals, new cliff faces and cones. And all the while the cones rising from this surging pit of flame spouted their incendiary gibbets toward the clouds and the very rock we stood upon cracked and shifted, offering new vistas of the magma beneath our feet. This was our picnic site as we ate the bread and cheese our host had packed, sipping wine from the glasses he had carefully wrapped and included in our bundle.

"We'd best head back," Reverend Haymark said at last, his voice hoarse, as if he had been shouting despite the fact of our almost total silence the entire time we had stood upon this hellish shore.

Mr. Clemens and I looked at each other then, as if we would protest, as if we would mutiny this decision and remain where we were, through the night, through the day, into the glory of another night in Pele's realm.

We did not mutiny, of course, although I believe we read that moment of madness in each other's eyes. Instead, we nodded our assent and backed away, watching the sea of flame as long as we could glimpse it, until sanity made us watch our feet and follow the bobbing lantern of our clerical guide.

I confess here that I had set my lantern down upon first sight of the fire-sea, and did not take it up again—nor give it another thought—when I left the vicinity of that terrible ocean. The reddish light had seemed so bright, my senses were so filled with the frightening grandeur all around, that I did not think of the lantern. I thought of nothing but the sights and smells that had overpowered me as nothing else in my thirty-one years had come close to so doing. Still holding my central position between the two men, noting idly that Mr. Clemens had brought his lantern and that the Reverend's bobbed along ahead with its usual regularity, I set my smoking boots upon the dark lava and trudged along, too fatigued and overwhelmed to think.

Thus it was a shock when Reverend Haymark's alarmed voice cried, "Stop!"

Both Mr. Clemens and I froze in our places, perhaps some ten feet apart. "What is it?" asked the correspondent in a voice that held some tension.

"We are off the path," replied the minister. I heard the quaver in his voice and my legs began to shake in sympathy.

Immediately, both Haymark and Clemens began holding

their lanterns to full extent without moving their feet, but all around us was blackness broken only by the glow of lava through narrow crevices.

"The surface is higher here," said Reverend Haymark. "We are far above the deep core. The lava is rotten, a thin shell. I noticed the difference in sound as I walked. I confess that I was not paying attention."

Mr. Clemens and I said nothing. Finally the correspondent said softly, "If we retrace our steps . . ."

Reverend Haymark's lantern swung in desperate arcs, sometimes illuminating his terrified face. "That would be very difficult, sir. We have been taking broad steps, jumping from hummock to hummock. A misstep here would send us crashing through, falling a thousand feet to the deep lava below."

"I think eight hundred would answer for me," said Mr. Clemens, repeating his weak joke of several hours earlier.

I felt that I could not breathe, so terrifying was the thought of being lost on this treacherous crust. "We could wait for dawn," I said, but dawn was hours away and even as I said it, I knew that we could not stand here through the long night.

"Perhaps we can walk carefully back until we find the path," said Reverend Haymark and took a single step before breaking through the crust.

My scream must have been a pitiful thing set against the roar of lava and hiss of steam escaping all around us in the night.

ELEVEN

Long as the lava-light
Glares from the lava-lake,
Dazzling the starlight;
Long as the silvery vapour in daylight,
Over the mountain
Floats, will the glory of Kapiolani be mingled with
either on Hawa-i-ee.
                    —Alfred Lord Tennyson
                    "Kapiolani," 1892

Security chief Matthew "Matt" Dillon was not in a bad mood
when he passed through the doors marked AUTHORIZED PER-
SONNEL ONLY and trotted down the ramp into the catacombs
beneath the Mauna Pele. Dillon had worked for the FBI briefly,
then—in a rare shuffle—for the CIA for seven years before entering private security work. His area of expertise had been antiter-
rorist tactics, specifically terrorism targeted at large installations.
To be an expert in protecting such installations, Dillon had
become an expert in terrorizing them. His services had even been
offered to the military when the idiots around President Carter
had been planning the rescue of the hostages held at the occupied
American Embassy in Iran. Dillon had always been glad the Army
had not taken the FBI up on its offer and involved him in that
monumental fuck-up.

Dillon had been a private consultant for five years when Pete
Briggs, who had taken a course in executive protection from him
the year before, approached him about working for Byron
Trumbo. Dillon had no interest in such a job—static security work

bored his ass off—but Briggs pressed, they flew him in a private jet from San Diego to New York, Trumbo personally interviewed him, the job sounded interesting—more a troubleshooter around Trumbo's widely scattered empire of businesses and casinos and hotels than a simple security director—and the money was twice what he was making as a consultant, even in those rich times of executive kidnappings and shootings. Dillon had said yes.

For a year or two it had been fun, jetting around the world looking into blackmail threats and security breaches, exposing thieves in Mr. Trumbo's casinos and counting houses, even laying some muscle on Mr. T's less savory enemies when it came down to that. Dillon had never had a problem working in the gray areas of the law, or even descending into the black outside the law when the job demanded it. Trumbo had seemed to sense this, and used Dillon accordingly.

Then, six months earlier, the disappearances had begun at Trumbo's Mauna Pele Resort and Dillon had been on the next plane west. His plan was to arrive unofficially to get a sense of the place. At first it was a lark, soaking up the sun, sitting at the Shipwreck Bar all evening, generally playing the idiot tourist while he scoped out the resort and tried to figure out what was going on. It didn't tell him much. Stephen Ridell Carter was running a tight ship. Mauna Pele's security chief at that time, a local Hawaiian ex-cop named Charlie Kane, had been lazy but not totally incompetent. The local cops had looked into all the obvious angles—disgruntled ex-employees, local crazies, someone with a grudge against Trumbo personally—but nothing panned out. After a week of fruitless undercover work, Dillon had identified himself to Carter, Kane, and the local authorities and worked with them. Still nothing.

The failure had frustrated him. After Trumbo had fired Charlie Kane and asked him to assume the position of resort security director "until this thing's ironed out," Dillon had accepted, thinking it would be a few weeks at most. Leaving the mystery open had not been his style.

Now, more than six months later, Matthew Dillon was sick of Hawaii, sick of the Mauna Pele, sick of sunshine and fresh air and the crashing surf. He wanted to get back to New York in the winter with its grimy streets and surly cabdrivers. He wanted to trouble-shoot one of Mr. T's casinos in Las Vegas or Atlantic City, working through the night in an interior world where no one knew if it was night or day or gave a shit.

But now this. Body parts turning up on the golf course. The three missing New Jersey guys. The astronomer disappearing in great gouts of blood. Matthew Dillon grinned and hurried down the service tunnel, patting the holster on his hip as he moved along. This was more like it.

The astronomer's office was unlocked. Dillon slipped the 9mm Glock out of the holster and pushed the door open gently.

Pete Briggs was standing in the center of the room, holding a ten-pound sledgehammer and rubbing his massive chin. Dillon slid the semiautomatic back in the holster. "You really going to knock down that wall?"

Briggs did not turn his head. Dillon knew that the big man looked like some half-wit linebacker but was fairly canny. And a good personal security man. Dillon knew lots of worse profession-als when it came to watching someone's back.

"Yep," said Briggs.

"The local cops will shit bricks."

"Yep," Briggs said again, obviously not interested in how the local cops would react. He shifted the sledgehammer from his left shoulder to his right and looked at Dillon. "I've been waiting for you."

Dillon raised a thick eyebrow.

Briggs nodded toward a six-cell flashlight. "I figure it might be best for one of us to hold the light while the other knocks down the wall."

Dillon picked up the flashlight. "OK."

Briggs lifted some plastic goggles from the desk, put them on, shoved the desk aside with one massive hand, set the sledgeham-mer appraisingly against the widest section of the crack, and said, "You'd better stand back."

There was not much room to stand back in, but Dillon moved to the far wall and raised the flashlight.

"Pull your piece, too," said Briggs.

Dillon looked at the other man. "Why? Do you think whatever got Wills is going to come out of that crack to get you?"

Briggs did not smile. "Keep your flashlight and the Glock aimed on the hole as I widen it," he said.

Dillon did not like taking orders, but he shrugged and pulled the 9mm pistol from its holster. The overhead lights were bright enough in this small room, but he aimed the flashlight at the hole, holding it in his left hand directly above the pistol in his right hand just as he had been trained, both flashlight beam and barrel swiveling together. "Ready," he said.

Pete Briggs raised the sledgehammer and swung it full force against the wall.

Eleanor had watched the sun set into the ocean from the beach near her *hale* and then walked to the Shipwreck Bar for a drink. There were a scattering of guests sitting around, occupying only a few of the many tables set out under the thatched roof of the bar or on the flagstone terrace overlooking the beach. Eleanor sat by herself at the edge of the terrace, ordered a gin and tonic, and sipped it as the sky to the west shifted through pink to purple to a dying violet. Palm trees cut serrated silhouettes against the sky. Eleanor could see the glow to the east as the volcano light illuminated the ash cloud, which had shifted direction again, bringing an overcast to the Kona Coast. The beach and walkways were empty until a single Hawaiian runner, clad only in a traditional loincloth, ran down the path carrying a long torch with which he lighted the many gas braziers and torches that lined the walkways. The flames whipped and sizzled in the rising wind.

She was lost in thought—about the day, about the dog and its grisly toy, and about her strange quest here, when she looked up to find Cordie Stumpf standing over her with a bottle of beer and a glass in her hand. "Hey, Nell, mind if I join you?"

"Of course not," said Eleanor, thinking, *Nell?* She rather liked it. Each generation of spinsters in her family had acquired a nickname by which she was known through her later years—Aunt

Kidder, Aunt Mittie, Aunt Tam, Aunt Beanie—Eleanor thought that she could live with "Aunt Nell."

"That was quite a runaround this afternoon, wasn't it?" said Cordie, sipping her beer.

Eleanor nodded, still watching the fading sky.

"Trumbo definitely wanted to sweep the whole thing under the rug," said Cordie. "The cops haven't contacted me. Have you seen 'em?"

"No," said Eleanor.

"I bet Trumbo hasn't even called them."

"Why wouldn't he?" said Eleanor. Far out to sea, a sailing ship was a triangular silhouette against the fading violet on the horizon. Despite the wind coming up, the ocean seemed perfectly calm, waves hardly breaking against the sand fifty feet away.

Cordie shrugged. "Probably trying to avoid the publicity."

Eleanor shifted to look at the other woman. "How can he do that? We're bound to tell someone soon. We could call the local police tonight . . . right now."

Cordie poured more beer, drank, and licked foam from her thin lips. "Yeah, but we won't. We're on vacation."

Eleanor did not know if Cordie was joking.

"Besides," said Cordie, "I think Trumbo's trying to sell the place. Maybe he's just trying to hold off the news until he unloads it on those Japs I saw him driving around this morning."

Eleanor winced at the word "Japs." She said, "How do you know about Byron Trumbo?"

"The *National Enquirer* and *A Current Affair,*" said Cordie. "Haven't you heard about his wife and girlfriend troubles?"

Eleanor shook her head.

"It's worse than old Donald Trump a few years ago with whatshername. Trumbo's in the process of divorcing a wife who was *smart*—she helped him build his empire—or at least that's what her lawyer says. And then he started running around with this supermodel . . ."

"Maya Richardson," said Eleanor, and drank the last of her gin and tonic.

Cordie grinned. "You *do* read the *National Perspirer.*"

"Just scan the headlines when I'm in line at the supermarket."

"Yeah," said Cordie. "Uh-huh. Well, *A Current Affair* says that Trumbo is having a new affair with a younger model. One that Maya hasn't found out about yet." She waved at the waiter. When the young man came over, Cordie showed him the card entitling them to free drinks for the rest of their stay and said, "We'll try one of Mr. Trumbo's favorite drinks. Pele's Hair."

"You mean Pele's Fire," said the waiter. He was blond, handsome, bronzed by the sun.

"Whatever," said Cordie. "Bring two." She watched the waiter's rear end as he retreated.

"I'm not sure I should mix my drinks," said Eleanor.

Cordie's eyebrows went up. "Oh, did you want one?" She waited a moment and smiled. "Well, do you have an appetite after what we saw today?"

Eleanor hesitated. "I'm beginning to doubt what we saw today."

"Oh, don't doubt it," said Cordie. "We saw what we saw. And I've seen weirder things."

Eleanor started to ask what weirder things, but Cordie spoke up again, "And did you notice the dog?"

"Only that it was black," said Eleanor. "And large. Like an oversized Labrador."

Cordie leaned closer. "I saw it early this morning. Just as it was getting light. The same damn dog was running down the beach."

"Oh, yes," said Eleanor. "You asked me if I'd seen a black dog. I'd forgotten until now."

Cordie nodded. "Did you notice its teeth? That's why I asked you this morning if you'd seen it."

"Its teeth?" Eleanor tried to remember. The dog had stood in front of them for only a few seconds before bolting off into the lava fields. She remembered the shock of realizing what was in its jaws, and the sense of something *wrong* about the animal, but nothing specific about the teeth. She shook her head. "What about its teeth?"

Cordie leaned back as their drinks were set down. When the boy was gone, she said, "It had human teeth."

Eleanor blinked.

"It did," said Cordie Stumpf, and pulled the tall drink closer to her. It was red, with a slice of orange floating in it. "As God is my witness, the damned dog had human teeth. Like dentures. The critter smiled at me this morning on the beach."

"You must be mistaken," said Eleanor.

"Uh-uh," said Cordie. "I've had me as many dogs as I've had men in my life, and I know what they look like. This thing didn't look right the first time I saw it. When it grinned at me this morning, I saw why. I might not have noticed this afternoon—what with that guy's hand hanging out of its mouth and all—but I knew what to look for, and I did, and they were human teeth all right."

Eleanor felt slightly dizzy. She liked Cordie Stumpf and did not want the other woman to be proven crazy. To hide her confusion, she pulled the tall drink to her, removed an umbrella and sprig of mint, and sipped it. "It's sweet. I wonder what's in it."

"Everything," said Cordie. "It's like a Long Island Iced Tea with cherry flavoring and about four more kinds of alcohol thrown in. Two of these and I'll be dancing naked on the bar."

Eleanor tried to picture that, then quickly put the image out of her mind.

"Speaking of dancing naked," said Cordie, "what do you think about that Paul?"

Eleanor swallowed. "What about him?"

Cordie smiled. "He's got the serious hots for you, Nell."

No one had ever used that phrase in Eleanor's presence to the best of her recollection. She took a few seconds to reply. "You're mistaken."

"Uh-uh," said Cordie.

"I have no interest in Dr. Kukali," said Eleanor. She heard how stuffy it sounded—a professor reprimanding a student—but she could not help it.

"I know," said Cordie, still smiling slightly. "I can tell. But I'm not sure Dr. K. can. Men are as dense as bricks sometimes."

Eleanor decided to change the subject. "Anyway, Dr. Kukali

said that he was driving back to Hilo this afternoon. He only lectures at the Mauna Pele once a week.''

"I don't think so," said Cordie. "I think he's still here tonight.''

Eleanor took another sip of the drink. It was too sweet, but rather pleasant. "Why do you say that?''

Cordie nodded her head toward the entrance to the terrace behind Eleanor. "Because he just came in the bar and is coming over to our table.''

June 14, 1866, Kilauea Volcano—
When the Reverend Haymark broke through the crust of dried lava, my first thought was—"He will volatilize, and the resulting flames shall consume us all!" It was an unworthy thought. And the hypothesis remained untested, since the portly cleric fell through only to his outflung arms.

"Do not move to save me!" cried Reverend Haymark. His altruism was obviously much more evolved than that of either Mr. Clemens or myself, as neither the correspondent nor I had made or considered the slightest move to save our guide. Indeed, I doubted at that moment if I was capable of taking another step.

The cleric extricated himself with a great amount of heaving and wheezing, and crawled away from the hole on hands and knees. The glow of magma shone up through the jagged aperture. Rising carefully to his feet and relighting the lantern he had dropped, Reverend Haymark said, "Look around for the path. It is harder and more dried than this surface.''

Mr. Clemens and I cast around wildly, without moving our feet on the treacherous surface, but as far as the lantern light extended, the surface looked to be the same. Whatever different surface the path had offered, it was invisible in lantern light. We were lost without hope on this thin crust above a bottomless lake of lava.

"Quickly," cried Reverend Haymark, "douse the lanterns.''

The correspondent looked as dubious at this suggestion as I felt, but we followed our portly guide's example. A moment

later, all was darkness except for the hellish glow from the lava
lake we had departed and from the many cracks and fissures
around us.

"I did not notice that we had strayed from the path by the
look of the surface," explained Reverend Haymark, his voice
hushed, as if any loud noise would send the three of us hurtling
through the rotten surface. "It was the sound."

"How do you mean?" asked Mr. Clemens.

"The path was worn smooth. The untraveled areas retain
these fine lava needles. Listen." He moved his boot along the
surface and we could hear a fine rasping as these tiny needles
were crushed under his boot. "It was this sound that made me
realize we had gone astray."

I looked around in the darkness. Perhaps the path would be
visible once we had found it again, but it was invisible now.

"Close your eyes!" cried the Reverend Haymark and did so
himself, swinging his boot in small circles while he kept his
weight on his left leg.

Mr. Clemens and I immediately saw the wisdom of our
guide's maneuver, and we closed our eyes and began searching
out the telltale crunching sound with our boots. If anyone had
been watching, it would have been a humorous sight—the three
adventurers each standing on one leg in the hellish darkness,
each moving a single leg in slow, cautious, ballet-like movements,
eyes closed, each with an indelible expression of fear each time
we took a step to increase the range of our searching. I expected
to break through with each step and was certain that I could hear
a general creaking, as if the entire surface was preparing to
collapse under us like a shield of rotten ice.

"I've found it!" cried Samuel Clemens. The Reverend and I
opened our eyes to see the correspondent with his right leg fully
extended, his boot scraping an area far to our left. I did not see
how he managed to keep his balance in such a comical pose.

"It sounds different," he said. "I will have to take another
step to see if my ears are trustworthy. It could be a thinner
layer."

"Please be careful, Mr. Clemens," I said, realizing the
absurdity of the statement even as I spoke.

The correspondent gave me a look, his eyes bright under those heavy brows. The red glow made him look like a mischievous demon.

"Miss Stewart," he began earnestly.

"Yes?"

"If the crust does not hold me, would you carry back a message to California?"

My heart lurched. "Yes, Mr. Clemens."

His voice was doleful. "Would you please look up all the young ladies I have ever wooed and tell each that her name was upon my lips when I went to my fate?"

There was no answer to such impertinence, so I said, "Take your step, Mr. Clemens."

The correspondent took a long hop and landed on both feet, like a child playing at a game of leapfrog. The surface held. Mr. Clemens crouched, felt the surface with both hands, and announced, "This is the path. I can see where it leads from this angle."

The half dozen or so paces it took for the Reverend Haymark and myself to join Mr. Clemens on the solid surface constituted the longest voyage of my life. Eventually, after we had ascertained that it was indeed the path we had followed to the lava lake and we had gotten our breath back, we lighted our lanterns and proceeded more carefully than before. The final few hundred yards across the hot surface and narrow fissures, seemingly so frightening during our voyage out, seemed child's play after the terrors of Hale-mau-mau and our subsequent misadventure.

It was almost sunrise when we climbed the last of the thousand-foot staircase and emerged on the crater rim. Hananui was waiting there, coming awake at our approach like some loyal dog happy to see its masters. I had thought that our guide had stayed by his post out of professional loyalty, but it seemed from his excited babble that something extraordinary had occurred at Volcano House in the middle of the night.

"Easy, easy," said Reverend Haymark, laying his large hands on the Hawaiian's shoulders as if he were calming a child. "Tell us slowly."

"Missionaries, they came up from Kona," panted the little man, his eyes wide in the lantern light. "They running away."

Mr. Clemens was in the process of lighting a cigar, as if he had waited until we were safely out of the crater to celebrate. "Running away from what?" he said.

"From Pana-ewa!" gasped Hananui. "From Ku and Nanaue!"

Reverend Haymark took a step back with a look of dislike, if not outright disgust on his florid face.

"What?" said Mr. Clemens, puffing his cigar alight. His face bore an expression of what may have been professional interest.

The cleric waved one hand in dismissal. "These are local gods," he said, his voice contemptuous. "Demi-gods, really. Monsters."

Mr. Clemens stepped closer to the guide, who was obviously terrified. "What about these fellows?" he said.

Hananui shook his head. "Loose. All loose. They kill many people below Kona village. Kill most of missionaries. Those at Volcano House, run away. Run to Hilo Town."

Mr. Clemens's cigar jerked upward and his eyes gleamed with the eager mischief I had seen earlier in the crater. "You say there are missionaries who've been murdered on the Kona Coast?"

Hananui nodded but such a fact was obviously not the cause for his distress. "The gate to Milu is open," he muttered.

Reverend Haymark turned his back on the smaller man. "I believe that Milu is their god of the Underworld," he said. "A sort of Pluto."

Hananui was both nodding and shaking his head in alternate motions. "Milu place. Milu Underworld. Milu land where ghosts live."

Reverend Haymark sighed and lifted his lantern. "We should be getting back. If something has happened to the Kona missionaries, we should hear about it."

Thus we trudged the last few hundred yards to the waiting hotel, Reverend Haymark and I in the lead—too exhausted to speak—and Mr. Clemens bringing up the rear with the babbling Hananui, the correspondent with his arm around the little

Hawaiian, asking more questions and listening to our guide's babbled responses. I was too tired to care.

Byron Trumbo and his people were halfway through a long, relatively formal dinner—formal meaning that Trumbo was dressed in "Aloha Wear" of clean Hawaiian shirt, chinos, and high-top sneakers—with Hiroshe Sato and his people when the bad weather and bad news started flowing in.

The weather evidently came from the east, sliding in on brisk winds under the volcano plume that had filled the sky since early evening. By nightfall, the palm fronds were dancing wildly below the seventh-story level of Sato's dining *lanai* and it began to smell like rain. The rain was not a problem—the dining area of the *lanai* was covered with a roof and sturdy awnings—but the wind made conversation and serving complicated.

Then Will Bryant's assistants began filtering in with more bad news, most of it also coming from the east. Bryant would listen to the assistant, wait for an opportune moment in the general discussion, and then dab at his lips with a linen napkin and come whisper in his boss's ear.

During the shrimp course, the whisper was, "Mrs. Trumbo and her lawyer want to talk to you. They're in the Ali'i Suite. Mrs. Trumbo insists that you meet with her tonight."

Trumbo merely shook his head and Will went off to deal with the bitch by himself. Ten minutes later he was back and whispered, "She insists that it be tonight. She says that it's important. Koestler will be with her. If you don't come to talk to her, she says that she'll come over here and interrupt the dinner. She knows about Sato."

"Fuck," Trumbo whispered, and smiled at Dr. Tatsuro across the table, who looked up startled. Trumbo's own divorce lawyer, Benny "Raw Meat" Shapiro, was still in New York. Caitlin was not playing by the rules.

At seven forty-five, while they were having sherbet between the soup and the fish courses, Will whispered, "Ms. Richardson has just arrived at the hotel. We've given her the Premiere Tahiti Hale on the Point."

Trumbo nodded. The Point of the peninsula was as far from

the Big Hale and Caitlin as they could put Maya. Luckily, the ex-model was used to luxury and being waited on—the Premiere Tahiti Hale had its own pool, chef, and full-time butler—so Maya should not have any reason to come up to the main building.

"She says that she needs to speak with you," whispered Will Bryant.

"Tonight?"

"Immediately," said Will.

"Fucking Christ," Trumbo whispered back, and smiled again at Dr. Tatsuro, whose head was now bobbing like one of those dashboard doll's.

At eight-thirty, during the main course of prime beef raised at the Parker Ranch just up the Kohala Coast, Will Bryant whispered, "Bicki's landed. She's on her way here." Usually, Trumbo's assistant preferred titles and last names, but Bicki had been—at least for the time Trumbo had known her—only "Bicki," a rising model who had joined the ranks of Prince, Madonna, and the other one-namers. Trumbo had liked the simplicity of that—it counterbalanced the nose ring and pierced tongue that his newest interest had sported in the past month or so. Trumbo hated the feeling of kissing Bicki and encountering the tiny steel balls on the upper and lower surfaces of the girl's tongue. She insisted that he should think of it like rock candy, but Trumbo didn't much like the idea of kissing someone with lumps of candy in her mouth either. So he just skipped the kissing part—it had never been that important anyway. But he did order her not to pierce her nipples or any parts south. Bicki had sulked, but complied.

"Where are we going to put her?" he whispered to Will.

"We have the old construction shack," said his assistant.

For a second Trumbo thought that Will was joking, but then he remembered the comfortable home they had erected on the extreme south end of the bay during the construction of the Mauna Pele. The "construction shack" was actually a three-bedroom home sitting just beyond the fourteenth hole, a few hundred yards beyond the edge of the lanes of *hales*. No one had used it but Trumbo during his visits while the resort was being built. The shack had no beach, but it was on a low rise with a beautiful view of the bay and the south peninsula. The house was now used only for the occasional visits of lecherous VIPs like Illinois' Senator Harlen, who wanted to stay totally out of sight with their underaged companions.

"Good idea," said Trumbo. "Bicki's too stupid to notice how isolated she is. Make sure that the place has a cook and valet."

"I've seen to it," whispered Will, and started back to his place at the table.

"Oh," said Trumbo, wiggling his finger to bring his executive assistant back. "Who has Briggs assigned to watch Bicki and Maya?" Trumbo didn't care if the Mauna Pele Killer carried off Caitlin *and* her fucking lawyer.

Will Bryant came back to his boss's side, crouched next to the chair, and seemed to hesitate a moment before whispering, "I've assigned Myers to Ms. Richardson and Courtney to Bicki."

"*You've* assigned them? Where's Briggs?"

"Well, we have a bit of a problem there."

Sato, Dr. Tatsuro, and Sunny Takahashi were all looking at Trumbo across their haunches of beef. Trumbo sincerely believed that if he heard the word "problem" one more time he would throw up. He leaned closer to Bryant, trying to look totally calm and indifferent as he did so. "What problem?"

"Mr. Briggs and Mr. Dillon seem to have disappeared," whispered his assistant.

Trumbo concentrated on not ripping out clumps of hair—his own or Will Bryant's. "I told Briggs and Dillon to knock down that wall in the astronomy office."

Will nodded. He was also smiling, just another Trumbo lackey whispering happy trivia to his boss. "Yes. The wall's gone. So are Briggs and Dillon. There's some sort of cave there. Mr. Carter asked if you wanted to send someone in after them."

Trumbo considered this for two seconds. "Fuck 'em," he said. He turned back to his guests. "Damn good meat, isn't it?"

"Very tender," said Hiroshe Sato.

"Very good," said Sunny Takahashi.

"Very dericious," said Old Man Matsukawa.

"Very bad for arteries," said Dr. Tatsuro.

*   *   *

With the coming of the storm, Eleanor, Cordie, and Paul Kukali had moved their discussion from the Shipwreck Bar to the main dining room just inside the Whale Watching Lanai in the Big Hale.

Paul had been shy about approaching them, but he felt that he had to apologize for what they had seen and been through that afternoon. Before Eleanor could speak, Cordie had invited the curator to join them and the discussion continued into the dining room. Outside, a strong wind from the east was whipping the palm trees and shaking the bougainvillea.

Paul explained that he had stayed over the extra night to make sure that there was some follow-up to their report.

"We should call the police ourselves," Eleanor said.

Paul smiled. "I did. Charlie Ventura, the sheriff in Kona, is a friend of mine. He said that it would be in the state police's jurisdiction . . ."

"Yeah," Cordie interrupted. "Hawaii Five-O. Book 'im, Danno."

Paul smiled again. "That's a slightly different department. But anyway, Charlie wasn't sure that the state police would get anyone up here today. Their people are busy with the problems the road closing is creating between here and Hilo, and Charlie's people are busy with the influx of tourists on the North Kona Coast . . ."

"But they'll send someone?" said Eleanor.

Paul nodded. "Charlie did point out that no one has been reported missing here for a while. And he mentioned that Samoan boy who drowned . . ."

"Three weeks ago."

"Yes."

"Well," said Eleanor, "at least you've gone around Mr. Byron Trumbo. I hope you don't lose your job for it."

Paul Kukali showed his strong, white teeth again. "It's no great loss. I still have my teaching job at the university. The extra money has been nice . . . it's allowed me to buy a place of my own near Waimea . . . but that wasn't the real reason I took the job anyway."

They had chatted a bit about his property near Waimea, about preserving archaeological sites, about this and that, and then the rising wind and hunger drove them into the dining room.

"I guess it'd take more than a hand to put us off our feed," Cordie said as they walked to their table near the window. "Maybe if the dog'd come back with more pieces we'd've been put off enough just to have a snack, but as it is, I'm hungry enough to eat a horse."

"I can't recommend the horse here," said Paul, "but the *a'u* is quite good."

"Isn't that the lava stuff?" said Cordie. She put on black-rimmed glasses to peruse the menu.

"No," said Paul, "that's *a'a*. *A'u* is marlin or broadbill sword-fish. It's expensive, but excellent."

Cordie set the menu down. "Okey-dokey. I ain't payin', as the owner of the whorehouse used to say. Mr. Trumbo is. *A'u* it is."

Paul also ordered the *a'u* and Eleanor decided on *ulua*, a large, flat-headed fish she had tried under different names in South America and elsewhere.

The waiter asked if they would like a drink, and before any-one could decline, Cordie ordered them all another Pele's Fire. After a moment, the talk turned to Eleanor's job.

"Dealing with the Enlightenment philosophes," said Paul, "you must be put off by the mythopoeic universe of my ances-tors."

"Not at all," said Eleanor. "The philosophes were put off by the mythopoeic mind-set that had preceded them—that is, the Christian and Judaic—but they labored to return to an essentially pagan point of view." She sipped the tall red drink and smiled as the warmth spread through her. "Albeit, with a rationalist twist."

"Yes," said Paul, "a turn toward the rational-scientific."

Eleanor nodded. "For the philosophes, the mythopoeic mind-set was a veil to be pierced by a systematic criticism such as the Greeks had codified and the Romans had mandated."

Cordie Stumpf watched them like a spectator at a tennis match.

"But the mythopoeic was a phase to grow out of," insisted

Paul, toying with his salad. "A veil which clouded as much as protected."

Eleanor nodded again. "Yes. But with the loss of that veil we
also lost the iridescent sheen of immediate experience, the quality
of reification that imbued everything—in your ancient culture
and mine—with the excitement of knowing things as living powers."

"Your ancient culture?" said Paul.

"Pre-Christian Europe," said Eleanor. "The mystical Scots.
And some of my lineage is Native American . . . Sioux, I believe."

"Still," said Paul, "to the Hawaiians, *everything* was a living
power . . . a source of *mana*. It seems difficult to imagine Diderot
or Voltaire or Lessing or Rousseau or David Hume having any understanding of this epistemological worldview."

The waiter took their salad dishes away. The three sipped
water from long-stemmed glasses. Beyond the open windows, the
wind had brought the surf up to audible dimensions, the sound as
strangely lulling as the movement of palm fronds.

"The struggle between the mythopoeic and the rational certainly predates the Enlightenment era," said Eleanor, feeling the
warmth from the silly Pele's Fire drinks filling her entire body
now. Part of her mind thought it was strange to be wearing a short-
sleeved silk blouse and to be dining by open windows in a warm
breeze on what was still a winter evening. "In Lucretius's *De rerum
natura,* his constant theme was repeated thus—'This dread and
darkness of the mind therefore require not rays of the sun, the
bright darts of day; only knowledge of nature's form dispels
them.' "

Paul smiled again. "Yet the ancient Hawaiians who lived
along this very shore fifteen centuries ago had an intimate knowledge of nature—plants, animals, the creatures of the sea, the volcano."

Leaning forward as if awaiting her opportunity to join in,
Cordie said, "Tell us about the volcano."

Paul Kukali blinked. "Kilauea or Mauna Loa?"

"Both."

"It's unusual for them to be so active at the same time," said the curator. "Those of us on the Big Island get used to the eruptions. They're more or less constant, and usually threaten only the structures that people have put in foolish places."

"Is the Mauna Pele in a foolish place?" asked Cordie.

Paul hesitated only a second. "Not according to most of the studies done. This area has had volcanic activity . . . even lava flows . . . but not in this century. As you can see, even during the heavy activity, all you see here are the ash cloud and reflected light."

Cordie slurped the last of her Pele's Fire. "I saw this movie once . . . it starred, I think, Paul Newman and Ernest Borgnine and James Franciscus and a bunch of those stars that used to be in those old disaster movies like *The Towering Inferno* and *Airport* . . . and it was all about some tropical resort that got buried in lava."

Both Paul and Eleanor waited for the punch line.

"Well," said Cordie after a moment, "it seemed to fit in with what we were talking about."

Paul shook his head. "It was a mistake to build the Mauna Pele, but I don't think it will be buried in lava anytime soon." He sounded almost regretful.

"I would like to see the volcanoes up close," Eleanor heard herself saying. She realized that the alcohol in the drinks had affected her more than she had noticed.

"It's difficult," said Paul. "Volcanoes National Park is closed now due to the severity of the eruptions . . . people were flocking there by the thousands and many of the gases from the volcano can be deadly."

"Wasn't there a case of King Kamehameha's enemies once being struck down by such poison gases?" asked Eleanor. It was beginning to rain softly, the noise on the roof of the *lanai* quite pleasant. The smell of wet vegetation was almost erotic.

"Yes," said Paul. "In 1790, Chief Keoua was returning from an attack on Kamehameha's allies and decided to divide the army into three parts and meet again at the caldera to make offerings to Pele. When two of the groups caught up to the first third of the army, they found them all dead—men, women, and children—

from a cloud of poisonous gas that had rolled down the mountain-side.''

Eleanor said, "That can't have done much for morale."

Paul shook his head. "The next year Keoua surrendered, he was murdered and his body was offered as sacrifice, and Kamehameha consolidated his control over all of the islands."

Cordie finished her drink. "Was that far from here?"

"What's that?" said Paul.

"Where the army was gassed?"

"No. Actually, it's up the slope on this same southwest rift zone. The footprints of Keoua's retreating army are still visible in the solidified mud."

Their food arrived. For a few moments, the only conversation was in praise of their fish courses. Then Eleanor said, "I can see why it's hard to get close to the volcanoes now."

Paul paused in the act of lifting his fork. "The way to see the eruption is by helicopter. Of course, every chopper on the island is booked up for weeks in advance. They're flying out of the mega-resorts north of here and out of Hilo. Air tours that used to cost a hundred dollars are going for five and six hundred now."

Eleanor shook her head. "Too rich for my blood. And I won't be here weeks from now."

Paul lowered the fork. "I might be able to arrange something."

Eleanor glanced at the curator. There seemed to be nothing calculating in his eyes or demeanor. "Really," she said, "it's not important and I . . ."

He raised a hand. "I have a friend," he said, "who flies his own helicopter on Maui. He's going to be on the Big Island tomorrow and he owes me a favor. Of course, it might be late in the day, but that's the best time to see the eruption . . . at night."

"I wouldn't want to inconvenience . . ." began Eleanor.

Paul waved away her protests. "No, I think it's a good idea. I'd like to see the eruptions myself, and this would be a perfect opportunity. Seriously, if you don't *want* to go, that's fine . . . but otherwise I'll arrange a little tour for sometime tomorrow evening."

Eleanor hesitated only a second. "That would be marvelous."

She turned to Cordie. "You'd be interested in seeing the eruption, wouldn't you?"

"Not much," said Cordie. "I don't like fire, I don't like explosions, and I hate flying. You go, and tell me how it was."

Eleanor and Paul both tried to persuade her, but she was adamant in her refusal. "My idea of vacation doesn't include getting dropped into a lake of lava from no helicopter," she said and the matter was closed.

They paused a moment to listen as the storm roared more wildly outside. Palm fronds whipped back and forth just beyond the terrace wall. Lightning flashed and the lights went out. There were already candles on the tables, so there was no commotion among the few diners, but waiters quickly brought hurricane lamps with brighter candles. Soon the room was filled with a softer, more intimate glow. Lightning continued to ripple to the south and west now.

"Does this happen often?" Eleanor asked the curator. "The power, I mean."

"Occasionally. The resort has its own backup generators for vital things—refrigerators, the lighting in the catacombs, Mr. Trumbo's executive suites . . ."

"Catacombs?" said Cordie, perking up like a bird dog.

Paul Kukali explained about the underground service areas.

"I'd like to see that," said Cordie.

Paul sipped his wine. "I believe that there's a tour on Wednesday."

"I don't like tours," said Cordie, "but I'd like to see these catacombs."

The curator smiled. "My office is down there. We can go that way after dinner, if you like. I'm sure that it's against the rules to bring guests there, but I'm already in trouble with the boss today so . . . what the hell."

They toasted that with their wine. When they paused again, Eleanor said softly, "What can you tell me about Pana-ewa, Nanaue, and Ku?"

Paul set his fork down. "Why do you list those names?"

"I've read about them," said Eleanor.

The curator nodded seriously. "Monsters," he said. "Gods. Spirits." He looked at Cordie Stumpf. "There's no old Hawaiian burial ground here, but these creatures were supposedly entombed near here."

Cordie's eyes were bright. "Tell us."

Sighing, his face illuminated by the flickering candle flame, Paul told them about Pana-ewa, Nanaue, and Ku.

TWELVE

The stars, the moon are on fire;
The cold months burn;
Dust circles on the island, the land is parched.
The sky hangs low, rough seas in the pit—
The ocean tosses: lava surges in Kilauea
Waves of fire cover the plain;
Pele erupts.
                    —traditional Pele chant,
                    translated by Marjorie Sinclair

Briggs and Dillon were a hundred feet into the lava tube, flashlights illuminating the trail of blood on black basalt, when Dillon said, "This is fucked."

Both men had their pistols out—Dillon his 9mm Glock semiautomatic, Briggs a .38 Police Special—and Dillon still held the flashlight. When the section of wall had finally tumbled outward, revealing the cave and the smear of blood leading away from the light, Briggs had set down the sledgehammer and stepped across the masonry and Dillon had followed. The lava tube was smoother than most caves, the ceiling about nine feet above the floor, with striated strips where lava had dried and receded on either side. The regular bunchings reminded Dillon of the muscular wall of an intestine. The thought was not reassuring.

They had advanced professionally enough, like two cops going into a crack house where a homicide suspect was waiting— pistols up and braced, Dillon's flashlight swinging, their backs and shoulders touching as they covered each other.

Nothing moved. The cave was free of stalactites or stalagmites. The floor was a polished basalt and it seemed to rise slightly as it twisted out of sight to the right, in the direction Dillon thought was toward the ocean. The wide trail of blood led away down and to the left.

"This is where we call for backup, right?" Dillon had said as they stood together, pistols aimed toward the curve of cave wall where the blood trail disappeared from sight.

"Yeah," Briggs had said, and began moving toward the curve in the tunnel. "But let's just look around the bend. Whatshisname . . . Wills . . . might be there."

Dillon had the choice of either following or letting the larger man march off into the darkness. He had followed. Five minutes, two bends in the cave, and a hundred feet later, he wished he'd let Briggs go off in the dark. "This is truly fucked," he suggested again. His arms were getting tired holding the Glock in firing position while steadying the flashlight. The two moved as quietly and carefully as they could—Dillon recalled from the training sessions years ago that Briggs was very fast and light on his feet for a big man—and they paused every few seconds to listen and check behind them. The flashlight beam whipped across smooth black basalt and dark lava striations.

"Whatever got Wills dragged him a long way," whispered Briggs. Both had been straining to hear any sound.

Dillon nodded. Blood still gleamed in the flashlight beam. "You ever see that movie . . . *Alien?*" he whispered back.

"Shaddup," said Briggs. "Shine the light down here." The bodyguard crouched next to the smear of blood on basalt, reached out, and lifted a bit of cloth.

"What is it?"

"Part of the poor fucker's suit, I'd guess. Gray. Linen."

"Yeah, Wills dressed pretty well."

"It's wet," said Briggs. "Like . . ."

"Like what?" Dillon moved the flashlight in quick arcs, never leaving any area dark for long. He could see about thirty feet from curve to curve in the tunnel.

"Like it's been chewed," said Briggs.

"Yeah," said Dillon. "Well, I'm heading back. I figure that if I call in all of my security people, we can field thirty men in here. With radios and automatic weapons. Whoever or whatever got Wills might have dragged him miles from here. These tunnels go on forever."

"Yeah?" said Briggs. He carefully set the piece of chewed cloth back in place. "You pussying out on me?"

Dillon sighed. Teach these no-necks as you might, they still confused testosterone with brains. "Call it that," he said. "I'm going back to call for reinforcements and the flashlight's going with me. You can stay here if you want." He started backing down the tunnel in a half-crouch, swinging the light as he went.

Briggs waited only a few seconds before following, backing toward Dillon with his pistol still raised toward the darkness. Dillon half expected some melodrama then—perhaps half a dozen crazed Hawaiian nationalists with axes charging around the bend in the cave—but there was only the sound of their own feet and breathing until they came around the last twist and saw the gleam of light spilling into the cave from the astronomer's office. Dillon was careful to keep pivoting, keep checking behind them and then flashing the light quickly in the opposite direction. When they got to the crack in the wall, he even leaned over to make sure that nothing was lurking in Wills's office. It would be poor form if they screwed up and got killed this close to safety. The office was empty, the overhead fluorescent lights terribly bright after the darkness of the cave.

They paused for a minute at the tumbled wall, still standing in the tunnel. "Mr. T is going to shit bricks," said Briggs.

Dillon shrugged. It wasn't their problem.

"We can't really put thirty men in here," said Briggs. "Mr. T's got his ex here and his other main squeezes are going to be here soon. They'll need security. Plus he's got some of your guys backing up Sato's guys."

Dillon nodded. "OK, so we put ten guys into the tunnel with radios and Mac-tens and we make this the command center. The point is it's not you and me with one flashlight stumbling around like a couple of dorks in one of those monster movies. You know— 'Let's split up, you go that way, I'll go this way'—that kind of shit."

Briggs grunted. "What do you think did this? How did it cram Wills's body through that narrow crack?"

"How the hell do I know . . ." began Dillon. Then the lights went out.

They reacted quickly, each man dropping into a crouch, pistol extended. Dillon had kept the flashlight on and now he swept it up and down the length of the tunnel. "You back into the room," he whispered. "I'll follow. Cover me when I come through."

Briggs had just stood up to step through the crack when Dillon heard the sound. "Shhhh!" he whispered. Briggs froze, pistol sweeping back.

Something was scraping and wheezing in the direction the blood trail had led. Dillon went to one knee and steadied both Glock and flashlight. The beam stayed steady on the bend in the cave wall.

"What the fuck?" whispered Briggs.

The sound grew louder. It was a snorting, wheezing, huffing sound, and whatever made it was *large*. Dillon imagined a sumo wrestler with asthma.

"Two warning shots," he whispered. He thought that Mr. T would prefer the perp alive.

"Yeah," Briggs whispered back, "I'll put my first two warning shots through the fucker's head. You put yours in his chest."

Dillon did not reply. The wheezing, scraping, huffing, snorting was louder, closer, certainly no farther than just around the bend. So there would be no surprises, he took two seconds to sweep the flashlight to their right, then swung it back to the left. Something sharp-edged scraped on stone. Feet, perhaps. Hooves? It sounded like more than two feet. Dillon could hear the actual breathing now, a heavy rasping beneath the huffing and wheezing. He had already made sure that a cartridge had been racked into the cylinder of the semiautomatic and that the safety was off. Now he thumbed back the hammer. Part of his mind noticed that the flashlight beam remained absolutely steady.

The snorting and heavy breathing paused for a moment just around the curve of wall, the scraping sound hesitated, and Dillon realized that he was holding his own breath as well. Briggs crouched next to him, both huge hands cradling the .38.

Suddenly the wheezing started up again, the scraping intensified, and something very large came around into the light.

"What the fuck?" said Briggs, and stood.

The pig was gigantic, at least four feet high at the shoulder and five or six feet long. Dillon could only guess at its weight—perhaps four hundred pounds on the cloven hoof. Its legs seemed far too skinny to support such bulk. It stopped twenty-five feet away, still wheezing, its strange eyes gleaming bright red in the flashlight beam.

"What is this shit?" said Briggs, taking one hand away from the .38.

"Careful," said Dillon, still crouching, the light and Glock steady. "The hills are filled with wild pigs . . . wild boars. They're goddamned dangerous."

The pig in the flashlight beam looked huge but not especially dangerous. It seemed to be blinking in confusion at the bright light. There was something strange about its eyes. The animal ambled a few feet closer.

"Give me a fucking break," said Briggs, still holding the pistol at full cock but lowering it. "Are you telling me this fucking pig cracked through the wall, dragged Wills out through an eight-inch crack, and ate him?"

"No, but . . . shit!" said Dillon. He had just realized what was wrong with the pig's eyes. There were too many of them. At least four on each side of the huge snout—the eyes small and close together, but visibly separate now as the pig got within twenty feet of them. Dillon swung the flashlight beam away for two seconds. The eyes still glowed red as if from their own flames.

Dillon swung the beam back just as the pig's lips pulled back. The teeth there were not swine teeth; they looked like something out of a jaguar's jaw—all long canines and incisors. The teeth also gleamed.

"Jesus . . ." said Briggs, and brought the .38 back up.

The pig moved impossibly fast then, its hooves scrabbling across blood and black lava, its teeth gleaming as it rushed them.

The tunnel echoed with explosions and flashes of light as Briggs and Dillon opened fire.

June 15, 1866, Volcano House—

A very strange day. I am so exhausted from the previous night's excursion and today's wild decisions, that I can hardly find the energy to bring pen to paper.

If I slept at all last night, it was a fitful tossing, filled with visions of the Pit and nightmares of demons. All of us were awake early, even we three pilgrims of the crater, in order to hear more of the terrible ordeal of the five missionaries who have taken refuge here on their flight to Hilo.

Mr. Clemens, Reverend Haymark, Hananui, and I arrived back at the volcano hotel shortly before dawn, the three of us too weary from our ordeal even to speak to one another, but amazed to find the Volcano House alight with lamps and filled with chattering people.

Hananui had not been exaggerating the seriousness of the matter. Five members of the Kona Mission—three women, a young boy, and an old man—had arrived in the middle of the night with two Christian natives who had risked their lives in leading the *haoles* (white people) to safety over the volcano. There are easier ways to Hilo—a rough path running along the saddle valley between the great volcanoes of Mauna Kea and Mauna Loa is the shortest—but the missionaries were sure that they would be ambushed if they went that way, so they endured the much longer and more difficult route of the volcano.

I should mention the fugitives' names: Miss Charity Whister (sister of the Reverend Whister of Kona), Mr. Ezra Whister (Reverend Whister's elderly father), Mrs. Constance Stanton (Mrs. Whister's married daughter), Mrs. Stanton's nine-year-old son, Theodore, and Mrs. Taylor, sister of the assistant pastor of the mission. All of the fugitives are in a distressed state, but Mrs. Stanton has best summarized the terrible events of two nights ago which sent this band fleeing across the volcanic highlands.

It seems that Reverend Whister (whom Reverend Haymark had met briefly in Honolulu) and his band of missionary families had been landed in Kona ten months earlier. While the savages along this trackless coast were, in Mrs. Stanton's opinion, in dire need of assistance toward salvation, it seems that a previous ministry had already taken root in Kona. Reverend Haymark later explained that this was the Kona church of the famous Reverend Titus Coan, friend and advisor to the even more famous Reverend "Father" Lyman of Hilo. Even I had heard of Mr. Coan during my sojourn in Hilo: the amazing pastor has—not once but several times—made the 300-mile circumnavigation of the island by foot and canoe, establishing outrider churches as he did so, baptizing, by his own count, some 12,000 adults and 4,000 infants into the Universal Church. In light of this, the natives' loyalty had all been turned toward the Reverend Coan and his successors, boding hard times for the simple white-washed church of the more severe ("less liberal" were Mrs. Stanton's words) preachings of Reverend Whister. After ten months of laboring in the baptismal vineyards, Reverend Whister and his supporters had managed to save only a single Hawaiian soul—and even he had backslid upon the celebration of some pagan holiday and had to be excommunicated by a disappointed Reverend W. All in all, the Whister Ministry in Kona had seemed a failure. Thus it was only one month earlier that the Reverend W. had taken his wife, sister, daughter, son-in-law, and two other families of white Christians, and abandoned their first church, moving south along the Kona Coast into the less visited regions south of Kealakekua Bay, where Captain Cook had been slaughtered in 1779.

Mrs. Stanton sounded bitter upon relating these facts to us, as if Fate had pulled a particularly unpleasant trick on her father and his supporting family. (Mr. Stanton, her husband, was in training to become a minister himself, and it seems that her father, Reverend Whister, had held some fame in Amherst, Massachusetts, from whence the hapless missionary troupe had come.)

At first, the transplantation had seemed effective. The Hawaiians living in coastal villages amidst the desolate lava fields held no special love for Reverend Coan, and were willing at least

to come each Sunday and listen to the Reverend Whister's
sermons of imminent fire and brimstone. Indeed, the minister's
particular brand of fiery rhetoric seemed to appeal to these
heathen, living as they did literally in the shadow of the volcano's
wrath. I would venture a guess that this past month's increased
activity of Kilauea—the very activity which had brought me to
this island—had also increased Reverend Whister's appeal to the
frightened locals.

Then, two weeks ago, the threats began. Mrs. Stanton
related the bullying and terror that local followers of Pele—the
fire goddess whom I have mentioned in these notes—brought
upon the Christian families just settling their lives at this South
Kona outpost. The church, Mrs. Whister interrupted her tears to
tell us at this juncture, was just in the process of being erected.

It seems that the local *kahunae* (or priests) of Pele were a
massive brother and sister—"massive" I say because Mrs.
Stanton swore that each weighed at least four hundred
pounds—who had finally perceived the minister and his
congregation as serious rivals for the affections and loyalty of
their Pele worshippers. According to Mrs. Stanton, the first
intimations of the coming terror were propagated in the form of
"warnings" from the Pele priest to Rev. Whister. The priest
ingenuously warned the minister that something terrible was
about to happen, that the very gates of hell had recently opened
in that region and that the Christians—the "non-believers
unprotected by Pele's benevolence" were the heathen priest's
words—would be in great danger.

"What kind of danger?" Mr. Clemens had asked at that
point, straddling his chair in a most ungentlemanly manner and
leaning forward with that malevolent glint which correspondents
evidently acquire upon hearing of someone else's misfortune.

Mrs. Stanton had explained that the priest had formulated
some nonsense about there being an opening to the Hawaiian
Underworld nearby, an opening that Pele had once sealed up in
a battle with the evil gods and malevolent demons that had once
wandered the coast. According to the priest, the natives had
forsaken that section of the Kona Coast for centuries, these

demons were so active. It had taken Pele's generous act of
sealing the Underworld before Kamehameha's people could
return to the area. "All nonsense, of course," Mrs. Stanton had
snapped. "The flimsiest of fantasies to conceal the villain's real
intentions of terror."

Here, to everyone's surprise, our Hilo guide had
interrupted. "No, no!" he had cried, forgetting his place among
white people. "The Underworld of Milu exists! There were two
entrances—the cave in Waipio where the dead enter to become
ghosts, and the opening in Kona where the vilest demons once
escaped! Madame Pele did very good thing to seal Kona
entrance to ghost world!"

"Silence!" the innkeeper had shouted, visibly outraged by
the native's rude intrusion. But Mr. Clemens had silenced the
innkeeper in turn, holding up an imperious hand to keep our
host from further berating the frightened guide. "Hananui," Mr.
Clemens said gently, "it's all right. Tell us who or what lives in
this Underworld."

Hananui had glanced at the glowering innkeeper and the
fiercely frowning missionaries, but he had gone on gamely, "It is
as I say last night—Milu, he king of the Underworld, Pana-ewa be
very bad demon—reptile man, Ku—he sometimes come as dog.
All very bad ghost peoples down there."

Mr. Clemens had nodded, obviously wanting to hear more
but unwilling to irritate Mrs. Stanton or her flock further. I
should mention here that Miss Whister was present but
contented herself with weeping, the child, Theodore, and his
great-grandfather Ezra were sleeping, and Mrs. Taylor, the third
woman, said nothing during the entire time—merely sat and
stared fixedly at some internal vision.

Lips thin and white from the rude intrusion, Mrs. Stanton
continued:

"The warnings . . . the fantasies . . . were conveyed to my
father, Reverend Whister, a fortnight ago. Then, four nights ago,
the terrible events began . . ."

Here even the redoubtable Mrs. Stanton showed signs of
breaking down, but the innkeeper brought her a glass of water

and she continued despite the torrents of emotion welling in her.

"At first there were the . . . sightings. Strange things in the streets of the village at night."

"What kind of strange things?" inquired Mr. Clemens, his legs spraddled across the chair as if he were still riding a horse.

"I was just arriving at that, sir," said Mrs. Stanton between thinned lips. "The natives bore terrified tales of strange animals. A large . . ." She glanced reproachfully at Hananui. ". . . a large lizard. A wild boar. Some kind of frightening raptor." Again she glared at our Hilo guide. "A black dog. All nonsense, of course."

I found my heart beating wildly as she conveyed these facts. Something about our setting on the lip of this bubbling volcano made this tale, even in the cloudy light of day, all the more unsettling.

"It was nonsense until the nightmare began," continued Mrs. Stanton. "My husband was the first to die."

There were at least a dozen of us in the room and yet there was almost complete silence at this point, as if no one but Mrs. Stanton were breathing. Indeed, she took a deep breath then before continuing. "Four nights ago, there came a terrible screaming from the village. Our shack was the closest . . . Father and Mother live in a more substantial home up the hill near the temporary church. August, my husband—Mr. Stanton—seized the musket and resolved to go see what the fuss was about. I begged him not to go. I told him that no heathen life lost in whatever altercation then occurring was worth risking a Christian life. He patted my hair ribbon then, told me that we had come to this far-off place to prove precisely the opposite, instructed little Theodore to watch the homestead until he returned, and went out with Kaluna, one of our converted Hawaiians.

"August did not return that night. The village was filled with roars and shoutings. I was sure that we would all be killed . . . Theodore, Mrs. Taylor and her husband up the hill, Father, Mother, all of us . . . but the others did not respond to the noise, and I was too terrified to go for help in the dark.

"Come the morning, I took Theodore and we ran for Father's house. Father took the men—Grandfather, Mr. Taylor, two of the converted Hawaiians who could be trusted—and went into the village. They found Kaluna at the edge of the village, his head encrusted with blood, alive but with no memory of the night. They found August in the lava fields . . ."

Here Mrs. Stanton did break down. Reverend Haymark comforted her. There was to be no more of the terrible news for a while.

The two Hawaiians who had led the fugitive Christians had filled in the missing parts to the innkeeper, who later told Mr. Clemens, who later told the Reverend Haymark. All of the men tried to spare me the details of this horror, but by stationing myself at propitious locations in the small hotel lobby, I was able to hear the whispered reports.

Mr. Stanton had been found dead in the lava fields, his throat cut like some animal that had been drained of its blood. That night, the whites had congregated in Reverend Whister's larger home near the temporary church. According to the Hawaiians' whispered descriptions, it had been a night of pure terror—strange sounds, monsters creeping through the lava boulders, inhuman screams—all of it lit by the backglow of the same Hale-mau-mau eruptions I had witnessed just last night. Things had scraped and clawed at the grass hut of the terrified whites—Mr. Taylor and Reverend Whister had held ancient muskets at the ready while the women tended the flickering lanterns—but although the walls would not have held out a determined rat, nothing had entered. The Reverend Whister had told them all that this was a sign of Jesus's power against these forces of darkness—although whether he had been referring to vengeful natives or actual demons, no one knew.

That morning—only four days ago! Even as I partied and chatted with missionary families in Hilo!—the Christians had timorously gone out of their house to find that all of their horses had been slaughtered in the night, throats cut, legs severed. (This part was whispered most softly by the innkeeper describing it all to Mr. Clemens and Reverend Haymark, as if the disfigurement of horses were far worse than the slaughter of poor Mr. Stanton.)

Despite this grisly discovery, Mr. Taylor had insisted on

taking one trustworthy man and leaving for Kona, vowing to
bring help back the next day. Mrs. Taylor had argued against this
plan, but was kissed on the hair ribbon and overruled. Reverend
Whister evidently agreed with the course of action, realizing that
with his elderly father and the child along, the party would not
make Kona in two days, whereas one man traveling alone, even
on foot, could reach the village in twenty-four hours of hard
walking.

Mr. Taylor and the native, the same Kaluna mentioned
earlier, left about ten a.m. About five o'clock that afternoon,
Kaluna returned—again alone. The native, voice shaking and
hands palsied with some terrible emotion, said that a huge
reptile with the eyes of a man had leapt at them from a rock not
four miles from where they now stood. Kaluna said that Mr.
Taylor had fired the musket into the creature at a distance of
less than six feet, but the reptile thing did not hesitate. Kaluna
said that Mr. Taylor's head had fractured with the sound of a
coconut being halved—his exact words—and that the creature
had been so busy devouring the Christian, that he—Kaluna—had
been able to escape, injuring himself by falling in the sharp lava
fields. Kaluna said that small dwarf-like beings had pursued him
for two miles, but that he had escaped.

At this point, the extent of Reverend Whister's gullibility
had apparently been reached, for he accused Kaluna of lying, of
being an agent of the Pele priests. Kaluna denied it. An argument
ensued between the injured Hawaiian and the outraged
missionary. Kaluna had lifted his knife—to make an oath upon it,
explained the Christian natives who had helped the others
escape—but Mr. Whister had misinterpreted the gesture and
fired his musket into the hapless Hawaiian's body. It had taken
Kaluna several hours to die.

Then it was nightfall again. Once again Reverend Whister,
his terrified wife, his uncomprehending, aged father, his
daughter, his grandson, his sister, and the crypt-silent Mrs.
Taylor endured the shufflings and wheezings and roarings and
scrabblings. Finally, as the natives explained to the innkeeper,
the women, child, and grandfather were sleeping in the second

room of the house when a terrible noise arose from the room where Reverend Whister and his wife were standing guard. There were screams. Inhuman noises. The sound of a musket being discharged. More screams. Mrs. Stanton had tried to open the door, but at that moment friendly natives had broken through the back wall and spirited the shocked survivors to safety, urging them up the trail through the lava into the night. Behind them, the church and house they had recently vacated could be seen burning in the night. They had arrived at the Volcano House after some forty hours of travel across some of the worst terrain in the world. There had been no sight of pursuers, although the guides reported strange sounds among the lava fields and ghostly glows in the rocks behind them.

Thus ended the tale. It was terrible enough to set Master McGuire and the Smith twin conferring with Hananui for an immediate departure for Hilo. The innkeeper also decided to leave that morning, locking up Volcano House and leaving it to the mercy of the winds and vapors. The natives—both the innkeeper's servants and the two loyal guides of the Christians—were terrified at the prospect of traveling again at night, but willing to do so if it meant putting even more distance between them and the Horror along the Kona Coast.

Just minutes ago, as everyone finished their preparations for leaving, I heard the incredible spoken on the veranda between Mr. Clemens and Reverend Haymark. "I am not going back to Hilo with you," said the correspondent. "I must see what has happened. Whatever the truth of this terrible event—and I suspect it is nothing more supernatural than the vengeance of a jealous village shaman—it promises to be a bigger story than the sinking of the *Hornet!*"

Reverend Haymark had frowned at this selfish view of an obvious tragedy, but then surprised me by saying, "I will go with you. Hananui, McGuire, the hotelkeeper, Smith and the others can safely see the women down the mountain to Hilo."

The correspondent was also obviously taken by surprise at this announcement and announced his willingness to proceed into danger alone. Reverend Haymark brushed aside the comments. "I am not going to watch out for you, sir. I met the Reverend Whister and his son-in-law in Honolulu. We do not yet definitively know their fate. Much of what I hear is womanly panic and native superstition. I owe it to Reverend Whister and the others to see if anything can be done. If nothing else, they deserve a Christian burial. I am sure they will send a fast schooner around from Hilo, arriving shortly after you and I would get there. There should be no great danger."

The two men then shook hands. I went to my room and packed, pulling on my hardiest boots and most rigorous riding skirt. Mr. Clemens and Reverend Haymark do not yet know it, but I will be accompanying them to the Kona Coast.

Sato and his entourage retired to their suites after the interminable dinner and Byron Trumbo was free to deal with his disasters by 10:30 P.M. He and Will Bryant took the elevator to his wife and her lawyer's suite on the north side of the Big Hale. Outside the suite, Trumbo touched Will's arm. "Five minutes. Not a goddamn minute more. It has to be some emergency . . . I don't care what you make up. Five minutes." Will Bryant nodded and disappeared behind the potted palms.

Trumbo rang the buzzer to the suite, putting on the most affable face he was capable of this night. Myron Koestler opened the door. The lawyer's frizzy gray hair was tied back in its usual ponytail and he was wearing a thick terrycloth bathrobe with the Mauna Pele volcano crest on it. He was holding a glass with what looked like several fingers of Scotch in it.

Trumbo let his affable face slip. "Got comfortable enough yet, Myron? You and Cait tried the Jacuzzi yet?"

The lawyer smiled thinly. "She's been waiting for you."

"Yeah," said Trumbo, and swept into the suite. Everything was gleaming leather and combed cotton under recessed spots. The marble tiles and lush Persian carpets seemed to give off a light of their own. The storm winds ruffled long curtains away from the floor-to-ceiling windows along the west wall. Trumbo could hear the rain, and smell it over the scent of sandalwood and polish. "Where is she?"

"On the terrace."

To Trumbo's irritation, the lawyer followed him out onto the covered *lanai*. The view here in the daytime was north toward the shoulder of Mauna Loa and the white-capped summit of Mauna Kea beyond. Tonight it was just the tops of whipping palm trees illuminated by the occasional lightning flash.

Caitlin Sommersby Trumbo was also in a Mauna Pele robe and nursing a drink. Straight vodka on ice, Trumbo knew. She sat on the chaise longue with her feet up, one leg raised, showing an expanse of impossibly smooth thigh. The reading lamp near her threw her long, honey-blonde hair into a cascade of highlights. Trumbo felt the old stirrings that had made him marry her in the first place . . . that and the fact that she was worth several hundred million dollars on her own. It was too bad that she was a bitch.

"Cait," he said. "Great to see you."

For a moment she only stared. He used to think that her eyes were a cornflower blue; now he knew they were a glacier blue. "You kept me waiting," she said at last. Trumbo had never been able to analyze that tone: it was part pouting debutante, part spoiled daddy's girl, part ice queen, and part imperious business exec. But it was all bitch.

"I was busy," said Trumbo, hearing his voice fall into the old tones of truculence.

Caitlin Sommersby Trumbo blew air through her elegant nose.

Before she could speak again, Trumbo tried to take the initiative. "You know that you're violating the terms of the separation by being here."

Her eyes glinted. "You know that I'm not. This isn't a residence of yours. It's a property. And a hotel."

Trumbo smiled. "And with Myron here . . ." He nodded in the direction of the lounging lawyer. "You'd better be careful, Cait. I may have video cameras installed in the bedrooms."

She raised her chin. "I wouldn't put it past you." She looked at the lawyer. "The Big T here always enjoyed *watching* more than *doing*."

Trumbo realized that he was grinding his molars. "What do you want?"

"You know what I want."

"You can't have them," said Trumbo. "They're attached."

"I want the Mauna Pele."

"You can't have it, either."

She raised her chin higher. "We've made you a fair offer."

Trumbo laughed. "Cait, Cait, Cait . . . I spent more than eighty million dollars on the fucking *landscaping.*"

"Don't you dare use obscenity with me."

"I wouldn't fucking dream of it."

Koestler cleared his throat. "If I could suggest something . . ."

"Shut up, Koestler," said Trumbo.

"Shut up, Myron," said Caitlin.

The lawyer settled back in his chair and sipped his Scotch.

"Look, Cait," said Trumbo, trying to make his voice sound reasonable, "I know why you're here, but it's counterproductive. You'd do better to wait until I unload this place on the Japs and take your blood-money share of it rather than try to get the Pele at fire sale prices now."

His estranged wife sipped her vodka and stared at him over the rim of the glass. "I want the Mauna Pele."

"Why? You never came here. It's not like you have a sentimental attachment to it. And you know as well as I that it's a fucking money loser."

"I want it," said Caitlin Sommersby Trumbo in a tone that left no room for argument. "If you sell it to me, you get something. If you can't sell it, I may end up with it under the terms of the settlement anyway."

Trumbo laughed again, but the sound was more hollow this time. "You'd never get it. I'd burn the fucking place down first. And I *will* sell it."

Caitlin smiled sweetly. "Does your Mr. Sato know about all of the murders here in the past year?"

"Disappearances," said Trumbo.

"Six murders," she purred. "This place is riskier than Central Park at night. And I don't believe your Mr. Sato or any of his investors would want to buy Central Park."

"You stay away from Sato . . ." began Trumbo, amazed to find that he could speak through gritted teeth.

"Or what, T?"

"Or you'll find out how dangerous the Mauna Pele can be . . ."

"I heard that!" cried Koestler, rising to his feet. His hairy legs showed through the flap in the robe. "That was a threat. I was witness."

"That was a warning," said Trumbo, turning toward the ponytailed divorce lawyer and pointing a blunt finger like a revolver. "And I'll warn you . . . this place may not be safe. There's weird shit going on here. I've got security men around Sato and his people, but I can't spare any for unexpected visitors."

"Another threat," said Koestler. "We can take this to court and . . ."

"Shut up, Myron," said Caitlin. She aimed her pale gaze at Trumbo. "You won't sell then?"

Trumbo returned her gaze with equal intensity. "Cait, there was a time when I would have given you the Pele. Hell, I almost did at Christmas three years ago. Now I wouldn't let you have it if my hair was on fire and that was the only way I could put it out."

The door buzzed. Koestler went to open it. "Boss," said Will Bryant, holding a phone out toward Trumbo, "I'm sorry to bother you, but Dr. Hastings is on the line from the Volcano Observatory. He says that the lava flow from Mauna Loa isn't moving as far south as they'd predicted. He says that it's following the old rift zones toward the Mauna Pele."

Trumbo sighed. "I'll take it outside." He pointed a finger at Cait. "I mean it when I say don't fuck with this sale."

She set down her empty glass and gave Trumbo a glance that would have frozen hydrogen. "And I mean it when I say I'll have the Mauna Pele."

Trumbo turned on his heel and went out with Will Bryant. In the elevator down, he glanced at his watch. "Bicki will sit out in the construction shack and watch TV until dawn, but I've got to get out to Maya before she comes hunting for me." He looked at his assistant. "Lava flowing toward the Mauna Pele? I said an emergency, but . . . Jesus, Will."

Will Bryant looked at his boss and handed over the phone. "I wasn't kidding. You need to call Hastings back. He says that we should evacuate the place tonight."

THIRTEEN

At the time when the earth became hot
At the time when the heavens turned about
At the time when the sun was darkened
To cause the moon to shine
The time of the rise of the Pleiades
The slime, this was the source of the
earth . . .
—from the Kumulipo, creation chant

Eleanor almost did not accompany Cordie Stumpf and Paul Kukali into the catacombs.

Dinner had been pleasant, despite—or perhaps because of—the storm raging beyond the *lanai* and the hurricane lamps with their warm circles of candlelight. When the power came on almost an hour later, the few diners on the terrace blinked at the relative brightness of the few soft electric lights. At first, Paul had seemed reticent to discuss the various myths that Eleanor had asked about, but as he realized that there was no hint of condescension from the Oberlin history professor, he visibly warmed to the subject. He explained the difference between *moolelo*—the oral tradition of the gods' exploits, so powerful that it could be recited only in the daylight—and *kaao,* simple tall tales of human heroes, stories fit to be told around the bonfire at night. He discussed the hierarchy of Hawaiian animism: the *aumakua,* or important family gods; the *kapua,* or children of the gods, who dwelt among the mortals much as had Hercules and the other Greek demigods; the *akua kapu,* who, like the ghosts of mainland Native Americans, merely frightened people and presaged bad luck; and the *akua li'l,* literally "little spirits," who rounded out the almost endless Hawaiian pantheon as animist personifications of trees, waterfalls, forms of weather, and all the other aspects of nature.

"It all has to do with *mana*," said Paul, sipping his coffee as the last of the dishes were cleared. "Stealing *mana*, preserving *mana*, and discovering new sources of *mana*."

"Power," said Cordie, who had been listening intently.

"Yes. Power of the individual. Power over others. Power over the environment."

Cordie made a noise. "That ain't changed much over the years."

The waitress, a heavy, unsmiling Hawaiian woman with the nametag "Lovey" pinned to her *muumuu*, asked if they would be interested in dessert. Eleanor and Paul declined. Cordie said, "Heck, yes," and the three listened to the litany. There were numerous elaborate desserts, most seeming to deal with coconut, but Cordie chose an ice cream sundae . . . with coconut shavings. When it arrived, Eleanor realized that she wished *she* had ordered it. She asked Paul, "Where does someone like Ku fit in?"

The curator set down his coffee cup. "Ku is one of the oldest Polynesian gods who migrated here by canoe with the early Hawaiians—the god of war. Very fierce. Human sacrifices were made to him. He could assume various shapes when he walked among mortals."

"Including a dog?" asked Cordie, licking her spoon.

Paul Kukali hesitated a visible second. "Sometimes. In fact, quite specifically as a dog. Are you thinking of the one we saw today?" He smiled to show the irony in his question.

"Sure," said Cordie. She did not return the smile.

"Then I'm afraid I have to disappoint you," he said. "Ku . . . or at least his canine incarnation . . . was killed by the high chief Polihale centuries ago. Ku's body was cut into two pieces and then turned into stones . . . they can be seen on Oahu to this day."

"You can kill a dog but you can't kill a god, can you?" said Cordie. She had finished the sundae. There was the faintest trace of ice cream on her upper lip.

Paul looked at Eleanor. "Voltaire and Rousseau would disagree, I think."

Eleanor did not respond to the quip. Instead, she said,

"Would the Ku dog be sent to the Milu Underworld when it died?"

The curator hesitated a longer moment this time. "Some *kahuna,* priests, would say yes. Some would say no."

"But Milu is where ghosts of humans go?"

"Yes."

"And where some of the *kapuas* and *mo-os* were contained?"

Paul rubbed his nose. "I mentioned *kapuas* earlier, but I don't remember talking about *mo-os.*"

"What's that?" said Cordie.

Paul answered, "*Mo-os* or *mokos* are serious demons. They can control nature as well as take various forms. And yes, the *kapuas* and *mo-os* were banished in the Milu Underworld after a fiery battle with Pele." As if to punctuate the words, lightning flashed nearby and thunder rolled through the open windows. The three smiled at one another.

"Enough of this," said Paul, looking around at the empty *lanai.* "We seem to have closed down the place. But at least the electricity is back on." He looked at Cordie. "Did you still want to see the catacombs tonight?" His tone suggested that it was late.

"Yeah," Cordie said at once.

Paul nodded. "Eleanor, would you like to see them?"

"I think not. I'm a bit sleepy. I think I'll head back to my *hale.*"

Paul gestured toward the rain, now coming down harder than before. "You said that you're in one of the *hales* on the south side of the resort, didn't you?"

"Yes, beyond the Shipwreck Bar and the little pool." Eleanor looked at the curator, curious as to what he was about to suggest.

"It's a long walk in the rain," he said. "They have complimentary umbrellas here, but the service tunnels . . . the catacombs . . . have an exit just a few yards from your *hale.*"

"I don't mind . . ." began Eleanor.

"Oh, come along, Nell," said Cordie.

Eleanor hesitated only a second. "All right, if it's a shortcut."

The three stood. "It will be," said Paul. "We can see you to your door and then I'll walk back to the Big Hale with Mrs. Stumpf. And we'll see the underground complex along the way."

They left the restaurant, nodding to Lovey and the maitre d' as they went. The rain was pounding on tropical vegetation beyond the open walls of the empty lobby. Paul took them to the elevator and they got off in the basement. He led them down a long ramp to a door marked AUTHORIZED PERSONNEL ONLY, inserted a security card in a scanner until the light on the box blinked green, and they continued down the ramp into the catacombs.

"What's this shit about evacuating the Pele?" Trumbo roared into the phone at the venerable Dr. Hastings.

The scientist sounded tired. "I merely suggested to Mr. Carter and Mr. Bryant that you be apprised of the situation and consider the alternative. The civil authorities have already warned the residents of Ocean View Estates and Kahuku Ranch . . ."

"Those are south of here," said Trumbo.

"Yes," said Dr. Hastings, "but several lateral fissures have opened, some of which may divert the secondary lava flow as far north as Keananuionana Point."

"That's still south of here," said Trumbo.

"Yes, but with each secondary flow comes the possibility of further lateral activity. I should remind you that in April of 1868, the entire area upon which you have built your resort was the focus of tsunami, lava flow, and a catastrophic slump along the Hilina Pali fault system . . ."

"I should remind *you*," said Byron Trumbo, "that I don't give a good shit what happened in 18-fucking-68. I want to know what's happening *now*."

There was a long enough silence that Trumbo and Will Bryant listening in thought that the elderly vulcanologist had hung up. Then Hastings continued, as if he had never been interrupted. "The 1868 event, consisting as it did of simultaneous fountainings of both Mauna Loa and Kilauea, is perhaps most analagous to the current situation along the southwest rift zone. Missionary families living almost exactly where your resort is now situated, Mr.

Trumbo, recorded that the earth rolled under their feet like an ocean swell for long minutes and that every man-made structure along the South Kona Coast was toppled. Following that, a mud slide traveled three miles in less than three minutes and carried away every village along the coast. Minutes after that, the ensuing tsunami crashed in, bringing waves sixty feet high, and washed the muddied ruins out to sea. Five days later, the epicenter spread from Kilauea to Mauna Loa, the larger volcano erupted in full force, and lava suddenly poured from a new fissure just above where Kahuku Ranch now stands."

"So?" said Byron Trumbo. "What's your point?"

The volcano expert sighed. "You had better consider evacuating your resort if this activity continues."

"The governor hasn't said anything to me," said Trumbo.

"Nor will he, Mr. Trumbo. The governor is—as is everyone else on this island—afraid of you. He does not wish to give you news you do not want to hear."

Trumbo snorted. "But you aren't afraid, Dr. Hastings."

"I am a scientist. It is my job to acquire the most reliable data and pass on our assessments based upon that data. It is *your* job to vouchsafe the lives and safety of your guests and staff."

"Yeah, it is my job, Dr. Hastings," agreed Trumbo. "I appreciate you remembering who is responsible for what."

The vulcanologist cleared his throat. "But having said that, I should add that I will go to the media as soon as the data says clearly that there is a threat to life and property along your section of the Kona Coast, Mr. Trumbo."

The billionaire put his hand over the mouthpiece and cursed vehemently. Then he lifted the phone again. "I understand, Dr. Hastings. And I know you were scheduled to visit us here at the Mauna Pele tomorrow, but I see now that your duties will prevent that."

"On the contrary," said the scientist. "I look forward to briefing your guests on the . . ."

"Never mind," said Trumbo, his voice flat. "You just keep carrying on up there. We'll carry on down here. And call me first if the lava heads this way, OK?" Trumbo thumbed the hang-up button before Hastings could reply. "OK, Will, I'm taking the golf cart out to see Maya on the peninsula . . ."

"It's raining," began the assistant.

"I don't give a shit if it's raining. I'll take the radio, you keep yours so we can stay in touch. I want you to go down and see what the fuck's keeping Briggs and Dillon in the service tunnels."

Will Bryant nodded.

"When I'm finished with Maya, I'm going to head out to the construction shack and see what Bicki wants. I'll talk her into leaving tomorrow, so make sure her plane is ready to take off after breakfast. Then tell Bobby Tanaka to meet me up in the suite . . . we're going to burn some midnight oil getting this deal ready to close tomorrow. I want Sato and his buddies to have signed and flown off into the sunset within thirty-six hours. Any questions?"

Will Bryant shook his head.

"Good. See you in an hour or so." Trumbo headed for his golf cart and the peninsula.

"Most of the offices down here are closed at this hour," Paul Kukali was saying, "but the laundry is going strong and the bakery will get busier after midnight."

The three strolled through the warren of tunnels. Only one golf cart had passed them, the two women in it greeting the art curator by name.

"The staff seems to get along all right," Cordie said.

"I know most of the people here outside of work," said Paul. "Molly and Theresa were students of mine briefly in Hilo. It's a big island but a relatively small community."

"How many people?" asked Eleanor.

"Around a hundred thousand, but a third of those live in Hilo. In terms of population density, this is the emptiest island in the chain."

They turned left down a different tunnel, pausing for a moment outside the busy laundry. Eleanor smelled bleach and heated linen. Ions from the driers tickled her sinuses.

"Does Mr. Trumbo have difficulty finding workers?" asked Cordie.

"Yes and no," said Paul. "No, there's no shortage of people who want the relatively high hotel wages . . . the island's been in a serious recession for decades. Unfortunately, with the loss of the pineapple and sugar industries and with little or no indigenous business to replace them, working-class residents have to go into the service trade. But yes, Mr. Trumbo has trouble finding people because of the relative isolation of the resort and . . ." He paused.

Cordie ended the sentence. "And because of the reputation of the Mauna Pele being dangerous?"

"Yes." Paul smiled slightly. "Here's my office . . . nothing of interest to see in it, I'm afraid. And here's the astronomy director's office . . . strange, Mr. Wills's door is open . . ."

At that moment the lights went off.

Eleanor had once been in a cave in France where they had shut the lights off for several minutes to show people the effect of total darkness. She still had nightmares about those moments. Now she found herself holding her breath, her chest hurting with the pressure of the blackness around her.

"Damn," said Paul. Then: "Just stay put. There are emergency generators for the lights down here. They should be on in a second or two."

It stayed pitch-black.

"I don't understand," said Paul. "The emergency lights are self-contained. They should be on . . ."

"Hush!" came Cordie's voice in the darkness. "Listen."

Eleanor strained to listen. The sounds that had filled the corridor a few minutes ago . . . ventilation whispers, the rumble of the industrial washing machines and driers in the laundry section, the slight hum of the fluorescent strips in the ceiling, the snatch of conversation from the bakery . . . everything was gone. The silence seemed as absolute as the darkness. It was as if the few people they had seen had vanished with the light.

"I don't . . ." came Paul Kukali's voice.

"Hush up," Cordie said.

Eleanor heard it then, to their left, although she had thought only the wall and a few locked offices were to their left. It was a strange sound, part shuffle, part wheezing, part oily sliding along stone. Eleanor felt her hands ball into fists even as her eyes strained to see in the heavy darkness.

There came the sound of keys being shuffled. "Stay here," said Paul in the darkness. "I'll feel along the wall until I find my office. There's a flashlight in the drawer there. I'll . . ."

"Don't move," came Cordie's voice and there was something flat and authoritative enough in her tone to keep the other two frozen in place. Suddenly a light flared and Eleanor swiveled to see Cordie Stumpf crouching on one knee, a flaring cigarette lighter in her raised left hand. Eleanor was so relieved to see the light . . . to *see* . . . that she did not react for a second when Cordie reached into her straw shoulder bag and lifted out a revolver. The pistol looked absurdly heavy and long-barreled as Cordie, still on one knee, raised it and pointed it in the direction of the sliding, shuffling sound. Whatever was making the noise stayed just beyond the circle of light. Now Eleanor could hear voices from around the bend in the tunnel, back toward the laundry complex.

"Move the light this way," said Paul, a shadow to their left, "and we'll find my office."

"No," said Cordie, and again the tone would brook no argument. "Don't move." She came up off her knee, her ugly dress billowing around her, the lighter held high, her right arm rigid with the pistol rock-steady. The short woman walked quickly toward the source of the shuffling sound. Eleanor followed just to stay within the blessed circle of light.

Eleanor saw the eyes gleaming first. Cordie did not pause in her advance.

"Holy shit," said Cordie Stumpf.

It took a moment for Eleanor to recognize the bearded man slumped against the tunnel wall as the security director who had interviewed them hours earlier . . . Dillon. Now the short man stared at them dully, as if he were in shock. Eleanor saw the reason as Cordie stepped even closer. It looked as if the security director had been in an automobile accident: his clothes were torn almost to rags—the right sleeve of his blazer was missing and the white shirt beneath it torn into strips—and there was blood on his face, hands, chest, and matted in his wild hair. Saliva drooled from the man's open mouth into his beard.

Paul rushed over and cradled him as Dillon slumped even lower along the wall, his polished shoes sliding out across the floor. "We've got to get him to a doctor," said the art curator.

Cordie suddenly wheeled and lifted the lighter and pistol in the direction from which they had come. Footsteps were advancing rapidly toward them in the dark.

June 17, 1866, Along the Kona Coast—
I have not made entries during the past two days because the conscious hours have been too unrelentingly filled with events, the events themselves too extraordinary to put into any sort of perspective, including the private perspective of this journal. Even now, as I set pen to paper in this wretched hovel within earshot of the booming surf, straining to hear the night sounds of the unbelievable horror begin again above the background noises of ocean and wind-tossed coconut palm, knowing full well that these night sounds may presage our terrible death, I can scarcely credit my own senses or memory.

It seems an age ago that I impulsively insisted upon accompanying the correspondent and the cleric on their mission of mercy and curiosity to the Kona Coast. Amazingly, their protests were neither lengthy nor vehement. Perhaps our adventure of the night before had made them see me as a capable companion in any adventure they might devise.

I almost wish now that this had not been the case.

At any rate, we departed late that morning from Volcano House, Hananui, McGuire, Smith, the innkeeper, and the Christian guides escorting the fleeing missionaries back to Hilo. Half a dozen horses and a comparable number of mules had been kept at the volcano hotel so at least all of the whites were able to ride on the last leg of their flight eastward. Both the hotelkeeper and his primary servant had muskets, which they loaded before departing.

There was some discussion about arming our little party. The Reverend Haymark waved off the innkeeper's suggestion of keeping one of the muskets, but Mr. Clemens obviously thought

that it was not a bad idea. In the end, the correspondent accepted the loan of a revolver.

"You've fired a weapon?" the innkeeper asked, obviously dubious of the correspondent's abilities. "Were you in the war?"

Mr. Clemens looked up from inspecting the ancient revolver. "Sir," he said, his Missouri accent deepening, "I had the honor of joining the irregular militia to serve the Confederacy."

"Ah," said the innkeeper, nodding in understanding.

"I deserted after three weeks," added Mr. Clemens.

"Mmmm?" said the innkeeper, his eyebrows rising.

Mr. Clemens set the pistol in the pocket of his coat and raised one long finger. "And the South fell."

I might mention here, before depicting the terrible images of the next few days, that while Mr. Clemens's humor might be trying, it was rarely absent. One instance might be the "Volcano Book" which we were asked to sign despite our hasty departure. While some of the comments written therein were valuable in their observation of the particulars of the eruption, most were rubbish. Examples include—"Not much of a fizz" or "Madam Pele in the dumps" or "a grand splutter." These usually had English signatures. The American contributions tended to be more breathless—"9 June, 1865 . . . Descended the crater and paid a visit to Madame Pele. Found the small lake in great action, it put me in mind of the sea in a troubled state. The sight is awful as well as grand and sublime . . ." Or this, dated 4 August, 1865: "Professor William T. Brigham, together with Mr. Charles Wolcott Brooks, went down into the crater and passed the night within ten feet of the boiling cauldron. The scene was truly grand. Professor Brigham and Mr. Brooks were startled out of a sound sleep in the morning by a violent puff of sulfurous vapor, from which they left in a remarkable hasty manner, leaving blankets etc. behind them."

I copied these verbatim to give a context for Mr. Clemens's entry:

Volcano House
Friday, June 15, 1866

Like others who came before me I arrived here. I travelled the same way I came, most of the way. But I knew that there was a protecting Providence over us all, and I felt no fear. We have had a good deal of weather. Some of it was only so-so (and to be candid, the remainder was similar).

My traveling companions Reverend Haymark and Miss Stewart from Ohio—But, however, details of one's trifling experiences during one's journey thither may not always be in good taste in a book designed as a record of volcanic phenomena, even if one such subject of observation smokes and the other is given to an outpouring of fiery temperament; therefore let us change to our proper subject.

Visited the crater, intending to stay all night, but the bottle containing the provisions broke and we were obliged to return. But while standing near the South Lake—say 250 yards distant—we saw a hump of dirt about the size of a piece of chalk. I said in a moment, 'There is something unusual going to happen.' But soon afterwards we observed another clod of about the same size; it hesitated— shook—and then let go and fell into the lake.

Oh God! It was awful.

We then took a drink.

Few visitors will ever achieve the happiness of two such experiences as the above in succession.

While we lay there, a puff of gas came along, and we jumped up and galloped over the lava in the most ridiculous manner, leaving our blankets behind. We did it because it is fashionable, and because it makes one appear to have had a thrilling adventure.

We then took another drink.

After which we returned and camped a little closer to the lake.

I mused and said, 'How the stupendous grandeur of this magnificently terrible and sublime manifestation of celestial power doth fill the poetic soul with grand thoughts and grander images; and how the overpowering solemnity.'

(Here the gin gave out. In the careless hands of my esteemed clerical companion and amateur guide, who had broken through the lava crust in diligent search of the Fiery

Pit of Sulfur and Brimstone of which he had so often and so
fondly preached, the bottle broke. Dismissing our dangling
guide from further service on the grounds of his being
careless with our provisions, Miss Stewart from Ohio and I
both decided that I should terminate all further
philosophical musings.)

Reverend Haymark laughed loudly at this vain attempt at "wit,"
but I record it here merely to show the disposition of my
traveling companion even at this most serious hour.

None of the natives would accompany us to the leeward
coast, although Mr. Clemens offered them an impressive bribe.
All of them were terrified, including Hananui. In the end, we set
off with a hastily drawn map provided by the innkeeper, our
horses laboring under several days' worth of provisions garnered
from the Volcano House stores.

The first part of our ride down the volcano was uneventful,
although fantastical enough with the geysering lava behind us
and the long trailings of sulphurous vapors hanging above us like
foul-smelling clouds. Mauna Loa loomed to our right, its summit
at almost 14,000 feet some ten thousand feet above her smaller
sister of Kilauea. We could see no lava from it, but a cloud rose
from the caldera and plumed westward as if in ill omen to our
task.

The land here on the leeward side of the island is almost
unutterably boring, with lava field following lava field, the
cooled *pahoehoe* lava molded in a thousand ungainly attitudes,
the basalt buttresses and silent cinder cones creating a landscape
comprised of equal parts Dante and Pittsburgh coalfield. The
trail—part of an ancient Hawaiian path the locals called
Ainapo—wound southwestward between the massif of Mauna
Loa and the sea cliffs to the south. For the first few hours there
was almost nothing to be seen but the black lava except for a few
scruffy-looking scrub trees which the Hawaiians call *ohi'a*, and
some hardy ferns—*ama'u*—which Reverend Haymark says grow
on lava fields which are less than a year old.

Because this section of trail was less traveled and more

rugged than the path between Hilo and Kilauea, we covered fewer than twenty miles by the time tropical darkness fell. I should take a moment to describe that sunset: we had traveled far enough west that the leeward coast of the Big Island had come into view far below, the vista north along its shoreline obstructed only by the lower limb of Mauna Loa's southwest ridge; from our vantage point still two thousand or more feet above sea level, we could see the southernmost point of the island and the great expanse of ocean to the south and west. The afternoon had been clear, the wind turning about from the west and blowing the volcanic clouds away from us, and now nothing but azure sky separated us from the straight horizon so far to the west of us.

We paused in the process of making camp and tethering our tired horses to watch the sunset, the sun a perfect red orb hesitating along the horizon like a suitor loathe to bid a loved one good-night. Finally it disappeared, slowly devoured by a ragged line of dark cloud just above the horizon. I had been watching the departure of the sun with a lyrical eye, but Mr. Clemens must have been observing with the trained gaze of a former riverboat pilot, for he said drily, "If the wind holds, that bit of cloud may bring us problems before morning."

His warning hardly seemed likely as we ate our dried beef, performed our evening ablutions as best we could among the *a'a* boulders, and prepared to sleep, the horses tied to a lone *lauhala* tree by their long tethers, our saddles inverted for pillows, and the sky a canopy of blazing stars above us. While washing my face where rainwater had accumulated behind a weathered boulder, I overheard the men discussing the merits of standing watch that night. Reverend Haymark was not in favor of the idea due to fear that it might alarm "the lady." Mr. Clemens barked his laugh and said, "I rather think that there are very few things on this planet that would spook this particular lady." I admit that I was not sure how to take this comment, although I know that I resented his facetious tone when he used the word "lady."

At any rate, neither stood guard, although I got the

impression that they were trusting the horses to that task. I believe that my horse would have stood sleeping through an attack by whooping Red Indians, so sluggish was the beast.

In the morning, Mr. Clemens's prediction was confirmed, as we were awakened before first light by a steady downpour. With nowhere except the single *lauhala* tree to shelter, we gave up trying to make coffee over the tiny fire the correspondent had started, and loaded our bedrolls and saddle-bags for the day's descent. Already I was having second thoughts about the wisdom of my self-inclusion on this odd trip. As the horses picked their way south and west over slippery lava fields, the sound of their hooves echoing amongst the *a'a* boulders, I remained all too aware that had I accompanied the others, I would already be basking in the comforts of Hilo.

Little did I know then how unimportant mere comforts would seem a few hours hence.

All that day—yesterday—we picked our way lower, traversing the southernmost ridge of Mauna Loa and coming out onto the highlands above the Kona Coast. From our vantage point a thousand feet above the sea, we could see the patches of brilliant green where the coconut palms marked the fertile band of soil near the ocean cliffs. I say cliffs, because even from this distance we could see the maddened toss of surf where the angry Pacific encountered the steep and rocky shoreline. Only a few beaches and bays were visible up the ten or so miles of coastline we could see, the vast majority of the coast being given over to cliffs where no ship or longboat could put in. It was somewhere down there that the Whisters and the Stantons and the other families had met their doom. These glimpses were made through rising clouds that boiled in from the west, their edges curling against the great mass of volcano behind us.

"I thought this was the dry side," Mr. Clemens remarked laconically.

"It is," said Reverend Haymark, water dripping from his short-brimmed hat. "This is most unusual for June."

"Odd how weather always chooses the unusual for its commonplace," muttered the correspondent. We picked our way lower and the clouds seemed to descend with us, the day growing gloomy and dusky hours before its late-evening sunset.

Reaching a sort of wooded shelf some half mile in from the sea cliffs, we struck a foot path winding through the trees and thicker shrubbery at this elevation. "This is the main trail between Kona and the missions at Kau and South Point," said Reverend Haymark, turning the nose of his horse north.

"Are we almost there?" I asked, alarmed to hear myself ask the whining entreaty of all undisciplined travelers.

"Another eight to ten miles," said the cleric, shifting in his saddle. "I am afraid that with the horses being so tired and the weather so inclement, we shall not make the mission village by nightfall."

"Perhaps that is for the best," remarked Mr. Clemens, and it took me only a moment to see his point. We did not know what awaited us there. If the villagers were still up in arms, if they had indeed slaughtered the mission families, it would hardly be wise to arrive on their doorstep a few minutes before nightfall.

Reverend Haymark nodded. "There is a place only a mile or two north of here, I believe. A site of pagan ritual. I believe we can find shelter there."

And thus we arrived that evening at the great *heiau* where the terrible events of that night would take place.

Our entry into the *heiau* was foreboding enough: we had to follow the trail between two high stone walls, down the very passageway—Reverend Haymark observed in sad tones—where the heathen priests had dragged their sacrificial victims to slaughter on the steps of that huge pile of stones which awaited us.

"Kamehameha the Great built this before going on to conquer Oahu," said the cleric as our horses paused at the base of the terrible structure.

"I dreamed about Kamehameha last night," said Mr. Clemens in a tone that was far from jesting. "I dreamed that a gaunt muffled figure appeared at our campsite and led me back into the crater at Kilauea. There, in this underground chamber, my spectral guide pointed to a great boulder and cried, 'Behold

the grave of the last Kamehameha!' I remember setting my
shoulder to the stone, the great boulder shifted, and there were
the mummified remains of the great king."

"A disturbing dream," said Reverend Haymark, mopping his
florid face with a handkerchief and glancing my way.

"More disturbing yet," said the correspondent, his voice
serious in a way I had not yet heard, "the dead king set a bony
hand upon my shoulder and tried to speak, his voice attempting
to escape withered lips that had been sewn together. The sound
was more a terrible human groan, but I was sure that he was
trying to warn me of something."

"It seems a poor time for ghost stories," I said, glancing up
at the wall upon wall of sacrificial stones rising above us.

Mr. Clemens seemed to shake himself out of reverie. "Yes,"
he said absently. "I am sorry."

Surprised by his apology—the first of the trip—I distracted
myself by estimating the size of this *heiau*. It lay in the shape of
an irregular parallelogram more than 200 feet long, and the
walls, built of lava stones situated without mortar, were some 12
feet wide at the bottom and 20 feet high, tapering to a width of 6
feet at the top. This was on the *mauka* or landward side; on the
sea side, the walls had tumbled in places, and were only 7 or 8
feet high, flat on top to facilitate the chiefs and priests in their
ceremonies here. There was an inner court on the south end, and
Reverend Haymark commented that here was where the
principal idol stood—Tairi, fierce in aspect, helmeted and
festooned with red feathers, Kamehameha's chosen war god. It
was here that the people were sacrificed by the
hundreds—perhaps thousands—to facilitate the king's goals.

The rain was falling more heavily now and I confess that my
spirits were as dampened as my clothes and body. Everything was
gray and dripping. The place seemed worse than devoid of
life—it was *draining* of life, if that makes any sense.

There were three long-abandoned grass shacks set fifty
yards or so north of the foreboding *heiau*, and it was here, in the
least dilapidated hut, that we decided to tether the horses and
spend the night. Out of the rain, Mr. Clemens managed to use

the drier bits of the decaying shack to start a small fire on the dirt floor, and we managed to boil coffee to have with our salted meat and mangoes. I would have preferred tea, but the hot liquid did serve to revive all of our spirits, and as the darkness fell we discussed what we might find during the coming day. Reverend Haymark was of the opinion that the local *kahuna* had conspired to terrify the missionaries, but that it was quite possible that Reverend Whistler and the others were still alive.

"What about the monsters?" asked Mr. Clemens. "Hananui's reptile man and dog man and all the rest?"

Reverend Haymark showed his scorn of such superstition.

"It would certainly make a better story than surly natives," suggested the correspondent.

I sniffed at this. "Why must journalism always concern itself with the grotesque and unsettling?"

Mr. Clemens smiled. "Miss Stewart," he said, "death and dismemberment, madness and cannibalism, these are the good Christian topics that make illiterates learn to read newspapers. The more bizarre the event, the better the breakfast reading."

"But surely," I said, "this is a sign of our sensationalist age."

"Yes," agreed Mr. Clemens, "and of all ages before us and all ages to come. Nations grow and die, machines are invented and fall to obsolescence, fashions bloom and wither like last summer's flowers . . . but a good murder before breakfast, Miss Stewart, this is the stuff of eternity. If this story is half as sensational as the tale of the *Hornet*, I would be able to sell it to any paper, be it 1866, 1966, or the year 2066."

I shook my head at this nonsense. At that moment the horses began to cry and whinny in the unmistakable expression of pure equine panic.

FOURTEEN

Pana-ewa is a great lehua island;
A forest of ohias inland.
Fallen are the red flowers of the lehua,
Spoiled are the red apples of the ohia,
Bald is the head of Pana-ewa;
Smoke is over the land;
The fire is burning.
—Pele's sister's chant to Pana-ewa

Byron Trumbo lay naked and exhausted, flat on his back with the covers kicked aside, watching the wooden blades of the fan turn overhead while Maya dozed in the crook of his arm. Both were covered with a thin film of sweat. Trumbo was breathing through his mouth, still trying to catch his breath. He had forgotten how tiring these reunions with Maya Richardson could be.

The woman lying with her head on his chest was tall, thin, young, beautiful, famous, rich, and passionate beyond Trumbo's imaginings. He had been sleeping with her for a little more than two years, promising to marry her almost as long as that, and staring at her picture next to his in the gossip columns and tabloids for as long as he could remember. Trumbo was not sure when he had grown tired of Maya, only that he had: tired of her relentless beauty, tired of her model's professional narcissism, tired of her clipped British dialect and wicked British wit, tired of her undaunted passion and indefatigable sexual technique. Bicki had been the answer—the black, teenaged rock singer somehow balanced Caitlin's lovely bitchiness and Maya's mannered beauty. Bicki's selfish, awkward sexual tendencies somehow made Caitlin's frigidity and Maya's wild abandon more tolerable, even interesting. It was odd how it took the combination of the three women in Byron Trumbo's life to make one satisfying relationship for him, but it did, and he accepted it. The hard part was to maintain it.

He had no illusions that Maya would ever accept Bicki's existence if it came to light, so Trumbo had made damned sure that it would not come to light. Only recently had the tabloids been hissing and whispering about a new Trumbo relationship, and it was lucky that Maya was too much the lady to read the tabloids.

"Mmmmmm," moaned the supermodel, stirring from her doze. She ran elegant fingers through the hairs on Trumbo's chest.

"Mmmmm yourself," said Trumbo, and patted her on her perfect butt. "Move your head, kid. I've got to get dressed."

"Nooo," whined Maya. She rested on her elbow as Trumbo sat on the edge of the bed. "You have to stay the night."

"Sorry, kiddo. Will and Bobby Tanaka and the others are waiting. We've got hours of work to do before tomorrow morning's session with Sato."

"Mmmmm," said Maya. "Don't you like my little surprise?"

Trumbo had pulled on his pants. Now he looked over his shoulder at her. Her breasts were small but perfect, the nipples pink and perfect. She did not pull the sheet up.

"Coming here to surprise you, I mean," she said, each syllable emphasized with her precise British accent. Maya's press kit said that she had been raised and had gone to school in England, but Trumbo knew that she had grown up in New Jersey. The dialect came from six months of intensive tutoring when she was seventeen and had just gone professional as a model.

"Yeah," said Trumbo. "I like it. Only I'm busy as hell. You know how important this sale is." He stood to find his shirt. The fan turned slowly overhead.

"I won't get in the way," she said with only a hint of a pout.

"I know you won't, kid." He pulled on the loose Hawaiian shirt and began buttoning it. "You're out of here in the morning."

"*No!*"

"Yes."

"You've promised me a vacation at the Mauna Pele for two years."

"Jesus, Maya, your timing stinks. You know I'm trying to unload this place."

She pulled the sheet up. "That's why I wanted to see it before you sold it."

Trumbo shook his head and looked for his sandals. "You need to get out of here in the morning."

"Why? Is someone else here?"

Trumbo stopped and turned slowly. "What do you mean by that?"

Maya leaned out of the bed, pulled something from her straw bag, and laid it on the sheet with long fingers.

Trumbo picked up the tabloid, glanced at the front page, and tossed the paper aside. "This is bullshit. You know it is."

"I know you told that to Cait when the papers started talking about us two years ago."

Trumbo laughed. "You can't be serious. I don't even *listen* to that kind of music. I've never even seen this woman on MTV."

"No?" said Maya, and there was something strange and brittle in her tone.

"No," said Trumbo.

"Good. Because if I found out that there was something to that story, I'd give the tabloids something to write about." Maya leaned out of bed again, one perfect breast coming free of the sheet, and pulled something else from her bag.

"Christ," said Trumbo, staring at the nickel-plated little automatic in her perfect hand. The pistol was small, probably a .32-caliber, but Trumbo had respect for all calibers of automatics. "Are you shitting me, kid?"

"I shit you not," said Maya in her crisp British tones. "I really have no intention of being made a fool of, Byron. Trust me."

Trumbo felt something like rage rising in him. He had had about enough of this. Things were getting out of hand. He took half a step toward the bed, ready to take the pistol away from this spoiled bitch and spank her until she screamed.

The radio buzzed and squawked where he had tossed it on the wicker chair. Trumbo paused and then picked it up. "Yeah?"

"Boss," came Will Bryant's voice, "you'd better get back here."

Trumbo continued to glare at Maya. She was not aiming the pistol at him, but had rested it on her raised knee and was inspecting her long nails. Trumbo's palm itched in expectation of the spanking. "Why?" he snarled into the handset.

"It's Briggs and Dillon," rasped Will's voice.

"What about them?"

"You'd better get back here."

"In a minute," said Trumbo, and thumbed the radio off. He pointed a blunt finger at Maya. "Give me that."

The supermodel's eyes flashed. "No."

"You'll fucking shoot yourself."

"Maybe." Her accent slipped a bit when she was angry. "The tabloids would love that as well."

Trumbo took a step toward her and then stopped. "Look, honey . . . I'll be honest with you. Caitlin's here. With her lawyer. They arrived tonight without warning."

Maya's lips thinned. "That bitch? Why?"

"She's trying to queer the deal with Sato. She and Koestler have gotten an investment group together and they think they can steal the Pele from me at a ridiculous price . . . threaten me into selling."

Maya's eyes changed, deepened. "Doesn't she know you at all, Byron?"

"No," said Trumbo. "Now put that thing away."

She dropped the automatic into her bag. Trumbo considered grabbing the bag, but then left it alone. "I need your help, kiddo."

"How?" She raised her head and the soft light from candles illuminated her perfect cheekbones.

"Amscray tomorrow. Don't let Caitlin find you here and add that to her list of things to get vengeance for."

Maya's perfect lower lip pouted out.

Trumbo sat on the edge of the bed and caressed her leg through the sheet. "Listen, kiddo. It'll just be another month or so. Then this shit will be over and we'll get married. Once I sell the Mauna Pele, things will be back on track. We'll honeymoon anywhere you want. Trust me."

Maya cocked her head at him. "Then it's not true about this . . . this Bicki person?"

"I've hardly even *heard* of her."

Maya leaned forward, rubbing her short hair against his forearm. "All right. But you have to come back here to sleep tonight."

Trumbo hesitated only a second. "Yeah. Sure. But give me the gun."

Maya pulled the bag out of his reach. "No. I've heard scary things about this hotel. You told me yourself that people have disappeared here."

Trumbo sighed. *Then why the hell did you come, you little dipshit?* "Honey," he said, "I've got two guys out there in the rain guarding your *hale* right now."

Maya glanced toward the uncurtained windows.

"They can't see in," said Trumbo. "We're twelve feet above the ground and there's nothing to the west but rocks and the Pacific. But you don't need the gun."

"I'll keep it until you get back."

Trumbo shrugged. He recognized the tone. He was glad that most of the people he had to negotiate with were men. "OK, kiddo, but it'll be late. I've got a shitload of work to do."

Maya slid lower so her huge eyes were just visible above the sheet. "I'll wait up," she said.

Trumbo leaned forward and kissed the top of her head. Outside, pausing on the porch and listening to the rain pounding the thatch on the roof of the huge *hale,* he thumbed the radio back to life. "Will?"

"Yeah, boss. Over."

"What the shit is all this about Briggs and Dillon?"

Static rasped for a moment. "I'm not sure this frequency is secure . . ."

"Just tell me."

"Dillon's in the infirmary. Briggs is missing. Over."

Trumbo leaned on the porch railing. The surf crashed against lava rock not thirty feet from the *hale*'s front door. Lightning flashed somewhere behind him. "What happened? Over."

"We don't know yet. Dillon can't talk. There may be something down in the . . ." Static crashed over his assistant's voice as lightning flashed again and thunder rolled over the palm trees.

"Will? Can you hear me?"

"Yes. Over."

"I'm going over to see . . ." Trumbo paused and looked at the closed door behind him. "I'm going over to the construction shack before coming back. Have Fredrickson send another man out here to guard Maya's *hale* and tell him to meet me at the shack in about forty-five minutes. Tell him to wait outside."

"All right, Mr. T. But I think you might want to . . ."

"I'll see you in about an hour," interrupted Trumbo. He pocketed the radio and bounded down the stairs to the covered golf cart. The little vehicle's single headlight illuminated a thin cone of rain and thick vegetation as he turned the humming cart around on the asphalt path and headed back down the peninsula. Thirty feet down the path he paused to talk to a dark figure huddling under a tree. "Michaels?"

"Yessir." The security man wore a soaked windbreaker and a baseball cap that was dripping water from the bill.

"Where's the other guy?"

"Williams is over on the north side," said the security man. "We take turns on the patrol."

Trumbo nodded. "Fredrickson's sending another man. You got a radio?"

"Sure," said Michaels, touching his earphone and the small unit clipped to his belt.

"Have them bring out another gun for you," said Trumbo. "Give me yours."

"Another . . . sure," said the security man, reaching under his windbreaker and pulling out his weapon. He handed it over. "It's a Browning, Mr. Trumbo. Nine-millimeter. There's a safety catch on the . . ."

"Yeah, yeah," said Trumbo. "I own one of these. You get on the horn and tell Fredrickson to send you out another."

"Yessir."

Trumbo started to hum away but looked up as he realized that Michaels was jogging along beside him. "What?"

"Uh, Mr. Trumbo, sir . . . I was wondering . . ."

"What?"

"Well, sir . . . I was wondering that if . . . I mean, after you're through with it . . . I mean, could I get the automatic back? My first wife gave it to me. It has . . . you know . . . sentimental value."

"Jesus Christ," said Trumbo, and drove off into the downpour.

June 17, 1866, Along the Kona Coast—
We were sheltered out of the storm in the abandoned hut near the ancient *heiau* when the horses began to rear and whinny in panic. Reverend Haymark jumped to his feet and Mr. Clemens reached into his coat pocket to extract the large pistol loaned to him at Volcano House. All three of us stood at the open doorway and peered into the dark and rain.

Torches were moving among the stone avenues of the *heiau*. Above the noise made by the terrified horses, I could make out the sound of drums and nose flutes raised in some wild tune. Moving as one, the three of us stepped onto the veranda. Reverend Haymark tried to calm the horses as Mr. Clemens and I stood looking at the moving lights amidst the maze of stones.

"Kapu o moe!"* came a cry from the direction of the moving torches. *"Kapu o moe!"

"What is that?" I whispered.

Still stroking the horses' noses, Reverend Haymark whispered back, "It is a warning cry to close one's eyes or lie prostrate. I believe it is used only in royal processions or by the Marchers of the Night."

"The Marchers of the Night?" whispered the correspondent. The pistol was still in his hand. His eyes were bright. "Ghosts?"

"The natives believe that their former royalty returns from the dead in these marches," said the Reverend, his voice rising a bit to show his lack of fear of these superstitions. "Sometimes the gods themselves march."

Just beyond the nearest stone wall of the *heiau*, the torches

and music passed our clearing. Wind whipped at the trees as if a cyclone were blowing from the landward direction at the same time the storm blew in from the sea. In spite of Reverend Haymark's soothing, the horses continued to pull at their tethers and show the whites of their eyes.

"Come," I said and impulsively set off into the rain. Mr. Clemens followed at a jog. Reverend Haymark called something but then made sure the horses' tethers were secure and moved quickly across the clearing after us.

We had to walk some twenty yards to reach the end of the wall that separated us from the *heiau*'s entrance and courtyard, and when we came around the obstruction, the procession had moved on. We could see the torchlight and hear the chanting and music from the opposite side of the heathen structure.

A bit out of wind from my rush across the clearing, I said to Mr. Clemens, "They do not sound ghostlike."

"Perhaps," said the correspondent and pointed to the pathway where we stood between the walls.

The day's rain had turned the narrow path to a slough of mud. Our own footsteps around the south end of the wall to this point were quite clear, as was the sucking sound as Reverend Haymark waded up to us. Of the procession that had just passed, there was no sign in the oozing soil.

I touched my cheek. "Could they have come another way?" I knew the answer. Beyond us was the massive structure of the *heiau* itself. For the torches to have been visible, the procession must have passed down this muddy avenue.

"We should turn back," said Reverend Haymark, panting heavily. The rain ran from his hat and shoulders. "We have no lantern, no candles."

As if in response, lightning flashed on the rocks and palms around us.

"I must see this," said Mr. Clemens. I noticed that the pistol was back in his coat pocket. The correspondent started down the path and I followed. Reverend Haymark muttered something but came along.

By the time we reached the north side of the *heiau*, the

procession had moved into the forest beyond. The call of *"Kapu o moe"* was still audible, but further away. We followed the path into the trees. Foliage had dropped from the palms far overhead and now littered the ground. Mr. Clemens peered upward in the darkness. "How did they cut these? And why?"

"Tradition has it that when the gods march, nothing may be suspended above them," said the cleric. "But tradition also has it that the gods are not accompanied by music when they march. Only the dead chiefs march to music."

In the intermittent glare of lightning I could see Mr. Clemens raise a bushy eyebrow. "Reverend, for a man of the cloth you seem to know much about the beliefs of these non-believers."

"I have had the pleasure of working with Mr. Hiram Bingham in Oahu on his compendium of ethnological treatises concerning the Sandwich Island natives and their quaint beliefs," said Reverend Haymark a bit stiffly.

Mr. Clemens nodded and pointed in the direction of the receding procession. "Well, if we don't skedaddle after them, this is one compendium of quaint beliefs that's going to leave us behind. I am curious what these Sandwich Islanders find so important that it is worth coming out in the rain and getting their feathers wet for."

We followed the path into the jungle, each lightning flash showing our footsteps quite clearly in the unsullied mud. The way was littered with branches and boughs, as if some invisible force had sheared off everything above the procession, even though most of the trees were sixty feet tall and taller.

Some quarter of a mile north of the *heiau* and we were all ready to turn back. The storm had moved inland and left no source of illumination. I cursed myself for not bringing candles from my saddle-bag. Although the torchlight had become visible again far ahead, we never seemed to catch up to it. The music was no longer audible. At least the rain had all but stopped, leaving only the dripping from the jungle around us. My dress was soaked quite through to the stays of my undergarments.

We had stopped in a small clearing to discuss turning back,

when a final flash of distant lightning revealed the scene around us. The path curved to the east and downhill from this point, obviously heading toward one of the few beaches we had seen from our vantage point higher on the volcano. Torchlight was visible on the distant beach through the last screen of trees and brush before the path descended a cliff face. Also visible was the small clearing in which we stood. Branches and boulders were strewn across the lush grass, as were a few fallen coconuts looking like hairy severed heads. Even as I thought of this grisly allusion, I noticed a real head lying in the grass, then saw the pale shoulders. I believe that I stifled a scream even as Mr. Clemens showed a startled expression in the lightning flash and reached into his pocket for the pistol.

Around us in the clearing lay at least half a dozen naked bodies, all frozen in the uncomfortable attitudes of death.

The lightning flash ended. The darkness of the jungle descended once again, unrelieved by starlight or even by the distant glow of Kilauea, shrouded as that was by the moving storm.

At that moment, in the darkness, I heard Mr. Clemens curse some yards from me, heard Reverend Haymark clear his throat some yards beyond that, and distinctly felt a cold hand grasp my ankle in the tall grass.

It was lucky, Eleanor thought later, that Cordie Stumpf did not fire her heavy pistol at the footsteps in the dark. Eleanor was certainly spooked enough that she might have, had she been pointing the weapon toward whoever or whatever it was advancing toward them in the catacombs.

A tall young man with an expensive suit and neatly tied-back long hair stepped into the small circle of light. Cordie lowered the pistol.

"Mr. Dillon!" said the young man, and quickly crossed to where Paul Kukali held the injured security chief upright against the wall. The young man ran his hand in front of Dillon's unblinking eyes and looked at the others. "What happened?"

"We don't know," said Paul. "We were just passing through when the lights went out."

"Who are you?" Cordie asked the young man. She put the pistol back in her straw bag.

"Will Bryant. I'm executive assistant to Mr. Trumbo. You're the contest winner . . . Mrs. Stumpf, right? What are you doing with that revolver?"

Cordie smiled. "You tell me, Mr. Bryant. Ain't this the place where guests disappear like canapés at a cocktail party?"

Will Bryant grunted and said to Paul, "Will you help me get Dillon upstairs?"

"Of course, but . . ." At that moment the lights came on. Cordie squinted at the glare and flipped the cover on her lighter.

"The staff infirmary is down here," said Paul.

Bryant shook his head. "We're going to shut down the service tunnels for a while. We'll take Dillon to the guest medical services in the Big Hale."

"He'll need a real hospital," said Cordie.

Will Bryant and Paul each took an arm and helped the security chief to his feet. Dillon did not protest, but he showed no interest in the maneuver. "Yes," said Trumbo's assistant, "but we'll have the staff doctor look him over first. Did Mr. Dillon say what happened?"

"He said nothing," offered Eleanor. She pointed down the corridor toward an open door beneath the sign that said DIRECTOR OF ASTRONOMY. "He came from that direction."

Will Bryant nodded and said, "Dr. Kukali, can you hold him for a moment?" As the art curator held Dillon upright, Will walked down the corridor, glanced inside the astronomy office, and slowly closed the door. "OK," he said upon returning, lifting one of Dillon's limp arms over his shoulder.

The corridor filled with people from the laundry and bakery, everyone milling toward the exit. "It's all right," announced Bryant, identifying himself to the workers. "Supervisors report to Mr. Carter's office. Everyone else has the night off." There were expressions of relief as the local workers disappeared up the stairways and ramp into the Big Hale.

"I was in the main corridor when the lights went out," Will Bryant was saying as they helped Dillon into the elevator in the basement of the Big Hale. "I saw the flicker of your light and walked toward it. I didn't mean to scare you."

"You didn't scare me," said Cordie.

"I really think you should leave the weapon at the main desk for safekeeping until you leave," said Trumbo's assistant. "It's against the law and hotel policy for guests to carry concealed weapons."

Cordie grunted. "I bet it's against hotel policy for dogs to be carrying around people's hands and for the main security guy to get all clawed to shreds, isn't it?"

Will Bryant said nothing.

"I'll keep my pistol," said Cordie. "If Mr. Trumbo don't like it, please tell him for me that he can kiss my serene Illinois ass."

Bryant smiled slightly. "Here we are." They helped Dillon off the elevator and down a tiled corridor to the medical suite. Bryant had called ahead on a small radio and Dr. Scamahorn was waiting in the hall. "Thank you for your help," Bryant said to the women. "Dr. Kukali, could you please wait a moment so I could talk to you?"

Paul looked at Eleanor. "I was going to escort the ladies to their room and *hale*."

"We don't need an escort," said Cordie. She swung her heavy bag over her shoulder. "Give us that umbrella there and I'll walk back to Eleanor's shack with her."

Eleanor started to point out that she needed no escort, but something in Cordie's tone told her the other woman wanted to talk. They passed out of the open lobby of the Big Hale together, down the staircase past the Whale Watching Lanai, and along the path toward the beach. The storm had let up considerably and only a light rain was falling. The Big Hale was a blaze of lights behind them; the path was illuminated by gas torches and low electric lights lining the way. They did not speak as they wound their way through the tropical vegetation south of the Shipwreck Bar past dark *hales* on their stilts. The porch light on Eleanor's *hale* had come on automatically, but the rooms were dark behind shutters. Eleanor unlocked the door and turned to say, "Did you want to . . ."

Cordie put her finger to her lips, pulled the pistol out, motioned Eleanor aside, and stepped into the *hale,* flicking on the lights as she did so. A second later she said, "Come on in. I didn't mean to get melodramatic, but it's been a weird day. I figured if something was gonna jump somebody, it might as well try jumping somebody carryin' a gun."

Eleanor moved past the shorter woman and turned on the lights by the bed. The *hale* was small but very comfortable-looking, as neat as she had left it hours earlier. No . . . neater . . . someone had turned down the bed and left a flower on the pillow. Eleanor picked up the blossom and waved Cordie over to a wicker chair on one side of a small desk by the shuttered windows. Eleanor sat in the other chair and laid the flower on the desk. "Did you want to talk?"

"Yeah," said Cordie, and put the pistol away again, pulling something larger from her bag. She set the bottle on the desk between them and went down the short hall to get glasses from the vanity.

"Sheep Dip," said Eleanor, reading the label. "Is this for real?"

"Damned straight it's for real," said Cordie, setting down two glasses and dropping into her chair. "It's an eight-year-old single-malt Scotch that the locals pot-distill in England. Do you drink whiskey?"

Eleanor nodded. She'd enjoyed single-malts in Scotland during her trips there and had developed a taste for expensive whiskeys while she was seeing a pilot friend years before. She had never heard of Sheep Dip.

"It and Pig's Nose are my favorites," said Cordie. "Better'n Glenlivet and those better-advertised brands." She poured three fingers for each of them and handed Eleanor her glass.

"No ice?" said Eleanor. "No water?"

"With single-malt?" said Cordie, and snorted. "No way. Bottoms up, Nell."

They both drank. Eleanor felt the smooth whiskey spread a warm path to her stomach. She nodded. "What do you want to talk about?"

Cordie sat back in her chair and looked out through the shutters for a moment at the vegetation crowding the window. When she turned back, she raised her glass and said, "I'm ready to talk about why we each came here. Not the bullshit reasons, but the real ones."

Eleanor looked at the other woman for a moment. "All right," she said at last. "You first."

Cordie swallowed whiskey and smiled. "My reasons are sorta stupid. To catch some of my childhood, I guess."

Eleanor was surprised. "Your childhood?"

Cordie laughed. "I had a weird childhood, I guess you might say. Part of it had a . . . sort of an adventure. When I heard about the weird stuff going on here at the Mauna Pele . . . well, maybe I thought I could have some more adventure."

Eleanor nodded. "But you found that you can never go home again."

"Thomas Wolfe," said Cordie, and refilled their glasses. She looked up at Eleanor's startled expression. "Well, maybe I read some of those *Great Books*. And yeah . . . you're right . . . it isn't the same. But that's not the only reason . . ." She stopped and stared into her glass.

"What?" Eleanor said softly.

"I've been working pretty hard since I was a kid," said Cordie Stumpf, stirring the amber whiskey in its glass. "You see, I grew up almost living in a garbage dump, so it was sorta natural that my first job was driving a garbage truck in Peoria. I married the guy who owned the company." She paused a moment. "When he died, I took over the business and my second husband married me *because* of the company. We expanded it together. When we got divorced, Hubie got the house and a big chunk of money, and I kept the business. My third husband . . . well, he had his own disposal business, and I guess you might say that we sort of merged." Cordie smiled, drank the glass empty, and poured more Sheep Dip. "Come on, Nell. I'm way ahead of you."

Eleanor drank and listened.

"Well, the last few years, what with the boys grown and all, it seemed like running the company was all there was to life. You know what I mean?"

Eleanor nodded.

"Three months ago I sold the business. And then, two months ago, I got cancer," said Cordie. "Ovarian cancer. They said they had to take my ovaries out. I said, 'Go ahead . . . I don't have any more use for them.' And they did."

"Ahhh," said Eleanor.

Cordie rubbed her lower lip and then ran her finger around the rim of the glass of whiskey. "I recovered real quick from the surgery. I've always had a strong constitution. They said they thought they'd got it all. They thought I'd beat the odds. Then I won this Vacation with the Millionaires contest and I figured that luck was still with me. That same day, I went in for my checkup and my doctor said that they're afraid the cancer's spread. I was supposed to start the chemotherapy and radiation treatment this week, but I got them to hold off six or seven days while I came here."

Eleanor looked at the other woman in the dim light. She knew the poor prognosis for ovarian cancer patients once the cancer had spread. Her mother had died of the disease. "God damn it to hell," Eleanor said carefully, and drank the last of her Sheep Dip. Cordie nodded and poured three more fingers.

"So I was sort of hopin' that the Mauna Pele'd have some monsters," continued Cordie. "Or at least an axe murderer or something. You know, something scary but . . . *outside*. Something you could fight the way I . . . well, something you could fight."

"Yes," said Eleanor.

"You know, today when I was looking at this place, I was thinking . . . why not a hospital like this for cancer patients to take their treatments and relax and recuperate on the beach? Most of the hospitals I know are like the one in Chicago I'm goin' to . . . prisons under snow."

Eleanor said, "You mean a luxury hotel like a hospice?"

Cordie shook her head. "Hospice? Uh-uh, that's like a place to die while the dyin' specialists tell you what stage you should be on, ain't it? You've had your denial, now get on to acceptance, kid, we got others waitin'. Well, fuck that. I'm just talking about a cancer hospital where you can watch your hair fall out and get a tan at the same time, that's all."

Eleanor nodded and moved the shutters aside. The vegetation outside was still dripping. The smell of wet jungle was sensuous and a bit sad. "It would be expensive," she said. "It would have to be a hospital for rich people."

Cordie laughed. "Naww. *Cancer* is expensive. Do you believe those bullshit hospital bills? This place would just cost airfare . . . and maybe there'd be some . . . like scholarships to get the poor schmucks here. A cancer-vacation-of-the-month lottery. Something like that."

Eleanor held her glass out to be refilled. The Scotch had spread through her like a slow flame. "I think Mr. Trumbo has other ideas. It appears that the Japanese shall inherit this patch of earth."

"Yeah." Cordie rubbed her lip again. "Just what the world needs, more golf condos." She looked up suddenly. "Nell, you ever been in love?"

Eleanor was startled but tried not to show it. "Yes," she said. She did not offer to elaborate.

Cordie nodded slowly, as if satisfied with the simple answer. "Me too. Once. Oh . . . I've loved people. Two of my three husbands. All of my boys. That's a sort of love that either is there or it ain't. But I've only *been* in love once. When I was just a kid." She was silent for several moments and the only sound was the soft dripping of rain from the palm fronds outside. "I don't think he even knew it," she said at last.

"You never told him?" Eleanor sipped the Scotch.

"Uh-uh. He was another kid in this little town we lived in. He went away to Vietnam, got himself hurt real bad, and then became a priest. A Catholic priest. One of the kind that doesn't get married or screw."

"Oh," said Eleanor. *Have you checked the headlines?* she wanted to say *There's been more screwing than we might have thought.* Out loud she said, "Have you talked to him since he became a priest?"

"Naw," said Cordie. "I haven't even been back to that town in years. Somebody told me that he'd quit being a priest a few years ago and got married, but it doesn't matter, does it? The reason I mentioned it was, the last few weeks I've been thinking about all the things people with serious cancer think about. Missed chances . . . wasted lives . . . all that shit.''

"Your life hasn't been wasted," said Eleanor.

"Damn straight," agreed Cordie. "My boys'd agree with you. Raising them while runnin' the garbage business kept me busy.'' She set down her empty glass. "Okay, Nell, what about you. Why'd you come here?''

Eleanor rotated her glass in her hand. "You don't think I came here just on vacation?''

Cordie's lank hair moved as she shook her head. "I *know* you didn't come here just on vacation. You're not the type that hangs around mega-resorts in your time off. I'd say you're more used to trekking in Nepal and doing eco-tourist shit up the Amazon.''

Eleanor grinned. "Guilty as charged. Nepal trekking two years ago and three years before that. Amazon eco-tourist shit in '87.''

"So?'' Cordie poured the last of the Sheep Dip. "Why are you here?''

Eleanor reached into her bag and pulled out Aunt Kidder's diary, setting it carefully on the table, avoiding any moisture there. With two fingers she slid it across to Cordie.

Cordie hesitated. "Can I open it?''

"Yes.'' Eleanor watched the other woman fish a pair of glasses from her purse and flip through the ancient journal, skimming at first, then reading entire paragraphs.

Cordie whistled softly. "This ties in to a lot of the weird shit going on now.''

"Yes,'' said Eleanor.

"This Lorena Stewart,'' said Cordie. "Is she somebody important that I should know about? Like, was she Abe Lincoln's second wife or something?''

Eleanor laughed easily. "No, not that important, although she wrote some wonderful travel books that are all but forgotten now. Lorena was a distant relative of mine. When she grew older, everyone knew her as Kidder because of her sense of humor and the fact that she always wore white kid gloves.''

Cordie touched the book gently with her fingertips. "So why are you here?"

Eleanor paused, amazed even through the whiskey glow that she was talking about all this. "There are several mysteries in that book," she said at last. "The easier mystery . . . the *outside* mystery . . . of what Aunt Kidder wrote about. And the more difficult mystery of why she did not marry Samuel Clemens."

"Samuel Clemens," said Cordie. "That's Mark Twain, isn't it?"

"Yes."

"I went to Hannibal once," said Cordie. "Sort of a pretty little river town."

"Yes, I've been there as well," said Eleanor. *Once every two years,* she did not add. *Visiting the writer's childhood home and the dusty museum there as if there would be some clue about Aunt Kidder's decision.*

"And Mark Twain wanted to marry this Lorena Stewart?"

"Well . . ." Eleanor paused again. "You may read it if you wish." Since Aunt Beanie had given her the journal . . . the talisman . . . when she was twelve, Eleanor had shared it with no one, loaned it to no one.

Cordie nodded slowly, as if she understood. "I'm much obliged, Nell. I'll read it tonight and get it back to you tomorrow, safe and sound."

Eleanor glanced at her watch. "My God, it's after one o'clock in the morning."

Cordie stood, steadied herself with one hand on the table, and put the journal in her bag. "Hey," she said, "it doesn't matter. We're on vacation."

"I hate for you to walk back to the Big Hale by yourself."

"Why?" said Cordie Stumpf. "The rain's stopped."

"Yes, but . . ." said Eleanor. "But there are . . ."

"Monsters," said Cordie, and grinned. "I hope so. Goddammit, I hope so." She pulled the revolver out, hefted it, and put it back as she moved to the door. "I'll see you around tomorrow, Nell. Don't worry about Aunt Kidder's diary. Anything that wants it will have to get me first."

"See you tomorrow," called Eleanor as the other woman disappeared into the jungle down the curving path.

FIFTEEN

Fire-split rocks strike the sun;
Fire pours on the sea at Puna;
The bright sea at Ku-ki'i.
The gods of the night at the eastern gate,
The skeleton woods that loom.
What is the meaning of this?
The meaning is desolation.
　　　　　—Hi'iaka's chant to Pele

It was after five when Byron Trumbo got to bed, tumbling in beside Maya for an hour of half-sleep before getting up and showering. He had a seven o'clock working breakfast with the Sato Group.

The scene at the construction shack had been out of one of his adolescent fantasies. Bicki had met him at the door—naked—and had leapt for him even before he could close the door or window shutters. The hot tub had been bubbling on the seaside veranda, and Trumbo had carried the diminutive rock star to the tub and dropped her in, peeling off his clothes to join her. She had pulled him in before he'd gotten his undershorts off.

Trumbo never underestimated his own libido or stamina, but ninety minutes of Bicki passion on top of the evening with Maya and the trying day had him ready to slip beneath the hot tub bubbles. Finally he had extricated himself, dressed himself, given Bicki the spiel about Caitlin trying to ruin the Sato deal—a spiel lost on the young singer: Bicki took no interest in Trumbo's dealings—and tried to convince her to leave in the morning.

"Awww," pouted the seventeen-year-old, "I just got here."

She draped one long, mocha leg over an oversized pillow and said, "Did ah surprise you, T?"

"You surprised me," said Trumbo, buttoning his Hawaiian shirt. "And don't call me T."

"OK, T," said Bicki. "Ah won't call you T. Why do you-all want me to leave?"

Trumbo paused. Bicki was from Selma, Alabama, and he usually enjoyed her unself-conscious southernisms. Tonight they grated on him as badly as had Caitlin's damned New England vowels and Maya's fake British accent. And, in the height of passion, he'd forgotten her goddamned pierced tongue and tried to French-kiss her and almost leapt out of the hot tub when he'd encountered two tiny metal balls in there. "You distract me, kid," he said. "I need my wits about me for this deal."

Bicki ran her thigh up and down the pillow. "Ah'm not interested in your *wits*, T."

It's mutual, thought Trumbo. He said, "I know, kid, but this is a sensitive deal."

Bicki ran long fingers up his thigh. "But ah know about sensitive things, T."

Trumbo intercepted her fingers, kissed them, grabbed his radio and the 9mm Browning from the floor, and went for the door. "I'll check in on you in the morning, kid. But tomorrow you head back to Antigua." At least Bicki preferred sleeping alone.

"Tomorrow," drawled Bicki, "is anothah day."

Trumbo paused at the door, shook his head, and jogged through the dying drizzle toward the golf cart, where he jumped half a foot in the air and reached for the Browning in his belt as a figure as dark as the night stepped out of the jungle and seemed to float toward him.

"Shit," said Trumbo, sliding the Browning back in his waistband with shaky fingers. "Don't scare me like that."

"Sorry, Mr. Trumbo," said Lamont Fredrickson. The African-American assistant security chief was dressed all in black. Trumbo had forgotten he had given orders for the man to meet him here almost an hour earlier. Trumbo glanced back at the unshuttered windows, through which Bicki was more than visible as she lounged on the bed in a pool of yellow light.

"Enjoy the show?" asked Trumbo.

The security man had enough sense not to answer or grin.

"What's the word on Dillon?" asked Byron Trumbo.

Fredrickson touched his earphone and shrugged. "Mr. Bryant hasn't said."

"Briggs?"

"Haven't heard."

Trumbo sighed. "All right, here's what I want you to do. If Dillon's out of it, you take over security."

"Yessir."

"Your first priority is still to keep Sato and his boys from being killed by whoever's chopping up guests and staff."

"Yessir."

"Your second priority is to keep Ms. Richardson and the young lady in the construction shack here alive and well and away from each other and my ex-wife. Got that?"

"Yessir."

"Your third priority is to keep your men as much out of sight as possible. We don't want Sato thinking that this is an armed camp. And don't say 'Yessir.' "

"Yessir. I mean . . ." Fredrickson nodded.

"Your fourth priority is to find the fucks that are doing this to our people and stop them. Do you get my meaning on that?"

"You mean work with the police and Five-O, sir?"

Trumbo mimicked the man's tone. "No, I don't mean work with the police and Five-O, sir. I mean *stop* them. Shoot them."

Fredrickson frowned. "Yessir. Uh, Mr. Trumbo . . . shouldn't there be a fifth priority? I mean a first one, really."

"What are you talking about?" Trumbo had settled into the golf cart. The seat was wet. He switched on the power and squinted back toward the Big Hale, visible across the curve of dark bay as a glow of lights above the palms. Somewhere up there Caitlin was probably in bed with that bloodsucking Myron Koestler.

"I'm talking about you, sir," said Fredrickson. "If Mr. Briggs is gone, who's going to watch your back?"

Byron Trumbo sighed. "I'll watch my own back. You just keep on your toes and keep your men on theirs." Trumbo left the security man standing in the rain and drove back to the main building alone, through the carefully planned jungle of the "South 40" where the lower rent *hales* stood dark and silent on their stilts, past the small pool and the large pool and the Shipwreck Bar, and then up the winding path past the Whale Watching Lanai and into the belly of the Big Hale.

Will Bryant met him in the main lobby.

"How's Dillon?" asked Trumbo.

"Some serious cuts, a broken collarbone, tooth marks on his forearm that go to the bone. Dr. Scamahorn says that he's in shock."

"Tooth marks?" Trumbo paused a minute by the elevator. "What kind of tooth marks?"

Will Bryant shook his head. "Dillon didn't say and Scamahorn couldn't tell. Something large."

"Something large," repeated Trumbo. "Great. Where's Briggs?"

"It looks like something dragged him down the tunnel. Mr. Carter and I went down with two men, but we didn't . . ."

"Wait a minute, wait a minute. What tunnel?" They were in the elevator riding to the top floor.

"The one behind the wall in the astronomer's office. You remember, you told Briggs and Dillon to check it out."

"Yeah, but I didn't tell them to get dragged away or end up being gnawed on." They stepped out of the elevator and moved quickly down the hall toward the Presidential Suite. "So Dillon's out of it, Briggs is missing in this fucking tunnel, and we're stacking up sedated eyewitnesses to all this shit like cordwood in the infirmary."

"Right," said Will Bryant. "Dr. Hastings called again, but I told him that you were unavailable."

"Amen to that," said Trumbo. He nodded at Bobby Tanaka and the others in the living room of the suite and then went in his bedroom to change into slacks and a polo shirt.

"But Hastings said that the lava flow is moving laterally. He's most concerned about outgassing . . ."

"The only outgassing I'm worried about," said Trumbo, "is from Hastings. Do you have the amended contract ready?"

"Bobby and I were just going over it."

"Good. We're meeting with Hiroshe and that little asshole Inazo Ono at seven and I want to get down to the short strokes."

"Ono's a tough negotiator," said Will.

Byron Trumbo showed all of his teeth.

At six-thirty, Trumbo stepped out of the shower in Maya's Samoan Bungalow. The model squinted at him from the sheets. "Are you kidding?"

"Never kid, kid," said Trumbo. "Today's a big day."

"Why, what's happening today?"

"Well, first off, you're heading back to your modeling gig in Chicago."

"My next job is in Toronto."

"OK, you're headed back to Toronto."

"I rather think not."

"I rathuh think yes."

Maya stood with no hint of modesty and walked nude to the open screen doors of the east-facing veranda. Sunlight washed her perfect skin in gold light. "I'll ask again, Byron. What is happening today?"

Trumbo kissed her on the neck. "Everything," he said, and moved past her out the door.

He had no idea how accurate that statement would turn out to be.

June 17, 1866, Along the Kona Coast—

I did not scream when the hand grasped my ankle. Mr. Clemens had extracted his revolver and I could hear him curse softly and begin to move my way in the darkness, but I said, "No! Stay where you are." I bent down in the moist grass, gently unclasped the hand from my ankle, and followed the smooth curve of forearm to shoulder with my fingers. "Reverend Haymark," I said softly, "do you have a light?"

We had brought no candles, but I heard the rasp and then saw the sputter of flame as he ignited a Lucifer match and hurried toward me. The native lying at my feet was bleeding from a cut on the scalp and his eyelids fluttered with pain. He was little more than a boy . . . he *was* a boy. And quite naked.

"We must get him back to our hut," I said softly. The torches of the ghostly procession were some hundred yards away, but we could not guess who might have remained behind. "How are the others?"

"Dead, I fear," said Mr. Clemens. The correspondent had moved from body to body in the dim glow of Reverend Haymark's second match, checking each pale corpse with a matter-of-factness which seemed to belie his dismissal of his past military service. He and the cleric came over to crouch next to the boy with me. "He's been struck by a stone or dull weapon," said Mr. Clemens, running his hand over the moaning child's skull. To me, he said, "You are right. We should return him to the hut where we can inspect the wound by candlelight." The correspondent then said to Reverend Haymark, "Can you carry him by yourself?"

The portly cleric handed me the few remaining matches and I struck one in time to see him easily lift the boy. I looked at Mr. Clemens. "Are you not returning with us?"

The correspondent's eyes were bright. He nodded in the direction of the unearthly glow. "I will see that and return shortly."

"Perhaps I should . . ." I began.

"No," said Mr. Clemens. He turned around and disappeared into the darkness and rain.

The horses were nervous but still tethered in their place when we returned to the dilapidated hut. There was no bed, table, or even pallet of straw in the shack, but Reverend Haymark set the boy gently in the driest corner while I lit two candles and hunted in my saddle-bag for clean linen that would serve as a bandage. Taking the cleric's place next to the boy, I cleaned the wound as best I could with rainwater, staunched the bleeding, and bound a torn strip of cotton petticoat around the child's head. I looked up to find Reverend Haymark removing his coat.

"What is it, sir?" I asked.

"If his nakedness offends you . . ." said the blushing cleric, holding his coat out like an offering.

I waved it away. "Nonsense. He is a child of God. Innocence can never offend."

Pulling his coat back on, Reverend Haymark looked out at the night. The rain had stopped but the wind still lashed the palms. "I am not sure that these events hold much innocence."

The boy revived then. At first he moaned and spoke in his own tongue, but when his eyes focused on us he managed a passable English. His name was Halemanu and he had been baptized into the *Ora loa ia Jesu* or "endless life by Jesus" at the Reverend Titus Coan's Kona Mission when he was six years old . . . seven years earlier by the somewhat confused account I could elicit from the boy. Halemanu lived in the village of Ainepo north of here toward Kealakekua Bay where Captain Cook was slaughtered.

By this time we had brought the boy some water to drink and mango to eat and he sat up, his bare back against the grass wall of the hut, and babbled at us in his pidgin English. His eyes were bright, perhaps due to the concussion he had suffered or the great fright he had survived.

Halemanu had traveled south with his uncle and several warriors from the village because of a warning from their *kahuna*, or medicine man, that great evil was stirring along the Kona Coast near Honaunau, the City of Refuge. For Halemanu it had been his first adventure as a man.

The day before, yesterday, the party of men had reached the unnamed village where the Reverend Whister had built his church. The church was empty. The village was empty. Halemanu's uncle recognized the signs that evil beings had been loose upon the land. The group had come further south, thinking to visit a village in Kau where Halemanu's uncle knew dwelled the *Pele kahuna*, women who assuaged the goddess and who would understand such things as demons loosed upon the land. Night had fallen and the storm had found the party of five men and a boy far from shelter, but rather than stay in such an evil place, Halemanu's uncle and the others had chosen to press on to Kau through the night.

The Marchers of the Night had found them here, a mile

from the *Pele kahuna*'s village, near the ancient *heiau* which stood just outside our hut.

"Nonsense, boy," said Reverend Haymark. "You are a Christian. Certainly you no longer believe in such childish superstition."

Halemanu looked at the cleric as if the man had dribbled nonsense syllables. "There were two *Ka huaka'i o ka Po*," continued the boy. "Two groups, two Marchers of the Night. We try hide, but they come on us before we can go away into the *a'a*. First come the *aumakua*, the old *ali'i*, chiefs and warriors who all died long time ago. The dead chiefs, they led by an *alo kapu*, a dead chief whose face had been sacred so that no one—not man, not animal, not bird—could pass before him without being killed. We hear the *aumakua* shouting *'Kapu o moe!'* to warn the living relatives, but we no can run. My uncle, he tell us to take off all clothes and lie on back and close eyes. We do this. *Aumakuas* come pass, I hear flute, hear drum, hear the *manele*, the litters carrying chiefs not *alo kapu* or *akua kapu* . . . those be chiefs not kill us to walk before or walk behind. I hear ghosts cry *Shame!* at our nakedness. We all have our eyes closed, but I hear dead chiefs say *They shame us by lying uncovered. Do not touch them!* Then Marchers of the Night, they march on. But then come along another *Ka huakia'i o ka Po*. This time there no music and no *aumakua* shouting *"Kapu o moe!"* I open my eyes just enough to look and see torches—these much brighter than others, these torches red and carried five in front, five in middle, and five in back because five is perfect, complete number—the *ku a lima*. I know even before my uncle whisper for us to stay in grass that this *Ka huakia'i o ka Po* is a March of the Gods. The gods come walk six across, three male gods, three female gods—and my uncle, he whisper that he think that *Hi'iaka-i-ka-poli-o-Pele*, Pele's youngest sister, is in the first row. Then Uncle warn us to shut eyes and lie as if dead."

Here Halemanu paused to drink some water and I looked at Reverend Haymark in the dim candlelight. The minister was frowning and he shook his head at me as if to say that we should credit little or none of the injured boy's story. I glanced toward the open doorway. Water dripped from the sagging veranda of our shack, but the rain had stopped. There was no sign of Mr. Clemens.

"When the gods marched past, there was no music," repeated Halemanu, "only the lightning that was their torches and the thunder that was the chanting of their names and great deeds.

"They pass us on same path as dead chiefs go on, but the gods do not shout *Shame!*, they shout *Kill them!* And the ghost warriors who walk with the gods as protectors step out of line as they came to each man in our party, and a god would cry *Strike!*, and the man would leap up from the grass, but the ghost warrior would strike him down dead with his ghost club. Until finally, only ones alive were my uncle and me, and my uncle, he whisper, 'Halemanu, do not run when they call strike.' Then the god call *Strike!* when the guard come to my uncle, and my uncle do not run, but ghost warrior took club and struck his skull in anyway. Then ghost warrior come to me and god call *Strike!* and . . ."

"How did you know they were ghosts and gods?" interrupted Reverend Haymark.

Halemanu blinked in the candlelight. "The gods very tall," said the boy. "Their heads almost touch coconut palms. The ghosts much shorter, but also tall . . . maybe seven feet. And their feet do not touch ground."

Reverend Haymark made a noise.

"Go on, Halemanu," I said, still mopping blood from his brow with a wet cloth. "What happened when the god called 'Strike'?"

"Ghost warrior raise club to hit me. Even though Uncle die when he not run, I do what he say and do not run. Then one of gods—a female—she cry, *No! He is mine!* Ghost warrior not stop club all way, but pull aside so it just strike me little bit. God, she call again, *No! He is mine!* And guard go away with gods. I try to wake Uncle, but see that rain fall in his eyes and he not blink. All other men dead too. Then I do not remember until I see lightning flash and *nani wahine* god standing above me in *nui muumuu.* I touch your leg to thank you. But you are not god who spared me, are you?"

"No, Halemanu, I am not a god," I said. "And you must rest."

The boy's fingers tugged at my sleeve. "No, we must not stay here! The gods and dead chiefs are here because of Pana-ewa and *mokos* come up from Milu. Pele's sister, Hi'iaka, and other gods and *kahuna* here to build new *heiau* to fight Pana-ewa. They will fight terrible battle. Pana-ewa have many bodies. He eat soul of *wahine*. If you stay here, you all die before sun come up."

At that instant there was a crash behind us and Reverend Haymark and I whirled to see a form explode through the doorway and crash to the floor, tumbling one of the candles into extinction in his fall. It was Mr. Clemens, his usually wild hair in even wilder disarray, his eyes wide, and his clothes muddied.

"Miss Stewart!" he began, voice actually shaking. "Miss Stewart!" he said again.

"Are you hurt, sir?" I asked, kneeling next to him as I had knelt next to the boy minutes before.

"No, I am not hurt, Miss Stewart. But I have seen . . ." He broke off with a strange laugh.

"What have you seen, Mr. Clemens?"

Then he grasped me by my upper shoulders and pulled me closer. I confess that I felt a surge of alarm as well as a strange exhilaration at the unexpected contact.

"I have seen wondrous things, Miss Stewart. Wondrous things!"

Despite the late night and the bottle of Sheep Dip consumed, Eleanor awoke at seven-thirty with only a hint of headache. Scotch, she knew, was good for minimal hangovers.

Instead of going to the breakfast *lanai* or the beachside coffee shop, Eleanor used the small coffeemaker provided in the *hale* to set the coffee on while she dressed for jogging. She thought that it was a nice touch that the resort provided each *hale* with packages of fresh Kona coffee beans and a grinder. She drank one cup while standing on the small porch. Birds screeched and fluttered amidst the palms; peacocks strutted on the path below; the surf was audible through the thin screen of foliage to the west; to the east, the sky was blue above the thick *a'a* fields beginning mere yards beyond her raised *hale*. Eleanor could see a line of haze to the south, but the sky above the southwest ridge of Mauna Loa was clear.

Leaving the rest of the coffee on the warmer as an incentive, Eleanor left the *hale* behind and began jogging slowly south along the path, past the artificial lagoons and the smaller pool and the fourteenth hole to the petroglyph fields. Another quarter of a mile and she was beyond the artificial oasis of trees and shrubs, winding through head-high *a'a* boulders and catching occasional glimpses of painted figures and *piko* holes as she passed. Eventually the paved trail moved closer to the cliffs, and Eleanor felt the refreshing touch from the tall streamers of spray that lifted thirty feet from the rocks below. Rainbows danced in the air around her. Another quarter of a mile and the path ended at a sign warning guests that this was the property limit of the Mauna Pele Resort and that further travel on the lava fields would be dangerous. Eleanor paused at the asphalt turnaround for a moment, noticed a rough cinder path winding away through the boulders toward the cliffs, and continued on, jogging slowly through the rough rocks.

Ten minutes later and she came out on a peninsula looking north toward the Mauna Pele. The cliffs were higher here, at least forty feet above the water, and with no bay or lagoon to break the force of the wind and tide, the Pacific Ocean smashed itself against the rocks with a tangible fury. Eleanor stood, running in place, and admired the view.

To the north, the Mauna Pele was a verdant cluster of palms and bright foliage spreading back from the picture-perfect bay, the Big Hale set against the foothills of Mauna Loa with the Mauna Kea volcano rising above it farther to the north, its summit glittering whitely. The distant foothills and rising ridges showed a combination of rough rock and tough, brownish shrubs—not at all a tourist's vision of Hawaii. Eleanor thought it breathtaking.

To the south, increasingly rugged cliffs curved away to the east. The great southwest ridge of Mauna Loa blocked the sky, and now Eleanor could clearly see the plumes of smoke and ash that streamed south from the lava flows there. Another gray pillar of smoke caught her eye—this one more substantial than the ash plume and rising like a stratocumulus from the coast to an altitude of forty or fifty thousand feet. Eleanor realized that she was looking at one or more steam clouds from where the lava met the ocean just around the bend of the coast, perhaps ten miles away. The sight gave her goose bumps as she thought of the wild energies of creation that were being unleashed there.

Eleanor continued south along the coast trail, jogging easily now, thinking about things.

In the light of day, she was surprised to her core that she had loaned Aunt Kidder's journal to Cordie Stumpf. While she recognized the unlikely friendship with the strange woman from Illinois—she *liked* Cordie—it still remained totally atypical for her to let anyone read the diary. Since Aunt Beanie had entrusted the journal to her more than three decades earlier, Eleanor had shared it with no one. She wondered at her motivations for doing so now.

Perhaps I need an ally. Eleanor grunted at the thought and wiped sweat from her eyes.

The obvious ally in whatever was to come should be Paul Kukali: Hawaiian, well educated in the myth and history of the islands, well acquainted with the people and groups Eleanor would have to make contact with sooner or later . . . not to mention handsome and charming and sexy in his smooth way.

Eleanor grunted again and shook her hands to loosen circulation further. She had known many men like Paul Kukali, and while they were invariably interesting and charming, none could understand why his charm had not worked on the lonely, now middle-aged teacher named Eleanor Perry. Meanwhile, she needed Paul's contacts, and the feeling came perilously close to that of using the art curator.

Nonsense, thought Eleanor, *it's to his benefit even more than mine that we solve this old mystery.*

The rough trail had narrowed to the point where it was less a trail than a series of false trails through the rocks. Eleanor decided it was time to turn back. She had stopped to catch her breath and was leaning forward with her hands on her knees when she heard the noise.

It was a strange sound, as explosive as the surf but not synchronized with the crash of waves on rocks to her right. First would come the surf crash and then, ten or fifteen seconds later, this second burst of sound, as of a giant exhaling. Eleanor turned to her right and picked her way through the *a'a* to the source of the noise.

It was only a hundred feet or so from the cliff edge. Eleanor saw the spume of spray first, like a whale spouting. She moved across the wide slab of wet stone and crouched next to the blowhole. The sequence was always the same: first the crash of surf to her right, then a wailing as of tormented souls crying out or like a hundred flutes and oboes being blown by non-musicians, and then the spout of spray so fine that it was almost atomized. The water burst from the blowhole with the force of a high-pressure hose and Eleanor moved back quickly the first few times it blew, suddenly aware that to be caught in that explosion of spray would mean being lifted and thrown bodily through the air for dozens if not hundreds of feet. But when she had the timing down, knowing that there would be a minute and more between bursts, she crouched next to the hole and peered into it.

Obviously a lava tube connecting to the sea. Eleanor could hear the slap of the sea as waves surged in the narrow passage thirty feet below. Some dynamic of the lava tube channeled the explosive surf up this crack in the rock to the small aperture where she crouched. Satisfied with the explanation and not wishing to get wetter than she already was from the spray, Eleanor was about ready to leave when she heard something else above the wail of wind and water.

Voices. There were voices in the lava tube.

Eleanor stepped back as the geyser of spray exploded upward. As soon as the spouting ceased, she moved back to the crack and lowered her face to it.

Voices raised in rhythmic argument or actual chanting. Trusting the surge of water not to come off schedule, Eleanor lowered

her head and shoulders through the hole and realized that the
fissure extended downward for fifteen feet or so and then leveled
off into the ceiling of a cave. The lava tube was deeper and much
narrower toward the sea, the ridged cavern rising like a ramp toward this blowhole. Eleanor realized that the last hundred feet or
so of the lava tube was not much more than three feet across. It
widened and leveled off as it moved inland under the lava field.

Blocking the blowhole as she was, Eleanor could not have
seen this in the darkness. It was not totally dark. The gleam of
torches or some greener light illuminated the lava tube in the
mauka, or landward, direction. She heard the explosion of surf
from the opposite direction and suddenly pictured the high-pressure blast of water hurtling her way. She had tarried too long. Fingers slipping on wet rock, Eleanor scrabbled to pull her head and
shoulders up the crevice before the geyser smashed her like a
huge sledgehammer.

Her shoulders had just come free when heavy hands fell on
her back.

"Are you shitting me?" Byron Trumbo was just preparing to
putt when Will Bryant brought him the news of the escaped murderer.

"I never shit you," said his assistant.

Trumbo frowned, putted, missed, putted again, missed, and
putted in, falling two strokes behind. Hiroshe Sato could not hide
his smile. Trumbo stalked off the green, pulling Will by his elbow.

The morning session had gone well. The Sato Group had
opened the negotiations three weeks ago with a bid of $183 mil-
lion for the Mauna Pele. Trumbo had insisted on $500 million for
the resort and adjoining property. The discussion now hovered at
$285 million. When it hit $300 million, Trumbo was prepared to
agree. He would use the capital to shore up his appalling losses in
Atlantic City and Las Vegas, get out of the casino and hotel business, and get back to the basics of stock and real estate.

Then, as he was lining up his putt on the fourth hole of the
northern golf course, Will Bryant had whispered in his ear, "Sheriff Ventura is here."

"Fuck," Trumbo muttered after he told the Sato people to go ahead to the next tee. He walked back under the palms to where Ventura was waiting. The Kona sheriff was so tanned that he looked like a Hawaiian, but Trumbo knew that the man had grown up in Iowa.

"Charlie, you look great," said Trumbo, shaking the other man's hand. During the construction of the Mauna Pele, Trumbo had taken it as his personal duty to get to know all of the Kona Coast's politicians and law enforcement people.

"Mr. Trumbo," said the sheriff, pulling back his huge hand. Ventura was at least six-three and had never cut the billionaire much slack.

"Will says that you've got some news about Jimmy whatshis-name . . . the killer."

"Kahekili," said Ventura. The sheriff's voice was flat. "And you know as well as I that the allegations were silly. Jimmy Kahekili could slice somebody up in a bar fight if he was drunk enough, but he's no serial killer."

Trumbo raised an eyebrow. "So you say. But Will tells me that you came out here to warn me about him anyway."

Charlie Ventura nodded. "I got a call from the district attorney in Hilo. They let Jimmy go last night. The judge reduced the bail from fifty thousand dollars to a thousand because of the lack of evidence, and Jimmy's family made bail."

Trumbo waited.

"This morning Jimmy's cellmate told a trustee that Jimmy took the whole thing kind of personal," said Ventura. "Evidently Jimmy had convinced himself over the past couple of weeks that you were responsible for his troubles and he told this trustee that he was coming after you when he got out."

Trumbo sighed. "Can't you do something?"

Ventura made a gesture with one hand. "The state police have put out a notice that Jimmy's to be questioned about the threats, but so far no one can find him."

"He lived around here, didn't he?" said Trumbo.

"Yep. Right down the road in Hoopuloa. I've already spoken to Jimmy's mother and two brothers this morning. They say they haven't seen him and I've passed the word to him that if he shows up at the Mauna Pele or makes any more threats, I'll bring him in myself.''

Trumbo said nothing. He remembered that Kahekili was a big man . . . larger than the sheriff . . . a giant. He had once chopped up a South Kona bar with two axes, wielding one in each hand.

"Anyway,'' said the sheriff, ''I know you have tons of security around here, Mr. Trumbo. So you might alert them to watch out for Jimmy. He's a hothead and he knows the country around here.''

"Yeah,'' said Trumbo, thinking of his missing bodyguard, his still-comatose security chief, and the dickhead who was in charge of things now. ''Thanks, Sheriff.''

"One other thing,'' said Ventura. ''Have the state police been here about the dog and the hand?''

Trumbo blinked. *How the fuck does he know about that?*

Ventura took the billionaire's silence as a negative. ''They should be here sometime today to interrogate the witnesses and take a statement,'' said the sheriff.

"Good,'' said Trumbo. He thought, *That fucking art curator. His ass is grass.*

"I'll be in touch if there's any news about Jimmy,'' said Ventura.

"You do that,'' said Trumbo, and turned back toward the tee. Will Bryant was hurrying toward him. Trumbo stopped him six feet away with one blunt finger aimed like a pistol barrel. ''If this is bad news, I may have to kill you.''

His assistant nodded, swallowed, and said, ''Three things, boss. First, Mr. Carter talked to Hastings again and has taken it on himself to warn the guests that the lava flows are causing potential problems. 'Possible airborne toxic events,' Carter's calling it.''

"That little shit,'' breathed Trumbo. He would fire the manager and the art curator at the same time. ''Is anyone listening to him?''

Will rubbed his upper lip. ''This morning we had seventy-three paying guests. Forty-two of them have checked out.''

Trumbo grinned. The ground felt slippery under his golf

shoes, as if he were standing on a board that was resting on a field of marbles. Trumbo seriously thought that he might be losing his mind. "Tell me that's the worst of the three things, Will."

Bryant said nothing.

Trumbo continued grinning. "Go on."

"Second, Dillon's missing."

"Missing? Whaddya mean? This morning he was sedated in the infirmary."

Will nodded. "Sometime after eight he clonked Dr. Scamahorn on the head with a bedpan and made a run for it. The nurse says that he's still in his hospital gown."

Trumbo looked out at the *a'a* as if he might see the hairy little security director running from boulder to boulder with his ass peeking out. "OK," he said. "No big deal. Tell Fredrickson to watch for his old boss while he's watching for Jimmy whatshisname with an axe. What's three?"

Will Bryant hesitated.

"Come on," snapped Trumbo. "Sato's waiting for me. What's three?"

"Tsuneo Takahashi," said Will.

"Yeah," said Trumbo, rubbing his eye. "Hiroshe said that Sunny was up late partying with some of the girls. He slept through the breakfast and missed the tee-off. Sato's pissed at him. So?"

"He's missing," said Will Bryant. The assistant took a breath. "Sunny had a private room on the fourth floor of the Big Hale . . . evidently the others in Sato's group are used to his partying and like to keep him away from the business . . . but Fredrickson checked and says that something smashed the *lanai* doors sometime before dawn. The suite is torn all to hell. It looks like all of Sunny's clothes are still there . . . just no Sunny."

Trumbo lifted his graphite putter in both hands and bent it without thinking. "Don't panic," he whispered.

"Excuse me, sir?" Will leaned closer.

"Don't panic," Trumbo whispered, even more softly this time. He continued to bend the five-hundred-dollar putter as he walked back toward the tee for the fifth hole. "Don't panic. Don't panic."

SIXTEEN

E Pele, eia ka 'ohelo 'au;
e taumaha aku wau 'ia 'oe,
e 'ai ho'i au tetahi.
Oh, Pele, here are your 'ohelo berries;
I offer some to you,
some I also eat.
　　　　　　　—traditional Pele chant

Mrs. Cordie Stumpf, née Cordie Cooke of Elm Haven, Illinois, awoke before dawn with no hangover but with the constant pain she had ignored for two months now. Cordie went for a walk as the light came up and the birds came alive with noise. Cordie did not jog. The thought of running around when you did not have to was absurd to her.

Cordie waited for the breakfast *lanai* to open and had a huge breakfast of pancakes with coconut syrup and Portuguese sausage and scrambled eggs and whole wheat toast and three glasses of the excellent orange juice they served here and several cups of coffee. The leather journal that Nell had given her the night before was in her bag, but Cordie did not take it out while she ate. She had not looked at it before turning in last night. Cordie did not read many books, but this one she planned to read straight through.

After breakfast, Cordie wandered past the garden-level shops of the Big Hale. Most of the expensive little boutiques were closed, as were the beauty salon and the massage therapy center. Cordie began to wonder if the locals had decided not to come to work.

Stephen Ridell Carter came up to her as she was headed for

the beach. "Mrs. Stumpf," he began, nervously glancing at a list of names on his clipboard, "I'm pleased I caught you."

"Me too," said Cordie. "I always like getting caught."

The manager looked a bit nonplussed at that, but went ahead with what was obviously a spiel he had repeated many times that morning. It seemed that the twin volcanic eruptions had sent lava within a dozen miles of the Mauna Pele. Mr. Carter was sure that there was no immediate danger, but upon advice of the world's greatest volcano authorities, the Mauna Pele was suggesting that its guests might want to head homeward or transfer to another fine hotel with the assurance of a full refund of their fees.

"I'm not payin' anything," Cordie reminded him. "I'm vacationing with the millionaires."

Mr. Carter smiled. "Quite. But I assure you that the remaining vacation time will be honored when this . . . minor risk . . . has passed."

"That include the airfare I won? They going to fly me back a second time for free?"

The manager hesitated only a second. "Of course."

Cordie showed her small teeth in a grin. "Well, thanks but no thanks, Mr. C. I'm here and I guess I'll stay."

"But if there is any way . . ."

"Nope, thanks anyway," said Cordie, tapping the thin man on his linen-suited arm. "I got to get me to the beach. I have a bunch of reading to do."

Cordie did not actually read on the beach itself. Her skin was still red from the previous day's sunburn and she did not want to expose the journal to direct sunlight and salt air. Instead, Cordie found a lounge chair on the grassy, parklike area twenty yards in from the beach south of the Shipwreck Bar, sheltered and shaded by palms, but within a short walk of refreshments. Settling back in the cushions, making sure that her cover-up shielded her sunburned thighs from the solar rays, Cordie opened the book and began reading. She was a slow reader, but by late morning she had reached the account of events along the South Kona Coast recorded 130 years earlier.

June 18, 1866, In an unnamed village along the Kona
Coast—

The night and day since last I wrote seem like the
half-forgotten sights of a world with which I have long since
ceased to have aught to do. In truth, I believe that I have
exchanged my tenure in a world of beauty and sublimity for a
place in hell. But even such an excursion as a descent into hell
demands the honest traveler tell his tales, and so I shall.

Last night, the heathen temple, after the rain, after the
rescue of Halemanu, after the return of wild-eyed Mr. Clemens
. . . it all seems so long ago. But that is where I last had time to
set pen to paper, and that is where I must resume.

"Wondrous things!" Mr. Clemens had exclaimed,
and—ignoring the native child's pleas that we leave that place at
once—Reverend Haymark and I urged the correspondent to
share the events of the past half hour.

"The past half hour!" Mr. Clemens had said, removing his
watch from his waistcoat pocket and checking the time. At seeing
that he had indeed been gone from us for half an hour's span,
Mr. Clemens began laughing wildly. Reverend Haymark stepped
closer, squeezed the maniacal correspondent's upper arm with
what I could perceive was a powerful grip, and handed him a
silver flask.

"Whiskey?" said Mr. Clemens, pausing in his laughter long
enough to hold the flask under his nose.

"For medicinal purposes," said the cleric. Our Reverend
Haymark had been a man of many surprises these past few
nights.

Mr. Clemens drank deeply and wiped his mustache with
shaking hand. "You must forgive me," he said, gazing at none of
the three of us directly as he spoke. "You will understand when
I . . . when I tell of the wondrous things I saw."

The three of us spectators sat silent as the redheaded young
newspaper man spoke in his strangely lyrical Missouri accent.

"Although I could plainly see the torches on the beach, it
took me a while to work my way down the cliff face without
being detected. It was here that all my years of being a boy

served me in good stead. Secrecy and stealth are a boy's middle
name. By and by I reached the bottom of the hill and sought out
a vantage point from which I could spy without being spied upon
in return. An S-shaped rock, a sort of split boulder near the point
where the trees ended and the sand began, served that purpose
most admirably. I set up housekeeping there not two hundred
feet from where the torches burned and the ghostly figures
cavorted. Now that I have come through it, I admit that I was . . .
well, perhaps frightened is too strong a word for the emotion in
my breast . . . but I admit to a certain shortage in the saliva
department and a surplus of urgency elsewhere.

"What I saw then was enough to make a Methodist of me.
First there were the marchers . . . the chanting and music-playing
Marchers we spied from this very hut . . . another set of
Marchers made up, it appeared, of seven-foot giants whose skin
glowed the same pearly light as their uncanny torches . . . and
more sets of Marchers that arrived even as I crouched behind my
boulder. At that moment I would have sold my soul for the
meanest spyglass I had ever used from my pilothouse . . . sold it
and be welcome.

"There must have been a hundred or more Marchers there.
Both the human-sized ones and the larger variety were present in
both male and female form . . . they wore almost no clothes and
the torchlight and my fuddled mind were clear enough for this
identification. Some were obviously royalty, for they stood or sat
or reclined on the stretchers—those open palanquins I have seen
the native royalty in Oahu travel in—carried by slaves and gave
orders while the others worked feverishly. Royalty is the same
the world over and it is usually found horizontal.

"But the workers . . . I must say they worked with a will. As I
watched, these slaves . . . for it was obvious to this son of the
South that they were slaves, even though they shared the same
skin color as their masters . . . these slaves disappeared into the
jungle and reappeared in much the same frenzied manner as I
have seen ants come and go from a particularly busy anthill.
Each time these teams of slaves emerged from the jungle they
struggled under the weight of a stone block some four feet

square, similar if not identical to the stone blocks we observed in the abandoned temple which lies just outside this hut in which we shelter. I watched as the gods . . . for this is how I thought of the seven-foot-tall figures, so noble was their posture and bearing . . . pointed to the spot on the beach where the first stone blocks should be placed. The slaves hurried to do so, and then scurried back into the jungle for still more loads of blocks.

"And so I watched the construction of an entirely new *heiau,* for such it was. I soon recognized the shape . . . the broad steps for sacrifice, the walls for defense. Ah . . . I see in your eyes that you cannot believe such a thing. How could an entire temple be built in the space of half an hour? Thus you may understand my amazement, Miss Stewart, Reverend Haymark, for I stayed hidden behind my boulder and watched this frenzied construction for hour after hour. At one point I marveled that the dawn had not risen to interrupt these titanic labors, but when I removed my watch to check the time—just as I did moments ago before you—only ten minutes had passed from the time I had last checked the hour before descending the cliff. I was sure that the device had failed. Indeed, upon checking the second hand, I found it frozen in place.

"More hours passed. The trees and thickets at the base of the cliff were filled with slaves straining under their burdens. The beach was busy with gods and royal islanders supervising the construction. The torches flickered. The drums beat. The chanting rose above the crash of surf. Hours passed. The *heiau* neared completion. It seemed as if the sun had been eclipsed so that entire days could pass under the cover of darkness. I checked my watch. Twenty-five minutes had passed. I stared for long minutes until the second hand twitched, vibrated, and then surged forward a single second.

"Finally, incredibly, the temple was completed. The gods and chiefs and warriors and their slaves gathered around it. As if on some celestial cue, the wind roared in from the sea at twice its previous ferocity. Torches flickered and died. The scene was now lit by the glow from the unearthly bodies of those present. When I was a child in my small town in Missouri, we would gather lightning bugs on a summer's evening and bring them to our room in a jar. This light was not unlike that glow: pale, greenish, redolent of death.

"What happened next is the wondrous part. It was difficult to see from my place of concealment, but the music ceased, the chanting halted, and the pale forms on the beach arranged themselves according to some hierarchy . . . as if waiting. They did not wait long. Several figures emerged from the sea. The glowing chiefs and gods on the beach made way for them as the figures made their way from the surf to the beach, from the beach to the *heiau,* from the base of the *heiau* to its upper terraces. I say figures because the forms which emerged from the sea were . . . fantastical . . . to say the least. The central figure was in the shape of a man, but even from my distant vantage point I could see that it was far too large to be a man, and far too insubstantial. He . . . it . . . appeared to be formed of . . . well, fog. Sea spray. Cloud. Some insubstantial vapor."

Here the boy, Halemanu, exclaimed, "Pana-ewa!"

"Nonsense," said Reverend Haymark. "Pana-ewa is a myth."

The boy did not even look at the cleric, but spoke to Mr. Clemens in a soft voice. "Pana-ewa has many bodies. *Kino-ohu* is his fog body. Pana-ewa attacked Hi'iaka, Pele's sister, with his fog body."

"Well," said Mr. Clemens, pausing in his tale long enough to strike a Lucifer match and light one of his cigars, "the figure I saw tonight had a body of fog. Swirling fog. I could see the glow of the tall bodies through this swirling fog. And he was not alone. The retinue which accompanied him from the sea included a normal-enough looking man—a native—who wore a sort of cape over his shoulders. By and by, as events proceeded, those on the sand below brought a bleating goat to this man, who lifted it to the fog-shape above . . ."

"Pana-ewa!" breathed Halemanu.

"Yes," said Mr. Clemens, puffing his cigar alight. "Pana-ewa, we will say. This caped fellow lifted the live goat as if in offering to Pana-ewa, and then dropped the cape he was wearing and set the goat on his back, as I have seen shepherds do when carrying one of their flock. Only what happened next . . ." Mr. Clemens stopped and cleared his throat, as if overcome by some emotion.

"What?" I asked, glancing toward the dark window. A small bird had landed there and its fluttering had startled me.

"The goat began bleating more pitifully, terribly . . . and with that frenzied noise there came another sound . . . a cracking and rending, as if of bone and sinew. And then, even from my distant vantage point, I could see that the goat was . . . disappearing."

"Disappearing?" repeated Reverend Haymark. The cleric was still holding the small silver flask which Mr. Clemens had returned to him.

"Disappearing," affirmed Mr. Clemens in a stronger voice. "Being swallowed up by some sort of . . . aperture . . . on the man's back. I could see now that the woven cape had concealed a massive hump where the fellow's spine should be, and on that hump . . . an opening."

"A mouth," said Halemanu softly. "This is Nanaue. He is shark man. He sometimes serves Pana-ewa."

We all three stared at the child. Finally Mr. Clemens said, "There were others in this retinue . . . small men, twisted, gnarled in feature and form . . ."

"*Eepas* and *kapuas*," said Halemanu. "They very treacherous. Very treacherous. Also serve Pana-ewa."

Mr. Clemens removed the cigar from his mouth and stepped closer to the boy, staring down at him thoughtfully. "Another form had emerged from the sea," he said softly. "A dog. A large, black dog that stayed near the right hand of the fog-man."

"Ku," Halemanu said simply.

"Ku," repeated Mr. Clemens and sat down heavily on the dirt floor. He looked at me. "Then, when the goat had been devoured, the chanting ceased. The fog-man raised impossibly long arms and . . . I do not know how to describe this . . . he became . . . something else. I saw a tail. I perceived scales. I remember yellow eyes. The reptile thing still had arms and these remained raised. Then there was a stroke of lightning which blinded me for a moment . . ." Mr. Clemens seemed to notice the cigar in his hand. He returned it to his mouth, frowned, relighted it with a new match, and said, "When I could see again, the gods were gone, the chiefs were gone, the torches were gone, the dog was gone, the strange little gnomes were gone, and the fog-reptile man was gone."

I cleared my throat. "And the *heiau* was gone?"

"No," said Mr. Clemens. "The stone temple was still there. I looked at my watch. According to my own senses, many hours had passed . . . perhaps as much as a day. According to my watch, less than thirty minutes had expired. I came back here."

For a moment the three of us white people seemed to be only an assortment of wide eyes staring at one another. Finally, I said, "What do we do next?"

Halemanu tugged at my sleeve.

"In a moment, child," I said, still looking to the men for guidance. The tugging continued. Vexed, I removed my arm from the boy's grasp and said, "What is it?"

"We go now!"

"We will confer . . ." I began.

The boy shouted, "We go now!"

It was Mr. Clemens who calmed the child with a touch. "Why must we go now?" he asked.

Halemanu pointed to the window. "Birds. Little birds."

I looked over at the black square. The birds had gone. I smiled at the boy's fear of some of God's gentlest creatures.

"Birds be brothers of Pana-ewa!" said the boy, his voice rising again. "Birds gone. Pana-ewa come!"

Eleanor jerked her head and shoulders from the hole despite the pressure of hands on her back and quickly pulled back just as the geyser exploded from the fissure. Soaked through but not struck by the full force of the blast, she wheeled on the man standing next to her. It was Paul Kukali, his sunglasses spattered with droplets.

"God*dammi*t," roared Eleanor, her fists coming up. "What

the *hell* do you think you're doing?" Behind her the geyser roared, peaked, and fell back to nothing.

Paul took off his glasses and gave her a sheepish look. "I am sorry, Dr. Perry . . . I saw you, thought you were in trouble, tried to help you out . . ."

"By *pushing* me?" snapped Eleanor. She realized that her hands were still raised, her fists clenched. Her heart was pounding and she could feel the adrenaline coursing in her. If it had come to hitting Paul Kukali, she would not have tapped uselessly at his chest like some idiot female in the movies. Years ago, Eleanor had been assaulted in Port-au-Prince. It had been a simple mugging— the beating had not been serious and she had not been raped— but the experience had been sufficient to send her to self-defense classes that summer, and she took a refresher course at least once a year. If she had used her fists on Paul, she would have gone for the throat, the bridge of the nose, and several other sensitive areas.

"I was not pushing you, Dr. Perry," Paul said softly. He was wiping his glasses. Water beaded in his curly hair. "I was trying to get your attention. Did you not hear me call your name?"

Did I? thought Eleanor. She had been intent on the glow and movement in the cave. That and the sound of water rushing toward her. She said nothing.

"I am sorry if I startled you," said Paul, setting the glasses back in place. "These lava tube blowholes are dangerous. I was afraid you did not know about the surf coming through."

"I did," Eleanor said tersely. She lowered her hands. *I need his help.* "I'm sorry if I lost my temper. You startled me."

Paul nodded. "I understand. Again, I apologize."

There came a rushing sound and both of them moved away from the blowhole before the geyser spouted again. "Why were you way out here?" asked Eleanor, wringing the hem of her soaked T-shirt as they walked.

Paul smiled. "Actually, I was looking for you. My friend Sheriff Ventura was here to ask some questions of us about the . . . ah . . . the dog. I found Mrs. Stumpf, but we couldn't locate you. A groundskeeper told me that he'd seen a lady jogging on the trail and I came out to see if it was you. I noticed the sneaker prints beyond where the paved trail ended and caught a glimpse of you from the peninsula cliffs.''

Eleanor looked at him for a moment. "I'm sorry I wasn't around."

Paul shrugged. "It doesn't matter. Charlie's probably gone by now. I gathered that it was an informal investigation on his part anyway. We can call him later. Actually, I had another reason for looking you up."

Eleanor waited. They were walking back along the cliff face. She thought of what she had seen in the cave and wondered if Paul knew about it.

"I finally got in touch with my friend—the helicopter pilot," said Paul. "As I guessed, he's busy all day in Maui but could come over about dusk to give us a ride to the volcano."

"Oh," said Eleanor. "Good." She had almost forgotten about the ride to the volcano. She hesitated a second. "Paul . . ."

"Yes?"

"I have a favor to ask . . ." She stopped as if embarrassed.

The art and archaeology curator raised both hands, palms out, and said, "After frightening you like that, I would grant any favor. Name it."

"I would like to visit local *kahuna*," said Eleanor. "Preferably ones involved with Pele."

Paul Kukali stopped walking. His smile had faltered. "*Kahuna?* Priests? Why, Eleanor?"

She stopped and faced him. "I have a strong personal reason. I need to talk to them."

The curator smiled again. "Are you thinking of converting from rationalism?"

Eleanor raised a hand and stopped just short of touching his arm. "Paul, I know it's a big favor on top of the other help you've given me . . . given both Cordie and me . . . but it would mean a lot to me." In the silence, Eleanor watched her own reflection looking back at her from Paul's glasses.

"Why do you think I know *kahuna?*" Paul said at last.

Eleanor chuckled. "I guess I think you know *everybody*. If you can't, you can't. I understand. It was worth asking."

Paul sighed. "There are some . . . they live some miles from

here . . . toward the south where the lava flow is. They may have
been evacuated. When would you want to go?''

Eleanor put her fists on her hips and grinned. ''As soon as I
change clothes?''

Cordie would have kept reading straight through Aunt Kidder's journal if the child's screaming had not interrupted her. The
noise was coming from the beach. The view was partly blocked by
palm trees and a grassy knoll, but Cordie could see a young boy—
perhaps seven—running back and forth on the beach and screaming. There seemed to be no adults around. She vaguely
remembered two children coming by half an hour or more earlier; one of them had been carrying an inflatable raft of the sort
one would lounge on in a swimming pool.

Cordie dropped the journal in her tote bag, hefted the bag
onto her shoulder, and leveraged herself out of the lounge chair.
The child's screaming had not abated, had grown wilder if anything. Cordie moved quickly to the beach.

The boy ran up to her, hands folded together in terror. His
face was red from screaming and streaked with tears. Cordie
looked around once more for parents or a lifeguard, saw no one
else, and gripped the screaming child by his skinny forearms.
''Hey, now,'' she said. ''Calm down, little buddy.''

The child continued to cry. He pointed out toward the glare
of the lagoon. ''My bro . . . bro . . . brother,'' he stuttered through
his sobs. ''I to . . . told him . . . not to paddle out so fa . . . so far.''

Cordie shielded her eyes and squinted into the noon glare.
There was a boy out there on the inflatable pool raft. The kid had
his knees up on the float so the thing was bent almost in two, pillow and bottom end sticking up out of the water. He looked only a
year or so older than his brother and was plainly terrified. Perhaps
he had reason to be—the raft had floated more than a hundred
yards out and seemed to be picking up speed toward the open
ocean.

Cordie looked up and down the beach. Incredibly, there were
no other guests and the lifeguard chair was empty. *Hell of a lawsuit
for someone if the kid drowns,* she thought. She caught a glimpse of

someone behind the counter at the Shipwreck Bar, but the shack was too far away to shout to and the bartender had his back to the beach. Cordie saw the kayak beached near the lifeguard station.

"Go get your parents," Cordie said to the sobbing seven-year-old. "I'll go fetch your brother." To herself, she said, *Shit.* Cordie had never learned how to swim.

The kayak was made out of fiberglass and had a single round hole for its occupant to sit in. Cordie almost did not fit. It was a struggle to shove the little boat off and then clamber in, but she managed. She dropped the double-ended paddle, but it floated and she paddled the kayak over to it with her hands and picked it up. Luckily there was almost no surf today.

The boy had not gone for his parents. He was standing ankle-deep in the water and shouting something else at her. Cordie turned to listen.

"Gregory paddled out there because . . . because . . . because of the *shark*!"

"Shark?" said Cordie, and realized that she was lifting her feet in the kayak. She squinted out toward the raft. It had floated another fifty yards toward the opening of the bay now and high surf *was* breaking out there. "I don't see any shark," she shouted at the crying boy. It was hard to see in the glare, but no fin had been visible. The area where the boys had been swimming was the manta pool, where the winged creatures were drawn in at night by the lights and had become accustomed to feeding in the day. "Maybe it was a manta," said Cordie. "They don't hurt you." She didn't *think* that a manta hurt people.

The crying boy shook his head. "It was a *shark*. Only it didn't have a fin. And it had feet."

Cordie's flesh grew cold despite the 85-degree temperature. "OK," she said, "go get your parents like I said. I'll bring your brother in." She hesitated a second. "Hey!" she called to the running boy. "Throw me that straw bag." For some reason the thought of leaving Aunt Kidder's journal behind bothered her.

The boy wheeled in the sand, picked up the bag, and tossed it out over the water. Cordie had to lunge, but she caught it with two fingers and pulled it in without spilling the contents. She shifted her thighs and crammed the heavy bag down into the cockpit. Then she leaned forward, alternated strokes on the double-bladed oar, and began paddling toward the screaming child.

"You're shitting me," Byron Trumbo said to himself. They were on the seventeenth hole of the north course, almost back to the clubhouse; Hiroshe Sato was winning by five strokes and obviously pleased with himself, when Trumbo looked up to see the giant Hawaiian standing on the edge of the green. The man was shirtless and must have weighed at least five hundred pounds. He was carrying an axe.

"Ahhhh," said Hiroshe Sato, looking up from marking his ball and obviously seeing the apparition. "So."

Trumbo glanced behind him. Bobby Tanaka and Will Bryant were half a fairway back with the second party. It was just Hiroshe, Inazo Ono, and old Matsukawa on the green with Trumbo. The giant Hawaiian passed the axe from hand to hand as a child would a short baton. Trumbo felt his belt under his Hawaiian shirt: the radio was clipped on one side, the 9mm Browning was tucked in the waistband. It had made for an awkward golf game.

"Relax, Hiroshe," said Trumbo, grinning at the other billionaire. "This is a fellow we use to clear shrubs. I had a job for him. You go ahead and putt. I'll just be a moment." Trumbo set a marker down, dropped the ball in his shirt pocket, and confidently walked toward the giant. On the way he unclipped the radio, switched to security frequency, and said, "Fredrickson? Fredrickson?" Only static. "Michaels? Smith? Dunning?" Nothing.

Twenty feet from the giant, Trumbo switched to another frequency. "Will?"

"Yes, boss?"

"Get up here. Bring reinforcements." Trumbo set the radio back on his belt and stepped closer. The giant watched him approach. Trumbo saw that the man wore some sort of necklace or amulet of bone . . . large teeth gleamed in the bright sunlight.

Stopping five feet from the huge Hawaiian, Byron Trumbo said, "You've got to be Jimmy Kahekili."

The giant grunted and shifted the axe to his right hand. Trumbo thought that the man's belly was larger than some cars he'd owned. Rolls and wrinkles of fat hung from his neck, chest, and the inside of his arms.

"So, Jimmy Kahekili," said Trumbo, glancing at his watch, "what do you want? I've got to get back to my friends here."

The huge Hawaiian grunted again, and Trumbo realized that the grunts were syllables, the syllables formed words. "You stole our land," the giant said.

"I paid for this fucking land. And I pay the salaries of your friends and neighbors who work here."

The big man raised the axe to waist height. "You stole all our land. All of the islands. You stole our country."

"Oh," said Trumbo, sighing and letting his right hand go to his hip, only inches away from the grip of the Browning. "You're talking about all that U.S. imperialism shit. All right, we stole your country. So what? That's what countries do, asshole. They steal other people's countries. Besides, I wasn't around when that happened." Trumbo tried reading the Hawaiian's eyes to see if and when the man was going to act, but the man's eyes were hidden by folds of fat.

"You destroyed our fish ponds, *haole*." The grunts came quickly now.

"Fish ponds?" said Trumbo. "Oh, yeah . . . but I saved the petroglyphs."

The Hawaiian grunted. "You have none of the spirit of *malama* the *'aina* . . . the care for the land. You rob and destroy for profit."

Trumbo stared at the larger man a moment and then shrugged. "All right. I won't argue with you. I'm a capitalist . . . an entrepreneur. Robbing and destroying for profit is my thing. So your queen got whacked by the Marines a hundred years ago and now I bulldoze some run-down old fish ponds. What are you going to do . . . chop me and my friends up with your axe?"

Jimmy Kahekili made a rude noise that may have been assent and lifted the axe with both hands.

Trumbo was thinking, *The clip carries nine slugs. I don't think that will be enough.* He wondered how fast a five-hundred-pound behemoth could run. Aloud, he said, "I have a better idea for you."

This time the giant's grunt may have been interrogative. Trumbo took it as such. "Look, Jimmy," he said, half turning and gesturing toward the Japanese waiting forty feet away, "I'm getting out of the hotel business. These guys are the ones you'll be negotiating with in the future. I don't think it will help your little nationalist scheme to chop up the head of their corporation. They might not be as amenable to your ethnic and cultural sensitivities if you send their patriarch home in a bunch of Glad bags."

A softer grunt.

"But I have sympathy for your goals," said Trumbo. "In fact, I'll show you how much sympathy . . . ten thousand dollars' worth."

The folds of fat squinted at Trumbo.

The billionaire held his hand out. "I shit you not. All you have to do is keep your fellow Hawaiian patriots off my neck for another few days . . . a week at the most . . . and the check is yours. Hell, the money is yours today, and I'll make it cash. I trust you."

A grunt. The axe shifted.

"OK?" said Trumbo. "Let's shake on it." He held out his hand. After a moment, the giant extended the huge roll of fat that was his arm. Trumbo's hand disappeared and for a moment the billionaire had the image of his arm being wrenched off his body—*Wouldn't Caitlin just love that?*—but then his hand reappeared again.

Will Bryant came up with Michaels and Smith. The two security men had their hands under their suit jackets. "Ixnay on the unsgay," said Trumbo. "Will, would you accompany Mr. Kahekili here back to the Big Hale and have Mr. Carter give him ten thousand dollars from the incidental cash fund? List it under grounds maintenance."

"Boss?" said Will Bryant.

"You heard me." Trumbo smiled at the giant. "Thank you for dropping by, Jimmy. We'll talk soon."

Trumbo turned his back on the Hawaiian and walked back to the putting green.

* * *

Eleanor returned to her *hale* and switched off the coffeemaker, showered quickly, pulled on cotton slacks and a T-shirt,
and rushed to meet Paul at the Big Hale. Along the way she
glanced to see if Cordie was out and about, but she did not see the
woman on the beach or at the Shipwreck Bar or *lanai*.

In the lobby, she said, "I'd like Cordie Stumpf to come
along."

"Of course," said the curator. He seemed resigned to never
being alone with the history professor.

Eleanor rang Cordie's room but there was no answer. She
peeked into the Whale Watching Lanai, but the restaurant was
empty. The entire resort seemed emptier than usual. Leaving a
message with the desk clerk telling Cordie that she would see her
in the afternoon, Eleanor caught up to Paul between the praying
bronze disciples guarding the entrance.

"I'm afraid we'll have to rent a Jeep," he said. "I have my
Taurus here, but the roads where we're headed are a bit rough."

"I have a Jeep," said Eleanor. She jangled the keys she had
just picked up from the front desk.

"Mrs. Stumpf?" queried Paul as they walked out under the
porte cochere and into the perfume and color of the bougainvillea hedges that lined the road and walkways here.

"Can't find her," said Eleanor. "I guess it's just you and me,
sir."

Paul Kukali smiled.

Eleanor stopped in surprise as they came into the parking
lot. Her Jeep was one of only half a dozen or so vehicles on the
expanse of tarmac. "It looks like the place emptied out overnight."

Settling into the passenger seat of the Jeep, Paul said, "That
was another reason I was looking for you this morning. Mr. Carter
is warning the guests of possible danger with the lava flows."

Eleanor dropped onto the hot seat but waited a second
before turning the key in the ignition. "Lava flows? But aren't they
still miles south of here?"

"Yes, but there is always a problem with toxic gases. And Dr.
Hastings . . . Mr. Trumbo's man at the Volcano Observatory . . .

believes that other flows are moving down this southwest rift but have not reached the surface yet.''

"Lava tubes," said Eleanor.

"Precisely."

Eleanor chewed on her lip as she started the Jeep and drove down the long lane, past the north course, past the gardens and tennis center and rows of bougainvillea. She caught a glimpse of one group on the golf course and a single gardener working, hat shading his face, but other than that, the grounds and tennis courts seemed deserted. Beyond the golf course, the road deteriorated and wound through the desert of high *a'a*. With the blue sky above and the shoulder of Mauna Loa ahead of them, the miserable road and rough lava fields did not seem as threatening as they did when Eleanor and Cordie had arrived at night.

A security man stepped out of the guardhouse and nodded at them as they left. "Someone's still working," said Paul as they turned right onto Highway 11.

"Are people not coming to work?"

Paul's sunglasses turned in her direction. "Some still are. Many aren't."

"Is it the volcano or the weird goings-on at the Mauna Pele?" asked Eleanor. No traffic passed them headed north on the highway as they drove south. She could see the cliffs and peninsula where she had jogged.

"People around here are used to the volcano," said Paul. "It's the weird goings-on they don't care for."

They continued south past Puuhonua O Honaunau, the socalled City of Refuge. Beyond the tiny roadside town of Kealia, the only signs of habitation were one or two shacks along the highway and the narrow roads running east to the villages of Hoopuloa and Milolii. Paul said that both towns had been evacuated because of the lava flow.

Miles before they could see the lava, Eleanor marveled at the amount of smoke and steam rising ahead of them. It was a wall of blue-black smoke and—seemingly directly ahead of them—a tower of white steam that rose fifty thousand feet or more. It was frightening to continue driving toward such a dynamic sky.

There was little warning of the roadblock. One minute the Jeep was humming along at forty-five miles an hour, the wind ruffling Eleanor's short hair, and then they came around another curve and barricades, flares, and two Highway Patrol cars blocked their way two hundred yards ahead. Eleanor slowed and pulled up to where an officer was standing by the first flare.

"Road's closed, ma'am," said the officer. He was Hawaiian but had startling blue eyes. "Lava flow's cut it here and farther east. Best you head back. Oh . . . hello, Paul."

"Eugene," said Paul Kukali. "I'm surprised there aren't more folks down here rubbernecking."

"We had our share." The officer grinned. "Some of the big resort hotels sent down tour buses up until this morning. But there's a warning of gases and more flows back from the way you come, so they've stopped that. Most of the tourists are over on the Hilo side. That and helicopters." As if to punctuate the state trooper's words, a jet copter roared low over the lava fields to their right, swooping out and around the rising column of steam.

"Can I show Ms. Perry here what *pahoehoe* looks like when it's fresh?"

"Sure," said the officer. "Just park over there on the shoulder. Don't get too close. We had a lady from the Mauna Lani tour bus keel over and faint this morning. The heat's pretty bad, still, and the gases are tricky."

Paul nodded. Eleanor parked the car. They walked down the highway past the barricades and state police vehicles.

"This is incredible," said Eleanor. It was. A wall of gray lava covered the highway to a height of eight or ten feet on its way from Mauna Loa to the coast a mile or so east. Smoke still rose from the convoluted gray surface. Where the thick folds of *pahoehoe* reached the asphalt of the highway, the orange glow of active lava could easily be seen, like light from under a doorway. Tiny flakes peeled off the cracking, shifting rope lava and fluttered away on currents of hot air even as Eleanor watched. The entire surface was cracking and shifting as it cooled. Grass near the flow was burned black or actively smoking, and shrubs on both sides of the highway were either burning or standing as charred stubs. Luckily the smoke was blowing south, away from them, but the heat was so intense that they had to stop fifteen or twenty feet from the wall of gray lava. As Eleanor looked, folds and curves of seemingly cooled lava hatched like an egg and the yolk of molten fire flowed out and onto the highway or smoldering grass. Anything the lava touched burst into flame.

"Incredible," she said again, shielding her face from the heat.

"This flow crossed the highway yesterday morning," said Paul. "There were already at least five flows south and east of here cutting the road."

Eleanor peered up the shoulder of the volcano. Most of it was obscured by smoke. "Can they see it coming?"

"Usually. But this particular flow emerged from a lava tube only a couple of miles uphill. It caught the authorities by surprise. That's why they evacuated Milolii and Hoopuloa. They're just not sure what the volcano has in store."

Eleanor looked toward the southwest to where the steam cloud rose. "I wish I could see where this hits the water." Glancing back toward the police, she said, "Does this mean we can't see your friends, the *kahuna*?"

Paul Kukali hesitated. "There might be a way. With a Jeep. Knowing these old men, I don't believe that they'll let the *haole* authorities chase them off their land. But we'll have to cross that." He gestured with his right hand toward the wall of smoke and fire between the highway and the coast.

"Cross that?" Eleanor's voice was high. "You mean the old *a'a*?"

"I mean the new lava flow. This first one, at least."

"How can we cross that?" She stepped back as another gray egg hatched out of a blast furnace.

Paul shrugged. "With the Jeep we can get to the lava flow and decide if we can. It's the only way we can see the *kahuna* you wanted to talk to. It's up to you."

Eleanor looked at the curator a moment. Heat waves rippled between them. If he wanted to dissuade her without arguing, this was a clever way. "Let's do it," she said.

They hurried back to the Jeep.

* * *

Cordie was halfway to the boy on the raft when she saw the shape in the water. It was nearer to the terrified child than to her and it swam lazily about fifteen feet under the surface. It was white. Even from this distance, Cordie could see the huge mouth and the rows of sharp teeth. The kid on the beach had been right; it was a shark.

Water spattered her face and forearms as she paddled furiously. Cordie had got the rhythm of it now, feeling the fiberglass kayak slicing through the water as she shifted the stroke from left to right, left to right. Muscles in her back protested at the exertion and her forearms were aching. Cordie felt the sharp lines of pain in her lower abdomen that had been pulling tighter since the surgery. She ignored that pain as she had for weeks. Leaning forward over the streamlined hull, feeling her breasts pressing against the fiberglass, Cordie paddled harder.

"Look out!" screamed the boy as she drew within thirty feet. "The shark!" The child almost pitched off the jackknifed raft as he pointed.

"Careful!" cried Cordie as she let up on the frenzied paddling. She was out of breath. The kayak slid forward over slow swells as she caught her breath. She could feel the current that had pulled the boy so far out. If she let the kayak drift now, the tide or current or whatever it was would pull her out with the boy, both kayak and raft reaching the high waves breaking across the coral reef some thirty yards farther out. She could hear that surf now as a series of explosions; the spray drifted across the quieter water of the lagoon. When she looked back over her sunburned shoulder, the beach of the Mauna Pele seemed impossibly distant. "Careful," she cried again, voice more in control this time. "Don't fall off."

The raft had lost almost half of its air and the boy was driving out more of it in his wild attempt to keep his feet and legs out of the water. This child may have been a year or two older than his brother on the beach, but he was slim and pale with a sunken chest and a few freckles on his back. His short hair stood up in wet spikes. Now he pointed to the water again between the kayak and the raft. "It's back!"

Cordie had to lean out to see the thing. It was deeper now, perhaps twenty-five feet beneath the surface, but the water was clear. The shark teeth smiled at her from its open maw. But beyond the unmistakable mouth, the creature seemed deformed, twisted. Instead of the aerodynamically perfect shark's body with the powerful, bifurcated tail, this pale form seemed to have swellings and protuberances and no fins at all.

Like the back of a human with a shark's jaw where the top of the spine should be.

"Hang on to the raft!" called Cordie. "Don't move. I'm coming alongside."

"No!" screamed the child, obviously terrified at the thought of losing his precarious balance.

"I won't touch you till you're ready," called Cordie. The sunlight danced on the water and made her squint. She held up one hand to shield her eyes. The ocean swells were taller and broader here—one minute she would be three feet higher than the boy and the raft, another second several feet below him—but this was nothing compared to the violence of surf toward which they drifted. "Hang on," she added, stroking easily with the paddles. She wasn't sure how she would get him aboard when she got there . . . there was room for only one person in the kayak's little cockpit . . . but his raft was losing air fast.

"Look out!" the boy screamed again at the same instant that something hit the bottom of the kayak with tremendous force.

The light went blue. Sound suddenly seemed both amplified and muffled. Cordie felt the shock of water against her face and eyes and she realized that she had not had time to get a deep breath of air before the kayak had capsized. She knew at once that something had capsized her—she had seen a hundred outdoors documentaries on cable where some hunk in his twenties flipped his kayak while paddling down some wild rapids—only in the TV shows, the guy always flipped the little boat right side up again within seconds. Cordie struggled, but stayed upside down. Bubbles rose around her. The full weight of the kayak seemed to hold her down, keep her inverted. Twist as she might, she could not flip the boat right side up or get her head moving toward the surface four feet above her.

Cordie felt the last of her breath failing, saw spots in front of her eyes mixing with the cascade of silvery bubbles, and tried to pull her way out of the circular cockpit. She could not swim and knew that the water was deep here, but if she could get out and grab the hull of the kayak, she might be able to use it as a float, kick her way over to the boy.

Aunt Kidder's diary. The thought that it would fall out when she pulled herself free made the panic worse. She felt her heart pounding. Her chest ached with the urge to expel her breath and try to breathe in water.

Cordie stayed with the kayak and tried one last time to right herself, swinging her body to the left toward the silver ceiling of the surface.

She bobbed back and hung upside down. Something large and white swam by just beyond her focus.

With the last bit of air in her lungs, Cordie leaned forward as she had when she was paddling, set her chest against the fiberglass of the inverted kayak, grabbed the hull of the thing as if it were some sort of recalcitrant hoopskirt, and tugged with every ounce of her upper-body strength.

The kayak righted itself and Cordie choked in air, coughing seawater and retching, still leaning forward and holding the bobbing little boat upright by the force of her will.

The child was still screaming to her left. Cordie raised a hand to rub water out of her eyes and saw the inflatable raft sinking, the child pointing and shouting.

Hands came out of the water on either side of the kayak and seized the boat, rocking it. Cordie threw her arms out in a reflex action, trying to balance. The strong, brown hands twisted and the kayak flipped over to the right again, Cordie hitting the water hard.

She did not go under this time. Her arms and hands still splayed, she pushed off the water and righted the kayak. The boy was in the water up to his chest now, with only the front and back of the raft still inflated and pressed against him like leaking water wings. "Behind you!" he screamed and something hit the kayak hard.

Cordie heard a screech of rending fiberglass and the kayak

248 DAN SIMMONS

spun almost completely around. A white form split the water and dove again. Cordie could see the splintered hull, just above the waterline, where sharp teeth had taken an eighteen-inch bite out of her boat. The shark form circled the screaming boy once, brushed against his feet, and came hurtling back toward Cordie.

Cordie had trouble getting her arm down between her thighs and for a moment she thought the tote bag was gone, but then she found it and tugged it closer. She heard the water parting before and behind the attacking shark-thing just as she fumbled out the book, tossed it back in, felt the familiar heft of her ex-husband's long-barreled .38.

Teeth scraped along the side of the hull, sending long fiberglass splinters peeling back, and Cordie almost capsized again, but she flung her arm out—almost lost the pistol in that hand—kept her fingers on it, kept the weapon from submerging as she rocked back the other way, and then she was aiming the revolver with both stubby hands as the white form lunged at the boy's sunken raft. The child was treading water now and crying without sound.

Cordie fired four times, ceasing fire when the thing came too close to the boy. The shark form seemed to dive and for a sickening instant Cordie waited for the boy's body to be jerked under the water, pulled deep. Instead, the shark-thing disappeared beyond the sunken raft and the boy was still crying, still treading water.

"Swim!" screamed Cordie. "Here! Now! Do it!"

The boy swam. Water flew up from his paddling hands and feet, but he seemed to be making no progress. Cordie looked around for the missing kayak paddle, could not see it, realized that she could not use it with the revolver in her hand, and used her left hand to paddle the damaged kayak toward the boy.

There. The white form was hurtling through the water toward them from beyond the raft. There was a scream of escaping air as shark teeth bit through the raft and then the white form was hurtling the last twenty feet. Beyond the child's flashing feet, Cordie saw the open maw, blackness, triangular white teeth, white skin, arms, black hair.

She raised the pistol, steadied it as much as her pounding heart and the bobbing kayak would allow, and fired the last two bullets almost between the boy's kicking feet. She *heard* at least one of the slugs hit home—a flat, sickening sound, like a mallet striking dead flesh—and then the shark-thing dove deep.

The boy would have swum full tilt into the side of her kayak, probably knocking himself out, if Cordie had not reached out with her left arm and lifted him bodily from the water, depositing him across the hull in front of her like a deer on a fender.

"Straddle it!" she ordered. She dropped the empty pistol into her tote bag, looked around one last time for the kayak paddle, saw it floating with the current fifteen yards out toward the crashing breakers, thought, *Fuck it,* and began turning the boat around with her hands scooping water.

"Help me paddle," she said to the boy. He was straddling the kayak in front of her like a pale-legged frog, careful to keep his arms and legs out of the water.

"But the thing in the water will . . ."

"Help me paddle or I'll throw you back in," Cordie said in a totally flat, totally believable voice.

The boy began paddling and kicking with a will. With all six limbs working, they began making headway against the riptide or whatever it was.

The trip back to the beach must have taken ten minutes. For Cordie it was an eternity. She thought of Sam Clemens and his stopped watch and knew that if she had a watch that measured terror, days would have passed. Both she and the blubbering child kept checking over their shoulders, glancing from left to right, waiting for the hands or head or shark maw to explode out of the water right next to them.

There was no sign of the thing. They reached the shallows. "Help me pull this thing out . . ." began Cordie, but the boy leapt off the kayak and seemed to run across the surface of the last ten feet of water before galloping up the beach to his waiting parents and brother. The parents were blond and angry. They began to shout at the child even before he wrapped his arms around his mother's waist. The younger brother was smiling and smirking.

Cordie was sure that if she tried to get out of the damned kayak while it was still in the water, the shark-thing would slash in from the shallows, seize her, and drag her back out. "Hey, could you help me with . . ." she called to the family. They were walking away, their backs to her, the father and mother shouting and slapping at the wailing child.

"You're welcome," said Cordie. She took a breath, spilled the kayak over on its right, and flailed her way out of the tight cockpit.

Nothing attacked. She found sand under her feet, stood up, and righted the little boat before any more water slopped in it. She quickly dragged the thing up on the sand a healthy twenty feet from the water and then plopped down to inspect it.

Two jagged rents ran five feet up the left side of the hull and parallel splinters of fiberglass peeled back like wood shavings. Halfway to the bow, a section of the outer hull was bitten away with only a plastic inner liner remaining to keep the ocean out. It looked to Cordie like a bite taken out of a sandwich . . . if the biter's mouth had been three feet wide.

A shadow fell across her and Cordie jumped before realizing that it was just a lifeguard standing over her. He was one of those hunky twenty-five-year-old Adonis types with a perfect, all-over tan and sun-bleached hair and rippled stomach muscles above his orange swim trunks. He gaped at her and said, "What the hell did you do to our kayak?"

Cordie rose slowly, pivoted on one leg, and put the entire weight of her body behind the punch. She caught him high in his perfect, rippled stomach, just below the solar plexus. The hunk made a noise very similar to the sound she had just heard of the wind rushing out of the deflating raft and then he went down like a tossed-aside log.

"Why aren't you guys ever around when we need you?" asked Cordie. She pulled her tote bag out of the kayak, checked to make sure the pistol was in it, opened the journal and was infinitely relieved to see that somehow none of the pages had gotten wet, and carried the bag and book under the swaying palms to the Shipwreck Bar.

The bartender was Hawaiian and overweight and her age. He leaned on the counter and grinned at her as she took a stool. "Hey, Ernie," said Cordie. "Four Pele's Fires. Make them doubles. And remember that they're on the house . . . Mr. Trumbo's orders. And pour something for yourself."

When the drinks came, Cordie began sipping through a long straw as she carefully, almost reverently, opened Aunt Kidder's journal and began reading where she had left off.

SEVENTEEN

O Kamapua'a
You are the one with the rising bristles.
O Rooter! O Wallower in ponds!
O remarkable fish of the sea!
O youth divine!
—ancient chant to Kamapua'a the hog-god
who also changes into the fish
Humuhumu-nukunuku-a-pua'a

June 18, 1866, In an unnamed village along the Kona
Coast—

Even though the storm had passed, it seemed pure folly to
abandon our dry hut and circle of candle flame to go out into the
night on the advice of an injured heathen child who insisted that
two harmless birds had been the brothers and spies of the
demon-god Pana-ewa. Nonetheless, we left.

We discussed this for long minutes, both Reverend Haymark
and Mr. Clemens becoming more agitated as the discussion
progressed. Our cleric dismissed the child's statement as pure
nonsense. Our correspondent argued that the night had been
full of mystery and the boy's fears were no more nonsensical
than half the things we had seen since sundown. I held my
counsel.

Finally, both men turned to me. Reverend Haymark said,
"Miss Stewart, would you please bring this . . . this . . . literary
person . . . to his senses."

Mr. Clemens snorted and said, "Miss Stewart, if we are a
democracy . . . and I trust our Reverend Haymark still believes in

democracy . . . it seems that you hold the deciding vote to dispose of as you will."

I waited a second in silence. Halemanu watched me with terrified eyes. The two men watched me with varying degrees of clerical vexation and literary amusement. Finally, I said, "We shall go. Now. Tonight."

"But, Miss Stewart, certainly . . ." expostulated Reverend Haymark, his florid face growing even redder in the flickering candlelight.

"I cast my vote for leaving," I said, cutting off the protests with the decisiveness of my tone, "not because of fear of some Sandwich Island bogeyman, but because we have an injured child who needs assistance and . . . whatever else Mr. Clemens saw tonight . . . we are on heathen holy ground—or I should say, unholy ground—with marchers afoot who mean us no good."

Reverend Haymark paused in mid-expostulation to consider my argument.

"The boy says that he knows the way to the village only a mile or so north and east of here," I said. "It is the village his uncle's party had been attempting to reach. The child has relatives there and the so-called *Pele kahuna* woman may know folk medicine that could help him. If I do indeed cast the deciding vote, I vote that we embark for this village post-haste."

"Here, here," said Mr. Clemens.

I frowned at him as I gathered my few belongings. "I repeat that I do not fear any male," I said. "Much less a godless male made of fog."

Mr. Clemens colored and bit down on his cold cigar.

We left quickly but with no panic. The horses still showed the terror they had evidenced earlier when the Marchers of the Night were near, and it took both men to help me saddle my usually docile *lio*. Mr. Clemens set the boy on the saddle in front of him and the child seemed to be riding comfortably enough in spite of his head wound.

I confess that I all but held my breath as we clopped down the muddy lane between those evil stone walls. I half-expected some of the gods or demons or dead warrior chiefs from Mr.

Clemens's tale to leap out at us from hiding. It was dark enough for entire nations of heathen cannibals to be lurking behind those blood-soaked, ancient stones.

Nothing leaped at us. Halemanu pointed out a faint trail that ran east from the path we had been following north, and in the starless dark we proceeded up the volcanic slopes once again—Mr. Clemens and the child leading, my fidgety Leo following close to the tail of Mr. Clemens's horse, and the Reverend Haymark swaying along behind. I found myself checking over my shoulder repeatedly to make sure that the cleric remained behind us; that nothing scaly or shark-mouthed had plucked him from his horse and was even then leaning toward me. It was dark, but I could make out the minister's portly shape and clearly hear his asthmatic sighs.

After a while the stars came out in their tropical glory, and even by their dim light I could make out the shrubs and flowers that dotted the volcanic landscape around us: *ohias* and *ohelos* (a species of whortleberry), Sadlerias, polypodiums, silver grass, and a great variety of bulbous plants bearing clusters of berries that seemed to glow a necrotic blue in the starlight. There were various varieties of palm trees here—although no coconut palms—and a profusion of shrubs, fern trees, candlenut and breadfruit trees, but increasingly as we climbed, this floral vegetation gave way to at first subtle and then dominant flows and beds of the ropey lava called *pahoehoe*. We progressed slowly, the boy Halemanu seeming to rouse himself from a half-slumber to point the way, and our horses picking their way over the shelves and terraces of shrub-littered basalt with great care.

Once, about halfway to our goal, we all stopped and listened as there was a rhythmic noise some distance behind, as of a great party of men chanting under their breath, or perhaps the cadence of the surf—although we were far inland now.

"The Marchers?" whispered Mr. Clemens, but the boy did not answer and the rest of us could not.

We spurred our horses to less careful progress after this.

It was almost dawn when we arrived in the village—although

"village" is too grand a word for the half dozen ramshackle huts we encountered in the dark. There were no lights. No dogs barked to challenge our intrusion. For a moment we sat there on our horses, convinced that whatever had devoured the Reverend Whister's party had made short shrift of Halemanu's relatives in this village. But then the boy called out in that liquid torrent of syllables that was Hawaiian, and I could make out the words *wahine haole*, which was, of course, "white woman," and *wai lio*, which translated to "water for horse" in an interrogative way, and *tutu*, which I later learned meant "grandmother," and *Ka huaka'i o ka Po*, which I remembered meant "Marchers of the Night."

Suddenly there were a dozen shadows around us and hands pulled at us. For a moment I felt quite without volition, and I allowed these eager but seemingly not hostile hands to pull me off Leo, set me on my feet, and touch me with naive curiosity. I could hear Mr. Clemens and Reverend Haymark protesting, but they also were off their horses.

Halemanu's soft voice spoke again, one of the shadows near me replied in an old man's voice, and without further ado we were hustled through hanging fronds into the closest and largest of the huts.

The village obviously was not deserted. Eight old men, three younger women, and a *tutu*, or granny lady, as old as time took their places sitting in the long hut, their faces and wrinkled bodies now visible in the dimmest of lights from two tiny lamps of candlenut oil. They had pulled us down and now we sat with them, Mr. Clemens across the rough circle from me, Reverend Haymark near the door, and the weary child next to the crone at the darkest end of the hut. The old man next to Reverend Haymark spoke again. His toothless utterings may not have been understandable even if he had spoken in English, but Halemanu translated easily. "Grandfather asks why you are traveling on this bad night."

Mr. Clemens answered for us. "Tell him that we were traveling to the Reverend Whister's church and village."

The old man made more toothless noises in Hawaiian.

"Grandfather says that the church and village are killed. No one remains alive there now. It is a bad place. *Kapu*." Halemanu seemed older in his new role as translator.

Reverend Haymark said, "Ask Grandfather how it is that the minister and the people of the village were killed."

Halemanu spoke slowly, his eyes closed to the pain from his wound. Another old man in the circle barked an answer.

"My other Grandfather says that he and the other *kahuna* along this coast prayed them to death," said Halemanu without emotion.

"Prayed them to death?" repeated our cleric with obvious distaste.

"Yes," said Halemanu. "But the *haole* did not die when they were prayed to death, they only became sick. Which is why Grandfathers who were the strongest *kahuna* made the old chants and opened the door to the Underworld so that the *eepas* and *kapuas* and *mokos* and Pana-ewa himself could be loosed to rid us of the *haole* holy men."

"Rid us?" repeated Mr. Clemens. I felt my own heartbeat accelerate at the child's choice of words.

"Yes," said Halemanu and opened his eyes. "The Grandfathers ordered my uncle and the other warriors to fetch you back here for sacrifice. As the youngest of the *kahuna*, I was allowed to go. It was just bad fortune that we encountered the *Ka huaka'i o ka Po* on our short journey. They spared me because I carry the name of the most famous of the *aumakua* who serve Pana-ewa."

Mr. Clemens and Reverend Haymark attempted to leap to their feet then, but the old man near the door made a gesture with his little finger and the two strong men fell as if great weights had been set on their backs. Struggle as they might, they could not rise. I did not try.

"Halemanu," I began.

"Silence, woman," said the child in an imperious voice that sounded much deeper than any child's voice should.

The old men began to chant. The sound seemed to enter my body like a drug, the interior of the hut began to waver in the candlenut light, and my eyelids felt suddenly heavy. I could see Mr. Clemens and Reverend Haymark struggling to fight the chant and having no more luck than I.

At that moment I turned to look at Halemanu. The boy's body seemed to ripple, as a distant mirage does on a desert in midday, and then the flesh seemed to flow and shift, softening and pouring away like dark water down an invisible drain.

Fog remained. Fog shifted and flowed. Fog rose and took on the shape and silhouette of a man, albeit a man of impossible height, the form's head brushing the ceiling of the hut some ten feet above us. I watched the fog swirl in the candlenut light and when the voice came, it came out of the fog with the echo of a great beast roaring from a long tunnel.

"And now I claim what is mine! *Kapu o moe, haole kanaka!*"

The fog in the shape of a man lunged forward into our midst.

Eleanor turned the Jeep back up Highway 11 and drove a mile or so to the turnoff to Milolii and Hoopuloa. A police barricade stood astride the narrow access road.

"Don't go around it here," said Paul Kukali. "The *a'a* will tear your tires to shreds." He got out and moved the barricade. Eleanor drove forward and the curator replaced the heavy sawhorse.

The road was very narrow, very winding, and surrounded by the same desolate lava fields that separated the Mauna Pele from the highway. Eleanor drove slowly, half expecting the authorities to come around the next bend and order them back. There was no other traffic.

Milolii seemed to be a Hawaiian fishing village frozen in time. The few houses looked empty and quiet, and the only public establishment, a general store, had a large, police evacuation notice tacked to its door. The sign warned of the penalties of looting. The wind had shifted and smoke now drifted between the coconut palms and over the little houses with their galvanized-steel roofs. Outrigger canoes sat on a shady beach. Shafts of sunlight cut through the drifting smoke and made the scene look beautiful beyond words to Eleanor.

"Turn up that road that runs parallel to the beach," said Paul Kukali.

The "road" was a barely distinguishable pair of wheel ruts that ran through the tropical foliage and then across fields of ferns.

"The people here actually fish," said Paul. "One of the last real fishing villages in Hawaii. But they earn extra money by growing anthuriums and ferns. They had to truck in this soil. You can see that the lava fields don't support much."

Eleanor could see. The rude trail had left the rich fields and now bounced across crushed rock on the edge of the black-lava flows that stretched in all directions. Spray rose from where the ocean crashed into rocks a hundred yards to their right. Less than a mile ahead, the steam from the lava flow continued to climb into the stratosphere. The smoke was thicker now, billowing across the black basalt like tendrils of fog. Eleanor continued driving south parallel to the coast, careful not to slash tires on the *a'a* that edged the rutted path. After some minutes, when the smoke was almost too thick to continue, Paul said, "Stop."

They both got out of the Jeep and walked forward. Here was the same lava flow they had seen covering the highway, but it seemed twice as tall, covering the old *a'a* and *pahoehoe* as it did. Eleanor looked up at a wall of cracking, flaking, hissing, freshly congealed lava that rose at least a dozen feet above the ground and disappeared to the east and west in the smoke. Every shrub and small tree within thirty or forty feet of the flow had either burned away or was in the process of burning now. The grass smoldered. Fresh lava extruded from half a dozen low crevices and flowed onto the soil, igniting more grass. Eleanor thought it smelled like fall in the Midwest when she was a child and it had been legal to burn leaves. But beneath the pleasant, burning-leaves smell, something stank of sulfur and other noxious gases.

"I guess we don't drive across that," said Eleanor.

Paul stepped back and covered his mouth and nose with a red bandana. His eyes were watering. "The gentlemen you wanted to see live about a quarter of a mile beyond here."

Eleanor squinted at him. "And you think they're still here? With all this going on?"

Paul shrugged. "They're stubborn."

"So am I," said Eleanor. She walked up and down the edge of the flow, trying to find a section where the orange glow and heat were less noticeable. Finally she stepped close, shielded her face from the heat, and lifted her foot to a low bubble of gray rock. Chips flaked off the cooling lava and fluttered by her even as she set her foot down.

It was very hot. Eleanor wished she'd worn something other than her sneakers. But the soles did not melt and the crust of lava did not crack as she set her weight on the molded terrace of new stone. She stepped up. "I'm going to try to cross," she said, taking care to step on a firm ridge two feet higher.

Paul Kukali made a noise, but followed in her footsteps.

Eleanor crossed the lava flow slowly, stepping as carefully as if she were crossing a rushing stream on slippery rocks. Everywhere around her there were fissures through which the true heat of the still-molten rock below blasted at her. Smoke, steam, and sulfurous gases billowed from cracks and crevices, mixing with the general pall of smoke which had now obliterated the sun. She could feel the soles and sides of her sneakers softening, so she moved as quickly as she could, never resting on a hot spot longer than she had to. Eleanor tried not to think of what would happen if she broke through.

"Somewhere under here," said Paul Kukali about midway across the two hundred feet or so of lava, "the real lava is flowing like a river. The crust is thinnest above that flow."

"Thanks," said Eleanor, pausing to cough. "I was trying not to think of that." She took another step. To their right, the hissing and popping and sizzling of the lava meeting the cold ocean was like a radio picking up nothing but static turned to full volume.

Once the terrace did crack underfoot like rotten ice, and Eleanor had to not only draw her foot back in a flash but actually leap to a higher fold of gray rock five feet away to escape the blast of heat and lava that extruded. She stood shaking for a moment before going on. She had always appreciated Aunt Kidder and her adventures in wild parts of the world 130 years earlier, but now she had a visceral sense of the woman's courage in crossing the crust of Kilauea when the volcano was in eruption. *Perhaps*, she thought,

*it is more than spinsterhood that is handed down to each generation of
those of us following Aunt Kidder. Perhaps it's a gene for insanity.* She
took another step.

The fires on the north side of the flow made getting off more
difficult, but eventually she found a place where she could jump
from a terrace three feet above the smoldering grass. Eleanor
moved away from the heat and stood on solid rock for a moment,
feeling the slight shaking in her legs but also feeling the sense of
near levitation that adrenaline sometimes brings.

Paul came up to her. His face was streaked with soot from the
smoke—as Eleanor realized her own must be—and he was frowning. "Gosh," he said, "and we get to go back across it. I hope it
doesn't flow over your Jeep while we're visiting."

Eleanor took a breath. She probably should have parked farther from the flow. She was not yet volcano-savvy. *But I'm learning,*
she thought. They walked on through the wilderness of smoke
and *a'a,* following the tire ruts that had resumed on this side of the
flow.

The two old *kahuna* were standing outside their ancient Airstream trailer. They were both men, both Hawaiian, both in their
seventies . . . at least . . . and both wore jeans, faded western shirts
with snap pockets, and battered cowboy boots. The similarities in
their looks, expressions, and stances made Eleanor think that they
were twins.

"*Aloha,*" said the one who was smoking a cigarette—an incon-
gruous sight in the midst of all the billowing smoke that still concealed the sky, the ocean, and everything beyond a fifty-foot radius
from the trailer. "We have been waiting for you," he said, tossing
the cigarette down and grinding it under his boot. "Come inside
out of the bad air."

The trailer was not large and it smelled of bacon and grease.
The four squeezed into a breakfast booth, Eleanor and Paul on
one side, the two *kahuna* on the other. An old woman with a placid
gaze and white hair sat in the shadows on a sprung sofa at the
other end of the trailer. Eleanor nodded in the woman's direction, but the men—including Paul—ignored her.

Paul made introductions. "Eleanor, these are my great-uncles, Leonard and Leopold Kamakaiwi. *Kapuna,* this is Dr. Eleanor Perry. She wishes to speak to you.''

Leopold, the one sitting on the outside of the booth, folded his hands on the Formica table between them and grinned at her. A few teeth were missing, but the rest were very white. ''A doctor,'' he said, nodding as if pleased. ''It is good that you have come. I have a pain in my shoulder that I would like to have you make go away.''

''I'm not that kind of . . .'' began Eleanor, and stopped, realizing that he was putting her on. She returned his smile. ''You'll have to take your shirt off.''

The old man held up two hands as if shocked by her suggestion. ''No, no! *Mahalo nui,* but I never take my shirt off in front of a beautiful *wahine* until after a few drinks.'' He reached up to a nearby shelf and pulled down a bottle and four dusty glasses.

Leonard Kamakaiwi did not grin as he said dourly, ''Paul, is this your new *ipo?* Have you been *wela kahao?*''

Paul Kukali sighed. ''No, *Kapuna.* Dr. Perry is a guest at the resort.'' To Eleanor he said, '' *Kapuna* means 'grandparent' or 'old one,' but it also means 'those with wisdom.' Sometimes it is used loosely.''

Leopold cackled. ''Let me pour some wisdom,'' he said, and filled their glasses with a dark liquid.

They clicked glasses and drank. The fumes hit Eleanor at about the same time that the alcohol burned a path down her esophagus and set fire to her belly. She thought that it tasted like raw kerosene. ''What is it?'' she asked when she could speak again.

''Okolehau,'' chuckled Leopold. ''It means 'iron bottom.' It is made from the *ti* root. We used to brew it in the iron blubber pots. That is where the *hau*—'iron'—part of the name comes from.''

''Well, it certainly knocked me on my *okole,*'' said Eleanor, taking another drink.

Even dour Leonard joined in the laughter.

Leopold poured more in her glass and said, ''What do you want, Dr. Eleanor Perry?''

Eleanor took a breath and decided to play all of her cards. ''Paul tells me that you are *kahuna.*''

The two old men looked at her without expression. Eleanor took their silence as assent. "In which case," she went on, "I am curious whether you are *kahuna ana'ana* or *kahuna lapa'au.*" The former was a sorcerer who could command the powers of black magic. The latter was a priest who could heal people both physically and spiritually.

"Why?" said Leopold, showing his white teeth again. "Do you want someone prayed to death?"

Leonard made a hand motion dismissing his twin. "There are *kahuna* who share both powers," he said softly.

Eleanor nodded slowly. "Or twins who share them?" she asked.

The old men said nothing.

"It is none of my business . . ." she began.

"True, true," said Leopold Kamakaiwi with a smile. He sipped *okolehau.*

"It is none of my business," she went on, "but I think that you are trying to pray the Mauna Pele resort to death. I think that you opened up the Underworld of Milu and allowed the old demons to escape. I think that you have brought forth Pana-ewa and Nan-aue and Ku and others. I think that people are dying and you need to stop it." Eleanor stopped, feeling her heart pounding. She was very aware at that moment that she was miles from anywhere, alone with three men—all three of whom she suspected of being *kahuna*—and in the midst of raging lava flows. It was one of the reasons she had left word at the desk for Cordie about where she was going and with whom.

In the long silence that followed her speech, the hiss and crackle of the lava flow striking the ocean a quarter of a mile away was easily heard. Eleanor glanced at the grimy window above the table and saw smoke drifting by. The illusion was that they were flying through clouds. For all she knew, they might be flying through clouds at that moment, the *kahuna* taking her somewhere high on the volcano for sacrifice. *Steady, Eleanor,* she thought to herself. *Get a grip.*

Finally Leonard said, "We did not mean for people to die. You must believe that."

Leopold shrugged and poured more iron bottom. "To tell the truth, we did not think that the old magic would work."

Paul Kukali touched her arm. "It was not just Uncle Leonard and Uncle Leopold," he said. "*Kahuna* from all over the islands made the old chants on the same day. It was my fault. I told them that there was no recourse after the courts refused to save the fish ponds and the petroglyph fields. My uncles showed me that there *was* a recourse."

Leonard shook his head. "It was wrong. I said it was wrong. The *mokos* were better left buried. The gods were better left unsummoned." He took a long drink.

Leonard is the kahuna lapa'au, *she realized with a shock. The medical sorcerer. It is happy Leopold who commands the dark forces.*

As if reading her mind, Leopold grinned at her.

"Can't you stop it?" she said.

"No," both men said at once. Leonard went on. "All of the *kahuna* have tried for months. None wanted people to die. But the old chants worked to free the Underworld beings. We do not know enough to close the opening, to send them back to the darkness."

"Pele . . ." began Eleanor.

Leopold made a sweeping motion with his hand. "Pele is angry at us . . ." He gestured again, this time toward the smoke at the window. "But she does not listen."

"She has not listened for generations," Leonard said morosely. "We have lost the old ways. We have lost our pride. We do not deserve to have her listen to us."

Eleanor leaned forward. "Aren't there *Pele kahuna*? A secret order of women priests who intercede with Pele for you?"

Leopold squinted at her. "How do you know all these things, *haole*?"

"She reads," said Paul Kukali with a hint of irony.

Eleanor glanced at the curator and then looked back to the twins. "Am I wrong?"

"You are wrong," Leonard said flatly. "A hundred years ago there were *Pele kahuna*. Fifty years ago there were *Pele kahuna*. But they are all gone now. The women all died without passing on their secrets. There is no one."

"No one?" echoed Eleanor, feeling something like nausea rising in her. All her clever plan had just wilted away. She looked at the old woman on the sofa as if seeking help, but the woman's gaze remained so flat and inexpressive that Eleanor thought she might be blind.

"No one but Molly Kewalu," said Paul.

Leopold snorted. "Molly Kewalu is *pupule*," he said. "Crazy. Nuts."

"And she speaks to no one," said Leonard.

Leopold made the sweeping gesture again. "She lives high on the volcano where there is no road. It would take days to hike to her. The lava has probably claimed her already."

"How does she live up there?" asked Eleanor. "You can't grow anything. What does she eat?"

"The women keep her alive," said Leopold, and snorted again. "The women in the villages still think that she has *mana* and they have brought her food *manauahi*—for free—for fifty, sixty years. But she is just a crazy old woman. *Pupule*."

Eleanor looked at Paul but the curator shook his head. "Molly Kewalu claims she talks to Pele," he said, "but so do half the old Hawaiian women in the Alzheimer's wing of the hospital in Hilo."

"Still . . ." began Eleanor.

Paul made the same dismissive motion his uncle had used. "Eleanor, do you know the myth about not taking any rocks from the volcano so as not to offend Madame Pele?"

"Of course," said Eleanor. "It's the one thing about Madame Pele that every tourist knows. The goddess doesn't like her lava stolen. It's bad luck to take a stone, right?"

"Right," said Paul. "Every year the rangers at Volcanoes National Park receive hundreds of rocks in the mail. Most are from the mainland, but they come from all over the world . . . especially from Japan these days. Tourists pilfered them and now they're sending them back, complete with notes telling of the bad luck they've had since the theft. Four times a year the rangers have to take the rocks back to the volcano and leave them with offerings . . . usually a bottle of gin . . . to placate Pele. Eleanor, they get *thousands* of these guiltily returned lava rocks. Four times a year it's a procession of dump trucks filled with lava rocks."

"So?" said Eleanor.

"So there was no such myth, no such taboo," said Paul.

"No *kapu*," said Leopold.

"I traced the so-called legend back in one of my articles," continued Paul Kukali. "This 'ancient taboo' of not stealing volcanic rocks actually began in the 1950s . . . it was started by the driver of a tour bus who got tired of cleaning the lava dust out of his vehicle each time the tourists got off with their damned rocks."

Eleanor laughed easily, feeling the *okolehau* burn in her. "Is that true?"

"Yes," said Paul Kukali.

Eleanor made the same dismissive gesture that the men had been using. "So what does it have to do with Molly Kewalu?"

"Same bogus legend," he said. "She used to rave about being on a first-name basis with Pele, but she's just a crazy old lady hiding up there where no one can catch her and put her away."

"Hiding where?" asked Eleanor.

"In the empty region," said Leonard. "Ka'u. In a cave somewhere in the area of the ridge that the old people used to call Ka-hau-komo because there used to be two *hau* trees growing there where no trees can grow."

"*Hau*," said Eleanor. "Iron. As in ironwood."

Leonard grunted. "Molly Kewalu's cave is somewhere near the big stone called Hopoe by the old ones," he said. "For hundreds of years the stone was so perfectly balanced that the wind would move it. Our ancestors named it after Hopoe, the famed dancer from Puna who taught Hi'iaka, Pele's youngest sister, how to dance." He grunted again. "The stone fell over when Pele awoke and showed her wrath in 1866."

Eleanor touched the old men's hands, each in turn. They looked up from their drinks. "You released these spirits with your chants," she said. "Is there no way you can send them back to the Underworld?"

The hopeless look in the old men's eyes was an eloquent answer. The old woman said nothing.

Paul looked at his watch. "We should be getting back." He finished his drink. "If the Jeep hasn't been incinerated or buried."

Eleanor shrugged. "It's a rental." She nodded to the silent old woman as she left, irked that Paul and the other two men continued to treat her as if she did not exist.

Outside, the landscape was as surreal as before. The smoke was thicker and it blew past them more quickly as the wind came up from the south. The noise of the lava boiling away ocean was quite clear.

"*Kapuna*" said Paul to his grand-uncles, "the lava flows are moving quickly. They have evacuated all of the villages between here and the Mauna Pele. Will you not come back with us?"

Leonard Kamakaiwi glowered. Leopold Kamakaiwi laughed. The two old men went back into their trailer.

The lava field seemed hotter and even more treacherous on the return trip. Eleanor wondered if she would have heat blisters on her feet. A tree near the Jeep had begun to smoke in the heat from several new lava tributaries, but the vehicle itself was safe.

"We need to talk," said Paul as they reached Highway 11 and turned north. The afternoon light threw their shadow on the black rock to their right as they drove slowly on. The smoke was still thick here, the sulfur stench harsh.

"All right," said Eleanor.

"Mark Twain never wrote about the time in the 1860s when the Marchers of the Night built a *heiau* near where the Mauna Pele now stands," he said. "We . . . the *kahuna* . . . know of it only through chants and oral tradition. You found that out elsewhere."

Eleanor tried to change the subject. "Are you a full-fledged *kahuna*, Paul?"

The curator's laugh was cynical and dismissive. It reminded Eleanor of Leonard. "I will never be a true *kahuna*," he said, his gaze lost in the smoke that billowed ahead of them. "My Western education has robbed me of the level of belief necessary to learn. My rationalist *haole* eyes cannot see clearly."

"Yet you believe in what your uncles and the others have done at the Mauna Pele?" she said.

Paul looked at her. "I saw the dog . . . Ku . . . carrying the hand of its victim. I have seen other things at night there."

Eleanor did not ask about the other things. Not yet. Instead, she said, "Do I still get that helicopter ride?"

He laughed. "Do you still want it?"

"Yes."

"It's yours. My friend will be landing at the Mauna Pele in a few hours . . . about dusk. That is, unless the resort's forcibly evacuated by the authorities or buried in lava by then. Any other favors?"

"Just tell me who that old woman was," she said as they approached the entrance to the Mauna Pele. The smoke was lighter here, but still noticeable. The wind from the south was warm and sticky.

"What old woman?" said Paul. "You mean Molly Kewalu?"

Eleanor turned into the resort road. The security guard recognized them, snapped a friendly salute, and lowered the chain. They drove into the black *a'a* fields. The coast was less than two miles away, but it and the resort were lost in the smoke. "No," said Eleanor, "the old woman in the trailer with your uncles."

Paul looked at her strangely. "What old woman? There was no old woman in the trailer."

"Bra and panties are off," said Byron Trumbo. "Foreplay's over. Where's the fuck?"

Will Bryant winced at the vulgar metaphor. "Mr. Sato is concerned about Sunny."

"Shit," said Trumbo. Even through all the insanity, the negotiations had progressed pretty well according to plan. At three o'clock that afternoon, after a wonderful lunch on the private dining *lanai* on the seventh floor and a demonstration of the *hula* by five professional dancers Trumbo had flown in from Oahu, they had gotten back to bargaining. By four-fifteen, the price had been settled at $312 million and the papers had been drawn up. Sato had brought his phalanx of lawyers with him;

Byron Trumbo had eight lawyers on retainer but he hated traveling with them so much that he had Will Bryant do the vetting for
his side. Will had a law degree, as did Bobby Tanaka, and the two
spent a busy hour checking the fine print on the deal. By five-
thirty the contracts lay ready to be signed on the gleaming teak-
and-mahogany desk in the conference annex of the Presidential
Suite.

But Hiroshe Sato was worried about Sunny Takahashi.

"Shit," said Trumbo for the twentieth time that long day.
"Any word from Fredrickson on finding Sunny?"

"No," said Will Bryant. He was still going through a copy of
the contract that would turn the Mauna Pele Resort into a Japanese golf club and bail his boss out of serious financial trouble. His
tortoiseshell glasses and tied-back hair gave Bryant the look of an
earnest law student. His three-thousand-dollar Donna Karan suit
worked against that image.

"Any word on Briggs?" Trumbo had liked the bodyguard.

"No."

"Any word on Dillon?"

"No, still missing."

"Did you talk Bicki into leaving?"

"No. She went swimming."

"How about Maya?"

"She also insists on staying."

"Caitlin?"

"She and Mr. Koestler have been calling New York. Evidently
they still think that they can leverage you into selling at their price.
She's tried twice to get in to see Mr. Sato, but our security has kept
her out."

Trumbo lay back on the couch and set his high-top sneakers
on the cushion. "I'm tired."

Will Bryant nodded and turned to the next page of the contract. "You're sure you want the Sato payment to come through
our Miami Entertainment holding company?"

"Yeah," said Trumbo. "The taxes will be easiest that way;
we'll declare the loss through Miami Entertainment Inc. and then
liquidate it, I'll shift the bulk of the capital through the twin Cay-

man accounts, and we'll sell off the two casinos as part of the same deal. We'll amortize the whole mess that way for tax purposes and I'll have all the loose money to put into the Hughes Satellite Cable Service merger and refinance the Ellison deal."

Bryant nodded. "It could work."

"It *will* work." Trumbo sat up. "You don't think Hiroshe bought the story that Sunny was partying hard all night and is drying out somewhere with the girls?"

Will Bryant set the contract on the coffee table. "Well, Sunny's famous for partying. But he's also famous for being on time the next morning. Mr. Sato is all bent out of shape."

"Has Bobby been monitoring the tapes?" As a matter of course, Trumbo had bugged Sato's suite and phone lines. As a matter of course, Sato's security people had swept the rooms and phones and removed the bugs. Trumbo had used parabolic mikes from a hundred meters out to pick up voice vibrations on the windows of the suite and computers had reconstructed the conversations. He also used state-of-the-art fiber-optic video and audio devices no thicker than a human hair, hidden among the riot of plants in Sato's suite, and that information was also sent to tape recorders in Trumbo's suite. Bobby Tanaka and two security men had been monitoring the conversation all afternoon.

"Bobby says that Mr. Matsukawa is for dropping the deal," said Will, sipping ice water in a tall glass.

"That old fart," muttered Trumbo. "I wish the thing that got Sunny had grabbed Matsukawa."

"Inazo Ono is still hot for it," said Will. "And he *is* Mr. Sato's closest friend and chief negotiator."

Trumbo closed his eyes and rubbed the bridge of his nose. "For four million of my hard-earned dollars, that bastard Ono had *better* be hot for the deal. And Hiroshe will probably give him a big bite of the golf resort here as a reward for all the tough negotiating."

"Yes," said Will. "Well, everything's in order except for the signing."

"It's got to be today," muttered Trumbo, his eyes still closed. "That damned smoke from the volcano is getting worse and I don't think that we can hold things together another day. How many guests are left?''

"Hmmmm," said Will, checking his notebook. "Eleven."

"Eleven," said Trumbo. He sounded close to a laughing fit. "Five hundred fucking rooms and we've got eleven paying guests."

"Mr. Carter *did* warn people . . ."

"Carter!" said Trumbo from behind closed eyelids. "Is that fruit still around?"

"Yes, well . . ." said Will, finishing his ice water. "Technically, you haven't fired him yet."

"I may just have him killed," said Trumbo. "Which reminds me. What happened to that fat Hawaiian with the axe . . ."

"Jimmy Kahekili."

"Yeah," said Trumbo. "Did he leave?"

"No," said Will. "The last I heard, he was down in the kitchen eating pastries. He still has the axe. Michaels is watching him."

"Good. I'm glad he's still around. With people like Caitlin and Myron Koestler and Carter still around here, we may have use for Mr. Kahekili." Trumbo smiled as he massaged his brow.

"Do you have a headache, boss?" asked Bryant.

"Does the pope shit in the woods?" Trumbo sat up as his radio buzzed. It was the security frequency. "Trumbo here."

"Mr. Trumbo," came Fredrickson's voice, "good news. I've found Sunny Takahashi. Over."

Trumbo jumped to his feet, gripping the radio hard. "Is he alive?"

"Yessir. Not even hurt as far as I can tell. Over."

Byron Trumbo grabbed Will Bryant by the arms, pulled the younger man to his feet, and danced a jig. Then he released his assistant and thumbed the send button. "Great . . . get him here, Fredrickson. Pronto. You've got a bonus coming, kid."

Static rasped for a moment. "I think you'd better come here, Mr. Trumbo. Over."

The billionaire frowned. "Where are you?"

"In the petroglyph field. You know, where the jogging trail goes through the rocks south of . . ."

"Goddammit," shouted Trumbo, "I know where the fucking petroglyph field is. Why should I come there? Is Sunny with you?"

"Yessir. He's here. So's Mr. Dillon. Over."

Trumbo exchanged looks with Will Bryant. "Dillon's there?" he said into the radio. "Look, Fredrickson, I just want Sunny Takahashi back here as soon as possible, so don't fuck around with any other . . ."

"I really think you need to see this, Mr. Trumbo," came the security man's voice. It sounded strange, hollow, as if he were speaking from a barrel.

"Look, goddammit, just get that little Jap back here as soon as . . . Fredrickson? Fredrickson? Shit!" The frequency had gone to static. Trumbo headed for the door, picking up the 9mm Browning and checking its clip as he went. Will Bryant jumped to his feet to follow.

"No," said Trumbo, waving the other man back. "You stay here and get Sato and his people in the conference room and ready to sign. I'll be back with Sunny in ten minutes. I don't care if Takahashi has been lobotomized, we're going to get him presentable, give Sato a peek so that he knows his golden boy is all right, and then get those fucking papers signed."

"Roger, wilco," said Will. He headed for Sato's wing while Trumbo took the elevator downstairs.

Trumbo paused on the lobby floor and then hurried into the restaurant, then through it to the huge kitchen. Jimmy Kahekili was sitting at a stainless-steel counter eating cakes with one hand while holding the axe in the other. Michaels, the security man, was watching him like a hawk.

"Mr. Trumbo!" cried Bree, the chef, throwing his hands up in a flutter. "This . . . this . . . excrescence of fat . . . has been getting in my way for hours. Thank heavens you've come!"

"Shut up, Bree," said Trumbo. Then: "Look, I've got to go run an errand out in the petroglyph field and I want you to come as security."

"Sure, chief," said Michaels, buttoning his linen jacket over his gun.

"Not you," said Trumbo. He pointed at the five-hundred-pound Hawaiian. *"You."*

Jimmy Kahekili continued to eat cake with his pudgy hand
and to hold the axe at counter height with the other. He ignored
Trumbo.

"It's worth ten thousand more dollars to you," said Trumbo,
turning on his heel to head for the door.

Jimmy Kahekili wiped cake from his fingers onto his bare
chest with a dainty gesture, pivoted off the stool which had been
hidden by the mass of his body, and waddled to catch up.

Kahekili could not fit into a golf cart. Trumbo decided to
walk. The Hawaiian followed at a brisk waddle, his shadow falling
over the billionaire as they hurried through the garden and
turned south past the Shipwreck Bar.

They had just reached the large pool when Trumbo stopped
so suddenly that Jimmy Kahekili almost ran over him. The billionaire's shoulders sagged.

Standing in the walkway ahead of him were Caitlin Sommersby Trumbo, Maya Richardson, and Bicki. Myron Koestler
lounged against a coconut palm and smirked. All three women
had been talking rapidly until Trumbo had turned the corner.
Now all three folded their arms across their chests and tapped
their fingers against their elbows. Evening sunlight glinted on
long nails.

"Byron Trumbo," said Caitlin in her slow, perfect New England accent. "Just the man we want to see."

EIGHTEEN

Night is at Pana-ewa and bitter is the storm;
The branches of the trees are bent down;
Rattling are the flowers and leaves of the lehua;
Angrily growls the god Pana-ewa,
Stirred up inside by his wrath.
  Oh, Pana-ewa!
  I give you hurt.
Behold, I give the hard blows of battle.
—Hi'iaka's incantation against Pele's enemies

June 18, 1866, In an unnamed village along the Kona
Coast—

The creature of fog and night chose Reverend Haymark as
its victim and fell on him so quickly that even if Mr. Clemens
could have moved—and I could see that he was still held down
by invisible forces—it would have been too late to help. The
fog-man that had been the boy Halemanu leapt like a panther
pouncing and then seemed to surround the hapless cleric.
Reverend Haymark cried out, but it was a weak noise and
seemed to come from very far away. I tried to rise, to rush to the
cleric's side, but found myself held in place by the same sorcery
that had kept my two companions in check. Now there arose
from the thrashing silhouette of fog a growling and gnashing
sound such as I never hope to hear again. It was as if some foul
beast had been turned loose on a haunch of meat there in our
midst.

Finally Reverend Haymark's struggles ceased and the
fog-creature—Pana-ewa?—seemed to solidify, although the solid

was a blackness deeper than night. The growling and gnashing turned to the sounds of a foul beast drinking deeply, as if lapping water from some great gourd. Then the noise ceased.

The old man who had been sitting next to Reverend Haymark chanted something in ancient Hawaiian. The fog-beast seemed to slide away from our friend's lifeless body and suddenly . . . shift . . . until something large and scaly, not fully reptilian but far from human, squatted in the dark corner.

The old men continued to chant in their liquid language. I recognized the name Pana-ewa repeated frequently. The reptile-man seemed to sway with the chanting. Its human eyes shifted left and right in the candlenut light to watch Mr. Clemens and me almost mockingly. Its sharp teeth were moist. A long tongue flicked out to taste the air. I looked to Mr. Clemens for reassurance, but the correspondent had eyes only for the reptilian horror; the correspondent's mouth hung slack beneath his mustaches and his eyes were wide. I looked back at Reverend Haymark, but the cleric was absolutely motionless. I feared the worst.

Finally the old men ceased chanting and rose, one by one, to file out of the hut until only the old lady in the shadows, Mr. Clemens, myself, the body of our companion, and the thing called Pana-ewa remained.

It spoke. "Your ssssoulssss are mine, *haole*. I ssssshall return for them." And with that, the creature seemed to dig into the soft soil of the hut until it had disappeared from sight. As if released from invisible bonds, I almost pitched forward, so intense had been the restraints and so insistent my unconscious straining.

Mr. Clemens and I moved to the minister's side. While I felt for a pulse, the correspondent peered down the large hole the creature had used as an exit. "Curious," said the California reporter. "Very curious."

I looked up at him in shock. "Reverend Haymark is dead," I said. "There is no pulse." More shocking than the lack of pulse was the temperature of our former companion's body: the cleric's skin was as cold as ice. Frost could have formed on the poor man's staring eyes and his skin was as hard as frozen beef.

Mr. Clemens stepped closer and confirmed my diagnosis. "Dead as a cod," muttered the writer.

"He is not dead," said the old woman in the shadows. Her English was slow and accented, but proper.

I believe we both started at the sound. The crone had been so still and silent during the amazing events of the past half hour that we had all but forgotten her presence.

Mr. Clemens smoothed his mustaches. "I hesitate to disagree with a lady," he said to the old woman in the shadows, "but our friend is not only deceased, he is as cold and stiff as a frog in a Minnesota winter."

"He is not alive," the old woman said slowly, "but he is not dead."

Mr. Clemens exchanged glances with me. "Who are you?" I asked the crone.

She did not deign to answer. Outside we could hear the old men beginning their chanting once again.

"Why did your friends kill our friend?" I asked the woman. "Why have they called this demon forth?"

The woman made a rude sound in her throat. "These *kauwa kahuna*—these landless, brainless, pizzleless sorcerers—are not my friends. They are little men. They cannot see me. Only you can see me here."

Again I exchanged glances with Mr. Clemens. The old woman's statement was absurd, but everything that had happened this endless day and night was beyond sanity as we knew it.

"Are they going to kill us?" I asked Mr. Clemens.

It was the woman who answered. "They are trying to pray you to death even as we speak. Hear them? Their chants are useless."

Mr. Clemens looked at the rigid body of our companion. "Their summoning of a demon worked well enough."

The old woman made the rude noise again. "Summoning demons is child's play. They are children. Pana-ewa could steal the soul of only one of you, and they chose your friend, thinking him the most powerful because he was your *kahuna*." She spat into the dust. "They are fools."

I looked at the wide hole where the reptile creature had disappeared. "Will he . . . will it . . . return?"

"No," said the woman. "It is afraid."

"Afraid of what?" asked Mr. Clemens.

"Of me," said the old woman. And then she rose. She did not stand. She did not straighten. She simply rose, still in a sitting position, until she was floating some three feet above the earthen floor.

I stared and knew that Mr. Clemens's expression must mirror my own.

"Listen to me," said the old woman. "You must leave this place. Leave your friend's body here . . ."

"No, we cannot do such a . . ." began Mr. Clemens.

"SILENCE!" I was sure that the volcanic mountain must echo to the old woman's shout. It silenced Mr. Clemens, but outside I could hear the chanting continue in old men's wavering voices.

"You will leave your friend's body here," she said. "No harm will come to it. I shall watch over it myself. It is important that you retrieve his soul."

"His soul . . ." began Mr. Clemens, but then silenced himself.

"To do this," said the old woman, "you must go to the opening to the Underworld that these *kauwa* fools have opened in their arrogance and ignorance. They do not know how to close it. In their stupid attempts to drive off the *haole kahuna,* they have unleashed terrible forces.

"You will go to the opening to the Underworld and you will descend into the Underworld," she continued, her voice as rhythmic in its own way as the chant going on beyond the grass walls of our hut. "When you reach the entrance to the Ghost World, you will rid yourselves of the absurd *haole* raiments which you have draped upon your bodies . . ."

I glanced down at my skirt and vest and blouse and gloves and boots. What was absurd about this raiment? I had bought them in Denver at the finest stores.

"When you have rid yourself of your *haole* rags," said the

old woman, "you will anoint yourselves with the oil made from rotten *kukui* nuts. Ghosts do not like this smell."

Mr. Clemens raised his eyebrows at me but wisely held his tongue.

"Then you will make a rope of *ieie* vines and descend into the Underworld," said the floating crone. She held one finger up in admonition. "You must not let the ghosts and demons and gods there know that you are not ghosts yourselves. If you do reveal that you are living, Pana-ewa or his ilk will steal your souls and there is nothing I can do to help."

I closed my eyes in the hope that all this would turn out to be a dream. The distant chanting, the wind through the thatch of the roof, the sing-song of the old woman's voice—all this continued. I opened my eyes. The white-haired crone floated three feet above the candlenut flames.

"You must find not only the stolen ghost of your friend," she was saying, "but all of the *haole* ghosts which have been taken beneath the world since these fools opened the entrance two weeks ago. Take them all. If the entrance is to be sealed, no *haole* spirits can be allowed to remain in the domain of Milu."

Mr. Clemens and I both stood so that our eyes were level with the dark gaze of the floating old woman. "What if the men outside try to stop us?" asked the correspondent.

"Shoot them," she said tonelessly. I noticed for the first time that the old woman's lips did not move when she spoke. After all that had happened, this did not seem excessively strange.

Mr. Clemens was nodding as if all this made sense. "One thing," he said. "Or rather . . . a few things. Ahh . . . how do we find this entrance to the Underworld? And . . . ah . . . where would one buy rotten *kukui* nut oil and find some lengths of *ieie* vine?"

"GO!" commanded the crone, pointing toward the door. Her voice held the tone of a parent tried beyond patience by a child's mindless whinings.

We departed, both of us glancing back at the lifeless body of Reverend Haymark lying there in the dim light of the candlenut

flames. The old woman had returned to her place in the
shadowed recess of the long hut.

Outside, the old men looked at us as if surprised that we
were still alive. They interrupted their chant and came our
direction as Mr. Clemens untethered our horses and handed me
Leo's reins. Mr. Clemens pulled the revolver from his coat and
aimed at the bare chest of the chief of the little band. Mr.
Clemens cocked back the heavy hammer with an audible click.
The Hawaiian raised his hands, showed one tooth in a foolish
grin, and backed away.

"*Haole* magic works sometimes," said Mr. Clemens with a
grunt as he swung himself up on his horse. We rode out of the
dreadful little village the way we had come, picking our way
across treacherous lava terraces as we worked our way downhill.

Behind us, beyond the smoking volcano, the sky was growing
light in the east.

"What do we do?" I said when we were safely away from the
village.

Mr. Clemens tucked the pistol away. "The sane thing would
be to ride for Kona and help. It is the *only* sane thing."

I looked back at the dark rocks in the distance that hid the
village from sight. "But the Reverend Haymark . . ."

"Do you really think that we can bring him back to life?"
said Mr. Clemens, his voice as sharp as the rock our horses were
plodding through. "After all," he continued, "that sort of
miracle has not been performed adequately in some years."

I said nothing. There was a burning in my throat and I
confess that I felt perilously close to tears.

"Ah, well," sighed the correspondent. "None of this has
been sane. There is no reason to commence sanity now. We will
go to the Ghost World."

"But how do we find it?" I said, rubbing at my eyes.

Mr. Clemens reined his horse to a stop. Leo and I had been
following their lead and I had not looked ahead since leaving the
village. I did so now. Ten yards ahead of Mr. Clemens's horse,
floating above the *a'a* like a will-o'-the-wisp, a globe of blue fire
bobbed six feet above the faint trail, seemingly waiting on us like
a patient mountain guide pausing for tardy clients.

"Geddup," said Mr. Clemens and his horse began picking its way forward through the basalt. The will-o'-the-wisp floated ahead like a dog released to play.

Glancing at the slowly brightening sky, whispering something that might have been a prayer, I spurred my tired horse to follow.

A shadow fell across the page. Cordie Stumpf squinted up at the owner of the shadow.

"Interesting book?" asked Eleanor.

Cordie shrugged sunburned shoulders. "Characters are sorta interesting. Plot sucks."

Eleanor chuckled and sat on the chair next to Cordie's. The wind was blowing more out of the southwest now, leaving the coast relatively free of smoke. The sky above the palms was blue. Cordie had turned her lounge chair with its back to the beach so that the late-afternoon sunlight would illuminate the pages. The shadows of the palm trees were growing long across the grass. "Seriously," said Eleanor. "What do you think?"

Cordie marked her place with a magazine insert card and closed the leather journal. "I think I understand why you came here, Nell."

Eleanor looked at the other woman. Cordie Stumpf's moon-shaped face was pink with sunburn but there was a pallor beneath that and her lips were white. Eleanor knew that her friend was in pain. She set her hand on Cordie's freckled forearm. "Good," she said. "I thought you might understand."

"I read through it once and now I was just goin' through it again," said Cordie. "The details seem important."

Eleanor nodded.

"So what you been up to today, Nell? Sparkin' with the art curator?"

"You might say that." Eleanor explained about the day's visit to the *kahuna*. "When we came back, we talked for quite a while. It wasn't Paul's idea to invoke the old gods and open the doorway to Milu . . . their Underworld . . . but once his great-uncles suggested it, he went along. He's a *kahuna* himself, it turns out, but only a novitiate."

"That's like a priest-in-training, right?" said Cordie.

"Right."

"Well, did you tell him that your great-great-great-great-aunt saw his great-great-granddaddies fuck up the same way he and his uncles did?"

"No," said Eleanor. "But he knows that I have access to some information about that time . . . something about Mark Twain that was never published."

Cordie grunted.

"What about you?" said Eleanor. "Quiet day?"

Cordie smiled. "Yeah. Went kayaking across the bay earlier. Did a little swimmin'."

At Eleanor's look of surprise, Cordie told the story. She spoke flatly, without affect. When she was finished, Eleanor tried to speak . . . closed her mouth . . . shook her head . . . and tried again. "I think you ran into Nanaue," she said. "The shark-man."

Cordie smiled again. "I wasn't afraid of the man part. The shark part made me worry a bit." She lifted the journal. "Your Aunt Kidder didn't talk too much about Nanaue. Do you know anything more about him?"

Eleanor chewed on her lip for an absent moment. Finally she said, "Just what the legends tell."

"I don't know what the legends tell, Nell," said Cordie. "I just know that some dork with a hump on his back and teeth in the hump took a big bite out of my kayak. I'd like to hear background on it."

Eleanor regarded her friend with a searching gaze. "Cordie, you don't seem to be having much problem with this."

"*Au contraire, mi amiga,*" said the other woman. "I always have a problem when something tries to eat me for lunch."

"You know what I mean," said Eleanor. "A problem with the . . . improbability of all this. We're talking impossible things here."

Cordie's smile faded. She looked down at her rough hands. "Nell, I guess you might say that I've never quite grown out of my own little mythopoeic universe. Something when I was a kid sorta prepared me for . . . well, I guess it prepared me to trust my senses and not much else. Something in the water tried to *kill* me today. I want to hear what it was."

Eleanor nodded almost imperceptibly. "A long time ago, not long after the first Hawaiians settled on the islands, there was a sort of god named Ka-moho-ali'i . . . the King of the Sharks. As with most of the Hawaiian gods, he could appear in his original form—a shark—or as a human. Eventually Ka-moho-ali'i fell in love with a human woman named Kalei. He came out of the water on the north side of this island—the Big Island—and took on the form of a man and married the woman Kalei. They lived in the Waipio Valley, which is all the way across the island from here . . . on the north shore. When their child was born, it was a male child whom they named Nanaue. The child had a mild hump on its back and on that hump a birthmark . . . in the form of a shark's mouth."

Eleanor paused. Cordie smiled thinly. "Go on, Nell. I like your storytelling voice."

"Well, according to the legends, Ka-moho-ali'i returned to the sea, leaving his human wife behind . . ."

"Typical male," said Cordie.

"Leaving his wife behind, but warning her that she should never let anyone see Nanaue's birthmark or allow the boy to eat the flesh of animals. Kalei carried out her husband's wishes and protected Nanaue until he was a man . . . covering his increasingly humped back with *kapa* cloth and keeping meat from his diet. But when he became a man, he ate in the men's eating house and showed an insatiable appetite for meat. When he swam—which he invariably did alone—he transformed into more shark than man . . . some of the legends say that he was all shark, others say he still held some of the form of a man . . ."

"The second legend is right," said Cordie. "Go on."

Eleanor shrugged. "That's about it. Eventually Nanaue's secret was discovered. He had the bad habit of luring local people into the water . . . he especially liked fresh water like the pool under Waipio Falls . . . where he would attack and eat them. When the villagers turned on him, he escaped to the sea, but couldn't live in the ocean for long. The legends say that a band of *kahuna* chased Nanaue to Maui, near the village of Hana, and then on to the island of Molokai. Eventually he was captured and brought back to the Big Island. There the legends diverge. Some say that he was chopped to bits on the hill of Puumano. Others say that he was banished to the Underworld of Milu with the other demons and evil half-gods when Pele fought them in 1866.''

Cordie nodded and tapped Aunt Kidder's journal. "Yeah, well, I guess we know which version of *that* story holds water." She twitched a thin smile. "So to speak."

Eleanor sat back in her lounge chair. Her body ached, although from the day's mild exertions or its less-than-mild tensions, she did not know. The sky was gray to the east from the fires she had seen earlier, but the breeze from the southwest still kept the sky blue above the Mauna Pele. Eleanor tried to imagine just relaxing at this resort: playing tennis with someone, swimming in the beautiful bay without worrying about shark-men, jogging through the petroglyph fields without seeing torches underground, and taking walks after dark without waiting for something to come crashing out of the undergrowth. The thought seemed pleasant, but dull.

"I need to hear more about these legends," Cordie Stumpf said abruptly, handing the diary back to Eleanor. "If we're going to work together tonight, I need to know everything."

Eleanor sighed. "Yes. I'm sorry it's taken so long." She sat up. "You don't have to get involved in this, you know."

Cordie laughed her unself-conscious laugh. "Nell, kiddo, I *am* involved. And will be until we finish this business." She glanced over Eleanor's shoulder at the sun lowering toward the ocean horizon. "And I suspect that will be tonight. It may be wild around here after dark. We need a plan, girl." She looked back toward the Big Hale. "Are they still serving meals, or have the chefs been eaten by Pana-ewa or one of those critters?"

"Paul says that there are only a handful of us guests left," said Eleanor. "But the chef is still working and there are enough workers to keep the main restaurant going. Evidently Mr. Trumbo is having a big bash tonight and is paying out big bonuses to the staff that will come in."

"Good," said Cordie, standing and pulling her towel and wrap and large tote bag up with her. "I'm starved. What do you say to grabbing dinner with me and talking to me over a few cold Pele's Fires? I want to know everything you know about Ms. Pele."

Eleanor also stood, glancing at her watch. "I'm supposed to take that helicopter ride at dusk . . ."

Cordie's eyes glinted. "I think I know what you have planned for that. It's just about six . . . you have a couple of hours until sunset. Let's eat." When Eleanor hesitated a moment, she said, "It's probably going to be a long night, Nell."

Eleanor nodded, got to her feet, said, "See you at the restaurant in fifteen minutes," and headed for her *hale* to clean up and dress for the evening's activities.

Trumbo paused.

The three women blocked his path. Caitlin was wearing bleached cotton resortwear pants and blouse, the natural fabric fluttering slightly in the soft breeze that had come up from the south. She was carrying her Bally handbag and one hand was in the bag. Maya stood in the center of the trio; the model wore a flowery Hawaiian *pareu*—a yard and a half of simple cotton that she had wrapped around her like a skirt—over the same orange, one-piece swimsuit she had worn in her cover shot for this year's *Sports Illustrated* swimsuit edition. Maya's lips and nails were a liquid crimson. Bicki was dressed in high heels and a skimpy mocha two-piece swimsuit that almost perfectly matched her skin color. The effect was that she was nude except for the gold bracelet and rings. Her arms were crossed and her legs were set in a gunfighter stance.

"Hi, girls," said Byron Trumbo.

For a minute the only sound was the rustle of palm fronds and the wheezing of Jimmy Kahekili behind Trumbo. Then Caitlin Sommersby Trumbo spoke. "You miserable little fuck."

"You putrid little cocksucking twit *bastard*," said Maya. Her British inflection was heavy.

"Hey, T," said Bicki. She smiled, showing the grin that had launched a dozen MTV videos.

"Hey, Bick," said Trumbo.

"We've talked and decided, T," said Bicki. "We're going to cut off your balls and dick and each keep one as a reminder."

"Sorry, girls," said Trumbo. "I'm in a hurry." He started to move off the path to the left. The three women shifted left as fluidly as the front line of the Dallas Cowboys.

Myron Koestler pushed himself away from the tree he was leaning against and took a step closer. "Mr. Trumbo . . . ah . . . Byron, I'm afraid this complicates matters considerably. In light of this . . . ah . . . new development . . . I'm afraid that my client's reasonable demands must be . . . ah . . . revised upwards."

Trumbo put one hand on Jimmy Kahekili's arm. The Hawaiian's forearm was larger than Trumbo's thigh. "Jimmy," said Trumbo, stabbing a finger in Koestler's direction, "if that ambulatory hemorrhoid says one more word, I want you to take your axe and chop him into pieces small enough to feed to a mouse. *Comprende?*"

The mass of flesh behind Trumbo gave an anticipatory grunt. Koestler backed up quickly, looked at the women, opened his mouth as if to say that they were witnesses to the threat, looked at Jimmy Kahekili, and closed his mouth.

The women stayed in Trumbo's path.

"Look," said the billionaire, grinning slightly, "I'd love to stay and chat . . . I know you all want to know how you rated vis-à-vis each other . . . but I really have to hurry." He took a step toward them.

Caitlin took a polished semiautomatic from her Bally bag and aimed it at Trumbo's stomach. This weapon was larger than Maya's.

Trumbo stopped and sighed. "What? Was there a sale on those things at Bergdoff's?"

Caitlin braced the weapon with both hands. The other two women watched with no expression.

"No money in killing me, kid," said Trumbo. "They'll probably give you the same cell they reserved for Leona Helmsley and whatshername, the cow that did the diet doctor."

Caitlin raised the pistol until it was aimed at Trumbo's face.

"I really don't have time for this shit," said Trumbo, glancing at his watch again. He was supposed to meet Hiroshe for drinks before dinner. "Come on, Jimmy," he said, and walked toward the women.

Maya stepped aside. Caitlin swung like a rusty weathervane, arms still rigidly extended, pistol steady, tracking Trumbo as he passed. Bicki glared the way only proud African-American women can glare. Jimmy Kahekili glanced nervously to his left and right as he followed Trumbo through the gauntlet. Myron Koestler was standing behind a palm tree with only his pale fingers and pony-tail showing.

Trumbo walked a dozen paces, went around a bend and out of sight of the females, and let out his breath. "Come on, Jimmy," he said. "We've got to hurry and get Sunny Takahashi back before Sato gets cold feet."

"You one *lolo* buggah, brah. Dem *haole wahine* da' kine plenty *hu hu.*"

"Yeah," said Trumbo, jogging onto the paved path through the petroglyph field. "Whatever."

Fredrickson was waiting where the path ended and the *a'a* field began. The security man was gripping a semiautomatic in one dark hand and kept glancing over his shoulder at the lava field as Trumbo and the giant approached.

"Where is he?" demanded Trumbo. He saw that Fredrickson was gaping at Jimmy and his axe. "Never mind him, goddammit. Where's Sunny?"

Fredrickson licked his lips. "And Dillon . . . Dillon's here too."

"I don't give a shit about Dillon," snapped Trumbo. "I want Sunny Takahashi. If you've got me out here on a fucking wild-goose chase . . ." The billionaire and the huge Hawaiian took a step forward in unison.

Fredrickson backed into the lava field. "Uh-uh, Mr. Trumbo, sir . . . no. I mean, you've got to see . . . I mean, I didn't call anyone else because they said . . . anyway . . ." He turned and led them into the lava.

The pit was less than a hundred yards from the jogging trail.

From the looks of the tumbled boulders at the lip of the crater, the lava tube had collapsed only hours earlier. Fredrickson moved to the edge of the opening gingerly, his pistol raised. Trumbo followed impatiently. Jimmy Kahekili stayed well back.

"Now what the shit does this have to do with . . ." began Trumbo, and stopped.

The lava tube was not too deep beneath the surface here, perhaps fifteen feet. The seaward side of the cave had been covered by rockfall when the roof collapsed, but the *mauka* or toward-the-mountain side was still intact, a black ellipse opening into the earth.

Just inside that black ellipse stood Security Chief Dillon, Hiroshe Sato's good friend Tsuneo "Sunny" Takahashi, and a hog the size of a small Shetland pony. Dillon and Sunny were naked. Their bodies glowed from a pale green light, as if they had been dipped in phosphorescent paint. Their eyes were open but they stared straight ahead, blindly, as if in a trance. The boar stood between them. Its back was higher than Dillon's shoulder. The porcine apparition had a cluster of black orbs where each eye should be—Trumbo counted eight eyes in all. They glowed brightly, reminding Trumbo of Maya's orange swimsuit catching the evening light. The hog opened its mouth and grinned at them. Its teeth looked human—large, but human.

Trumbo turned and looked at Fredrickson. The security man shrugged helplessly. "He told me not to call anyone but you, boss."

"He?" said Trumbo. "Who the hell . . ."

"Me," said the hog.

Trumbo wheeled around and pulled the 9mm Browning from beneath his Hawaiian shirt. The hog smiled more broadly. Its eight eyes looked moist and happy.

"What's . . ." began Trumbo. He noticed that his voice was shaking ever so slightly, as was his pistol. He braced the Browning with his other hand.

"No, no, Byron," said the boar. "There's no need for that. We have too much in common to ruin the relationship that way." The voice was as deep as one would expect coming from a thousand-pound hog.

Byron Trumbo felt the sweat trickling down his rib cage under his loose shirt. He turned to look for Jimmy Kahekili, but the Hawaiian was gone. He had dropped his axe in his eagerness to leave.

"Pssst," said the hog. "Down here."

Trumbo turned back to the pit. The smiling hog and the two naked men were still there.

"Dillon!" shouted Trumbo. The ex–security chief did not twitch. The eyes remained open and glassy above the dark beard.

"No, no," said the hog again. "It's me you want to talk to, Byron."

Trumbo licked his lips. "All right. What do you want?"

"What do *you* want, Byron?" said the hog smoothly.

"I want Sunny Takahashi," said Trumbo. "You can keep Dillon."

The giant hog chuckled. The sound was like giant bellows being pumped while rocks rattled in a stone bowl. "Tsk, tsk, tsk," said the creature. "It's not quite that simple. We have to talk."

"Fuck talk," said Trumbo, and aimed the Browning between the creature's two clusters of eyes.

"If you pull the trigger," the hog said in conversational tones, "I will come up there, chew your intestines out, and munch on your testicles as if they were candy apples."

"You'll have to get in line," said Trumbo, holding the pistol steady.

The hog chuckled more deeply. "You want this one," it said, poking the mesmerized Japanese next to him with its snout.

Trumbo nodded and waited.

"He's yours when you want him badly enough," said the hog. The eight eyes blinked and the two glowing men turned and walked deeper into the lava tube, disappearing from sight. "All you have to do is come down and talk to me about it." The monstrous creature turned gracefully, almost daintily, and trotted a few paces into the darkness. It looked over its bristled shoulder and the eyes no longer looked playful. "But don't wait too long, Byron. Things are going to get interesting around here in a few hours." The hog trotted into the darkness.

Trumbo listened to the rattle of its trotters on basalt echo for a moment until there was silence. He lowered the pistol.

"Holy fuck, holy fuck, holy fuck," said Fredrickson, and sat down heavily on the lava. His face was more ash-colored than black at the moment.

"Don't faint on me, goddammit," said Trumbo. "Put your head between your knees. That's right."

Fredrickson looked up with wide eyes. "I thought I'd flipped out. Acid flashback . . . but I never took acid. He . . . it . . . that *thing* told me to call you on the radio . . ."

"OK," interrupted Trumbo, sliding the pistol back in his belt. "Did you tell anyone else?"

Fredrickson dangled his wrists on his knees and panted for breath. "Uh-uh. The pig said it would have my guts for garters if I called anyone else . . . that was its phrase . . . have my guts for garters."

Trumbo pondered that image for a moment. "OK," he said again.

Fredrickson looked up. Color seemed to be returning. "You aren't going down there, are you, Mr. Trumbo?"

Trumbo gave him a look.

"I didn't think so," the security man said hurriedly. "But if we got all of our guys and Sato's guys and some night goggles and Uzis and Mac-tens and some shit like that . . ."

"Shut up," said Trumbo. He looked at his watch. "Shit, I'm late for drinks with Hiroshe." He pointed at Fredrickson. "Stay here. Keep the channel open. I'll . . ."

The other man leapt to his feet. "No fucking way that I'm fucking staying out here by my fucking self in the fucking dark with some fucking talking slab of bacon down there in the fucking . . ."

Trumbo stepped forward quickly and slapped the man hard, twice. "You stay *here*. Do it and there's ten thousand dollars in it for you. Ten grand just for *tonight*. You can run like Stepin Fetchit if that thing comes out of its hole, but *let me know on the radio*. Got it? If you wuss out on me, Fredrickson, I'll spend whatever it takes to have you and your entire family . . . down to your fifth cousins . . . whacked. Do we understand one another?"

The security man stared, his gaze overwhelmed eerily reminiscent of Sunny's and Dillon's.

"Good," said Trumbo. "I'll send somebody out with food sometime before midnight." He patted the frozen man's shoulder and began walking quickly back toward the path and the Mauna Pele.

The wind had shifted out of the south again. It brought a hot, sticky feel to it, and Trumbo remembered that the wind was called a *kona* and was the namesake for this entire section of coast. The ash cloud from the eruptions were not a problem, but the smoke from the lava flows to the south were coming over the coast again in a heavy, gray cloud that felt like a low overcast.

It felt suddenly cooler, as if the sun had already set. Shadows disappeared as the smoke cloud thickened overhead, and a pall of twilight deepened over everything. The palm trees rustled and whispered to each other and a hot wind whistled through the *a'a*.

Trumbo glanced at his watch a final time and hurried back toward the darker oasis of trees.

"Where should I start?" said Eleanor as their second Pele's Fires arrived. They were sitting on the terrace of the Whale Watching Lanai watching the evening shade to sudden gray.

"Pele," said Cordie, raising her drink in salute.

"Hmmm . . . yes, well, Pele is your basic tutelary goddess with the usual assortment of implied powers and obligations . . ." began Eleanor.

"No, Nell," interrupted Cordie. "Don't give me the academic shit. Use your storytelling voice."

Eleanor took a sip of Pele's Fire, cleared her throat, and started again. "Pele is not one of the older gods, but she comes from the best family. Her father was said to be Moe-moea-au-lii, literally "the Chief Who Dreamed of Trouble," but he disappeared early on and doesn't figure into any of Pele's later tales . . ."

"Typical male," muttered Cordie, and sipped her drink. "Go on."

"Yes . . . well, Pele's mother was Haumea, sometimes known as Hina or La'ila'i. In her various forms, Haumea is the supreme female spirit, goddess of women's work and fertility, the mother of all the lesser gods and of all of humankind, and generally the female counterpart to all the male power in the universe."

"Right on," said Cordie, and lifted a clenched fist.

Eleanor paused and frowned. "You've had two of those drinks already. Are you sure you want to . . ."

Cordie reached over and tapped the back of Eleanor's hand. "Trust me, Nell," she said, her voice clear. "I can hold my Pele's Fires. Go on."

"Pele's powers were created out of the womb of the Earth Mother the ancient Hawaiians called Papa," said Eleanor.

"Earth Mother equals Papa," said Cordie, chewing on a swizzle stick. "OK. Keep going, Nell. I won't interrupt again."

"The ancients saw the universe balanced only in the embrace of opposites," said Eleanor. "Male light penetrating female darkness, begetting a universe of opposites."

Cordie nodded but said nothing.

"Pele came late to these islands," continued Eleanor, regaining her "storytelling" voice. "Her canoe was guided by Ka-moho-ali'i . . ."

"Hey, that's the shark king you were talking about earlier," said Cordie. "The old man of the brat who tried to eat me today. Sorry . . . I'll keep my mouth shut."

"You're right," said Eleanor. "Ka-moho-ali'i was Pele's brother. Back in Bora-Bora, where they both came from, he was also known as the king of dragons. Anyway, he helped lead Pele's canoe to Hawaii. She landed first in Niihau and then moved on to Kauai. Being the goddess of fire, Pele had a magic digging tool—I think it was called Paoa. She used Paoa to dig fire pits in which she could live, but the sea kept rolling in and quenching her flames. Pele moved down the island chain until she came here to the Big Island, where she eventually found Kilauea to be just right That's been her home for thousands of years."

Eleanor stopped as a wild screeching filled the air. Both women watched as a flurry of bright plumage showed where tropical birds were fighting in the branches below them. The two paused to sip their tall drinks.

"Anyway, before she settled here, Pele got in a huge battle on Maui with her older sister, Na-maka-o-Kaha'i, the goddess of the sea . . ."

"I never had me an older sister," said Cordie. "Just brothers. And they were all pains in the ass except for one who died when he was little. Sorry. Go on."

"Pele and her sister slugged it out until Pele was killed," said Eleanor.

"Killed?" Cordie looked confused.

"The gods have mortal sides," said Eleanor. "When Pele lost hers, she became even more powerful as a goddess. And because she died here in Hawaii, her spirit could be free to fly to the volcanoes of Mauna Loa and Kilauea, where she lives to this day."

Cordie was frowning. "I thought that Pele could appear as a mortal . . ."

"She can," said Eleanor. Their third round of drinks arrived. "It's just that she's *not* mortal anymore."

"I don't get it," said Cordie. "But go on. I'll drink. You talk."

"It gets complicated," agreed Eleanor. "For instance, Pele is the goddess of fire, but she can't *make* fire . . . that's a male prerogative. But she can *control* it, and she does on these islands. She has several brothers, also gods, who control thunder, explosions, fountains of lava, the so-called rain of fire . . . all the noisier and more dramatic but less powerful aspects of fire."

"Typical," Cordie muttered again.

"But Pele controls the great force of nature that is the volcano. Usually, Pele sleeps, but over the centuries she's helped certain human kings that she liked . . ."

"Kamehameha," said Cordie.

"Yes," said Eleanor. She pushed the third drink away. "I'd better avoid this. I'm already light-headed, and as you say . . . tonight will be busy. I can't let Paul and his pilot friend think that I'm a drunk."

Cordie shrugged. "I rarely give a shit about what people think." She looked up as the waiter returned to ask if they wished to eat in the restaurant or out on the dining terrace. "What do you think, Nell? I sorta like it out here tonight."

"I agree," said Eleanor.

They ordered. For an appetizer, Eleanor tried *ahi* cake, made of blended layers of marinated grilled eggplant, Maui onions, basil, seared *ahi*, and tomatoes, lightly sprinkled with a Puna goat cheese, and lemongrass dressing. Cordie ordered the potato-crusted lobster cakes with mustard vinaigrette. For a main course, both tried the caramelized Sonoma rack of lamb with fresh thyme and smashed potatoes.

"I used to call 'em smashed potatoes when I was a kid," Cordie said.

The food arrived quickly and was delicious. The two women spoke between bites. The sky began to darken. At one point, Paul Kukali stopped by the table, but only to tell Eleanor that it would be another half hour or so until the helicopter arrived. The curator seemed distracted as he nodded to each woman and left.

"OK, back to Pele," said Cordie as the dishes were cleared away from the second course. "Our problem is telling if she's on our side or if she's behind this shit at the Mauna Pele."

"Yes," said Eleanor, sipping water. "But you know what I think."

"Yeah, I read Kidder's journal."

Eleanor made a small gesture with her hand. She paused to look at that hand now in the horizontal sunlight. It reminded her of her mother's. *When did I get my mother's hands?* she thought. Shaking her head, she tried to focus. "We have to assume . . . or at least I want to assume . . . that these happenings are from forces opposed to Pele."

Cordie's small eyes were bright. "Yeah, but which of Pele's enemies are behind it?"

"I don't know," said Eleanor. She suddenly felt tired. "Pele had a lot of enemies. Besides fighting Na-maka-o-Kaha'i, the sea goddess, Pele's traditional enemies include Pliahu, the goddess of snow who lives at the summit of Mauna Kea. They had a falling-out several thousand years ago because they both loved the same man."

"Hrmm," grunted Cordie. Their desserts arrived. Cordie had ordered *lilikoi* cheesecake and had asked to try the lemongrass brûlée with the cashew cookie base. Eleanor had coffee.

"It seems from what we've heard that Pana-ewa, the reptile and fog guy, was behind this war and the one back in 1866," said Eleanor. "But as powerful as Pana-ewa is, he doesn't seem enough of a figure to lead a rebellion against Pele."

"Who else hates her?" said Cordie, digging into the cheese-cake.

"Most of the male gods," said Eleanor. "Even the older gods like Lono and Ku have become jealous of the devotion Hawaiians have given to Pele."

"Typical insecure males," muttered Cordie.

"What?"

"Nothing." Cordie tried the brûlée. "Oh, God . . . this is great. Want some?"

"Sure." Eleanor picked a bit of the brûlée out with her spoon, tasted it, and closed her eyes. "That is wonderful."

"Want some more?"

"No thanks." Eleanor sipped the strong coffee, feeling some of the alcohol buzz fade. "Where was I?"

"Pele and the male gods being jealous."

"Oh, yes . . . we saw that black dog, and Ku takes the form of a dog."

"How does the other one . . . whatshisface . . . Lono appear?"

"I'm not sure," said Eleanor. "Lono can be human, but I think he rarely appears in that form. He was the fiercest and most demanding of all the old gods . . . most of the human sacrifices along this coast were made to Lono . . . but I don't think he had any special bone to pick with Pele."

Cordie alternated bites of her cheesecake with spoonfuls of brûlée. "So Pele's enemy here could be Ku, the mutt, or more likely Pana-ewa and his demon buddies."

Eleanor watched the light fade on the treetops beyond the terrace. "Or someone else." She glanced at her watch and looked back at Cordie. Still a few minutes before she had to meet Paul for the helicopter ride. She found herself feeling tense about it. "Pele had a huge battle with her favorite sister, Hi'iaka, right along this coast somewhere. Again, it was a falling-out over a man. What?"

"I didn't say anything," said Cordie.

"Hi'iaka was Pele's younger sister who danced," said Eleanor, "and they got along very well. Hi'iaka remained loyal to Pele even though she was attracted to one of Pele's lovers, a human named Lohi'au. Pele thought that some hanky-panky had been going on and attacked Hi'iaka somewhere right along this stretch of coast . . ."

Both women looked out at the low sun and expanse of ocean. The ash-and-smoke cloud hung over the coast like a tarpaulin with the sun igniting the undersides of the cloud, tinting everything with an orange-red hue. The waves in the bay moved sluggishly, like an ocean of blood.

"Who won?" said Cordie. She had finished her desserts and now dropped her spoon in the brûlée dish with a satisfied clink.

"Hmmm? Oh, when Pele fought Hi'iaka? It was a draw, but Pele accidentally killed Lohi'au."

Cordie nodded. "It sounds like a Saturday night in Chicago. Typical domestic brawl."

"That tale had a relatively happy ending," said Eleanor. "One of Pele's god brothers found Lohi'au's spirit flying away over the ocean and brought it back to land, where he set it back in the body."

"Like in Kidder's journal?" said Cordie.

"I presume. Anyway, Hi'iaka and her new lover went off to Kauai together. But she might still hold a grudge. And she's a powerful goddess . . ."

Cordie folded her hands over her stomach and sat back in her chair. "I don't know, Nell. Somehow I don't think that Paul and these male *kahunas* managed to reach a female spirit. I think that they got some male-chauvinist-pig god workin' on their side."

Eleanor grinned broadly.

"What's so funny?" said Cordie.

"There is a pig god," said Eleanor. "Or at least a hog. Kama-pua'a. He's the quintessential male god . . . and Pele's enemy. Also Pele's lover."

Cordie leaned forward. The last rays of the dying sun made her sunburned face glow. "Tell me."

Eleanor shrugged. "The boar was the biggest land animal the Polynesians and the Hawaiians knew existed. It's the embodiment of male power. Kamapua'a takes the shape of a hog . . . or a hand-some man. He's a powerful god, although he likes to stay on the rainy windward side of the islands—he's associated with rain and forests and dark places—but his appetite is always getting him into trouble. Kamapua'a once tried to rape Pele's sister, Kapo, but Kapo got away by detaching her vagina and tossing it away as a decoy . . . I'm sorry, what?''

Cordie's round face had taken on an unreadable expression. "Nothin', Nell," she said. "I was just thinking how useful that would be . . . go on. This is better than *General Hospital*."

"It's just that Kamapua'a has also raped Pele dozens of times over the centuries," said Eleanor. "There's a place around the south end of the island in Puna called Ka-lua-o-Pele, where the land is torn and tumbled, and the legends say that this is where Pele lost the first great battle with Kamapua'a and where he . . . had his way with her."

"Screwed her," clarified Cordie. "Raped her."

Eleanor nodded. "I've seen pictures of the place. It looks like tousled bedsheets."

"Too bad Pele wasn't strong enough to fight the oinker off," said Cordie as the waiter cleared the last of the dishes.

"She might have been," said Eleanor. "It was a hell of a bat-tle—Pele's fires against Kamapua'a's deluges of rain. He even sent thousands of hogs to eat all the undergrowth so there would be nothing to burn. Pele turned his hurricane storms to steam. She covered his lands with lava. He fought back with more torrents. Pele was willing to be destroyed rather than yield to Kamapua'a. But the legends say that in the end her brothers—the ones in charge of the firesticks—saw that she was losing and ordered her to yield to him. They were afraid that all of the fires would be doused."

"Typical," said Cordie, and cracked her knuckles.

"Yes," said Eleanor, musing. "Kamapua'a would be a likely suspect, but he rarely comes to the leeward, dry side of the island according to . . ."

"Holy shit," said Cordie. She was staring over Eleanor's shoulder.

Both women stood and moved to the terrace railing. In the last indirect glow of sunset reflected from the lowering ash cloud, thousands of tiny filaments were drifting through the air, catching the sunlight like thin fibers of pure color. Cordie and Eleanor rushed out of the Whale Watching Lanai and onto the garden area between the Big Hale and the beach. Strands of the stuff lay in the grass, on the pathways, and in the foliage along the way. Clumps of the pliant fibers, many stretching a yard or more in length, lay in waves like a woman's hair.

"What is it?" said Cordie.

Eleanor shook her head. Now that the sun had set, the filaments had lost most of their color and seemed a faded red or polished silver gray. The impression of looking at a woman's hairpiece was uncanny.

"Pele's hair," said a voice behind them.

They turned to see Paul Kukali standing there. The curator still looked distracted and worried. His voice was flat. "It's a form of spun glass," he said, "created when Mauna Loa and Kilauea are in full eruption. Touch it . . . see how pliable it is? It rarely travels this far." He looked to the east, where the sky was brighter red than in the west. It was as if there were two sunsets this night. "The eruption must be worsening."

Eleanor touched the hairlike fibers a last time and stood. "Does that mean we can't go flying?"

"No," said Paul, "just the opposite. The chopper's here, although we'd better leave quickly before the ash cloud gets worse and they won't let us fly."

Eleanor turned to Cordie. "Are you sure you won't . . . ."

"Uh-uh," said the shorter woman. "I ain't afraid of much, Nell, but flying scares the shit out of me. I don't want to do it when I don't have to. I'll go out and watch you leave, though."

Paul had brought a golf cart and they rode back around the Big Hale, past the tennis courts and parking lot, through a section of the north golf course, to the heliport carved out of the *a'a* fields. Out here beyond the trees, the sky was lighter but the ash cloud remained a gray presence a few thousand feet above the ground.

The helicopter sat in the center of the asphalt circle, its rotors still turning slowly. It was much smaller than Eleanor had imagined, not much more than a bubble with a tail assembly and rear rotor. The wind from the southeast kicked at the orange wind sock hanging from the pole on this side of the landing circle. Because of the sky's reflection on the Plexiglas canopy, the pilot was visible only as the vaguest silhouette.

Eleanor turned and gripped Cordie's upper arm. "See you in an hour or two."

Cordie's eyes looked directly into Eleanor's. "You be careful, Nell. If you find who I think you're looking for, say hi for me."

Eleanor smiled, nodded, and followed Paul's crouched approach to the machine.

Cordie stepped back out of the wash of the rotors. She could not see the pilot from where she stood, but she watched as Paul crawled in first and then Eleanor strapped herself into the front seat. The helicopter's engine climbed in pitch, the rotors blurred, and the small machine seemed to leap into the air like a dragonfly. Cordie watched it circle the resort once at low altitude and then swing out to sea, humming south along the coast.

"Good luck, Nell," Cordie whispered. Then she turned back toward the oasis of gathering shadows that was the Mauna Pele.

NINETEEN

The bright gods of the underworld.
Shining in Vavau are the gods of the night.
The gods thick clustered for Pele.
                          —Pele's prayer

June 18, 1866, In an unnamed village along the Kona
Coast—

The sun had not risen above the mass of volcano at our
backs, clouds were gathering, but the sky had brightened to a
distinct gray by the time the will-o'-the-wisp guide brought us to
the entrance to the Underworld of Milu.

The last mile or so of that descent toward the coast followed
a raised macadamized road of uniform width. My tired horse
had been plodding along this highway for several minutes before
I heard the change in the noise his hooves made, and bothered
to look down in the lifting gloom. The road was paved with flat
stones, was obviously ancient, and had been constructed with a
high degree of engineering skill. The stones were worn and
smooth.

"It reminds me of those ancient paved highways leading out
of Rome which one sees in rotogravures," said Mr. Clemens,
letting his horse fall back to ride next to mine now that the path
had widened. Ahead of us, the sphere of burning blue gas
floated along like a hunting dog leading the way to the fields.
Our exhausted horses followed it with no sign of fear.

"I wish we were going to Rome," I said, realizing how worn
with fatigue and shock I felt.

"Hmmmm," said Mr. Clemens in a tone of agreement. "It

would seem a more pleasant prospect even to be visiting the
Pope than to have an imminent audience with the King of the
Ghosts."

Despite the warming air, I shuddered. "We should not jest,"
I said. Then, feeling that my tone might have been too harsh, I
asked, "Have you been to Rome?"

"Alas, no," said the correspondent, "but I hope to see all of
Europe before I grow much older. *If* I grow much older . . ."
Then he glanced at me with an expression that may have
suggested discomfort at alarming me. "Have you been to Rome,
Miss Stewart?"

I sighed. It was a tired sound. "I have just begun my travels,
Mr. Clemens. I have seen little of the world, and my main regret
in life is that I cannot live long enough to see it all. I had hoped
to see Rome on this voyage."

I could see my companion's eyebrows rise. "Yet you said
that you were headed west across the Pacific from here . . ."

"Yes," I said. "Having seen the Rockies and written a
description of my travels there . . ." I paused, shocked at my
indiscretion.

"You write!" cried Mr. Clemens. "A travel writer! A fellow
scribbler!"

I looked down at my hands, furious at myself for admitting
such a thing and for the blushes that burned my cheeks. "Only
certain journal entries I sent to my sisters," I said. "They were
bound . . . privately published . . . not a real book."

"Nonsense!" cried Mr. Clemens, his voice rising. "I have
been traveling with a fellow spirit without knowing it. Each of us
has abandoned honest work for the highwayman's pleasure of
the pen."

Knotting the reins tightly in my hand, I attempted to change
the subject. "From the Sandwich Islands, I had planned to go
on to Australia," I said. "Then back to Japan. Then perhaps
China . . . I have a cousin who is a missionary there . . . and then
India, and then perhaps overland to the Holy Land . . . and then
Europe . . . Rome . . ." I trailed off, aghast at my own
talkativeness.

Mr. Clemens was nodding as if impressed. "A respectable itinerary for a small lady traveling alone." He patted his coat pockets as if looking for a cigar, frowned, and said, "How long have you set aside for this circumnavigation?"

I raised my face to the fresh breeze blowing up from the forested areas lying between us and the coast. The sea was quite visible now, glowing in the reflected light from the sky. "A year," I said. "Two? More. It does not matter."

"There is nothing in . . . ah . . . Ohio to draw you back?" he asked.

Instead of answering directly, I said, "My father left a considerable endowment for me in his will. For some years I have suffered from chronic ailments. My doctor advised me to travel."

Mr. Clemens's eyes glinted. "Hardly imagining," he said, "that his patient would set off around the world." He raised one leg and set it sideways across the saddle horn in a languid gesture. His boots were dusty. "Had your doctor known what adventures the Sandwich Islands would bring, I doubt that he would have included them in his prescription."

Glancing to our right, desperate to change the subject, I said, "How strange. The surf is more than a mile away but one can plainly hear it."

Mr. Clemens glanced over his shoulder at the distant line of breakers far below. "Have you watched the heathen at their national pastime?" he asked.

I shook my head. The horses plodded along the smooth stones. The will-o'-the-wisp guide seemed almost ordinary in my haze of fatigue and shock at Reverend Haymark's death.

"Surf-bathing," said the redheaded correspondent, patting his pockets again as if some cigar had escaped his notice. Evidently none had.

"Ah," I said. "No, I have heard of it, in Honolulu, but have not seen it."

"A magnificent sport," said Mr. Clemens, resuming his normal posture in his saddle. "On my second day on Oahu I came upon a bevy of nude native young ladies bathing and surf-bathing in the sea, and went and sat down on their clothes to keep them from being stolen. I begged them to come out, for the sea was rising and I was satisfied that they were running some risk, but they seemed unafraid and went on with their sport."

I looked down and said nothing, looking away so that this brash young man would not see my smile. Suddenly the old woman's speech came back to me—'You will rid yourselves of the absurd *haole* raiments which you have draped upon your bodies . . .'—and my smile faded.

"By and by," continued Mr. Clemens, "the young men of the village joined the ladies and I became interested in their surf-bathing. Each heathen would take a short board with him, paddle out to sea for three or four hundred yards, wait for a particularly prodigious billow to come along, and then fling his board upon its foamy crest and himself upon the board. It was amazing to watch, Miss Stewart. The best of them—male or female—would come whizzing in toward shore like a bombshell, like a lightning express train! Meanwhile, the heathens would be balancing on one leg, waving to one another, doing handstands, braiding their hair, as their boards came roaring into land atop these amazing crests of surf."

Smiling once again, this time to show my incredulity, I said, "And have you tried this sport, Mr. Clemens?"

"Of course!" said the correspondent. He frowned at the recollection. "I confess that I made a failure of it. I got the board placed right—and at the right moment, too—but missed the connection myself. The board struck the shore in three quarters of a second, without any cargo, and I struck the bottom at the same time, with a couple of barrels of water in me. I suspect that none but the natives will ever master the art of surf-bathing thoroughly."

The sky was morning bright now, the sun just hidden by the peak of the volcano to the east, but the clouds moved in low and sullen from the sea and, despite the contrary winds, there was a stench of the firepit in the air.

I sighed again. I knew that all of my companion's badinage was to raise my spirits and to take my mind from the terrors yet ahead, but the sense of uncanny urgency remained as real as the floating will-o'-the-wisp that now left the ancient paved road and floated across the *a'a* field toward the coast. Our horses hesitated a moment, clearly reluctant to return to the effort of finding a way through the sharper stone, but we urged them on and they eventually obeyed. The ball of blue gas had seemed to wait for us until we entered the lava field, but now it floated on ahead again.

Striving to speak in the same light, offhanded tones that Mr. Clemens had been affecting, I said, "I'm afraid that I will have trouble leading the *haole* ghosts from the Underworld . . . I don't believe in ghosts."

Clearing his throat as if preparing for another anecdote, Mr. Clemens replied, "Nor did I, until a certain autumn night two years ago in Carson City when . . ." He paused and then reined his horse to a stop. Ahead of us, a steep wall of lava had long ago pitched a thousand feet in a fiery waterfall now cooled to stone to smooth itself into a circular amphitheater that led down to a broad bay. The surf crashed audibly some quarter of a mile below. In this amphitheater stood a coconut grove and a few ruined homes.

"I think that this may be Kealakekua Bay," Mr. Clemens said softly, as if we might be overheard. "Where they killed and cooked Captain Cook some years ago."

Whatever the bay was called, this strange circle of smooth and rippled stone was bisected by a single great fissure, a narrow crevasse which was obviously the collapsed ceiling of one of the many lava tubes we had encountered on our ride. Where the will-o'-the-wisp had disappeared, the ground fell away and the opening to the fissure was more like the entrance to a cave.

The horses would not come nearer than thirty feet to this fissure and entrance. We dismounted, Mr. Clemens hobbled the tired beasts, he pulled a longer coil of rope from his saddle, and we walked slowly to the opening.

The sense of a cave entrance was misleading; even here where the ground fell away in lava folds, the fissure was more vertical than cavelike. Because of the overhangs of rock where the roof had fallen in, it was impossible to see whether the crevasse was six feet deep or six hundred.

My companion had tied one end of the rope he carried around a small stone. Now he tossed it into the aperture at our feet. "We need a lead," he said, obviously distracted. The stone struck rock with less than twenty feet of rope played out into the opening.

"Good," said Mr. Clemens, pulling back the rope and coiling it with the ease of endless practice. "Mark twain, I think." He cast again, farther this time. "Yes," he said.

I showed my lack of understanding.

"An old riverboat term," said Mr. Clemens. "It means that the lead shows two fathoms ahead. Twelve feet. Deep enough for the keel to pass. Good news for the pilot. Actually, I like the term so much that when I submitted the *Hornet* article last week, I . . ."

"How shall we climb down twelve feet?" I asked, not wanting to interrupt but being much more interested in the task ahead than in quaint riverboat lore.

"The old hag said something about *ieie* vine," said Mr. Clemens. "But I thought that this rope would be a better . . ." He stopped, staring over my shoulder with an expression so peculiar that it made me spin around.

A young woman was standing not six feet behind me. I had not heard her approach, even though the pebbles and stone had scraped under our shoes. She was a native, young, beautiful, with glowing brown skin, bright, dark eyes, and flowing hair the luster of a raven's wing. She held two things in her slender hands—a stoppered gourd and a coil of what looked to be braided vine.

Before either of us could speak, the young woman said, "You must hurry. Pana-ewa and the others sleep for a short time after dawn, but they sleep lightly and wake easily. Quickly now, shed those *haole* raiments . . ."

The voice was young, vibrant, soft, liquid in its native handling of the English vowels . . . and it was unmistakably a younger version of the old crone's voice.

"Quickly!" said the beautiful young woman, gesturing with the hand that held the coiled vine. "Remove your clothes."

Mr. Clemens and I looked at each other.

"Will, I was arguing with a pig," said Byron Trumbo, tossing back his second vodka on the rocks. "A fucking pig."

Will Bryant nodded, glancing toward Hiroshe Sato and the others across the long buffet table. "I know," said Will. "Mrs. Trumbo refuses to leave and her lawyer insists that we . . ."

"Not *that* pig," said Trumbo, turning quickly and wiping his upper lip. "I mean a real pig. A hog. An oinker. A big, fucking swine."

Trumbo's executive assistant squinted at his boss and said nothing.

"Goddammit, don't give me that look!" roared Trumbo, loud enough that Sato and old Mr. Matsukawa and Dr. Tatsuro turned to stare.

Trumbo turned away, pulling Will with him. "Don't give me that *you're crazy* look," he whispered raggedly. "I mean just what I said . . . there was this giant hog in a hole in the ground and he was down there with Sunny Takahashi . . . who was glowing like some damn radium dial from the fifties, Will . . . and he had, I think, eight eyes. The pig I mean." Trumbo grabbed Will Bryant's upper arm. "You believe me, don't you? Tell me that you believe me."

"I believe you, Mr. Trumbo," said Will Bryant. He gently pulled his arm free.

Trumbo squinted suspiciously, but Will Bryant was nodding. "There are enough strange things going on around here," said the assistant. "If you say you argued with a pig . . . you argued with a pig."

The billionaire patted Will Bryant's shoulder. "That's what I like about you, Will . . . beneath that smooth Harvard Law School exterior there beats the heart of a real ass-kissing go-ahead-and-piss-on-me lackey. No offense, Will."

"None taken, boss," said Will Bryant. "But I have to tell you that we found Sunny Takahashi . . ."

Trumbo almost dropped the vodka bottle he was pouring

from. "He came back? Out of the hole? The pig let him come back?"

"I don't know about the pig," said Will, "but they found Sunny's body in one of the cold-storage lockers in the restaurant. Dr. Scamahorn says that it looks like he's been dead for about twelve hours. I haven't informed Mr. Sato or his party yet, because I knew you would want to. Security Chief Dillon's body was also found there. We tried to get you, but you weren't answering your radio. Scamahorn wants to do an autopsy after the authorities are notified and . . ."

Trumbo grabbed Will's arm again and pulled him farther from the banquet table. "Where's his body?"

"Who . . ."

"Sunny's!" said Trumbo, and lowered his voice again. "Sunny's. I don't give a shit about Dillon's. Where is it?"

"In the infirmary. Both bodies were taken up there about twenty minutes ago."

Trumbo prodded a heavy finger against Will's thin chest. "Get on the radio . . . no, go *personally*. See to it that Sunny's corpse . . . hell, both bodies . . . are returned to the freezer. Keep a lid on it. Don't tell *anyone*."

This time, Will Bryant did look strangely at his employer. "Boss, it's over. Mr. Sato will never sign now that his friend has been killed here. It's over. We have to . . ."

Trumbo backed Will farther away from the cocktail party. "Uh-uh. You don't get it. I *saw* Sunny Takahashi not thirty minutes ago. Admittedly, he was glowing and lurching around like a fucking zombie, but it was *Sunny*. If he's been dead and frozen for twelve hours like Scamahorn thinks, it must mean that the pig has his ghost held hostage or something . . ."

"His ghost?" said Will Bryant. The executive assistant did not drink alcohol, never had, but now he reached for the vodka bottle.

"Ghost, spirit, whatever the fuck," said Trumbo, keeping his voice as low as he could. "I don't know about this Hawaiian religious shit. But the hog was willing to give Sunny to me . . . he, it . . . the pig *knew* that Sunny was important to me and he was willing to deal. I mean, I don't know about Hawaiian pig gods or whatever, but I know when someone's willing to deal, and that fucking pig was.''

Will Bryant tossed back his vodka and nodded. "All right," he said, "but Sunny and Dillon are still dead . . .''

"Dillon can *stay* dead," hissed Trumbo. "But maybe the pig will give me Sunny back. He said that Sunny was mine when I wanted him bad enough. He said that all I had to do was go down there in the hole in the ground and talk to him . . . talk to the pig . . . about it." Trumbo trailed off, biting his lip.

Will set the vodka glass carefully on the counter. "We should get back to the party. Hiroshe and the others will be ready to eat."

Trumbo nodded distractedly. "But you think they'll sign if Sunny comes back?"

Will Bryant hesitated only a second. "All the paperwork's been vetted. The meeting room's still set up. Sato doesn't like to do business at night, but they're talking about wanting to fly out early tomorrow."

Trumbo's gaze was not on anything in the room as he nodded. "OK, well . . . I figure how to get Sunny back and we get the damn thing done before morning. OK, you go supervise getting the two bodies back in the freezer . . .''

Will made a face.

"Goddammit," said Trumbo, "you can wash your hands before coming back to the banquet. Just get the bodies back in the freezer. Maybe the pig will toss Dillon in for free. Don't let Scamahorn start an autopsy on either of the stiffs . . . Sunny wouldn't be much of a bargaining chip if I got his ghost back in but he was missing a brain or liver or something." He gave Will a light shove. "Go! I'll entertain Hiroshe and get everyone seated."

Will Bryant nodded and started for the back door to the suite. He paused at the door.

"What?" said Trumbo.

"I'm just wondering," mused Will. "What next?"

The lights went out.

Eleanor had taken off for the helicopter ride just after sunset and just before dark. The smoke from the lava fires was heavy. Vortexes from the small helicopter's rotors sent complicated spirals behind them as they circled the Mauna Pele once and then flew south along the coast.

Paul Kukali had scrambled into the backseat—more a narrow, upholstered bench with seat belts than a seat—while Eleanor had buckled into the single passenger seat in front. In the rotor noise and business of getting buckled in, she had missed part of the pilot's name in the shouted introductions. His first name, she caught, was Mike. Before the pilot pulled sunglasses from his denim shirt pocket and set them in place, Eleanor had caught a glimpse of the most startlingly clear gray eyes she had ever seen on a man. Mike appeared to be about her age—mid-forties—with tanned skin, a pleasant smile, a nicely trimmed beard, and strong forearms with surprisingly sensitive hands at the controls. The pilot was gripping a control stick between his legs and another control rod by his left leg. His sneakers were planted on pedals and Eleanor could see the ground through the Plexiglas of the bubble beneath his feet.

Paul Kukali had put on earphones and now he leaned forward and gestured for Eleanor to do the same. She took the earphones from a niche on the cluttered console between her and the pilot and slid them over her head, adjusting a small microphone in front of her as she did so.

"Is that better?" Mike was saying. "This machine is elegant, but she makes a lot of racket. It's easier to talk on the intercom. Can you hear all right?"

"Yes," said Paul's voice, tinny in her ears. Eleanor nodded and then said, "Yes."

"Well, OK . . . pleased to meet you, Eleanor," Mike said, and held out his hand. Obviously he had caught Paul's shouted introduction.

Eleanor shook hands with the man, blinking at the concurrent impression of strength and sensitivity in that brief contact.

"Shall we go?" said the pilot. "It'll be dark soon enough."

Eleanor nodded and within seconds the engine roar increased, the rotors blurred, and the little craft seemed to bounce once and then leap into the air with an agility that literally took

Eleanor's breath away and made her clutch the sides of the small seat. Her side of the helicopter had a flimsy door that Paul had pulled shut, but a sliding window in it was cracked open and it seemed that there was no barrier between her and the tops of the flapping palm fronds that seemed only inches away when they pitched forward and banked to their left as they climbed.

"You can grip that bar there," Mike was saying over the intercom to her, "but do keep your feet away from the pedals. Thanks."

Eleanor nodded again, feeling rather ridiculous. Then any self-consciousness fled and she watched out the bubble canopy ahead of them as they roared over the Big Hale and the Shipwreck Bar. Eleanor caught a glimpse of Cordie on the walkway three hundred feet below them, her moon-shaped face visibly pink as it lifted to watch the helicopter pass over, and Eleanor risked raising a hand to wave. She did not see if Cordie waved back. Then they were over the penthouse terraces of the hotel and crossing the beach. Eleanor saw the riot of palms below, the *hales* perched on their precarious stilts, the thatched roofs falling behind, and then they were out across the bay and she watched as the light green water changed to dark blue beyond the coral reef.

"Storm coming in from the west soon," said Mike, pointing out to sea. "About two hours, they say. Time for our little mini-tour and for me to get home."

"Where is home?" asked Eleanor. She heard her own voice booming in her earphones and realized that she had shouted into the microphone.

"Mike lives on Maui," came Paul's voice. She swiveled to look at the art and archaeology curator. Paul had his lap belt buckled, but the cabin of the helicopter was so small that when he leaned forward his shoulders almost touched Eleanor's and the pilot's. "Near Hana," he said.

"Kipahulu," said Mike. "No electricity. No water. No cable. We love it."

"Mike is married to a famous researcher and has two neat kids," said Paul. "Their house is this beautiful Japanese-style home set in the middle of the jungle there along the coast, and their nearest neighbor is Mike Love . . . the Beach Boy."

Eleanor nodded, although she was not quite sure if Paul meant a member of the old rock-and-roll group or some Maui personality.

"What kind of research does your wife do?" asked Eleanor.

"Medical," said the pilot, throwing two switches on the console in front of him and settling back comfortably.

They rushed south, a mile or so out from the coastal cliffs. The crash of surf to their left and flashing rocks reminded Eleanor of the opening of some old television series . . . *Magnum, P.I.* She smiled and watched as the petroglyph fields and the area she had jogged in that morning fell behind. She caught a glimpse of the blowhole spouting. "Do you give helicopter rides professionally?" she asked Mike.

The pilot grinned. There were pleasant laugh lines around his eyes, visible even with the sunglasses in place. "Sort of. I own the machine and contract out to Science City . . ." The sunglasses turned in her direction. "There's an installation way up on Haleakala . . . that's the huge dormant volcano on east Maui . . . and most of their work up there is astronomy and meteorology and classified stuff for the Air Force, but Kate . . . my wife . . . works at an immunology lab up there and I drive her to work each day. Up from our shack at sea level to ten thousand and twenty-three feet where her lab is."

Eleanor blinked at that image, traveling from tropical heat to arctic ice and back each day. "Why would they have an immunology lab so high and far away?" she asked.

Mike shrugged slightly. His right hand was easy on the stick while he seemed to be handling the pitch of the rotors with his left. "I guess they figure if some ugly bug gets loose up there, it dies. Meanwhile, Kate may be the only person in Hawaii who commutes to work in sandals and a goose-down parka each day." Mike turned his head and they banked in toward land, passing over a peninsula on which stone ruins and carved wooden figures seemed to stare out at the rising sea. "City of Refuge," he said.

A moment later they reached the first lava flow. Through the softening twilight and smoke, Eleanor could see the asphalt ribbon of gray highway inland cut by the wider gray ribbon of smoking lava flow. The coastal village of Milolii flashed under the helicopter's runners and Eleanor leaned forward to see the widening fan of glowing lava where the flow met the sea. The steam cloud still rose to fifty thousand feet or higher, a white and horribly solid column impaling itself on the sky less than half a mile to their right. "We won't get too close to that," came Mike's voice over the intercom. He moved the stick and they swung left with an amusement-park falling away that sent Eleanor's heart lurching higher in her body.

"There," she said, pointing through the Plexiglas. The lava flows seemed closer to the Airstream trailer of Leonard and Leopold Kamakaiwi, *kahunas*. Grass fires and flaming shrubbery seemed to surround the small structure, the orange flames reflected in the dull sides of the beetle-shaped trailer.

Mike circled lower. "Is this someone we should check on?"

"No, it's all right," said Paul. He pointed. "Their pickup is gone."

"Where could they drive to?" she asked, looking in both directions. To the southwest, the pillar of steam rose like a nuclear explosion. To the east, the lava flows from Mauna Loa fanned down the southwest rift zone, cutting the Belt Road in three places that they could see from here, separating the South Kona Coast from Ka'u and the south tip of the island more effectively than minefields.

"They're all right," repeated Paul. "Uncle Leonard and Uncle Leopold are stubborn . . . not crazy."

"OK," said their pilot. "Shall we do this? Shall we see the volcanoes?"

"Yes," said Eleanor. And then, without thinking, "Please."

They flew across the south tip of the island, keeping clear—as Mike explained—of the major ash cloud from the Mauna Loa eruption.

"Paul's probably explained that it's been a while since we've had major eruptions of Kilauea and Mauna Loa at the same time," said Mike as they climbed over the ridge running down the tail of the island like a serrated spine. The twilight was fading but the land ahead of them was on fire.

"Yes," said Eleanor.

"I think 1950 was the last time Mauna Loa sent lava down the west side like this," continued Mike. He had taken his sunglasses off and his eyes moved between the instruments and the rising land ahead. The helicopter continued climbing but remained a thousand feet above the tortured lava fields of Ka'u. "That stuff travels about five-point-six miles per hour . . . it can reach the coast in less than four hours. Plus, there are dozens . . . hundreds . . . of lava tubes carrying the molten rivers beneath the surface. I was ferrying some scientists up to Kilauea from Kona this afternoon and we watched as a whole new flow erupted up north, near your resort."

Eleanor was listening but her attention was being captured by the scene opening up ahead of them. Lines of orange-red fire as the scores of lava flows from the larger volcano on their left and the brighter eruption from Kilauea straight ahead sent rivers of flame twenty miles and more to the sea. Fountains of flame burning against blue-black ash clouds darker than summer storms. A thousand smaller fires from trees and fields of grass and—presumably—some human structures incinerating themselves in an instant of unspeakable heat.

"Believe it or not, I can pressurize this little thing," said Mike. "And I'm required to if we climb above Mauna Loa at thirteen thousand six hundred some feet . . . but I'll keep us lower. We can see both eruptions and stay off the oxygen."

Eleanor could already see both eruptions. From ten miles away, Kilauea was an overflowing lake of flame. Ash cones became visible in the gloom, illuminated by the fountains of sullen magma spurting from rents in Kilauea's flanks.

But it was Mauna Loa that held her attention. While the summit of the volcano—several miles north and a mile or so above them now—spewed a thick column of ash that drifted above them like a ceiling, it was the line of fissures running down the southwest rift that burned and glowed and flamed like cracks in the ceiling of hell. Eleanor saw ribbons of flame running six miles or more at a stretch, columns of incandescent gas pouring into the evening sky, wild lava fountaining nine hundred feet and more into the air down the entire six-mile slash of fissure.

"My God," she whispered.

"Yes," agreed Paul.

They passed over the fountaining wall of fire with little more than two hundred feet of safety. The helicopter lurched and surged from the updraft and Mike moved hands and feet in sure motions to steady the bucking machine. Eleanor could feel the heat through the soles of her shoes. "My God," she said again.

They passed just south of the caldera, still several thousand feet lower than the actual opening of Mauna Loa, and then rushed down the mountain toward the firestorm that was Kilauea.

It was dark enough now that both land and sea resolved themselves only as distinct darknesses between the innumerable rivers and tributaries of flame. Within each river there were ripples, fountains, textures of molten fire. The rivers of flame moved downhill in visible surges, sluggish, unstoppable. Ten thousand subsidiary fires burned along the path of each lava flow. Each flaming *ohi'a* tree became a distinct beacon, a part of the general burning but separate at the same time. The smoke shifted across the geysers and ribbons and rivers of flame like a torn curtain, sometimes temporarily occluding but never obscuring the fissures of flaming orange.

Mike flew them three hundred feet above the surging lake that was Halemaumau in eruption. Eleanor looked down at the steaming gases, the red geysers within orange fountains, the bubbling caldron of superheated magma, and thought about the engine failing, the helicopter autorotating down into that . . . and she willed herself not to think of it again. Heat pressed against the Plexiglas like a blast from an open hearth, and then they were beyond the lake of Halemaumau, beyond the overflowing crater of Kilauea, and following one of the lava streams downhill at a dizzying rate, banking around columns of black smoke that billowed up at them like giant tree trunks in the night.

"They're all active," Mike was saying. "All the spatter cones and old lakes . . . Mauna Ulu, Pu'u O'o, Puu Huluhulu, Pauahi Crater, Halemaumau . . . look there."

Eleanor followed his pointing finger and saw a lava dome rising like a serrated globe in a flaming lake to their left. The dome bubbled hundreds of feet above the *pahoehoe* surface and became something very close to a sphere—blood-red, ribbed with surging black that slid from the hemisphere in sheets of cooling lava—before beginning its slow collapse. But then she realized that Mike was pointing beyond the lava dome, beyond that lake of fire, to a fountain along the main fissure running down the southwest rift zone. Eleanor saw a tiny speck passing in front of that orange column and realized that it was another helicopter circling, an inconsequential mote drifting in front of a thousand-foot fountain of flame.

Mike toggled a switch and spoke swiftly into his microphone, voice clipped and precise. He switched the intercom back on. "The scientist I was ferrying up here earlier today estimated that more than a million cubic yards of lava was issuing from that one vent every hour. We mapped nine vents along that rift zone."

Eleanor shook her head, unable to speak.

"It's getting dark for real," Mike said. "I'd better get you good people back to the Pele and get myself home to dinner."

They flew west. Crossing the long spine of the island, Eleanor saw the storm clouds far out over the Pacific, but the western slopes of the volcano held the last twilight more firmly. The long fissures of flame were moving through a visible landscape here—the vast, high, lava desert that was Ka'u.

Eleanor amazed herself by reaching out to touch Mike's arm. He looked at her quizzically.

"Mike . . ." she began, and had to regroup. "This flight has been an extraordinary gift . . . I so much appreciate it . . . but could you possibly . . ." She took a breath. "Do you know the region around here called Ka-hau-komo?"

Mike glanced at his instruments, trimmed the ship with a deft touch, and looked back at her. "Ka-hau-komo? As in *hau* meaning 'iron'?"

"Yes."

"I've heard of it." He glanced down at the shadowy mountainside a thousand feet below. "It's somewhere down there, but we'd never find it in the dusk. The *hau* trees are gone, I think."

"Yes," said Eleanor, "but there is a large boulder there called Hopoe . . ."

"Eleanor," said Paul, his voice sharp in her earphones. "This is not a good idea."

She turned to face him. "I think it is, Paul. So do your uncles, but they are afraid to ask."

It was Mike who spoke. "I know the rock called Hopoe. We did navigation exercises off it when I was first certified here. Hard to find in this light, but it's right down . . ." He nodded toward the endless ridge of boulders falling away beneath them, two fissures running for miles on either side of the ridgeline. "Down there."

"There's a woman there," said Eleanor. "She might be trapped."

Mike's face was visible now primarily from the soft red glow of the instrument console in front of them. He looked concerned. "Molly Kewalu?"

"You know of her?" It was Paul's voice. Surprised.

"I thought she was a legend," said Mike.

"She is," said Paul.

"She's not," said Eleanor. "She's alive, she lives in a cave right near the stone called Hopoe, and she may need help."

"I could radio the search-and-rescue people," said Mike.

Eleanor persisted. "Would they go out tonight?"

Mike hesitated only a second. "No. First light at the earliest."

It was Eleanor's turn to point at the flaming cracks in the earth. The helicopter had flown around the west slope of Mauna Loa and the lava flows were very visible now, much broader than the rivers flowing from Kilauea.

"We have maybe five minutes where I can get a visual on Hopoe," said Mike, "but I think I can do it. It's right down there somewhere . . . near if not actually in that area beneath that big vent."

Eleanor realized that she was still touching the pilot's arm. She pulled her hand away. "Thank you," she said.

"It's too rough to actually land," said the pilot, his mind obviously rehearsing what he had to do. "I can let you out and circle, but it will be tricky. There's an emergency kit under your seat with a powerful flashlight in it. I can use the searchlight on the belly. But it will be rough down there . . ."

"I'll do it," said Eleanor. Her heart was pounding.

"We have room for one more," said Mike. "If Mad Molly Kewalu is there with her family and grandkids . . . forget it."

"It is just the old woman," said Paul from the back. His voice was flat. Emotionless.

"All right," said Mike. "Unless I'm off my mark . . . that's Hopoe about a mile ahead, one o'clock."

Eleanor strained to see but could make out only a wild tumble of boulders, each bigger than a house, all of them backlit by the lava flow that had scoured its channel through them on its fiery way to the sea.

"Hang on," said Mike. "We're going down."

Cordie was on her private *lanai* watching the storm move in from the sea when the lights went out. It did not surprise her. She had set the flashlight, candles, matches, and the hurricane lamp on the table near the lounge chair before the last twilight had faded. Now she used the flashlight to check the suite—the doors were locked and the windows secured—and then came back onto the *lanai* to light the candles. The wind was just picking up from the ocean, but even ten or fifteen miles from the storm front, she could see the outline of black stratocumulus backlit by lightning and knew the storm was a serious one. She wished Nell would get back. As long as the storm held off, she could hear the helicopter's return from the *lanai,* but Cordie had hoped her friend would return before full darkness fell.

Cordie set three of the candles inside, one for each room of the suite, and saved the hurricane lamp for the *lanai.* The wind was stronger now and palm fronds were rustling like a restless audience before a delayed final act. Cordie drew the .38 and a box of shells from her tote bag, broke the chamber, removed the empty cartridges, and began to reload.

There was a knock on the door.

"Just a moment," Cordie called softly, and slid the last three cartridges in place. She snapped the chamber shut, spun it, slid off the safety, and walked to the door. "Who is it?"

The answer was muted, but the voice was male.

Cordie left the chain lock on, held the pistol out of sight behind her back, and opened the door a notch.

Stephen Ridell Carter stood holding a hurricane lamp. "Mrs. Stumpf? I'm sorry to bother you, but with the electricity out, we are asking the guests to gather on the seventh floor."

"Why?" said Cordie. She did not open the door wider or take the chain off.

The manager cleared his throat. "Ahhh . . . we have a generator serving the suites up there, Mrs. Stumpf, and we thought it might be . . . ah . . . more comfortable."

"I'm fine," said Cordie. "The refrigerator might drip a bit when it defrosts, but the rest of everything's fine and dandy."

Carter hesitated. His perfectly combed hair gleamed in the candlelight, but his face looked older, more gaunt than it had the last time Cordie had seen him. "Well, actually, Mrs. Stumpf . . . ah . . . as you know, most of the guests have departed and we . . . ah . . . thought that security might be better if the few remaining guests . . . ah . . . gathered on the seventh floor."

"Security from what, Mr. Carter?"

The manager chewed his lip. "There are . . . ah . . . some unusual events occurring at this resort, Mrs. Stumpf."

"I'm aware of that, Mr. Carter." Cordie continued to hold the pistol out of sight.

"Are you sure you won't join us on the seventh floor? The suites there are . . . ah . . . even more comfortable than this one."

Cordie smiled at the man. "Thanks anyway, Mr. C. But I'm sorta used to the bed in this room. Plus, my friends can find me here. You go ahead." She started to shut the door.

Stephen Ridell Carter set two fingers on the door. Cordie waited.

"Mrs. Stumpf, you will . . . ah . . . be careful, will you not?"

Cordie brought the pistol into sight but did not raise it. "Yeah," she said. "I promise I will."

The hotel manager nodded and withdrew his hand. Cordie left the door open long enough to hear his footsteps echo down the tiled mezzanine. The atrium was very dark. She closed the door and went back out onto the *lanai*. The wind was stronger, the flame was flickering in the hurricane lamp, the palms were rasping more loudly below the terrace. "Come on, Nell," whispered Cordie, studying the sky above where the stars were beginning to be occluded by the advancing clouds. The red glow from the volcano tinged the stormfront. "Come on home, Nell."

There was a rasping below that did not come from palm fronds. Setting the pistol on the table, Cordie leaned far over the terrace. Something large and fast and four-legged ran from the jungle into the shadow of the Big Hale. A moment later, something larger followed—running on two legs this time but awkwardly, as if dragging a tail.

Cordie retrieved the pistol and returned to the railing. The asphalt path and terrace below were empty, the only sound the crackling of the torches that lined the walkway.

"Come on home, Nell," whispered Cordie.

June 18, 1866, In an unnamed village on the Kona Coast—
"Disrobe," the young woman had commanded us.

I think that until this moment, the entire adventure in the Sandwich Islands—the volcano, the temple at night, the dead *kanaka* natives, even the apparent death of Reverend Haymark—had seemed a dream, something I could and would write about with the detachment of a naturalist traveling in strange lands, something I could and would write about with a bemused, almost amused air which befits a white, Christian woman traveling in heathen lands. I would see things, I would remark upon things—*but I would not be affected by things*.

"Disrobe," said the beautiful native woman. "Quickly."

I thought of Reverend Haymark lying dead or comatose in the native hut miles above us on the smoking volcanic slope. I thought of the strange things we had seen and the fantastic events yet promised. I began unbuttoning my overvest.

"Miss Stewart," said Mr. Clemens, looking down at his boots, his fists clenched. "I think I . . . I mean, I know that I should descend into this chasm alone. It is no place for a . . ."

What it was no place for, I was never to learn, for the young

woman interrupted. "No! It must be a *haole* man and a *haole* *wahine*. The male ghosts will follow only the man. The female ghosts will follow only the *wahine*. Disrobe quickly! Pana-ewa and the others sleep . . . but not for long!"

Mr. Clemens and I turned our backs upon each other and removed our clothes. I took off my riding gloves, the short-brimmed hat the missionary families had given me in Hilo, the red silk bandana, my brushed leather overvest, and the whipcord riding skirt. Glancing covertly at Mr. Clemens, blushing furiously, I unbuttoned my heavy cotton blouse and set it on the heap of neatly folded clothes.

"Quickly!" said the woman. Her strong hands held the coil of vine and stoppered gourd. The light was rising around us, still occluded by ash clouds and clouds of the more normal variety, but definitely bright enough to read by now.

I wished I were in my guest room in Hilo or Honolulu, reading. Adventures, I decided, were better read about than lived.

I removed my underskirt, the bodice of my chemise, my cotton petticoat, my riding boots, and my heavy socks. Standing in my corset, pantaloons, and unlaced chemise, shivering more from embarrassment than from the cool morning breeze, I looked at the woman. I thought that I detected the slightest hint of a smile on the full lips.

"The old woman told you that to enter the Underworld of Milu you must be naked," said the beautiful apparition.

"*You* were the old woman," I said, marveling at the certainty in my voice.

"Of course," said the native. Turning to Mr. Clemens behind me, she said, "Hurry."

Feeling the heat in my cheeks, I unbound the stays in my corset, removed it, slipped out of my chemise, stepped out of my pantaloons, and laid them neatly with my other clothes. "Can we not wear footwear?" I asked, surprised again at the levelness of my voice. "We will cut our feet."

"Nothing," said the native woman. "Look at me."

Mr. Clemens and I both turned to stare at our interlocutor

while trying not to stare at one another. But still I noticed that the correspondent's chest was covered with a fine, reddish hair which gleamed like copper in the strengthening light. His face was flushed, his strong chin set with determination.

The woman—I truly believed her to be Pele at that moment—handed the coil of vine to Mr. Clemens. "The *ieie* vine will hold you," she said. "You must leave one end of it attached to the outer world or you will never escape the Kingdom of the Ghosts. Now, come closer."

We stepped toward the woman. I was intensely and absurdly aware of the warmth of Mr. Clemens's right leg near my own left one. His hands hung loosely at his sides. The native woman unstoppered the gourd. Forgetting our nakedness, Mr. Clemens and I stepped back quickly, raising our hands to our faces in a reflex but useless action against the stench which assaulted us.

"No, no," said the woman. "The *kukui* nut oil will keep the ghosts from looking carefully at you. They are embarrassed by bad smells."

"Then I trust there will be many embarrassed ghosts before the day's work is done," said Mr. Clemens. His face wrinkled in revulsion as the beautiful woman with the dark hair poured the stinking, viscous fluid from the gourd and rubbed it on the correspondent's hands and arms. "Rub it everywhere on your body," she commanded.

"Essence of polecat," my companion muttered, but he applied the reeking ointment.

Then it was my turn. The woman held the gourd out to me, spilling the buttery liquid on my upraised palms and bare forearms as if we were enacting some sacrament. Perhaps, in some heathen form, we were.

"Rub it everywhere," she repeated to me and tipped the gourd as I smeared the heavy fluid on my arms, throat, bosom, belly, thighs, and back. The sensation was not unpleasant. If it had not been for the almost unbearable stench of the rotten oil, one might have thought we were preparing for a massage in the Vapor Caves at a Rocky Mountain spa.

When we were finished applying the last of the reeking oil,

the young woman stepped back and appraised us with the smallest of smiles. "Very good. You smell like dead *haoles*."

Mr. Clemens brushed at his mustache. "Do dead *haoles* smell different than dead *kanakas?*" he asked, using the local word for the Sandwich Island natives.

Our guide ignored him. Her bearing was somehow both imperious and mischievous; it was as if we had encountered a princess of the ruling family who did not take her position with total seriousness. But her face was serious as she said, "Beware the hog."

"I beg your pardon?" said Mr. Clemens.

The woman took a step back. "Pana-ewa sleeps lightly. Nanaue, the shark boy, sleeps hardly at all. If Ku—the dog man—catches your real scent beneath the *kukui* nut oil, your souls will be forfeit." She turned to look directly at me. "If Kamapua'a awakes, he will rape you before killing you and eating your *hi-hi'o*."

I swallowed with some difficulty. My arms were across my chest, but I felt absurdly exposed and vulnerable. "Eat my *hi-hi'o?*" I repeated. The mind reeled at the possible translations of that simple Hawaiian word.

"Your traveling soul," said the woman who might be Pele. "The *hi-hi'o* is the *uhane*, the soul of the living, when it has left the *kino*. The body. If your *kahuna* friend had been killed by Pana-ewa, it would be his *lapu*."

"*Lapu?*" said Mr. Clemens.

"His ghost," said the raven-haired beauty.

I was confused. "Are the ghosts we are supposed to lead out of the Underworld *hi-hi'os*, the stolen souls of the living, or *lapus*, the ghosts of the dead?"

"Pana-ewa stole the *uhane* of your friend," said the woman, "thus making it *hi-hi'o*. The others will return to their bodies if they are *hi-hi'o*, or go to where Christian *lapu* go when they are freed from their bodies."

"Where is that?" asked Mr. Clemens.

The young woman's teeth were very white and regular. "Why do you ask me? *You* are the Christians, are you not?"

Mr. Clemens made a skeptical sound but was distracted

when the young woman handed him the coil of *ieie* vine and a coconut shell. The coconut had a plug in the top of it. "The shell is to capture your friend's *uhane*," she said.

Mr. Clemens and I looked dubiously at the coconut.

"Secure the vine with great care," said the woman, taking another step back. "It will be your only way out of the Land of the Ghosts."

"Secure it to what?" said Mr. Clemens, turning to look at the fissure and the nearly empty plain of lava around it.

Still conscious of my nakedness but somewhat distracted by the discussion, I also turned to survey the cave entrance. "The vine is not long enough to secure to those trees," I said. "Perhaps one of the boulders?"

Mr. Clemens cleared his throat as if to speak and turned. A second later, I did the same. The young woman I imagined to be Pele was gone. Ten yards away, our horses slept with heads bowed. Beyond them it was hundreds of yards of empty lava field to the ocean or the lava cliffs behind us.

At that moment, had we retained even a vestige of sanity, we would have donned our clothes and ridden out of that place. We could have reached Kona before nightfall and notified the authorities there of the strange insurrection occurring on their southern coast. Someone would have returned for Reverend Haymark's body.

We had no vestige of sanity left. The feeling was rather like standing on this empty lava amphitheater naked: chilling, exhilarating, somewhat buoyant.

Without speaking, we left our heap of clothes and walked the few yards back to the fissure. Seemingly lost in thought, Mr. Clemens once again inspected the vertical entrance to the cave, crouched gracefully, set the coconut shell down, and tied several loops of the vine around the one boulder that protruded sufficiently for the cord to pass around it. He tied off the vine in complicated knots made to look easy through obvious practice. At least fifteen yards of the braided vine remained.

"Miss Stewart," he began, not looking directly at me, "I still believe that I should go alone . . ."

"Nonsense," I said, crouching near enough to him that his

skin must have felt the heat of my own. "I believe her when she says that a man and a woman are needed to lead the male and female ghosts from the Underworld."

We looked at each other then, our eyes—I am sure—bright with something inexplicable. Who could have guessed that insanity carried its own logic and enjoyment?

We stood at the edge of the fissure. Mr. Clemens took the free end of the vine, looped it into a sort of lasso secured with a clever knot, but hesitated before slipping it over my head and shoulders. I realized that he would have to lower me into the chasm but that he did not wish me to be the first to descend into the darkness. I also realized that there was another reason that he hesitated before securing the line around me.

I took the braided rope and tugged it down over my shoulders and bosom. Mr. Clemens blushed, but secured the knot before the thick cord could tighten against my skin.

To break the momentary tension, I said, "Mr. Clemens, it occurs to me that the old adage 'Clothes make the man' has some veracity . . ."

He looked up at me in surprise.

"Naked people," I continued, "surely must have little or no influence on society."

For a second there was silence but for the distant surf; a moment later the crashing of waves was drowned out by the echo of my companion's laughter.

"Hush," I said, "or we shall awaken Pana-ewa."

He stifled his laughter but grinned at me. "Or Ku."

"Or Nanaue," I said, "the shark boy."

"Or Kamapua'a," he whispered. "The hog."

We continued smiling at each other for a long moment, and I must record here that a strange, intense energy passed between us. I am sure that it must have been the excitement of the moment, that surge of energy and sheer giddiness which soldiers record experiencing just before the battle, but it was also . . . something else.

Mr. Clemens tightened the knot and smoothed the length of vine out, speaking as he prepared to lower me into the chasm.

"Miss Stewart," he said, "this reminds me of the day not long ago in San Francisco when I happened upon a hotel fire. A lady was trapped on the fourth floor and all those around me had lost their head and were running uselessly to and fro. Only I kept my wits about me . . ." He paused to tug at the vine, checking the knot on the boulder. The vine held. "Only I had the presence of mind to go to a nearby tethered horse, remove the lariat kept there, toss the long rope to the hapless woman on the fourth floor, and shout instructions to her on how to secure it."

I backed to the edge of the fissure and waited there as Mr. Clemens took up the slack in the vine. "Yes?" I said.

He looked at me. His eyes were very bright under his expressive brow. "Well, then, once she had tied the line on, I shouted, 'Jump! I have you!' "

We stood there a moment, that strange energy rippling between us like the St. Elmo's Fire that had guided us here.

"Step back, Miss Stewart," he said softly, wrapping the vine once around my forearm and showing me where to hold tight. "I have you."

Leaning back, stepping off the boulder into nothingness, I began the descent into the Underworld.

TWENTY

O gods in the skies!
Let the rain come, let it fall.
Let Paoa, Pele's spade, be broken.
Let the rain be separated from the sun.
O clouds in the skies!
O great clouds of Iku! black as smoke!
Let the heavens fall on earth,
Let the heavens roll open for the rain,
Let the storm come.
      —Kamapua'a's war chant

E Pele e! Here is my sacrifice—a pig.
E Pele e! Here is my gift—a pig.
Here is a pig for you.
O goddess of the burning stones.
Life for me. Life for you.
The flowers of fire wave gently.
Here is your pig.
      —traditional chant to Pele

A sense of unreality had been building in Eleanor all afternoon, and now, as she jumped from the skid of a hovering helicopter to the broad surface of the tumbled "dancing stone" called Hopoe, that sense of unreality took on a delicious, dreamlike quality. *Dreamlike, but hardly calm,* thought Eleanor, crouching as the helicopter rose in a downblast of wind and blown grit. She felt the surge of adrenaline in her body acting like some sort of turbo-boost to her spirits. *This is being alive!*

Mike, the pilot, had given her ten minutes. His own fuel requirements and the approaching storm had made even that allowance marginal. In the meantime, he would circle above—"orbit" was the word he had used—and five flashes from Eleanor's flashlight would bring him back to the pickup area on the rock called Hopoe.

Eleanor flicked on the flashlight, testing it, and then turned it off. She had thought that it would be dark here on the mountainside, but the reflected volcano glow on the clouds above and the more fiery light from the lava flow less than fifteen yards away cast each rock, boulder, and fissure opening in a thick, bloody light. Eleanor picked her way from rock to rock toward the base of the giant boulder on which she had landed.

There was an open space at the foot of the huge stone and a darker shadow that may have been the entrance to a cave. Lava flowed by not ten yards down the hill from that entrance. Eleanor was amazed by the heat and rapidity of the flow; it moved like a mountain stream at flood stage, black and red rushing by at freight train speeds, the heat from the hurtling magma causing her to raise her forearm to shield her face. A hundred yards farther down the mountainside, lava geysered fifty or sixty feet in the air. Eleanor was reminded of fireworks displays she had seen as a child in her sleepy Ohio town, with the ground-display finale fountaining sparks and liquid fire like this. Not like this. A quarter of a mile lower, another geyser, taller and brighter, and below that, more flaming fissures and geysers, and so on to the invisible sea eight miles or more below. Eleanor wondered if this tidal wave of molten rock had reached the Mauna Pele Resort yet. She squinted upward, but could not see the helicopter in the clouds of smoke and ash. Pele's hair gleamed here and there, filaments strewn across boulders and bridging black fissures, each glasslike strand catching the hellish light.

"Eleanor," said a voice.

Eleanor turned quickly, seeing the form of a woman in the dark mouth of the cave. "Molly Kewalu?"

"Come in," said the woman, and stepped back into the shadows.

Eleanor glanced at her watch and hurried up the talus slope. She had less than seven minutes before the helicopter returned.

The cave widened half a dozen yards beyond the entrance. Eleanor noticed the carpet on the lava-smooth floor, the fine old table with two chairs, another rocking chair near an end table made of a packing crate, the books in other crates made into shelves, the kitchen area with its gleaming copper pots, the three hissing lanterns illuminating the scene with their warm light. The dreamlike quality of everything had not abated. Eleanor did not ask how the woman had known her name.

"Sit," said Molly Kewalu. Eleanor had expected her to be the old woman she had seen in Leonard and Leopold's trailer, but she was not. Molly Kewalu may have been the Crazy Old Woman of the Big Island, but she reminded Eleanor of a former head of the English Department at Oberlin. Molly's gray hair was drawn back in a tight bun and held in place with a beautiful tortoiseshell comb. Her face was almost unlined, and strengthened by exquisite eyebrows and a firm chin, and her eyes seemed more amused than mad. She was wearing tan chinos, a red silk shirt open at the throat to exhibit a turquoise necklace which looked of Navajo design, sturdy hiking boots, and a simple but elegant bracelet made of tiny shells.

"Please, sit," said Molly Kewalu, gesturing toward the rocking chair. The older woman pulled a table chair closer.

"I only have a minute," said Eleanor, settling back in the rocker and thinking, *Is this real?* It was real. She could hear the lanterns hissing, still smell the sulfur from the lava flow just outside the cave.

"I know," said Molly Kewalu. She leaned forward and touched Eleanor's knee. "Do you have any idea what you have involved yourself in, Eleanor Perry from Ohio?"

Eleanor blinked. "There is a battle," she said, voice small in the comfortable, hissing silence of the cave. "Pana-ewa and the other demons . . ."

Molly Kewalu lifted her hand to make a dismissive gesture. "Pana-ewa is nothing. *Nothing.* It is Kamapua'a who contests the rule of this island with Pele. It is Kamapua'a who has used the *haole* to prepare his way."

"Prepare his way," echoed Eleanor. There was a rushing of blood in her ears. "Even with Kidder and Mark Twain, it was . . ."

"The hog," said Molly Kewalu. "The men *kahuna* say that they worship Pele, but in their heart of hearts, they follow the hog."

"The hog," said Eleanor.

Molly Kewalu leaned closer and grasped the teacher's upper arms. "You have courage, Eleanor Perry of Ohio. You think you will descend into the Underworld of Milu as did your female ancestor."

Eleanor blinked again. *How does she know all this?*

"You will fail, Eleanor Perry. Your body will die before this happens. *But you must not lose your courage.* It is the quiet night-courage of women which binds our powers and balances the loud day-courage of men. Our courage is the source of the darkness that makes darkness, do you understand, Eleanor Perry of Ohio?"

"No," said Eleanor. She thought, *My body will die?* She said, "I want to understand, but I do not." *I teach the history and literature of the Enlightenment.* Has meus ad metas sudet oportet equus.

"Listen," said Molly Kewalu, and rose to her feet. She chanted softly:

"At the time when the earth became hot
At the time when the heavens turned about
At the time when the sun was darkened
To cause the moon to shine
The time of the rise of the Pleiades
The slime, this was the source of the earth
The source of darkness that made darkness . . ."

Creation chant, thought Eleanor. *Simple, common creation chant. Am I to die?*

"When space turned around, the earth heated," chanted Molly Kewalu.

"When space turned over, the sky reversed.
From the source in the slime was the earth formed

From the source in the darkness was darkness formed
From the source in the night was night formed.''

Union, thought Eleanor. *The womb of night. The birthing place of the universe in the clash of opposites. Even the war between Pele and Kamapua'a must continue.*

"From the depths of the darkness, darkness so deep," sang Molly Kewalu.

"Darkness of day, darkness of night
Of night alone
Did night give birth
Born was Kumulipo in the night, a male
Born was Po'ele in the night, a female.''

But the rape has to stop, thought Eleanor. *The balance must be reset or lost.* Part of her mind understood. Part of her mind did not care. *Must I die?*

"Born was man for the narrow stream," chanted Molly Kewalu. She touched Eleanor's hand. Eleanor rose and followed her to the dark cave mouth. Lava hissed and poured red light beyond. Somewhere above there was a roar.

"Born was woman for the broad stream
Born was the night of the gods.''

Molly Kewalu released her hand. "Go back, Eleanor Perry of Ohio. Go back and do what you must do. Have courage."

Eleanor turned, started to leave, and turned back in a panic. "No! You have to be there. To help."

"Someone will be there to help," Molly Kewalu said softly, her words all but lost under the hiss of lava. "There is always a midwife to help us when we are in pain."

Eleanor shook her head sluggishly. It had seemed so clear moments before. "You have to come . . ."

"Not tonight," said Molly Kewalu. Her finger lifted, pointed to the river of lava, traced its flow back up the volcano's flank.

"This night I must make offering elsewhere." She moved quickly forward, squeezed Eleanor's hand, and disappeared in the cave mouth.

Eleanor hesitated a second and then staggered blindly up the talus slope to the top of the tumbled rock called Hopoe, the Dancing Stone.

The helicopter hovered low a moment later, its blast of grit blinding Eleanor, its roar deafening her. Hands pulled her in. Someone was shouting something over and over. It took a moment for her to understand the English words; they struck her ear as if they were from a foreign tongue.

"No," she said at last, allowing Paul to buckle her in. "She was not there. No one was there."

"All right," said Mike, the pilot with kind eyes. The engine roared. They rose, tilted, flew away and down.

"Byron-san," said Hiroshe Sato as the Escargot Mezzanine arrived, snails baked in a sun-dried tomato pesto butter and white wine, "the electricity here seems unreliable." The hurricane lamps flickered down the length of the resplendent table. Waiters set out bowls of Malaysian shrimp salad featuring skewered tiger prawns served with *gadogado* peanut dressing with stir-fried vegetables over a bed of greens.

"Atmosphere," said Byron Trumbo. "There is a storm tonight, but the backup generators handle it." He nodded to Bobby Tanaka, who flipped a switch. The electric candles on the chandeliers blazed. Bobby turned off the lights. "We like the atmosphere of the candles," said Trumbo.

The white-liveried waiters set out a Grecque spinach salad for those who did not care for the shrimp. The onion-garlic-dill dressing with a hint of ouzo made Trumbo blink. Crumbled feta cheese added a nice contrast to the greens. Warm focaccia bread, straight from the ovens, was set in place. André, the aged wine steward, opened bottles and brought Trumbo the corks. Trumbo ignored them and gestured for the wine to be poured.

"We remain concerned about our friend Tsuneo," Hiroshe Sato whispered, leaning close so that no one else could hear him.

"As irresponsible as he is, it is unlike him to miss a business function."

"Yeah, well," said Trumbo, "I'm sure Sunny's OK. In fact, I'm certain he'll be back for the signing after dinner."

"Hrrgghh," said Sato, emitting that half-growl that Japanese men made on emotional but noncommittal occasions. He applied himself to the Malaysian shrimp.

"Excuse me a moment, Hiroshe," said Trumbo. He had seen Will Bryant entering the long room, talking to two security men. Trumbo pulled his assistant onto the terrace. The wind was roaring, clouds scudding above, illuminated by volcano glow.

"The bodies are back in the cooler," Bryant said softly. "We've got the seventh floor sealed off here. Michaels has people guarding the elevator, the stairways, and the mezzanine."

"What about Fredrickson?"

"He called in a few minutes ago," said Will Bryant. "He's spooked. He says a storm's coming. He wants to come in."

"Tell him to stay where he is," said Trumbo. He pulled Bryant a few steps closer to the railing. "Will, I've got a job for you."

The assistant waited. He was wearing his round Armani tortoiseshell glasses and his eyes looked large behind the lenses.

"You remember that cave I told you about? And the pig? And Dillon and Sunny Takahashi looking sort of like ghosts or zombies or something?"

Will Bryant nodded and waited.

"Well," said Trumbo, "the pig said that if I wanted Sunny, all I had to do was go down and get him."

Will Bryant nodded and waited.

"Will," said Trumbo, "I want you to go down and get him."

Will Bryant turned his head slowly until the owl-like eyes were looking directly at his boss.

"Now," said Trumbo.

"Ahhh," said the assistant. He licked his lips and started again. "I just put Sunny Takahashi's body in the freezer."

"Yeah," said Trumbo, brushing away that fact with a flick of his hand, "but I think the pig's got his spirit or some shit like that. You go down and get it and we'll see if we can get it back in the Jap's body in time for Sato to sign the deal tonight."

Will Bryant's eyes did not blink behind the round lenses. "You want me to go out in the storm, find the cave that Fredrickson's guarding, go down in it, talk to a pig, and get Sunny Takahashi's spirit back in time for the signing?"

"Yeah," said Trumbo, his voice relieved. When the instructions were clear, Will Bryant had never failed him.

"Fuck you," said Bryant.

Trumbo blinked. "What?"

"Fuck you." And then, as if an afterthought had struck him: "Boss."

Trumbo resisted the urge to grab the Harvard Business School graduate by his skinny throat and hurl him over the seventh-floor railing. He had essentially done that to his last executive assistant. "What did you say to me?"

"I said, 'Fuck you,' " said Bryant, his voice calm. "There are a lot of people dead around here, and I'm not ready to join them. It's not in my job description."

Trumbo was trembling with rage. He clasped his hands behind his back to hide their shaking. "I'll make it worth your while," he said through clenched teeth.

Will Bryant waited.

"Ten thousand dollars," said Trumbo.

Will Bryant laughed softly.

"All right, goddammit, fifty thousand," said Trumbo. He would send one of the security men to fetch Sunny, but those guys were too stupid to pour piss out of a boot. Bobby Tanaka was a wuss and he had fired Stephen Ridell Carter. It had to be Bryant.

Will Bryant shook his head and waited.

"Goddammit," breathed Trumbo, his face red and neck cording, "how much?"

"Five million dollars," said Will Bryant. "Cash."

Trumbo's vision narrowed to a long black tunnel decorated with red spots. When he could see again, he said, "One million."

"Fuck you," said his assistant.

It was kill the blackmailing little dust mite or leave. Trumbo wheeled on his heels and left, returning to the dinner party. Waiters were setting out the main courses of *opakapaka* with ginger-scallion crusts, and pan-roasted lamb chops with macadamia nut-coconut-honey crusts floating on star anise sauce.

"Are you all right, Byron-san?" asked Sato, his voice concerned. "Your face is the color of lobster." *Robser.*

"I'm fine," said Trumbo, lifting his knife and thinking how sweet it would feel sliding between a certain traitor's skinny ribs. "Let's eat the fucking food."

June 18, 1866, In an unnamed village along the Kona Coast—

For a moment I stood alone in the Ghost Kingdom of Milu. The lava tube extended away, but not into darkness. The walls glowed with a subdued phosphorescence. Faint sounds echoed from around the bend in the cave. The striated cavern floor was rough against my bare feet. I could smell the rancid *kukui* oil on my skin.

Hurriedly, I untied the knots, freed myself from the vine, and tugged the braided cord to let Mr. Clemens know he could descend. Sunlight reflected from the fissure wall above, but a rock overhang kept me from seeing my companion. I looked away as he let himself down the thick vine.

Glancing at each other, feeling somewhat less naked in the dim light here, we began walking toward the glow. "Still reminds me of lightning bug light," whispered Mr. Clemens. We paused at the bend in the cave, Mr. Clemens peering around before we went on.

He turned back, his mustaches veritably quivering with excitement. "Ghosts," he whispered.

"How many?" I whispered back.

"How many?" repeated Mr. Clemens. "How many? I don't know . . . about nine hundred eighty-seven thousand, six hundred thirty-one, I estimate."

I stared in shock.

"I don't *know* how many!" whispered Mr. Clemens in a loud tone. "A cotillion's worth. Perhaps a regiment. I am not accustomed to counting ghosts. There are enough for several bridge games with ample left over for a jury."

I made a face at his light tone at this serious juncture. "How do you know they are ghosts, Mr. Clemens? Simply because we were told to expect them here?"

The redheaded correspondent nodded, shrugged, and patted his bare chest as if searching nonexistent pockets for a cigar. "Yes, Miss Stewart," he said, "that and the fact that they glow like St. Elmo's Fire and I can see through them as if they were a thin broth. These are the primary clues, but I am no detective. They could be a Senate Committee in search of a quorum, but since they are naked, this seems improbable. I would put my money on ghosts." I hesitated and Mr. Clemens may have mistaken the pause for fear, for he said, "Shall we go on? Or return to the surface?"

"We shall go on," I said at once. Noticing the color high in Mr. Clemens's cheeks, I added, "Do not distress yourself about our state of dishabille, sir. Our worthy progenitors, Eve and Adam, were comfortable enough in this state."

Mr. Clemens made a soft, nasal noise and whispered, "This is true, Miss Stewart, and I am no biblical scholar, but I believe that Adam and Eve were on a first-name basis."

"Shall we proceed, Mr. Clemens?"

The correspondent turned and held out his arm. I linked mine with his. Thus we entered the realm of Milu, as cordially and casually as two well-dressed San Franciscans entering a formal ball. Ghosts, it seemed, spent the afterlife doing much the same sort of thing that had preoccupied them during life. The cavern widened here and scores of glowing figures were visible, all Sandwich Island natives as far as we could tell; some were sleeping, many were gambling or playing the type of games we had seen being pursued with stones in the dirt of Hilo and lesser villages, others rolling coconuts to hit a post and paying each other off in bones, while some were eating—many of these gathered around a huge bowl of the purple paste the locals call *poi*—and still others were merely strolling, men with men, women with women, and the occasional couple looking as if they were courting in death much as they must have in life.

Mr. Clemens and I proceeded slowly, staying to ourselves.

While we could not approximate the transparent quality of these spirits, some quality of the *kukui* nut oil imparted a glow to us that was not dissimilar to the spectral glow of those ghosts around us. Several times a spirit separated himself or herself from some activity and seemed to glide toward us, as if to welcome us to this place, but when each spectral form came within olfactory range of the rancid oil, the ghost would turn quickly and make a face, as if to say, "What a bad-smelling ghost!" It was after these occasions that I noticed that while the spirits in this huge cavern seemed to be speaking to each other—their mouths opened and closed, their jaws moved, their expressions changed—there was no audible conversation, indeed, no sound of any sort except the wind through the many fissures and crevices running from this main chamber.

Mr. Clemens reached over, squeezed my upper arm, and nodded in the direction of a side cavern. As if to dispute my conclusion about the silence of this spectral realm, a huge pig—the boar must have weighed well over a thousand pounds—was sleeping at the entrance to this subsidiary cavern. The hog's snoring was more than audible—indeed, the rasping and whistling of air rushing in and out of the creature's cavernous snout had been much of the noise that I had taken for the wind through the cavern's fissures.

Remembering the woman's warning about not waking the hog, I was ready to tiptoe in the opposite direction, but Mr. Clemens pointed and nodded again.

Behind the hog, in a deep niche in the cavern wall, stood several glowing forms that—while naked as the others—were obviously not the spirits of natives. Most of the *haole* spirits were male, but I could see at least one elderly woman in the congregation . . . for in truth, a congregation it was. A four-foot extension of lava that was relatively flat on top was obviously being put to use as a pulpit, and several of the ghosts appeared to be vying for preaching time at it. An older, taller spirit must have been the Reverend Whister. The aged female in the listening crowd must have been his wife. There were other men; I tried to remember the details of the story at Volcano

House—the taller of the young men might be August Stanton, the widow Stanton's late husband. The other young man might be Mr. Taylor. I winced upon recalling that they had found Mr. Stanton all but drained of blood and Mr. Taylor's demise had included having his head "fractured with the sound of a coconut being halved." They looked none the worse for wear in their spirit form, although there was a certain abstract quality around the eyes that may or may not have been with them in life.

Mr. Clemens nodded again and I almost exclaimed aloud as I saw the next speaker at the pulpit. Reverend Haymark's girth was as impressive unclothed as it had been beneath layers of missionary finery. Our former companion set his hands on the edges of the rock with the ease of someone familiar with the pulpit, leaned his weight forward, and began to mouth inaudible platitudes. The congregation listened with a certain zombie quality not uncommon in any Presbyterian church on a warm Sunday.

Mr. Clemens set his lips against my ear so that the noise of his whisper could not be heard even a few paces away. "How do we get him into the coconut?"

I shook my head. I had no idea how we were to get past the hog. Indeed, to gain access to the side cavern, one or both of us would have to step over the monster pig's snout. The thought made me shudder.

As if reading my mind, my companion leaned against me once again and whispered, "You stay here. I will endeavor to reach Reverend Haymark."

I answered by seizing Mr. Clemens's upper arm and shaking my head rapidly. Already more of the spirits were wandering near, despite the stench of our drying oil, and the thought of standing there alone while these dead things brushed against me was not supportable.

Mr. Clemens nodded his understanding and we began our slow voyage past the snoring hog. The cavern floor was irregular under our feet and I felt a mounting terror at the thought of suddenly losing my balance and pitching over onto the bristled mass of the thing. At close inspection, the hog was even larger than I had thought from a distance; it must easily have weighed a ton. The thing was like a small elephant with a hog's bristled hide and terrible head. As we reached the point where we would have to step over that head, I realized with a surge of vertigo that the sleeping beast had multiple eyelids . . . not two or four, but at least eight. I caught a glimpse of obsidian orbs beneath those lowered lids, and for a moment I was sure that the monster was only feigning sleep in order to draw us closer. Even as I lifted my bare foot to step over that snout, feeling the hideous, warm breath on my sole, my imagination supplied me with the sudden and certain image of those eyes snapping open, that mouth with its too-human teeth opening and then closing upon my ankle; I could hear the snap and rending of cartilage and bone as the hog swallowed my foot with a single gulp and then lifted that head the size of a barrel to devour the rest of my leg . . .

Mr. Clemens caught me before I fainted dead away. In my sudden vertigo, I had swooned toward the hog's bristled back, and only the former riverboat pilot's strong left arm held me upright. While we were clasped thusly, like two dancers in a slow pirouette, I regained my composure and then my balance.

We stepped over the hog and were in the deep niche in the cavern wall. If it awoke now—and I suddenly realized that a hog's sense of smell was sensitive and that it would certainly be awakened by our stench—we would be trapped with the other *haole* ghosts. I remembered the Pele-woman's comment that the hog would rape me and eat my *hi-hi'o* should I waken it. Once again my flesh rippled with revulsion and my skin went cold with giddiness; once again, Mr. Clemens steadied me with a strong hand on my bare back. Such intimacies would have been unthinkable an hour earlier; now they were welcomed.

We moved through the small congregation of Christian spirits. We had come for our friend, Reverend Haymark, but the old lady in the hut had ordered us to remove all of the *haole uhane* from the cavern so that Pele might resume battle with her enemies. I looked at Mr. Clemens, but it was obvious that he had no more idea how to move these glowing forms from this spot than had I.

The problem was solved for us. The Christian spirits disliked our smell as much as the *kanakas* had, and they made a path for us. Mr. Clemens led the way to the pulpit, where Reverend Haymark's ghost continued preaching to an unheeding audience. Our corpulent friend's spirit made me think of an unsuccessful waxwork imitation of the living man I had known. His mouth moved soundlessly until Mr. Clemens touched the spirit's arm. Immediately, Reverend Haymark's *uhane* turned as if summoned and stepped down from the makeshift pulpit, following Mr. Clemens as the correspondent threaded his way back through the crowd.

I tried this technique. It worked well. A mere touch on the arm of our kindred ghosts worked like a silent summons. The first time I touched one—the woman, Mrs. Whister, I presumed—I drew my hand back quickly. The spirit's arm was no more substantial than a breeze—a chilly breeze. But she turned obediently and followed me toward the hog's snout and freedom.

Half a dozen touches and the *haole* spirits followed us like goslings behind a mother goose. Mr. Clemens led the way, pausing only briefly before lifting his bare leg over the snoring pig's snout. For a second I feared that Reverend Haymark's ectoplasmic feet would wake the hog, but then I noticed that none of the spirits actually touched the ground as they walked.

When it was my turn to again pass the sleeping pig, I felt my heart pounding so loudly that I was sure the monster would hear it and wake. But I summoned my courage and once again lifted my leg over the ugly snout. I could see the creature's teeth now—huge, sharp, glistening. A small puddle of drool moistened the cavern floor where the monster slept.

I passed without incident. The following spirits did not even glance at the hog as they floated after me. I wondered what I would do if these ghosts spent the rest of eternity following me around. As we moved further toward the mouth of the cavern, Reverend Haymark and the other ghosts floating like tethered balloons in our wake, I decided that I would deal with that problem when faced with it in the outside world.

Some of the other ghosts followed our procession out of some sort of spectral curiosity. There was no cry or alarm sounded; indeed, there was no sound at all save for the monster pig's rasping breathing—a sound which receded but never disappeared no matter how far we traveled down the lava tube.

Most of the native spirits had turned back before we reached the base of our entrance fissure, but one—a handsome young man with blank eyes—continued to follow. I suddenly was certain that this was the loyal but hapless native named Kaluna whom the Reverend Whister had murdered by accident when the boy had lifted his knife to take an oath. It did not matter. The old woman had not told us to take any native spirits with us when we left, and, in truth, the young man's *uhane* did not try to follow as we left the fissure.

Mr. Clemens leaned close and whispered, "I will have to climb first and then lift you out."

The thought of being alone in the near-darkness with these glowing, mindless things did not please me, but I bit my lip and nodded agreement. Before climbing, however, Mr. Clemens did an incredible thing. Unstoppering the coconut shell the young woman had given him, he held it against the ectoplasmic persona of Reverend Haymark and began shoving and twisting the yielding specter. Incredibly, the shape of our former companion began flowing into the coconut like fog through a keyhole. Mr. Clemens worked harder, palpatating the cloudy remnants of the cleric into malleable forms to squeeze through the tiny opening. It was hard work—as Mr. Clemens said later—rather like folding a large sail into a small valise.

It—he—eventually folded. Mr. Clemens squeezed in the last ectoplasmic protuberance of the missionary, stoppered the coconut, and began to climb the vine.

"What of these?" I whispered urgently, gesturing toward the sightless congregation of the elder Reverend Whister, his staring wife, his vacant-eyed son-in-law, Mr. Stanton, the vacuous Mr. Taylor, and one or two others whose stories we did not know.

Mr. Clemens leaned back from the vine and whispered, "We had best leave them to get out as best they can. I think they have no bodies to return to, so they are on their own. From what the old woman said, they are *lapus*, ghosts of the dead, rather than a kidnapped *hi-hi'o*, spirit of the living, such as our friend." He panted slightly, holding himself nearly horizontal from the cave wall while hanging from the vine. I realized with a shock that I was growing accustomed to Mr. Clemens's naked presence. "Also," he said, returning his attention to the climb, "I don't think there's any more room in the coconut."

Mr. Clemens leveraged himself higher, out of sight. For the moment, I was alone with the glowing spirits who had followed me there, including the native Kaluna whose sad face registered the only emotion I had seen in the Ghost Kingdom of Milu.

Suddenly my pulse galloped and I whirled as if something had moved in the shadows. Images of Pana-ewa leapt to mind, but there was no lizard or creature of night and fog there in the lava tube.

It took me a second to realize that what had startled me was not a sudden presence but an absence.

The hog had stopped snoring.

Cordie heard the helicopter before she saw it. Then it came in once over the Big Hale, searchlight stabbing down over the palm trees and winking twice as if in hello to her, before the throbbing rotors passed overhead and the moving shape was lost to sight in the night.

Cordie knew Nell's plan. She knew that unless the old woman on the mountain had dissuaded her, Eleanor would be planning to descend into the Underworld to lead the *haole* spirits out so that once again Pele could battle her enemies without fear of hostages. Cordie also knew that Nell would have been working to persuade that jerk of an art curator to go into the cave with her—assuming that the old rule of one man and one woman to lead the spirits out was somehow still in effect.

Cordie did not care about the plan. She did not care about saving the Maune Pele Resort or the ghosts of the missing guests or any of it. She just wanted to get her friend Nell and herself out of this alive. With a growing chill, Cordie Stumpf realized that she would have to go to the heliport to warn Nell and Paul about the things abroad in the night . . . but to get to the heliport meant braving the dark and exposing herself to the things abroad in the night.

"Shit," said the little woman. She tugged her straw bag over her shoulder, checked to make sure that everything she needed was in it, and slipped the lock on the door.

The sixth-floor mezzanine was dark. She could hear laughter and music from the Trumbo party one flight up, but everything below the penthouse level was darkness and subtle sounds. Cordie was sure that the guest elevator was out of action, which meant six flights down on one of the stairways at either the east or west end of the Big Hale. The stairways were open to the night air, which should help, but the only illumination was from the lanterns and lights above and the hellish glow from the volcano to the east.

Enough to see giant pigs by, I guess, thought Cordie. She held the pistol in her right hand and locked the door to her suite behind her. She took four steps, frowned, and leaned against the railing to the central courtyard while she removed her sturdy shoes and dropped them in her tote bag. Her socks made almost no noise on the tile. *Better,* she thought.

Cordie moved quickly toward the stairway.

Eleanor barely remembered the last of the helicopter ride, so confused were her thoughts and emotions. The pilot seemed concerned about the whereabouts of Molly Kewalu, and Eleanor's repeated assurances that the cave had been empty did not seem to satisfy him. Paul's silence from the backseat spoke volumes of skepticism.

They circled in from the sea to approach the Mauna Pele. "Lights are out," said Mike, throwing a toggle on the console that stabbed a searchlight beam down into the night. Eleanor saw dark *hales,* the empty beach, an abandoned Shipwreck Bar, and garden foliage whipping in the rising wind.

"I don't know about leaving you here," Mike said as they approached the darkened heliport. "It doesn't look like they've even bothered to turn the backup generators on." They hovered while the pilot looked first at Eleanor and then at Paul Kukali in the backseat. "They'll probably order an evacuation in the morning anyway. Why don't I drop you at Kona on my way north?"

"We'll be all right," said Paul. The curator's voice was tired.

"I don't know," said Mike. "You saw that new fissure on the way down. There's an active geyser not three miles from here and God knows what's happening in those lava tubes."

"We'll be all right," Paul said again.

Mike hesitated another moment and then brought the helicopter down, using the searchlight to illuminate the empty landing area. The winds buffeted the little machine and Eleanor realized what skill it must be taking to land as smoothly as they did. When they were on the ground, Eleanor reached across and squeezed the pilot's hand where it rested on the control stick. "Thank you," she said. "This ride was very important. I will never forget it."

Mike looked at her and nodded, but there were unasked questions in those startling gray eyes.

"Will you have problems getting back to Maui?" asked Paul.

Mike shook his head and tapped his earphones. "The tower at Keahole is telling me that I have almost half an hour before the real storm sweeps in. Time enough to get north of it and make the crossing." He smiled at Eleanor. "The kids will have eaten, but Kate always waits to eat with me. Well, good luck, guys."

Eleanor and Paul unbuckled and clambered out of the machine, crouching instinctively to get under the idling rotors. The wind was strong even when they reached the edge of the heliport pavement and were outside the rotor blast.

Mike twinked on the red cabin lights, waved, and then darkened the bubble. A second later the rotor sound deepened, the agile machine seemed to balance on its skids, and then it was in the air and pitching away to the north, navigation lights blinking.

"Molly was there, wasn't she?" Paul said when the red and green lights disappeared in the low cloud.

"Yes." Eleanor hugged her arms to her and shivered, even though the wind was warm.

"What did she say?"

Eleanor started to speak and then hesitated. "I'm not sure," she said at last. "I remember her chanting something, but it was as if she was speaking to me on another channel at the same time."

"The *Pele kahuna* can do that," said Paul. "At least with other women." There was an undertone of bitterness in his voice.

Eleanor realized something. "You . . . you and your uncles and the other *kahuna* . . . you tried calling to Pele to rid the island of this resort, didn't you? You called Pele before freeing Kamapua'a, Pana-ewa, and the others."

Paul did not answer, but even in the dim light Eleanor could read the truth of her statement in his face.

"Things are out of balance," the curator said at last. "The old ways . . . the old chants . . . many do not work. Pele does not respond as she did to our ancestors."

"It is the rape," said Eleanor.

"What?" Paul seemed startled.

"The rape," Eleanor repeated, surprised at her certainty but certain nonetheless. "For centuries, your hog god . . . Kamapua'a . . . has raped Pele at his whim. It has thrown things out of balance. Their battles used to be part of the scheme of things, but the rape has ruined that." She looked at the paved path and the golf course beyond the bougainvillea in the darkness. "It is like this resort, too much of a violation."

Before Paul could speak, brilliant headlights swept over them. Both of them took a step back, but the vehicle roared up the access road and turned onto the heliport asphalt at high speed. Brakes screeched.

"I'd get in if I were you," Cordie called, leaning out of the Jeep. "It's gonna rain up a shitstorm here in a few minutes."

They both clambered into the Jeep, Paul in the back and Eleanor in the passenger seat, just as in the helicopter. They had turned and were driving back toward the Big Hale before Eleanor said, "This is my rental Jeep. I still have the keys. How did you get it started?"

"Hot-wired it," said Cordie. "And it isn't as easy as it looks in the movies, either. Trust me."

"Why?" said Paul Kukali.

"Why isn't it that easy? Well, for the first thing, the ignition wires aren't just dangling down there ready to be stripped and braided. Although with this stupid Jeep it wasn't much more . . ."

"No," said Paul. "I mean, why did you do it?"

Cordie glanced at them. Her lank hair was blowing back over her ears. "There are weird things loose tonight. But you know that. Or at least *you* do, Nell."

Eleanor nodded. "We have to go down there tonight. Into the Underworld."

"Tonight?" said Cordie. "Jesus Christ, kid."

"Impossible," called Paul from the backseat.

The Jeep pulled up under the porte cochere. The lobby was dark. Not even a candle glowed.

Eleanor twisted around in her seat. "Why impossible?"

Paul Kukali made a motion with his slender hands. "There is a short time in the morning when the gods sleep. Then the Underworld is unguarded. At night . . . Kamapua'a would eat your soul."

"Fuck Kamapua'a," said Eleanor. She thought, *Did I say that?*

Paul frowned. "Kamapua'a is part of our religion, Eleanor. He is as important a force as Pele."

"Perhaps," said Eleanor, "but he is also a rapist. And a pig." She took a breath. "If Pele is to stop him from slaughtering everyone on this coast, we have to free the *haole* spirits so she can act."

"Did Molly Kewalu tell you this?" asked Paul.

"Yes," said Eleanor. "No." She frowned and rubbed her brow. "It's hard to remember exactly what she said." Looking up again, she said, "But we have to go down there soon. And you have to go, Paul."

"I'll go with you, Nell," Cordie said softly.

Eleanor set her hand on the other woman's arm. "Thank you. But it has to be a man and a woman. You read Kidder's journal."

Cordie made a face. "Maybe that's out of date."

"No," said Eleanor. "A man and a woman. Paul . . . you started this. Will you go down with me?"

The curator sat in silence for a long moment. Cordie could hear the palm fronds rasping far above them. Lightning flickered behind the Big Hale. "Yes," he said at last. "But not tonight. It would be death. At first light."

Eleanor sighed, although whether it was from frustration or relief, even she was not sure. "All right."

"That's settled," said Cordie. "Now I have a suggestion."

The two listened.

"If this was one of them stupid movies my boys used to watch," she said, "we'd all split up now and head in different directions and the monsters or the guy in the goalie mask would pick us off one at a time. That's the point in the movies where I always start rooting for the monsters 'cause they're smarter than the good guys. Get my drift?"

"I agree," said Paul. "It will be chaotic tonight. We should stay together."

"Or leave," said Cordie. "I liberated the Jeep. We could drive up the highway thirty miles to the Mauna Kea, or Kona Village, or the Mauna Lani, and watch HBO until the sun comes up."

"No," said Eleanor. "Mike said they will probably evacuate this resort in the morning. If they did it before we got back, we would never get into the Underworld."

"Gee," said Cordie. "That would be terrible."

Eleanor stared at her friend. "You *read* Kidder's journal. You know how important it is."

"Yeah," said Cordie. "All right. But we stick together. I say we make a run for the west staircase, get up to my suite, light the lanterns, lock the doors and windows, and play poker till dawn."

"Agreed," said Eleanor. "But I have to go back to my *hale* first."

It was Cordie's turn to stare. "Why?"

"I left Kidder's journal there."

Cordie tapped the steering wheel. "Shit. OK, but we go back now. And we go together. And we come back here together."

The other two nodded and Cordie drove past the entrance to the Big Hale, down a service road along the south side, and then onto the garden path. The Jeep took up the entire paved path, but Cordie did not slow below thirty miles an hour as they swerved past the Shipwreck Bar and accelerated toward the *hale* area. Headlights illuminated thick foliage. It began to rain.

Pulling up in front of Eleanor's *hale,* Cordie slammed the Jeep to a stop, and said, "Paul, you get behind the wheel. Me and Nell may be wanting to leave in a hurry." She jumped out, pulling the pistol and a flashlight from her bag.

"Cordie, you don't have to . . ."

"Shut up, Nell," said Cordie. She played the light over the stairs and porch. "Even the torches weren't lit tonight. Come on. You open the door and step back. I'll use the light."

They did just that. Eleanor felt a trifle melodramatic, as if they had watched too many police shows on television, but Cordie seemed completely serious as she kicked the door wider and swept the interior with her flashlight, pistol raised.

The *hale* was empty and exactly as Eleanor had left it except that the bed had been made. She retrieved Kidder's journal, tossed her toilet kit and a few other loose things in her bag, zipped the bag shut, and they were out the door within a minute.

Paul had turned the Jeep around. Cordie jumped into the back and let Eleanor have the front seat. The Jeep accelerated up the narrow path toward the Big Hale.

The fallen tree lay across the asphalt trail just short of the Shipwreck Bar. "Oh, shit," said Paul.

"Go around it," said Cordie. "Put it in four-wheel drive and cut through the bush."

Paul shook his head. "No, it's too thick. Too many rocks and pipes. We've got to find another way."

"The beach," said Eleanor. It was only twenty yards to their left. If they backtracked, they could take the path by the small pool to the beach and then up to the Big Hale.

Paul nodded and put the Jeep in reverse. The falling tree would have landed on Cordie if he had not had the quick reflexes to slam on the brakes. As it was, Cordie went over the back of the Jeep and into the waving palm fronds of the fallen tree.

"Cordie!" cried Eleanor, half coming out of her seat.

"Oh, shit," said Paul Kukali again. Something in his voice made Eleanor turn.

In the headlights, clearly visible despite the pounding rain that reduced visibility to twenty feet or so, stood the huge black dog, the twisted shark-man, a reptile-shaped creature filled with swirling fog, and a hog the size of a small car. The hog and the dog smiled with glistening teeth. The shark-man turned so that sharper teeth were visible on his back. The fog creature showed a reptilian smile. Other things moved and crashed in the brush.

The Jeep's engine died. Paul set his hands slack on the wheel, his jaw sagging.

Eleanor tried again to climb over the backseat to see if Cordie was hurt, but before she reached the back of the Jeep, strong hands grabbed her arm and pulled her out of the vehicle.

"I am not allowed to touch you, woman," said the hog in a smooth bass voice. "But the others can." Pana-ewa swirled around Eleanor, his shape swallowing her.

The shouts, both male and female, soon turned to screams, but the Big Hale was several hundred yards away and not even screams could be heard over the sound of the storm and the band playing for Byron Trumbo's penthouse dinner party.

TWENTY-ONE

The stars were burning.
Hot were the months.
Land rises in islands,
High surf is like mountains.
Pele throws out her body.
Broken masses of rain from the sky.
The land is shaken by earthquakes.
Ikuwa, the showery month, reverberates with
thunder.
—chant attending the birth
of *Wela-ahi-lani-nui,* the first man

June 18, 1866, In an unnamed village on the Kona Coast—
No sooner had I heard the silence that bespoke the giant
pig's awakening, but the earth shook and I was thrown to the
floor of the lava tube. Rocks fell, stalactites tumbled, and the
ghosts around me swirled like phosphorescent plankton stirred
by a swimmer's kick.

At that second I was sure that I was doomed, destined to die
naked and alone in the Kingdom of the Ghosts, but a second
later the *ieie* vine snaked down with the loop already tied. Again
the earth shook and again I was thrown from my feet, but the
fissure above had not closed and I hurried to tie the loop around
my waist and to secure another loop around my wrist the way Mr.
Clemens had shown me. A second later and I was rising toward
the light, bruising my bare feet against the rough cave wall as I
kicked for purchase. The *haole* ghosts rose with me, whirling and
spinning like agitated dust motes in a shaft of sunlight. There

was a roar in the tunnel far behind me, although whether it was
the sound of the earthquake or of an awakened and infuriated
pig god, I could not say.

All thoughts of decorum had fled as I scrabbled and crawled
onto the fissure ledge, breathing in the humid air while being all
but blinded by the light. The earth continued to shake, there was
the stench of sulphur in the air, the sky was tinged a bloody
orange, spirits of the missionary dead flew into the light around
me and dissipated like fog in a strong wind, but at that moment
all of my attention was focused on the apparition before me.

I confess, I began laughing and could not stop. Still naked as
Eve and on my knees in an attitude no Christian woman would
hold for a minute even in solitude, I could not move I was
laughing so hard.

"What?" said Mr. Clemens, dropping the vine but still
holding the coconut gripped firmly under his arm. "I needed
them for traction to pull you up, Miss Stewart," said the
correspondent, blushing more furiously than any time previous.

I tried to stop laughing. I did. But it took several minutes,
with the earth shaking around us and the volcano in full eruption
behind me. The image of Mr. Clemens pulling so earnestly on
that vine, the coconut containing the immortal remains of our
missionary friend firmly clamped in his armpit, wearing nothing
but the tall boots he had taken time to pull on and his rising
blush . . . you will pardon me for my moment of hysteria.

Mr. Clemens held the coconut in front of him like a fig leaf.
"If you are quite finished," he said rather archly, "I suggest we
dress ourselves and leave this place. It seems that Madame Pele
has begun her day's work."

At this I did turn and look across the great amphitheater of
dried lava. Flames erupted from fissures less than a mile up the
mountainside. Lava flew hundreds of feet into the air and great
clouds of sulphurous gases drifted across the rocky landscape.
The stony terraces that had been only a residue of ancient lava
falls an hour ago were now red with molten streams, flowing and
dripping even as I watched. The lava would reach this point in
mere minutes, if it had not already, pouring underground
through the lava tube we had just vacated. It was a sobering sight.

It took us less than a minute to dress, although I admit to leaving some stays unfastened. It felt strange to have garments on again, as if my short time of Edenesque innocence with Mr. Clemens had awakened racial memories of our earliest days in the Garden. But I was glad for the sturdy riding skirt as I leapt astride the saddle. The horses were terrified by the noise and shaking and stench, but Mr. Clemens had tethered them with an expert hand and they had not succeeded in fleeing with the panic visible in their rolling eyes. We spurred the beasts on and headed north and east. Behind us, the lava flowed like a sudden spring flood, igniting the few shrubs and patches of grass that grew in the old *pahoehoe* field. We had no glowing will-o'-the-wisp to guide us on our return trip, but Mr. Clemens had taken notice of the way and although the horses were exhausted, they climbed the long slope with a determination spurred on more by the volcanic cataclysm behind us than by actual spurs. Mr. Clemens held the coconut firmly wedged against the pommel of his saddle as we rode. "It would not do to lose Reverend Haymark after all this trouble," he suggested at one point. "The coconut might roll into a grove of coconut palms, and after decanting the nut we chose and hauled miles back to the village, we might find that we had returned with a native horse trader or some such."

"That is not funny, Mr. Clemens," I said, although for some reason, most probably my severe exhaustion at this point, it did seem mildly amusing.

We rode on into the morning. Several times the entire island seemed to shake with such ferocity that we had to dismount and hold the terrified horses. Boulders careered down the slope, smashing every bit of shrub or small *ohi'a* tree in their way, while behind us, the clouds of ash and smoke served to hide the sun. Once, when we had paused thus and were holding the horses through sheer strength of will, Mr. Clemens pointed down the long slope toward the coast. At first I could make out little through the shifting smoke and cloud, but then I saw the cause of his alarm: from miles out at sea, a wave of gigantic proportions was rolling in toward land. At this point we were several miles above sea level and had nothing to fear, but the sight of this great wave—tsunami I believe the Japanese call them—quite took my breath away.

From our vantage point we watched as the giant curl of green water crossed the line of cliffs far below, then moved relentlessly across groves of coastal palms, snapping them out of sight as with a conjuror's sleight of hand and then moving on. At this distance the wave looked harmless enough, just a larger wave among many that had come before, but it was all too easy to imagine the terrible destruction it was wreaking as it passed. I thought of the temples we had seen and the village where we had spent the night—two sleepless nights ago!—and wondered if they lay in the path of that terrible marine juggernaut. The wave crossed the half mile of lava bowl we had left in such a hurry, and when the water struck the fissure of boiling lava, such a gout of steam rose that I confess that I flinched, as if Mr. Clemens, our horses, and I were to be parboiled like shrimp in a pot.

The steam cloud did not come within a mile of us, but it did obscure the most hideous part of the scene—the carnage of that great tsunami retreating to the sea, carrying huge trees, native homes, and living things miles out to the trackless depths.

We rode on. In the aftermath of such excitement, the fatigue which followed was even more absolute. Several times I awoke to find that I had been sleeping while sitting up in the saddle. My hands, legs, and feet were scratched and bruised from the climbing and cave exploring we had done *au naturel,* and we still stank from the rancid *kukui* nut oil that neither of us had taken time to rub off in our haste to depart, but not even this constant discomfort could keep me from dozing off as we rode.

In early afternoon, perhaps an hour from the village we sought, Mr. Clemens called a halt. At first I was too groggy with sleep to understand this delay—there were no earthquakes taking place and we had escaped the worst of the smoke and ash—but then I looked to my poor horse, Leo, and realized that his neck was arched and he was drinking. We had come upon a great rarity in this porous volcanic landscape—a temporary mountain stream of clear, cold water.

I immediately dismounted to drink. While little of the precious liquid made it to my mouth via my cupped hands, I hesitated to imitate Mr. Clemens's mountain-man method of simply lying on his belly and slurping up the water like a dog. I do admit, however, that his method was more efficient.

When we had drunk our fill and our horses were standing there dozing on their feet, I suggested to my companion that we use this bounty to clean some of the oil from our bodies. My tame correspondent agreed and we each adjourned to the relative privacy that a large boulder could provide—Mr. Clemens upstream and I down—and I proceeded to sponge myself off as best I could without actually undressing. Of course, by this time, the terrible odor had permeated the clothing that had been in contact with the greasy oil, so even though I was able to pull another riding blouse and clean pantaloons from my saddle-bags, the majority of our efforts were for naught.

We reconvened back at the stream and Mr. Clemens hefted the coconut. "I have half a mind to dip this in the water to let Reverend Haymark join in our ablutions," he said, but setting the coconut safely in his own saddle-bag, he added, "but the other half of my mind vetoes the proposition."

"Half of my mind believes that I am out of my mind," I said. My voice sounded drugged with fatigue even to me.

Mr. Clemens nodded. And then he did a strange thing, stepping forward quickly and raising his hand to my shoulder. I first thought that he was adjusting my collar or returning some errant strand of hair to its proper place, but instead his large hand merely rested on my shoulder while he leaned forward and kissed me.

I was taken totally by surprise. I did not protest. I did not pull back. Mr. Clemens kissed me again.

Finally I pulled back, flustered, setting my hands on his chest and pushing him away, although with little force.

Mr. Clemens shifted from boot to boot. "I apologize, Miss Stewart, but I have been wanting to do that since we were on the ship discussing cosmic topics by the light of the stars. I apologize for my presumption and awkwardness. I do not apologize for the affection that motivated the awkwardness. My intentions are of the highest caliber, and are not to be mistaken for momentary impulse."

I stood speechless. Finally I managed, "Really, Mr. Clemens . . ." which set my companion to more shuffling of boots and a blush which equaled the one I had laughed at not three hours earlier.

Setting my hair in place, registering my unhappiness with him through posture and intensity of my unfriendly gaze, I confess that my thoughts were whirling back to the sensation of his lips on mine, his strong but sensitive fingers on my shoulder.

"We should continue," I said at last, pulling the reins to wake Leo from his standing doze.

"I must apologize again, Miss Stewart, if you . . ."

"We will speak of this later," I said curtly—perhaps more curtly than I intended. The saddle leather creaked as I pulled myself into the awkward astride position I had been using since coming to the islands. Mr. Clemens rushed to help me, but I gained my seat and pulled back the reins. "We should hurry," I said. "We do not know how long the spirit of Reverend Haymark will remain efficacious in its temporary home."

Mr. Clemens made a sound which I took for assent; he mounted and we continued upward along the lava slopes of Mauna Loa with my thoughts as twisted and confused as the *a'a* lava which now surrounded us.

We arrived at the ramshackle village sometime in mid-afternoon. I was too exhausted to consult my watch. The village men were nowhere in sight, which relieved my anxieties somewhat. I was concerned that Mr. Clemens would have to shoot several of them to convince them to leave us alone. My brazen companion appeared to share this relief, for he seemed in higher spirits since my rebuke at the stream. He helped me off Leo, who was wheezing loudly in the way that horses do shortly before collapsing.

The old woman was waiting for us in the hut, as was the lifeless body of Reverend Haymark. I crouched by the cleric's corpse, looking carefully for the early signs of putrefaction that would convince me that the events of the past several hours had been an opium dream.

The missionary's body remained lifeless and cold to the touch, but exhibited none of the symptoms that twelve hours of true death would inevitably bring on.

"You have brought it," said the old woman in a way that suggested it was not a question. It soothed my nerves somewhat to see that she was no longer floating in the center of the room, but was sitting on one of the woven mats in the same manner as I.

Mr. Clemens held up the coconut.

"Good," said the old woman. I scrutinized her features, but was no longer sure that she was the same person as the attractive young woman at the fissure. I was too tired to care.

The old woman slapped me. Shocked, I raised a hand to my burning cheek.

"You must be awake to do this thing," she said. "You must understand and remember each step. If you make a mistake, the spirit of your *kahuna* friend will be lost forever."

I could only stare.

"I will do it," said Mr. Clemens, stepping between the old woman and me.

She shook her gray head. "Only the woman, the follower of Pele, can do this thing."

"I am not a follower of Pele," I said through shock-numbed lips. "I am a Christian from Ohio."

The old woman merely smiled. She lifted a gourd with a cloudy liquid in it. "Drink this," she commanded.

I looked doubtfully at the viscous liquid, but I drank. Within seconds, a strange energy surged through me.

"Now," said the old woman, "we shall begin."

There was a loud noise at the open doorway. Mr. Clemens, looking over my shoulder, said, "My Lord."

Filling the entire doorway was the giant hog from the Underworld of Milu. My heart stopped.

The old woman barely paused in her preparations. "He cannot enter," she said sharply. Setting her wizened hand on my head, looking at the hog, she said, "Kamapua'a, know that this *haole wahine* and all of her descendents have been set apart by my touch. They are under the protection of Pele. You may not harm their bodies."

The hog snorted in anger and then smiled. "But I can eat their souls."

"You may not enter," said the woman. "This hut is set apart from your power. I have invoked the force of Kilauea. You have no power here."

The hog pawed at the earth in his inhuman frustration.

"Attend me," said the old woman. "Each step must be correct, or your friend's *uhane* will be lost forever."

The chanting began then. The ritual commenced.

Cordie regained consciousness amidst a tumble of broken palm fronds. There was no interval of confusion: she knew exactly where she was and exactly what had happened the instant before she was knocked out. She remembered the creatures blocking the road, Paul's panic attempt to back the Jeep, the falling tree, and her own tumble out the rear of the vehicle. What she did not know was whether all of that had occurred thirty seconds earlier or three hours ago. It was still raining, although not as hard as it had been when they were driving back from Eleanor's *hale*. This meant little—the tropical rainstorms had changed temperament within minutes during the past few days.

Fighting the nausea that comes from such a bump on the head, Cordie thrashed her way through the tangle of palms and pulled herself up the rear bumper of the Jeep. Something small and wet and furry brushed against her leg and Cordie's hands involuntarily curled into fists before she realized that it was a rat. *They live in the damn palm trees. There were probably fifty of those filthy things running over me while I was out.* Cordie felt her skin shudder, but she set aside the thought. She had grown up as white trash, living on the outskirts of a dump where she played every day. Most of her adult life had been spent in garbage collection. She hated rats, but she was not unused to them.

Even before pulling herself to her feet, Cordie felt around for her tote bag. The long strap had been over her shoulder when the

Jeep slammed into the tree, but she remembered the bag flying away even as she went flying. She found it within thirty seconds, its Velcro tab still secured. Cordie fumbled it open and drew out the .38 and the flashlight. Her thumb on the hammer of the pistol, her head throbbing with the aftereffects of what must be a mild concussion, she came up over the back of the Jeep with both weapon and flashlight extended.

The Jeep was empty. Stepping through sharp branches, she worked her way around the driver's side of the stalled vehicle. The headlights still illuminated rain but there was no sign of the creatures. Nothing moved in the underbrush. Cordie came around to the hood of the Jeep, flashlight swiveling. Nothing in front of the Jeep. Rain dripped from foliage in the dark.

A low sound to her left made her drop to one knee and elevate the pistol barrel level with the flashlight beam. It came again—a moan. Cordie lowered the beam and saw a man's bare foot protruding from the flower bed. Small plaques set in the ground near the bare foot bore labels that Cordie could read even from this distance: "Hibiscus" and "Lantana" and "Hapu'u Fern." The man moaned again. Swinging the beam behind her again, feeling sure that she was the only person or creature standing in the immediate vicinity, Cordie approached the body on the ground.

It was Paul Kukali. The art curator's shirt had been torn off and his trousers had been shredded as if by long claws. The left side of his face was bruised and lacerated, one eye hidden by the purple swelling, his left arm was obviously broken in two places, a finger was missing on his right hand, there were deep cuts on his chest and upper leg, and his right ankle looked wrong, as if it had been twisted too far. "Jesus," whispered Cordie, "they did a job on you." She had never especially liked the man, had not fully trusted him for some reason, but she hated seeing him in this condition.

The art curator moaned again. Cordie leaned closer and set a hand on his bare chest. Despite the damage, the man's breathing seemed strong and clear and his heartbeat was solid. "Paul," she whispered, "where's Nell? Where's Eleanor?"

Paul Kukali moaned again. He was not truly conscious.

Cordie patted his shoulder and stood. She had received enough medical training to know that she should leave him in place and get help to him rather than vice versa; his back could be injured or there could be serious internal injuries that could kill him if she tried to move him. But Cordie also knew that in this insane place at this insane time, medical help would not be coming anytime soon. The creatures that did this to Paul might well find her before she got back to the Big Hale, in which case he could die out here in the dark.

"I'll be right back," said Cordie, and began searching the paved walkway and flower beds with the flashlight. There were footprints—human and otherwise—and torn flower beds, but no sign of Nell. Then, suddenly, the flashlight beam illuminated something pale several yards into the jungle twenty paces or so to the right of the fallen tree that had blocked their path. Crouching, keeping the pistol ready, Cordie moved under the low branches. The rain had intensified and fell from leaf to leaf with a patting sound that might have been soothing under different circumstances.

It was Eleanor. Her clothing was not ripped and there were no external signs of injury. Cordie set the pistol in her belt and felt her friend's wrist and throat. She laid her cheek on Eleanor's breast. Nell had no pulse. She was not breathing. Her skin was cold to the touch.

"Shit," said Cordie. Gripping the flashlight in her mouth, she pulled Eleanor's body through the mud and underbrush. By the time Cordie reached the path, she was gasping for breath and the throbbing in her aching head made her dizzy. She had to sit down on one of the stones lining the flower bed to let the dizziness and nausea pass. Then, lifting Eleanor with great tenderness, she carried the body to the Jeep and set it carefully in the wet backseat.

Paul Kukali had ceased moaning but he was still breathing. Cordie used a bandana to wrap around the bleeding right hand with the missing finger and then, taking care not to touch the shattered left arm, she half carried, half dragged the man to the front seat of the Jeep. Paul moaned loudly during this operation, especially when his broken ankle scraped along the ground, but he did not fully waken.

After using the shoulder harness to fix the curator in place and wedging Eleanor's body in the back so that it would not roll, Cordie leaned against the Jeep briefly to shake away the dizziness, tossed her tote bag on the floorboards, leaned over to hot-wire the ignition again, got the thing started after several minutes, and just sat in the driver's seat for a moment. The Jeep was blocked by the fallen tree in front and the smaller one behind. But the tree in front was a palm tree and the fronds were just a mass of foliage in the flower bed to the right.

Cordie set the Jeep in four-wheel low and drove over the fronds, cracking branches and pitching back and forth as she went. She half expected something to drop snarling from the trees onto her back, but she was too busy keeping the vehicle from pitching over to worry about it. Then she was on the paved path to the Big Hale and could see the dark hulk of the Shipwreck Bar ahead.

Cordie shifted out of four-wheel low and accelerated.

The five-piece Hawaiian band had initially refused to come to the Mauna Pele, but Trumbo had promised them an extra thousand and here they were, saxing and guitaring and *ukulele*-ing their way through the night, with the hurricane lamps providing a soft glow to the long banquet room and Sato's people scarfing down saki like it was going out of style. Trumbo welcomed the music, for it covered both the sounds of the storm and the unusual quiet of the almost abandoned hotel beneath the seventh floor. It also allowed him to think rather than talk.

The thinking was not terribly productive. According to the original schedule, Sato was supposed to have signed the papers that afternoon and this was to have been the celebration party for both sides. But although the terms seemed settled enough, Hiroshe Sato and his advisers were upset about Sunny Takahashi taking off and refused to sign until the kid returned. As far as Byron Trumbo could tell, Sunny wasn't really dead, but was a sort of ghost being kept in a lava tube south of the resort, guarded by a giant, talking pig who would give Sunny back if he—Byron Trumbo, billionaire—would come down to talk.

Weird shit, thought Trumbo. He was not superstitious, nor was he religious, and he had no interest in the paranormal, but he was used to weird shit. One did not amass a fortune of over a billion dollars without encountering weird shit. Nor did one amass such a fortune without the ability to focus, and what Byron Trumbo was focused on now was getting the contract signed and the Mauna Pele off his back so he had the capital to dig his way out of his current financial crisis. The talking pig could wait for rational analysis. So could that other talking pig, Caitlin Sommersby Trumbo, although he doubted if anything rational would ever pass between the two of them again.

Michaels, the acting security chief, had come by earlier to whisper in his boss's ear that Mrs. Trumbo and the other two ladies, along with the lawyer, Koestler, were together and guarded and safe on the seventh floor of the Big Hale. Trumbo had fetched the other two with the excuse that a hurricane was blowing in— which it looked like it was. He was sorry that the three women had finally stumbled across one another; Maya was not a great loss— the relationship was reaching the end of its natural arc anyway— but Trumbo had enjoyed the unusual pairing with Bicki. *Well, maybe that's not a total loss,* he thought, but quickly put the issue aside. He focused on the immediate problem.

The immediate problem was how to get Hiroshe to sign the deal. Trumbo suspected that despite the Sato Group's apparent obliviousness to the chaos around the Mauna Pele, Sunny's disappearance had been just the icing on their cake of vague uneasiness. Despite their vicious history right up to and through World War II, the modern Japanese affected this terror of violence and they could sniff it out.

On the other hand, Trumbo knew, young Hiroshe was trying to step out of his father's shadow, and this beautiful golf club on the Big Island of Hawaii was the shortest route. It would either turn him into a successful billionaire entrepreneur in his own right, or sink the old man's fortune. Byron Trumbo did not really give a shit which way that went as long as the resort got sold and he got the cash.

Trumbo wondered if he should have powered up the lights. He had guards around the emergency generator and it was working all right, but he had decided to save power for the elevator, the seventh-floor security alarms, and the lights in the conference room when the time came for the signing . . . if it came. Meanwhile, the Japs didn't seem to mind the hurricane-lamp ambience, so he decided to leave well enough alone.

The band was working up a sweat, Will Bryant had come back to the table but was wisely avoiding his boss's eye, and Trumbo was carrying on stupid conversation with Hiroshe, old Matsukawa, and Dr. Tatsuro, when Michaels came back. Trumbo despised having his ear whispered in, so he stepped away from the table for a minute.

"Two things," said the flustered security man. "First, Fredrickson is off the air."

"You mean he didn't check in when he was supposed to?"

"No," said Michaels, "I mean that he's off the air. We had him on an open band so all he had to do was break squelch if he got in trouble and . . ."

"Break squelch?" said Trumbo irritably. He hated it when people spoke professional or technical double-talk.

Michaels actually blushed. "That's an old 'Nam term, sir. It means we had him on an open band . . . the rest of us kept off it . . . and all he had to do was press the transmit button so we could hear him. That's the way we used to communicate in the boonies when we didn't want the Viet Cong to overhear our . . ."

"Yeah, yeah," said Trumbo. "Save me the war stories. So all Fredrickson had to do was push a button, but he didn't?"

"We don't know, Mr. Trumbo. He's off the air. It's as if something smashed his radio."

"Or ate it," said Trumbo.

"Pardon me?"

"Nothing," said Trumbo.

"Shall we send some men out, sir?" said Michaels. "Things are pretty quiet up here, we could . . ."

"No," said Trumbo. "If Fredrickson's still alive, he'll be doing his job and find a way to let us know if something comes out of that hole in the ground. If he's not . . . well, why waste men. Now what was the other thing you wanted?"

"There's a woman here to see you, sir."

Trumbo sighed. "Which one? Caitlin?"

"No, sir," Michaels said hurriedly. "One of the guests. Mrs. Stumpf."

Trumbo paused. "One of the guests? I thought they'd all lit out."

"Not quite, sir. Mrs. Stumpf was the contest winner who . . ."

"Yeah, I know," said Trumbo. "Well, tell her I'll catch her tomorrow after breakfast sometime."

Michaels shifted uncomfortably. "Well, sir, she says that it's very important. She says it's about the dog and the shark and the pig. She said you'd understand."

Trumbo looked back toward the dining room. Waiters were bringing around the dessert—ice cream made with local mangoes, chocolate mousse pie, and Kona espresso—and it looked as if his guests would be preoccupied for a few minutes. "OK," he said. "Where is she?"

She was in the suite's tiled anteroom. Trumbo had met this stocky little woman with the moon-shaped face when she and the curator and the other woman had reported the dog carrying human remains, but he was surprised at how much worse she could look with wet hair and dripping clothes.

"Mrs. Stumpf!" he said expansively, opening his arms but not actually hugging the dripping apparition. "We're so pleased you accepted our invitation to enjoy the more comfortable seventh-floor suite until the storm is over! What can we do to make your stay even more enjoyable?"

Mrs. Stumpf grunted. "Send your bodyguard away," she said.

Michaels bristled but Trumbo just smiled again. "Don't worry, Mrs. Stumpf, my associate is a trusted colleague. Anything you say will be held in confidence."

"Tell him to fuck off," said the little woman.

Trumbo blinked, his smile fading only slightly. "Fuck off," he said to Michaels. The security man blinked but disappeared out the door onto the mezzanine where the other security men waited.

"Now," said Trumbo, "what's this about sharks and pigs and whatever?"

Cordie Stumpf grunted again. "Byron, babe, you've got two problems. The first one is that your hotel is being overrun with mythological beasties right now. Before I parked my Jeep in the empty lobby, I saw wild pigs rooting through the gardens and that dog with the human teeth on the second-floor mezzanine."

"You parked your Jeep in the lobby?" said Trumbo. Regaining his composure, he said, "There is nothing to worry about, Mrs. Stumpf. I admit that things have been a bit . . . ah . . . unusual the past day or two, but they will be back to normal by tomorrow. I'll have my associate see you safely back to your suite." He set his hand on the woman's back, feeling the wet blouse and the solid muscles there, and began escorting her to the door. She did not resist.

"Oh," she said. "I did say that there were two problems."

Trumbo resisted the impulse to sigh. "Yes?"

Cordie Stumpf stopped, turned slightly, reached into her cheap tote bag, and came out with a long-barreled .38, which she jabbed into Byron Trumbo's ribs. "This is the second problem," she said softly, and cocked the hammer.

Trumbo regarded the problem without moving. "OK," he said at last. "How do we solve it?"

Cordie nodded toward the inner door. "We go in there, out the back way, and downstairs. You're going with me. You're keeping your mouth shut. You're not signaling to your lackeys. If you make any sign or give me any grief, I pull the trigger."

"You realize that you're fucking insane, don't you?" said Byron Trumbo.

"Yes," said Cordie, and pushed the barrel tighter against the billionaire's ribs. "Look at me."

Trumbo looked into those small, washed-out eyes. Earlier that day he had faced down a revolver in the hands of his outraged wife, but he had known the limits of her insanity. He saw no limits to whatever gleamed in this woman's eyes. "All right," he said. "I'm not going to cause any trouble. We'll go out through the back door. Just lower the hammer, would you?"

"I'll lower it when we get where we're going," said Cordie. Her voice was tired and flat, but firm. "Or when I have to squeeze the trigger."

Trumbo felt his flesh crawl at that, but he turned and led the way back through the suite, down the interior hall to avoid the banquet in the dining rooms. Cordie pulled the revolver out of his ribs, but only to set it in her tote bag. Trumbo could feel the muzzle poking him through the straw of the bag.

They went out the back door to the terrace. Trumbo nodded at the security men at the outer door and again at the elevator.

"Want us to go down with you, Mr. T?" asked a huge man at the elevator.

Trumbo shook his head and stepped into the elevator car with the little woman. The tote bag stayed against his ribs. "Which floor?" he said.

"Six."

Trumbo was surprised. He had expected the lobby. On the sixth floor, they walked to Mrs. Stumpf's complimentary suite.

"Paul Kukali got hurt real bad," said the woman in her midwestern drawl. "I left him with a couple of your security guys, who took him to a doctor up on your seventh floor."

"Dr. Scamahorn," Trumbo said automatically. "He's moved the infirmary up there to . . ."

"Yeah," interrupted Cordie, unlocking the door of her suite and motioning Trumbo through. She swept a flashlight around the interior and then opened the door to the bedroom. A woman's body was there under the handmade Hawaiian quilt.

"Jesus," said Trumbo, touching the cold wrist. It was the other woman who had reported the dog—Dr. Perry. Her skin was so cold that Trumbo thought she must have been dead for hours, perhaps in the sea. "What happened?" he said, and thought, *The fucking pig. Somehow it was the pig.*

"It was the pig," Cordie said tiredly, as if reading his mind. "But the pig couldn't touch her himself because of Pele's 1866 injunction, so he sicced Pana-ewa on her."

Trumbo looked at the little woman as if she had begun speaking Swahili.

"Never mind," said Cordie, leading him out of the room again. "I just wanted to check in on her. I think she'll be all right here. The critters don't think I'll return here. Actually, I don't think the critters give a shit about me."

"Critters?" said Trumbo. He was irritated and frustrated that this dumpy little housewife was leading him around at the point of a gun when he should be upstairs finishing the deal with Sato, but this development was enough of an absurd cherry on the surreal sundae he'd been eating the past few days that he was enjoying it in some bizarre fashion.

"Never mind," said Cordie Stumpf. On the dark mezzanine, she locked the door and listened for a moment. Trumbo listened as well, acutely aware of the pistol in his ribs again. There were scurrying sounds from the lower floors and once he thought he heard a low growl.

She moved him to the stairway. "Walk light," she whispered. Trumbo did so, his high-top sneakers making almost no noise.

This time they stopped on the first floor and moved through the dark lobby to the restaurant. It was locked. "Hope you got a key to this thing," whispered Cordie. Something moved in the shrubs beyond the kneeling Buddha figures across the lobby.

Trumbo considered denying that he had keys, but the noise in the shrubs decided him against that. He unlocked the door and locked it behind them when they slipped into the restaurant. Cordie scanned the long room with her flashlight beam, but her attention never wandered so far that Trumbo felt he could make a grab for the gun. *Soon.*

"Is that the kitchen?" she whispered, holding the light on a doorway.

"Yeah."

She motioned him forward and they moved through the swinging door into the kitchen. Stainless-steel counters and cabinets gleamed in the flashlight beam. "Pantry," she whispered. Trumbo led the way, wondering if the woman was some sort of crazed bulimic who was going to eat herself to death while holding him at gunpoint. As long as she did it quickly enough that he could get back to the Sato party, he didn't really care.

In the pantry, Cordie tried to switch on the lights but the electricity was still off.

"Anything I can help you find?" asked Trumbo, eyeing the row upon row of canned goods and other delicacies befitting a five-star restaurant. *Arsenic?* he thought. *Ground glass?*

Cordie hesitated only a second. "Anchovy paste," she said, holding the light on a lower shelf.

Trumbo blinked but obediently fetched the dark tube of paste when she waggled the revolver barrel at him.

"Better get two tubes," said the dumpy little woman. "And that long tube of garlic paste up there . . . yeah, that's it."

Trumbo pulled down the heavy commercial tube of liquid garlic. He felt like a henpecked husband in a supermarket.

"What's it say on that little black jar?" she asked.

Trumbo leaned closer and read it in the flashlight beam. "Marmite," he said. "It's this paste that some of our British guests like for breakfast on their toast and . . ."

"I know marmite," said the woman. "I had me some in London once. It's this black yeast stuff that smells like a mouse crawled in the jar and died a year or two before. And it tastes worse. Better take that jar, too."

Whatever kind of sandwich she's making, he thought, *I'm not eating it.*

"Cheese," said Cordie, and they moved to the cooler.

"Look," said Trumbo as they stood in front of the racks of dessert cheeses, "if you're hungry, come on back upstairs with me and you can join the banquet . . ."

"Shut up," said Cordie. She gestured with the revolver. "Some of that Limburger. And that blue."

"I'll need a knife to cut it," said Trumbo. He turned toward the kitchen.

"Cute," said Cordie, waving him back. "Use your hands. Better yet, bring the whole wheel of Limburger."

"This must weigh ten pounds," said Trumbo, still juggling the anchovy paste and garlic tubes while wrestling the stinking circle of cheese off the rack.

"You're a strong guy," said Cordie. She held the door open for him and kept the pistol trained on him as they crossed the dark restaurant again.

She paused by the door, holding it open a crack.

"Where now?" whispered Trumbo. He thought, *If she comes two steps closer, I can conk her with this fucking cheese.* The stench from the giant wheel of Limburger made him want to throw up.

Cordie was listening to a scraping sound from the second-floor mezzanine. "We'll take the stairs," she said. "Your security guys will come down to check if we use the elevator."

She started through the door and then stopped. "Heck and spit," she said softly.

"What?" said Trumbo, holding the garlic tube in place atop the cheese with his chin. The fumes made his eyes water. "You forget the bread?"

Cordie shook her head. "I don't have a coconut."

"Pity," muttered Trumbo. "Does that mean the picnic's off?"

She ignored him. "Where's the wine cellar? A fancy place like this has to have a wine cellar."

Trumbo nodded toward a door by the kitchen.

The wine cellar was set into stone behind the kitchen and although it was refrigerated, it had kept its cool temperature when the power failed. Cordie moved from rack to rack, shining the flashlight on corks and labels. "What's your best wine?"

Trumbo shrugged. "I have no idea." He peered at the exclusive racks she was illuminating. "This Lafite-Rothschild '48 is worth more money than you'll ever see."

"Okey-dokey," said Cordie Stumpf, and pulled the priceless bottle from its cradle. Reaching into her tote bag she removed a Swiss army knife, extruded a corkscrew, said, "Stand back there," and while Trumbo stood ten paces away, fuming, she held the bottle between her knees and uncorked it with one hand while holding the pistol on him with the other.

"Hey," said the billionaire, "that bottle's worth . . ."

"Shut up." Pulling the cork free and sniffing it, Cordie nodded like a wine connoisseur and took a swig. Then she poured the remaining wine onto the floor.

"Jesus!" shouted Trumbo. He was furious again. He started to set the cheese down and looked up into the flashlight beam and the black muzzle of the .38.

"Oh," said Cordie. "Did you want some?" She tapped the cork back in place.

"I'm going to put you in a looney bin for the rest of your miserable, fucking life," said Byron Trumbo in a tone he reserved for serious contractual arrangements.

Cordie nodded. "I'd welcome the rest, Byron old buddy. Pick up your cheeses." She whistled two bars of "What a Friend We Have in Jesus" while Trumbo hoisted his load.

"Just a minute," she said at last. "Paul Kukali said that you had people missing. You might want to bring a bottle."

"What the fuck are you talking about?" said Trumbo.

"Ghosts," said Cordie. "Transporting ghosts. This bottle's for mine. You might want to bring something if you have somebody you want to bring back."

"Transporting ghosts," repeated Trumbo. "That's the stupidest fucking thing I've ever . . ." He stopped. "Yeah," he said. "Maybe I do need a bottle."

"Just one?" said Cordie, passing her light over the shelves.

"Yeah. My hands are busy. Can you grab one?"

"Sure," said Cordie, and reached for one while keeping the pistol trained on him.

"Not the expensive ones," snapped Trumbo. "That cheap Gallo will do."

Cordie shrugged, retrieved the Gallo, and set the full bottle under his chin with the garlic and the anchovy paste. "Let's go," she said.

They took the stairs to the basement level.

"Fuck this," said Trumbo. "There's nothing down here but the . . ."

"Catacombs," finished Cordie. "Yeah, I thought it might be easier than trying to hike the mile or two through the storm up there. My guess is that all these lava tunnels connect, and I suspect that your guys got chewed up by something tunneling in here."

"What are you talking about?" said Trumbo.

"Go," said Cordie, nodding toward the pitch-black corridor.

"Fuck that," said Trumbo, backing against the corner. "I'm not going down there."

"Yes, you are," said Cordie Stumpf, and raised the pistol.

Trumbo stared. "You'll have to shoot me," he said. "There's no way I'm going to . . ."

The shot was unbelievably loud in the echoing space. The bullet nicked Trumbo's ear, taking the tiniest piece of earlobe with it, and ricocheted away down the concrete tunnel. The noise and the stink of cordite seemed to fill the world.

Trumbo dropped the tubes, the cheeses, the jar of marmite, and the bottle, frantically holding one hand in front of himself while feeling his ear with the other. "Don't shoot, don't shoot, don't shoot . . ."

"You ain't hurt," said Cordie. "Not yet. I figure I can aim at two or three soft spots and still have you function for a while. Now pick up the stuff."

Trumbo scrambled to pick up the food.

"Good thing for your ghost friend that the wine bottle didn't break," said Cordie, holding the light on him.

Trumbo made a noise.

"Let's go," she said, waving him down the dark tunnel. "It gets better."

Trumbo muttered something into the stinking Limburger.

"What was that?" said Cordie. "I didn't quite catch that."

"I said," said Trumbo, "I don't see how."

Behind the glare of the flashlight, the woman's voice was soft. "When we get to the place where the cave starts," she said, "we're going to strip ourselves naked and rub this stuff on us."

TWENTY-TWO

*It requires small play of the imagination to see
these lava beds all peopled with strange forms,
such as antediluvian monsters built up for our
instruction at the Crystal Palace. All manner of
creeping crawling things seem to be here: gigantic
lizards and monstrous, many-armed cuttlefish.*
—Miss C. F. Gordon-Cumming
"Fire Fountains," 1883

June 18, 1866, In an unnamed village along the Kona
Coast—

I knelt next to the Reverend Haymark's body while the old
woman sat across from me. Mr. Clemens watched. The pig god
and other unspeakable things thrashed through the village in
wild frustration at being barred from this hut by Pele's
command.

The old woman handed me the coconut holding our friend's
uhane. "You must be stern," she said. "The spirit will not want to
return to its body. It has become used to its freedom and will not
wish to be caged again. You must slap it into submission."

"Slap it," I said.

"Slap it," said the old woman. "And then you must slap the
spirit back into the body and keep it there until the body grows
warm. If it escapes while you are trying to do this . . ." The old
woman gestured toward the open door. "It will be eaten by
Kamapua'a or Pana-ewa and you will never see the spirit again.
Even now my lava fills the Underworld. In moments, my enemies

will have to leave this place. But the ghosts also will be entombed."

"Slap it," I said. Holding the coconut, glancing at Mr. Clemens for support, I asked, "Where does the spirit . . . how does it . . ."

The old woman touched the corner of Reverend Haymark's eye. "This is the *lua-uhane*, the 'door of the soul.' It is where the spirit departed the body . . . where Pana-ewa drew it out as you might suck milk from a coconut. The spirit will wish to return this way. *Do not allow it!* The spirit must return through the body's feet and be coaxed upward until it resides everywhere. Now take off your *kahuna*'s foot coverings."

I reached for Reverend Haymark's boots but stopped in confusion. I had never undressed a man, not even to remove my father's boots when he had imbibed too much, and it seemed wrong to do so now. Luckily, Mr. Clemens saw my confusion and leaned forward to remove the cleric's high boots and socks. In a moment, our friend's ten toes pointed skyward like pale grave markers. The thought of touching those cold, dead feet made my skin shudder.

The old woman set strong hands on my head and shoulder. "From this moment you are anointed as a priestess of Pele," she half spoke, half chanted. "You join the sisterhood of sorcery for Pele. You speak for Pele. I shall put the words in your mind. Your voice shall be my voice. Your hands my hands. Your heart my heart. Pele has spoken."

At that second I felt a great jolt, as if lightning had struck me. My exhaustion vanished. Power seemed to flow from my fingertips. I looked at Mr. Clemens and saw in his widened eyes that my own visage had changed, perhaps evincing the glow of energy and understanding that I felt at that second.

I unstoppered the coconut. Reverend Haymark's spirit flowed out like thick, gray molasses, first pooling along the floor and then rising into the shape of a man. I stood next to it as it coalesced. The old woman's murmurings became a distant background noise—or perhaps they were only in my mind. I do not know.

When the ghost had formed into its human shape, it rippled like smoke disturbed by a slight breeze and began drifting toward the door. I did not need the old woman's urgings to know what to do.

Standing between Reverend Haymark's spirit and the open doorway, I slapped at the ectoplasmic shape, my fingers contacting something but sliding into the smoky form.

The ghost turned back, but the lower half lost human form and began to swirl around the head of Reverend Haymark's corpse, spiraling like a cyclone seeking the corners of the body's eyes.

I roughly slapped it away. Finding that I could grasp the ghost, I seized its shoulders and dragged it to the bare feet. By this time the spirit had all but lost its human form and I felt that my burning hands were holding a tangible fog. I pressed that fog against the feet, feeling resistance at first but then sensing the resistance yielding, bending, and finally the osmotic penetration of the bare and vulnerable soles. It felt a bit like pushing some thick cream through a fine filter.

The spirit resisted for a moment and these words came unbidden to mind. I began to chant:

"O the top of Kilauea!
O the five ledges of the pit!
The *kapu* fire of the woman.
When the heavens shake,
When the earth cracks open,
Man is thrown down,
Lying on the ground.
The lightning of Kane wakes up.
Kane of the night, going fast.
My sleep is broken up.
E ala e! Wake up!
The heaven wakes up.
The earth island is awake.
The sea is awake.
        Awake you!
        Here am I."

At that moment, the earth did shake and the hut swayed back and forth like a grass skirt of a native maiden in one of their sensuous dances. I heard great crackling and rumblings, although whether it was earthquake or lightning or both, I do not know. Mr. Clemens was thrown to his knees, but he never looked away from the wrestling bout between Reverend Haymark's spirit and me. Somehow I knew at that second that Pana-ewa, Kamapua'a, and the other antagonists had been cast far away from this place, and the Underworld of Milu had been sealed off by flowing lava.

I concentrated on my work. Perspiration dripped from my nose and chin as I forced the ghost up the cleric's legs to the hips. Here the struggle intensified, as if the spirit were loathe to rise to the vital organs and allow the body to breathe and live again. I reached behind me as if knowing the old woman would be holding an earthen jug. She was. Taking fresh water from the vessel, I poured it over the body while chanting:

"I make you grow, O Kane!
I, Lorena Stewart, am the prophet.
Pele is the god.
This work is hers.
She makes the growth.
Here is the water of life.
E ala e! Awake! Arise!
Let life return.
The *kapu* of death is over.
It is lifted,
It has flown away."

Suddenly the resisting spirit ceased its resistance and seemed to slip easily upward as I slapped and massaged the dead missionary's sides and belly. I massaged the spirit down the limp arms and slapped the fingers until I felt the warmth returning there. Finally I rubbed the broad neck, massaged the jowls, and set my glowing fingers on the dead man's face and scalp.

A moment later I sat back, suddenly exhausted once again, the divine energy flowing out of me so abruptly that I lifted my fingers to the inside corners of my eyes to make sure that my own *uhane* was not escaping.

Reverend Haymark made choking noises and then his eyes flickered open. His lips moved. He began to breathe.

I believe that Mr. Clemens caught me as I swooned.

Standing in the astronomer's tumbled office, playing the flashlight on the shattered wall and the dark cavern beyond, seeing the blood smeared on floor and wall and ceiling, Cordie stepped back and said, "Okey-dokey, time to take your clothes off."

"Forget it," said Byron Trumbo. He would jump the bitch before submitting to this indignity.

Cordie sighed tiredly and raised the pistol. "Where do you want it then? In the thigh or that spare tire you're carrying around? Either way, I want you to still be able to walk." Standing too far back to be rushed, she cocked the hammer.

Trumbo began cursing as he unbuttoned his shirt. By the time he had his underwear off, he had used every phrase he had learned in his colorful life and had started improvising new ones. Behind the flashlight, Cordie was also disrobing. When he was down to nothing but socks and the dumpy little woman had only the gun, flashlight, and tote bag left, he said, "What next? You rape me?"

"Please," said Cordie, "I just ate a couple of hours ago. Take them socks off."

"If we go in there, the rocks'll cut my feet," said Trumbo, hearing something sickeningly like a whine in his voice.

Cordie shrugged. "The ghosts in there don't wear socks. I guess we can't neither. Peel 'em off."

Trumbo gritted his teeth and tugged the socks off. "You carrying that bag in? You think ghosts carry tote bags?"

"I don't give a whole big good goddamn," said Cordie. "I need it to haul my stuff. I'm not leaving Kidder's journal behind."

"Whose journal?"

"Never you mind," said Cordie. "Time for us to smell ourselves up. You first. Start with the garlic paste, I guess."

The next few minutes were beyond anything in Byron Trumbo's experience. Under the pistol's one-eyed gaze, he smeared on the semiliquid garlic, then rubbed on the anchovy paste. The smell made him gag.

"Now the cheese," said Cordie, applying the garlic to herself even as she held the pistol steady.

"Fuck it," snarled Trumbo, and began crumbling cheese. "It won't stick," he said.

"It'll stick. Keep smearing."

Trumbo smeared. The pungent Limburger caked on his chest. Crumbs gathered in his armpits and fell to his pubic hair. He rubbed his legs with crumbling handfuls of the stinking stuff.

"Great," said Cordie Stumpf, and took the remaining cheese to rub on her own body.

Trumbo tried not to look at that body. Since he had made his first million, the women he had chosen to see naked were physically attractive, as close to perfect as he could buy. Looking at this woman's small, sagging breasts, at the cellulite on her ass, at her fat thighs, and the twin scars on her belly, and at her stubby legs reminded him of his mother and of mortality and of all the things he thought he could put behind him forever. Suddenly Trumbo felt like crying.

Cordie ignored his glances. "Now the marmite," she said. "Put it in your hair and on your face."

Trumbo opened the jar and almost lost his banquet dinner then. It was not just the rotting yeast stink of the dark spread, but how it blended with the other stenches rising from his own skin. Holding his gorge in check by sheer willpower, he spread fingerfuls of marmite through his thinning hair and behind his ears.

"Go ahead and upchuck if you want," said Cordie at one point. "It'll just add to the smell."

Trumbo passed on the offer. "Why the fuck are we doing this?" he asked as he handed the marmite jar over. The damn cow kept the pistol just out of grabbing range.

"It's all in Kidder's journal," said the little woman as she rubbed the black paste in her stringy hair. "Ghosts don't like bad smells. They look away. If they knew we was still alive, they'd mob us and steal our spirits, just like Pana-ewa did to poor Nell." She tossed the empty jar aside. "Wish we had some herring in cream sauce. And maybe some cat food. The canned type. Puss'N'Boots would be good. That stuff always made me want to puke when I had a cat."

"You are fucking certifiable," said Byron Trumbo through gritted teeth.

Cordie nodded. "Okey-dokey, let's get going." She gestured toward the hole in the wall.

"You just expect me to hike down that lava tube with you until we find ghosts?"

"That's the plan," said Cordie, plucking a black gob of marmite from the wet bangs in front of her eyes.

"Why me?" said Trumbo.

"The rules say there's gotta be a man," said Cordie. "You seemed available. I'm sorry it's that way, but that's it. Life tends to be like that."

Trumbo considered this bit of philosophy for a moment and then tensed his muscles in preparation for a leap at her fat throat.

"Don't even think about it, By," said the little woman, holding the pistol steady.

Knotting his fists, Trumbo stepped through the broken wall into the cavern. "It's pitch-dark in here," he said, hearing the mild echoes.

"I'm coming," said Cordie.

Above and outside, in the earth, in the sky, and beneath the sea, the battle is joined.

The volcano Mauna Loa rises an impressive 13,677 feet above sea level, but beneath the waves the bulk of the mountain extends another 18,000 feet to the seabed. If the ocean were to be removed, Mauna Loa would stand as the 32,000-foot mountain it is, the highest peak on planet Earth. Kilauea, now in full eruption with its taller sister, Mauna Loa, would not stand at its modest 4,075-foot level but would be revealed as the 22,000-foot volcanic cone it truly is.

Now, from the permanent reservoir of seething magma more

than seven miles beneath the summit of Mauna Loa, internal forces squeeze great volumes of lava upward through rock so permeated by fissures that it resembles a giant sponge. This ejaculation of molten flame is so powerful that it triggers earthquakes across the Big Island and more than thirty miles out to sea.

In the Mauna Pele Resort, the tremors are strong enough to send earthquake-savvy Japanese scurrying to doorways while Will Bryant tries to contact either his boss or Dr. Hastings at the Volcano Observatory via cellular phone or radio. Neither answers. At the Volcano Observatory, Hastings and a score of other scientists are monitoring instruments showing the strongest earthquake readings since 1935 and the strongest simultaneous eruption of Mauna Loa and Kilauea since scientists began observing such proceedings on the island in 1832.

Along the southwest rift zone where the Mauna Pele Resort now lies, more than a dozen new flank eruptions are recorded in less than a dozen minutes as the tremendous pressure rising to the Mauna Loa caldera vents itself along fault lines which have long lain cold and dormant. While not explosive in the twenty-megaton range of Washington State's Mount St. Helens eruption of 1980 or the 1985 eruption of Nevada del Ruiz in Colombia, which killed more than 23,000 people, this lateral eruption is powerful enough to send lava geysering down the southwest slope of Mauna Loa in innumerable fountains, some rising 2,000 feet into the night sky.

Gases exceeding 2,100 degrees Fahrenheit are vented along the thirteen-mile fissure and great clouds of sulfurous steam billow among the flames and lava flows. Tens of thousands of strands of fibrous, silica Pele's hair drift on the heated updrafts and descend on the tropical forests and fern fields. Rock fragments are blasted miles into the air, the heaviest ones tumbling in the vicinity of the fissure but the lighter pebbles and particles traveling hundreds of miles out to sea on the resulting ash clouds.

All along the southwest rift zone running to the sea, ancient lava tubes are filling with fresh magma. Starting at the 12,000-foot level and running to the sea, rock made porous by tens of thousands of years of cooling and shifting is suddenly filled with lava and agitated by earthquake. Water-saturated rock miles above the lava reservoir explodes in a superheated instant. Steam clouds vie with sulfur clouds as the explosions continue down the thirteen-mile rift zone like a string of giant firecrackers. Over 700,000 cubic yards of lava is flowing, setting a new Volcano Observatory record.

In front of this lateral flow, forests burn. Highways disappear under 30-foot lava flows moving faster than a man can run. Houses vaporize. Abandoned cars and trucks rise like toys on the magma stream and are carried along at thirty-five miles per hour, paint steaming away in a toxic instant, interiors bursting into flame and gas tanks igniting in a minor counterpoint to the fountaining lava all along the flow.

Against this, Kamapua'a's tropical disturbance crashes onto the flaming coast like a stream from a garden hose turned against a three-alarm fire. Steam rises in ten thousand points where the monsoon downpour meets overflowing lava tubes, but mere rainwater will take millennia to prevail against molten rock sizzling along at 2,000 degrees. A tsunami might quench some of the flames, but Pele has planned the night's eruptions so that while the earthquakes are terrible to feel, no tsunami is created. Twenty-foot waves crash against the flaming cliffs, but no tidal wave arrives.

As part of Kamapua'a's age-old strategy, thousands of wild pigs are loosed on the land to eat the shrubs and vegetation, denying Pele fuel for her fires. Most of these pigs die in the first thirty minutes of this new lateral eruption, swallowed by carefully crafted tendrils of lava. Amidst the sulfur stench and steam roar, the night is filled with the *luau* scent of roasted pork.

Standing in the doorframes of the banquet hall of the Presidential Suite of the Mauna Pele, Hiroshe Sato watches the lava tendrils burning their way to the sea less than five hundred yards south of the resort and whispers softly to himself. "Hory shit," he says over and over.

"I think we're getting close," said Cordie. The tunnels had seemed to stretch for miles, one lava tube connecting with another until neither Cordie nor the billionaire had the foggiest idea of which direction they were heading. Each expected to arrive at the sea at any moment, or tumble into the volcano caldera.

Instead, they reached a point where the walls began glowing.

"This is a good sign," said Cordie, patting the tote bag she carried over her bare shoulder. "Kidder's journal says that everything glows in ghost country."

"Great," said Trumbo. His feet were scratched to shreds. His skin crawled with the stinking concoction she had insisted he smear on himself. Four or five times they had been thrown from their feet by earthquakes that dropped rocks and dust from the ceiling of the lava tube. Each second that passed, Trumbo expected a wall of lava to come barreling into them. "Ghost country," he said. "Just great."

The ghosts, when they found them, were somewhat of an anticlimax. Glowing forms—almost transparent, almost human-shaped—moved in pairs and small groups. As the cavern widened, hundreds of the spirits were visible—playing games, lying together, eating *poi*, gambling. "Just like in the book," Cordie said.

Spirits floated toward them and then swerved away as they came within range of the stench. Trumbo did not blame them.

Cordie came close, the pistol lowered, and whispered in Trumbo's ear. "We have to be quiet from now on. They don't talk. Or if they do, our ears can't hear them."

Trumbo nodded, thinking that he could grab the woman's arm and take the gun away from her now. *Why? We've got to get what we came for and get the hell out of here.* Despite himself, Trumbo had begun to admire the courageous little woman whose naked form he was getting used to. He realized that she was more dumpy muscle than fat, and that behind those tiny little eyes burned a will hotter than the lava that would probably soon consume both of them. *Fuck it,* thought Trumbo. Everybody had to die. This would be an unusual way to go. He was just sorry that he hadn't concluded the deal on the Mauna Pele. If he had to die, it would be better to die with that deal done.

The ghosts continued their play and work and silent conversations. All the ghostly forms were nude, male and female, and there were few children visible. Trumbo thought, *If this is the afterlife, I'll pass. It looks like Friday night in Philadelphia.*

"There!" whispered Cordie, almost hissing in his ear.

It took Trumbo a minute to see what she was pointing at. Then he noticed them in a side cavern—several spirits who looked more *haole* than the rest. It took Trumbo another minute to realize what these ghosts were up to: Dillon's ghost and Fredrickson's ghost and his ex-bodyguard, Briggs, were playing craps with invisible dice with three pudgy guys who looked like New Jersey car dealers. One of them seemed to be missing a hand. Sunny Takahashi's spirit appeared to be making side bets with invisible money. Some tourist types were putting with invisible putters and eating invisible food at an invisible table. The Mauna Pele's former astronomer sat reading an invisible magazine while two other middle-aged guys sat watching an invisible television, impatiently changing channels with invisible remote controls.

The spirit of Eleanor Perry stood alone, wandering, as if seeking a way out.

"Nell," whispered Cordie, and crossed the cavern to her. It took less than a minute to uncork the wine bottle and contain the spirit. The bottle seemed filled with smoke.

"Touch the others," whispered Cordie, "and they'll follow you out. But I think you have to capture the ones you want to put back in their bodies." She handed Trumbo the extra bottle.

Trumbo hesitated. Briggs and Fredrickson had served him well. Dillon hadn't really been killed, it appeared, just robbed of his soul. The astronomer and the other employees he recognized here had not deserved their fate. Sunny Takahashi's return meant money.

Trumbo took the Gallo bottle and squeezed Sunny into it. It was not as difficult as he would have imagined. All the while, however, the bearded ghost of Dillon flitted around him like a pesky fly. Finally Trumbo relented and uncorked the bottle. "Look," he whispered, "if there's room, I don't mind if . . ." The spirit flowed in like water into a boot.

Trumbo dropped the smoke-filled bottle into Cordie's tote bag. "Let's get the fuck out of here," he whispered, knowing full well that they would never find their way out via the route they had taken in.

Cordie nodded and turned. They both froze.

Kamapua'a stood blocking their way. The giant hog was grinning.

June 23, 1866, Aboard the U.S.S. *Boomerang*—

I read over my breathless, scribbled entries of less than a week ago and cannot believe that I wrote them. Those words and events belong to a different person, a different life.

The steam propeller has just put out from the Kona-Kawaihae docks on its slow voyage to Lahaina, where I expect to meet friends and take a week of rest at their upland plantation before going on to Honolulu and thence to the Orient via the Pacific Mail Steamer *Costa Rica*. Mr. Clemens and Reverend Haymark departed yesterday for Honolulu on the inter-island packet *Kilauea*, Reverend Haymark back to his mission on Oahu, and Mr. Clemens back to California via Honolulu. He has booked passage on the sailing ship *Smyrniote*, and Mr. Clemens informed me that he has full confidence that he shall reach San Francisco, since no ship with such an odd name would be welcome in Davy Jones's Locker.

Of the hours and days immediately after our rescue of Reverend Haymark, my memory is hazy, at best. I do not even recall penning those fantastic lines which precede this entry in my journal. The events of the resurrection of our comrade are dreamlike . . . no, beyond dreamlike . . . removed, as if they occurred to a fictional character.

I remember our arrival in Kona. I remember Mr. Clemens's proposal of marriage two evenings ago as we stood on the dock and watched the sunset. I remember my refusal.

My friend was hurt. I hurt for him. I remember removing my glove and touching his cheek gently. "May I ask why you cannot consider this offer, Miss Stewart?" he said formally, the hurt audible in his voice.

"Sam," I said softly. It was the only time I had ever or would ever use his proper name. "It is not that I do not wish to marry you . . . or that I do not love you . . . only that I *may* not marry you."

I saw the confusion in his face.

"When the old woman touched me," I began, knowing correctly that I would not be able to explain, "I felt . . . something. My destiny. I must travel and write and make a name for myself in the world, however small a name, and this would not be possible were I to become Mrs. Samuel Langhorne Clemens." I smiled then. "Or even Mrs. Thomas Jefferson Snodgrass or Mrs. Mark Twain."

My correspondent friend and true companion did not return the smile. "I do not understand," he said. "I wish to write. I wish to travel. I have already prepared a proposal to my newspaper that I travel around the world and send back the type of correspondence I have written here in the Sandwich Islands. Why could we not enjoy these things together while pursuing our separate professions, Miss Stewart?"

I could only sigh. How to explain to this fine, courageous man that he was a *man*—all things were possible for him—while I was a *woman*, and must *make* possible those things I wished to have.

But I admit that at that second, I wished to have him. Samuel. My brave companion. My love.

"I shall love you forever," he said next, as the sun fell beneath the earth's flat line somewhere toward the Orient. "I shall never marry another."

I touched his cheek again. How to explain to him that I was certain—I *knew*—that the fate he described for himself would be mine, while he would almost certainly choose another within a short time. His need for companionship was as tangible as the soft touch of his cheek against my palm.

I realize that I am dwelling on these personal things at the expense of describing Reverend Haymark's unceasing amazement at being alive, or our fantastic trek up the Kona Coast amidst fire and flame and earthquake, or the equal amazement of the Christian inhabitants of Kona and Kawaihae at our survival.

By tacit agreement, none of us discussed our true adventure. No mention was made of Pele or speaking hogs or of the Ghost Kingdom of Milu. The Sandwich Islands do not have a bedlam set aside yet—there is no formal asylum—but there are many isolated places they could have marooned us should we have spoken such things aloud.

I do not feel like writing about those hours and days after the resurrection and our return. I will mention how bereft I felt when I turned in that grass hut and found the old woman gone. I knew that I would be connected to her for the rest of my life—indeed, I suspect that my descendents, the female ones at least—shall share some such connection for generations to come. I mourned her leaving.

I mourned the departure of my one life's love yesterday. Mr. Clemens and I shook hands quite formally on the dock, with Reverend Haymark and the dozens of others watching. But I saw the emotion in his eyes. I trust that he saw the tears in mine.

There are tears in my eyes at this moment. I will not allow this. I will stop writing until I regain control.

A cockroach the size of a dinner spoon just marched from the pillow on my berth to the rough bit of wool they call a blanket. It watches me with beady eyes, sensing that I fear cockroaches and cannot bring myself to touch it.

It is wrong. I have faced beadier eyes and fiercer opponents. This vermin's days and moments are numbered.

Freedom from fear is a heady thing, stronger than whiskey, and it bodes ill for cockroaches here and everywhere on this wide planet.

"Byron," said the hog, "so nice of you to drop in." Its snout thrust in Cordie's direction. "Is this an offering to me?"

Trump glanced at Cordie and then back at the pig. "Sure," he said.

The hog made a sound in its massive throat. "I'll eat it in a moment. First, we have business to do."

Trumbo waited.

"I see you helped yourself to Sunny's soul," said Kamapua'a.

Trumbo shrugged. "It seemed to be self-serve."

The growling from the monster hog's belly might have been a chuckle. "Fine, fine," it said. "But there is still a price."

"My soul?" said the billionaire.

"Fuck your soul," said the hog. "I'm talking a trade."

Trumbo's eyebrows twitched, but he remained silent.

"When I best that bitch Pele and regain my control of this island," continued Kamapua'a, "I plan to take on human form for a decade or two. I will be free to roam the earth again. I have been watching from my underground cell as things have changed on the surface. In mortal form, I could be a chieftain of one of these tribes again, but I have other plans."

"A trade," said Trumbo.

The hog smiled more broadly. "Precisely." It took two steps closer, its trotters echoing on the hard basalt. Cordie could see the moisture on its broad snout and feel the warm bellows of its breath. "We can do a deal, Byron," it said in a conspiratory, male whisper. "You and I."

"Why should I?" said Trumbo.

The giant hog took another step closer. Its breath was unbelievably foul. "Because otherwise I will chew your guts and bones and set your miserable soul in the foulest reaches of this cave for all eternity," said the hog, its deep voice rising.

"OK," said Trumbo. "I'm listening."

The hog took half a step back. "You take Sunny's useless little *uhane* back to the Japanese, do the deal, and get your three hundred million dollars," the creature said. "You return here and we do a trade."

"What kind of trade?" asked Trumbo. "You want the money?"

The hog grunted. "The miserable *kahuna* summoned us to destroy you," it said. "But we had no intention of doing so. It is Pele whom I wish to destroy. You and I are alike, Byron. We were born to dominate. Born to subdue . . . women . . . the land. I understand your urge to bulldoze and rape. I understand it well. I don't want your money."

Trumbo nodded thoughtfully for a moment. "I still don't see what we'd be trading," he said at last.

Kamapua'a showed his grin. His eight eyes were bright. "We trade places for a while, Byron my friend. I become you. You become me."

Trumbo's face remained expressionless. "Let me get this straight . . . the deal you're offering me is that we trade places? That you get my body and I get yours?"

The hog nodded.

"You get to be a handsome billionaire with homes and women on three continents," continued Byron Trumbo, "and I get to spend a couple of decades as a giant, smelly pig living in a cave in Hawaii. Is that the deal?"

Kamapua'a's grin remained in place. "That's the deal, Byron."

Trumbo nodded. "And why the hell should I be interested in a deal like that?"

"First," grunted the pig in the voice that seemed to come from his belly, "you will be allowed to live. I will not devour your guts and bones. Second, I guarantee you that in my fifteen or twenty years in your body, I will enlarge your financial empire to a scale never before seen on this planet. You came down here as a man on the skids . . . desperately trying to shore up your tumbling empire by selling this miserable hotel for a few hundred million dollars. When you return to your body, you will *own* the world, Byron Trumbo. And that is not a figure of speech."

"I'll end up owning the world if I stay in my own body," said Trumbo.

The hog grunted. "Thirdly," he continued as if Byron had not spoken, "while you are King of the Underworld, you will have unlimited power over the ghosts and demons in this world. You will have power over the elements above, commanding the lightning, the tide, and the great tsunamis. You will taste power the likes of which you currently cannot dream of."

Trumbo rubbed his cheek. "Will I have all the powers you have now?"

Kamapua'a shook his great, bristled head. "I am not a fool, Byron. If you assumed all of my powers, you could cancel our deal anytime you wished and establish yourself as king of the world above. No, I will need the majority of my powers while in your body, using them to make you rich and famous beyond your wildest dreams. But I assure you that being Kamapua'a, lord of the

Underworld and of all he surveys, will be the high point of your life. And—as I say—when you return to your mortal form, you will inherit the riches and powers I have amassed for you."

"What if you decide to stay human forever?" asked Trumbo.

"No, no, no," grumbled the hog. "Your mortal form is acceptable, but it is mortal. I have no wish to die. I am a god."

"That's another point," said Trumbo. "My body will be old if you sublet it for two decades . . . almost sixty."

The hog's teeth gleamed slick in the dim light. "At the height of your powers, Byron. I will treat your mortal form with greater care than you do now. It will be fit, tuned to a fighting edge . . . after all, I would be disappointed if you wasted the empire I will earn for you. And you should be reminded that your brief stint as a god will prepare you for greater things than any mortal has ever achieved on the earth above."

"So that's it?" said Trumbo. "That's the deal?"

"That's the deal," said Kamapua'a. "If you say no, you die here and now and your soul will rot down here forever. If you say yes, you gain illimitable power and wealth and taste the magnificence of being a god. What do you say, Byron Trumbo?"

Trumbo seemed lost in thought for a long moment. When he looked up, his face showed resolve. "Well," he said, "since you put it that way, I say fuck you."

Cordie would not have imagined that a hog's face could show amazement. This one did.

"Fuck you and the sow you rode in on," said Trumbo for good measure.

The giant pig actually bellowed, its roar echoing from the lava tube ceiling. "Why have you cast all away to deny me, mortal?"

Byron Trumbo shrugged. "I was never that fond of bacon," he said.

The hog showed all of his large teeth. "I will take great pleasure in devouring both of you," it growled. "And then I will devour your ghosts."

"Look!" said Cordie, pointing beyond the hog.

The monster glanced over its own bristled back. The young Hawaiian woman who stood twenty paces away was not a ghost—

she was barely a woman, more a beautiful girl—but her dark eyes were bright and hard.

Kamapua'a snorted. "Be gone, bitch," the hog said to Pele. "You have no power here. This is my domain. These mortals are my dinner."

The young Hawaiian woman did not move or blink.

"Now," said Kamapua'a, returning his attention to Trumbo and Cordie. "Die." The monstrous form trotted forward on its little pig legs.

Cordie stepped between Trumbo and the wall of pig flesh, fumbled in her bag, and came out with her revolver. She pulled the hammer back just as the hog grunted another laugh.

"You must be joking," came the belly rumble. The thing wriggled its snout and the pistol flew from Cordie's hands, clattering against the cave wall. The pig trotted toward Cordie, its face and teeth filling her vision.

An earthquake threw both Cordie and Trumbo to the stone floor. Even the giant hog stopped and braced itself on its tiny hooves. The monster snarled over its shoulder at the silent Hawaiian woman. "*Damn* you, bitch. I tell you, you have no power here. I will deal with you in a moment."

Byron Trumbo and Cordie heard the rumble before they felt the heat. Something was rushing down the lava tube at them with the speed and noise of a freight train. Suddenly, an orange glow illuminated the walls.

"Lava!" cried Trumbo, and turned to run. There was no time.

Kamapua'a laughed and showed his backside to Pele. "Do what you want, bitch. They will die by my teeth before your pitiful fire reaches us." The hog snarled and leapt at Cordie.

Cordie had lifted out the wine bottle carrying Eleanor's soul, and now she uncorked it. Eleanor's form flowed out and around like smoke in a vortex.

The hog skidded to a stop on the rough floor. Other ghosts swirled and fluttered now, agitated by the approaching lava. The orange glow had intensified and the heat was terrible.

"*Move,* damn you!" bellowed the hog as Eleanor's ghost

swirled between him and Cordie. Less than a foot separated the hog's gnashing molars and Cordie's face, but the ghostly shape twisted and blocked his every lunge.

"You are forbidden to interfere with her," said Cordie, her voice small. "Pele has so commanded."

Kamapua'a roared in earnest then, and pieces of the cave ceiling tumbled down. The hog wheeled and lunged toward the stunned Byron Trumbo. The glow of the advancing lava illuminated the cave like an orange searchlight.

Eleanor's ghost shifted like quicksilver, interposing itself between the monster and the man. Again, Kamapua'a had to slide to a halt rather than violate the unbreakable *kapu* of Goddess Pele. The thing turned back to Cordie, who stood unprotected. The lava became visible behind her, swirling around the bend in a blast-furnace tsunami of molten rock.

"Quickly," said the young Hawaiian woman. "To my side."

Cordie bolted to the left of the hog, Trumbo to the right. Kamapua'a started to swing toward Cordie, the ghost of Eleanor blocked him; he reversed himself to catch Trumbo in his teeth, but again the smoky ghost form interdicted him. The hog's trotters slammed and echoed on stone. Both mortals were too fast. By the time the monstrous pig had wheeled on its oddly delicate little legs, both Cordie and the billionaire had sprinted the last twenty paces and were standing next to the Hawaiian girl.

"NO!" screamed the hog and the echo made the cavern shake worse than any earthquake. Kamapua'a put his massive head down, pawed the earth, and charged like an oversized bull in an undersized arena. Cordie and Trumbo both flinched, but the monster smashed into an invisible barrier three feet from the beautiful Hawaiian maiden.

The girl raised her hands. Her voice was as lovely as her aspect.

"O the top of Kilauea!
O the five ledges of the pit!
The heaven wakes up.
The earth is awake.

The sea is awake.
I, Pele, am the goddess.
This work is mine.
I bring the fire.
I bring the flame of life.
E ala e! Flames awake! Lava arise!
The *kapu* of rape and death is over.
It is lifted.
It is flown away.''

The *haole* ghosts flitted around Pele, Cordie, and Trumbo like a swirl of smoke, filling the air around them. Eleanor's ghost flowed back into its waiting wine bottle. Cordie slammed the cork back in. Kamapua'a bellowed again. Rocks tumbled and fissures opened. The wall of lava, when it covered the last dozen yards, arrived almost too quickly to be seen.

Cordie saw the bristles on the hog burst into flame in the second before the lava enveloped him, and then she was crouching, closing her eyes, feeling the heat of the molten rock and wondering that her last thoughts were not more important than *Shit!*

The lava flowed around them, the heat terrible but not the killing stroke it should have been. Cordie heard the monster hog's final scream but did not see it volatilized or borne away by the rushing lava stream. Magma surrounded their invisible shell of a barrier, flowing past in black and orange chunks. There was an explosion of steam behind them as the lava struck the ocean.

Then they were rising, the girl's arms raised, rising on a smooth, invisible elevator, passing up through the fissure and out the expanded blowhole as if such things were commonplace.

The girl lowered her hands. Cordie blinked and felt the sea breeze, smelled the rain. The barrier was gone. Behind and to the south, lava flowed and steam hissed, but there was nothing between them and the Mauna Pele a few hundred yards to the north.

"Come with me," Cordie said to the child and goddess. "I need your help." She lifted the bottle with its smoky soul.

The young woman shook her head. "You have the words."

She reached out and touched Cordie Cooke Stumpf's head. "You belong to the sisterhood of Pele. Go."

Byron Trumbo started to go but found that his legs were not ready. He sat down heavily on the smooth rock.

Cordie crouched next to him. "You all right?"

"Yeah." Trumbo saw spots.

"Put your head between your knees. That's better."

Trumbo stayed in that position until the spots receded. "It's probably the goddamn smell," he said, raising his face to the rain. "Hey, where is she?"

Cordie looked over her shoulder. The young woman was gone.

"She's up there," said Cordie, pointing to the orange glow that was the volcano. "Come on, I'll give you a hand." She pulled Trumbo to his feet.

"We'll bring Eleanor back," said Cordie, "and then I'll help you with your Japanese friend."

Trumbo shook his head. "Hell of a parlor trick. If we could patent it, we'd make a fortune."

"You've got a fortune," Cordie reminded him.

Byron Trumbo grunted. "Had one. The Japs are probably halfway to Tokyo by now."

Cordie made a fist and tapped Trumbo on the shoulder. "Are you saying you aren't capable of making a million bucks again even if you're broke tomorrow?"

Trumbo hesitated only a second. "Hell no," he said. "I know I could."

"And it'd be fun, wouldn't it?" she said.

Trumbo did not answer but a small smile turned into a grin. They began walking toward the Big Hale. After a moment, he said, "Jesus Christ, but we smell."

Cordie nodded. "Keep walkin'. The rain'll wash the worst of the stink off. We'll take a shower when we get to the hotel."

"I wish we had some clothes," said Trumbo, stepping lightly in his bare feet.

Cordie grinned at him. "You look all right naked," she said. "For a man."

TWENTY-THREE

The sky is established.
The earth is established.
Fastened and fastened,
Always holding together,
Entangled in obscurity,
Near each other a group of islands
Spreads out like a flock of birds.
Leaping up are the divided places.
Lifted far up are the heavens.
Polished by the striking,
Lamps rest in the sky.
Presently the clouds move,
The great sun rises in splendor,
Mankind arises to pleasure,
The moving sky is above.
—from the Kumulipo, creation chant

Cordie and Eleanor slept late, oblivious to the sunrise sounds of helicopters landing and taking off and landing again. It was the singing of birds that finally awakened them.

Eleanor came in from the couch to where Cordie was sprawled on the king-sized bed. Cordie was still dressed in the wrinkled shirt and jeans she had pulled on the night before. "Good morning," Eleanor said.

Cordie forced one eye open. Eleanor handed her a hot cup of coffee.

"Where did you find this?" Cordie asked, gratefully accepting the white mug.

"There's a coffeemaker in your kitchen. Some individual filter packs." Eleanor touched her head. "What a headache."

"Yeah," said Cordie, looking at her friend. "Do you remember much of . . . much of what happened?"

Eleanor managed a smile. "Of being dead, you mean? Of
coming back to life?" The smile faded. "No. Just the dreamlike
images we talked about last night . . . this morning . . . whatever."

"Besides the headache, how do you feel?" said Cordie.

Eleanor took stock. "Pretty good. The soles of my feet are
sore."

Cordie grunted. "I had to slap them pretty hard to get your
uhane back in there. It didn't want to go."

Eleanor shook her head. "You know what's strange? I never
believed in the soul or the afterlife."

"Me neither," said Cordie.

"You know what's stranger?" said Eleanor. "I still don't."

Cordie sipped her coffee. "I know what you mean, Nell. It's
like we were caught up in somebody else's universe here for a
while. It's not like it's . . . real. Universal. Whatever."

"I had the thought when I woke up," said Eleanor, "that it
might be hard for me to go back to teaching the Enlightenment.
But it won't. It may mean more to me now."

Cordie sipped her coffee.

"What do you say I get dressed and we see what's left of this
place?" said Eleanor.

"Good idea," said Cordie. She looked down at her wrinkled
clothes. "I'm dressed, but I guess I could take a shower and find
some fresher clothes."

"That's an interesting cologne you're wearing," said Eleanor.

Cordie made a face. "Eau de garlic anchovy Limburger," she
said. "Guaranteed to repel ghosts."

Eleanor stood holding the door. "I haven't really thanked
you. I mean, I don't know how . . ."

Cordie cut her off. "You know you don't have to, Nell. You
know."

Eleanor nodded. "Midwives. We are there when the other is in pain and needs us."

"Yeah," said Cordie, sipping the last of the dark brew. "Jesus, Nell, you make shitty coffee."

They toured the hotel together. The first floor was a riot of mud and tumbled furniture. The grounds were littered with fallen branches and trampled flowers. Lava flows were visible less than a quarter of a mile to the south and north, but the hotel grounds appeared to have survived intact, although bruised by the storm.

Workers and emergency crews swarmed everywhere, their yellow hard hats gleaming in the morning sun. A wind from the north had blown the ash cloud far south out to sea, although occasionally they caught the whiff of sulfur above the fresh scent of the ocean.

Television news anchors did stand-ups in front of the Mauna Pele's entrance. Microphones were thrust at them, but Cordie and Eleanor waved them off and went upstairs past sleepy security men.

They found Byron Trumbo in the ruins of the long banquet hall. Whatever had come through here had left a mess. The billionaire was looking out over the terrace. He was wearing shorts, a crisp Hawaiian shirt, and sandals. Will Bryant was with him.

"Hey, By," said Cordie.

Trumbo gave her a look. "I haven't forgotten last night."

Cordie smiled. "I wouldn't think so. I don't plan to. How's Paul?"

"They airlifted him out at first light," said Will Bryant. The assistant was dressed in a white linen suit that made Eleanor think of Mark Twain.

"How was he?" asked Eleanor.

"The medics said he'd be all right," said Bryant. "We've got all the injured out now. No fatalities last night."

"What about Caitlin, Maya, and Bicki?" asked Trumbo. "They make it through the carnage last night?"

"Yes," said Will Bryant.

"Shit," said Trumbo.

"They left together on Maya's jet at sunrise," said Trumbo's assistant. "They had Jimmy Kahekili with them."

"The giant Hawaiian?" said Trumbo. "Why?"

"They said something about paying the Hawaiian Liberation Front to assassinate you," said Will Bryant.

Byron Trumbo grunted.

Eleanor looked around. "What about the Japanese?"

"They were out of here *before* the sun came up," said Trumbo. "They're halfway across the Pacific by now."

"No deal?" said Cordie.

Byron Trumbo laughed. "They were talking about suing me for thirty-five million dollars."

"What spooked them in the end?" asked Eleanor. "The earthquake? The riot here? The lava flows coming so close?"

Trumbo grinned. "None of those things, really. Cordie, you remember when we slapped Sunny Takahashi's ghost back in his body?"

"Sure." Cordie was drinking her second cup of coffee.

"Well, I poured it out of that Gallo bottle in such a hurry, I forgot that there were two spirits in there. Later, when we did Dillon, remember how hard it was to get that fucking ghost in the feet?"

"Yeah," said Cordie.

Will Bryant looked at Eleanor. "Are sane people supposed to listen to things like this?"

"Don't ask me," said Eleanor. "I've been there."

"What about the ghost stuff?" said Cordie. She had changed into a white, cotton dress that looked surprisingly good on her.

"We got the wrong ghosts in the wrong bodies," said Trumbo. "So I dragged Sunny back to his loving friends, figuring Sato would sign anything after that, and all of a sudden Takahashi's voice starts talking like Dillon. Then Dillon comes in and starts yammering Japanese. And then all hell broke loose."

The four considered the morning light on the surviving coconut palms for a moment.

"Did you get them straightened out?" said Cordie.

"Nah," said Trumbo, walking over to the railing and stretching. "Both Dillon and Sunny decided they liked the new bodies. They're going to try them out for a while."

Will Bryant shook his head.

Trumbo turned to look at his assistant. "Didn't I fire your ass last night?"

"Well, actually, no," said Bryant. "After the Japanese freaked out and you and I had a few drinks, you told me that you thought of me like your own son."

"Bullshit," said Trumbo.

"I'm sure," said Will Bryant. "But you said it. You also said that anyone who would have agreed to go into that cave with a two-ton pig was too stupid to work for you, so I wasn't fired."

Trumbo scratched his head. "Shit."

Eleanor looked at the wreckage of the banquet. "What does this mean, Mr. Trumbo? Financially, I mean."

Trumbo shrugged. "Financially? Financially, I guess it means that I'm fucked up the ass. I guess it means that my wife will have my guts for garters and the Mauna Pele, too. I guess it means that I have to start all over, not from scratch, but from bankruptcy court." Suddenly he grinned at Cordie. "Not the worst fate, huh?"

Cordie set her coffee cup down. "Not the worst fate, By. But not the only choice, either. What was Sato's group offering when it got down to the short strokes? About three hundred million?"

Trumbo blinked. "Yeah. So?"

"I'll offer three hundred and twenty-five million and sign the papers this afternoon."

Byron Trumbo started to laugh and then stopped. "Are you going to pay cash?"

"If you like, although my people suggest a mixture of cash and stock options would work better for both of us."

Eleanor watched, puzzled, as Will Bryant twitched as if touched by a cattle prod. "Mrs. Stumpf from Chicago . . . Chicago . . . Cooke? Is it Cooke?"

"What?" said Eleanor, watching the sudden dawning of amazement on first Bryant's face and then Trumbo's. "What?"

"Cooke Removal Systems of Chicago," said Trumbo, slapping his forehead. "The biggest goddamn garbage business in North America. They serve every college between Nebraska and Vermont and half the big cities. Stumpf . . . whatshisname . . . he died a while ago and his wife ran the business. Rumor said that she always had."

"Rumor is right," said Cordie.

"It was sold just a couple of months ago," said Will Bryant. "A year after it went public. Three quarters of a billion dollars from Richie-Warner-Matsu."

"That was just the cash part," said Cordie. She leaned on the railing next to the stunned-looking Trumbo. "So what do you say, By? My people tell me that three hundred twenty-five is in the ballpark for this place." She looked around. "Even allowing for cleanup."

Trumbo's mouth opened. He closed it.

Eleanor spoke. "Cordie, do you . . . I mean, do you really want to go into the hotel business?"

"Hell no," said Cordie. "That would bore the panties off me. But remember what I said about how this would make a good hospital-slash-research center for cancer patients?"

"Hospital?" said Trumbo flatly. *"Hospital?"*

Cordie shrugged. "Every damn cancer treatment center in America seems to be in the slushy old rust belt. Why not have a place where people can get a tan while they get helped . . . even if they're dying?"

"Why not indeed," said Will Bryant to himself.

"Besides," said Cordie, "the economy of this island's in the crapper. It's never going to get better when the locals are just hired to be waiters and busboys and laundry people. If the Mauna Pele were an international oncology clinic and medical training center, maybe some of these local boys and girls would consider a career in medicine. Hell, I bet Byron Trumbo, Incorporated, would probably agree to pitching in a scholarship or two if the deal depended on it."

Trumbo looked at her.

"Well, what do you say, By?" said Cordie. "My lawyers should

be flying in by lunch. You want to draw up the papers by then?''
She held out her large, callused hand.

Trumbo looked at the hand, looked at Will Bryant, looked
back at the hand, and shook it.

As the two men conferred, Eleanor and Cordie took their refilled coffee cups and went downstairs and down the littered path
toward the beach. Once on the sand, they stopped to enjoy the
sight of the sunlight dancing on the clean water and the slow rolling of the surf.

"This will be a beautiful place to recover," said Eleanor.

Cordie only nodded.

"Do you have any worries about . . ." Eleanor gestured toward
the south.

"Kamapua'a?" said Cordie. "Pana-ewa? Ku? Nanaue 'the
shark-man?''

"Yes," said Eleanor. "All of them."

"Naw," said Cordie. She showed her small teeth in a smile. "I
don't think they'll want to fuck with the sisterhood of Pele again
for a few centuries at least."

Eleanor smiled and sipped her coffee. The sunlight was
bright and fierce against her skin. She slipped her sandals off to
dig her toes in the warming sand.

"Nell, you decided what you're gonna do for the next few days?"

"Yes," said Eleanor. "I came for a week's vacation. I don't
feel I've had it yet. I'm going to ask the new owner if I can extend
my stay until then."

Cordie rubbed her lip. "I have a feeling the new owner may
even comp you a room. She may even suggest we go swimming
later and have a drink at the Shipwreck Bar this afternoon to shoot
the shit."

Cordie kicked off her shoes and the two women began walking down the curving line of white beach, sipping coffee as they
went. Eleanor squinted and did her best Bogie imitation, getting
the lisping voice almost right. "Louie," she said, "this may be the
beginning of a beautiful friendship."

"You bet your ass," said Cordie Stumpf, and skipped a pebble
across the line of surf into the quiet lagoon.

Letter found in the back of Aunt Kidder's journal:

June 18, 1905
21 Fifth Avenue
New York, New York

Miss Lorena Stewart
3279 W. Patton Blvd.
Hubbard, Ohio

Dear Miss Stewart:

It is with a great sense of guilt and some trepidation that I finally respond to your kind note of one year ago. As you know, it was just a year ago June fifth, on a Sunday evening in Florence, that I lost my dear Livy. You will also understand that not a day has passed in that intervening year that I have not wished to join her.

But as we both learned those many years ago in the beautiful Sandwich Islands, the living have their duties to the living, and your beautiful and generous note of last year reminded me of that forgotten fact.

In your letter, you asked that I tell you someday how Livy and I met and how we came to be married. That someday has arrived.

You may remember that after we parted, I convinced my newspaper to send me on a 'round-the-world' voyage, from which I sent my early and crude correspondences to amuse the unwashed multitudes. Well, it was while I was in the Holy Land that I made the acquaintance of a young man named Charley Langdon. Charley showed me an ivory miniature of his sister one day, and I promptly fell in love with her.

I saw her in the flesh for the first time the following December. She was slender and beautiful and girlish—she was both girl and woman. Two years later we were married.

This sounds easy enough, but true love is rarely that unobstructed. I had connived to spend a week with the Langdons but spent almost no time alone with Livy during that frustrating week. It was on the carriage returning me to the railway station that Fate struck with the heavy-handed blow we know she utilizes so well. It seems that the back seat had not been well fastened and, when the coachman touched up the horse with a whip, Charley and I went over the stern of the wagon backward. Charley was the only one legitimately injured, but I feigned concussion and swooned until they carried me into the house and forced enough brandy down my throat to choke an Irish horse, but it did not diminish my unconsciousness—I was taking care of that myself.

To make a long, sweet story modestly short, I managed to stay in that unconscious condition until Charley and his other sister ceased their ministrations and turned over the stroking and massaging of my insensate brow to Livy. This I endured for as long as I could until my eyelids fluttered open and Livy and I said hello for the first true time.

I got three days' extension out of that adventure, and it helped a good deal. By and by, Mr. Langdon asked me for letters of reference and I furnished them as best I could. When Livy's father read those letters there was a great deal of pause. Finally he said:

"What kind of people are these? Haven't you a friend in the world?"

"Apparently not," I replied.

"Then I'll be your friend. I know you better than they do. Take the girl."

The engagement ring was plain and of heavy gold, engraved with the date February 4, 1869. A year later I took it from her finger and prepared it to do service as a wedding ring by having the wedding date engraved inside—February 2, 1870. It was never again removed from her finger, even for a moment.

Last summer, in Italy, when death had restored her vanished youth to her sweet face and she lay fair and beautiful and looking as she had looked when she was a girl and a bride, they were going to take that ring from her finger to keep for the children. But I prevented that sacrilege. It is buried with her.

I tell you this, Miss Stewart, because over the decades when my dear Livy has asked—as all brides must eventually ask—if there had ever been a rival for her hand and affections, I eventually told her about us: about the aroma of sandalwood

coming down from the forests above the sea, about the light a
volcano makes and how pleasant it is to survive it, about our
dream of descending into death's kingdom to retrieve the uhane of
our minister friend.

It comforts me, somehow, to know without believing that Livy's
spirit awaits me somewhere.

And it has comforted me, Miss Stewart, to know that my
boylike disappointment at your refusal on my stammering proposal
that long-ago June day was misdirected. It has comforted and
pleased me over the years to read your wonderful travel books—I
believe that Unbeaten Tracks in Japan: An Ohio Lady's Visit to the
Court of Japan, An Ohio Lady's Life in the Rocky Mountains, and
Across the Wide Sahara by Camel and Moonlight were my
favorites, although I confess that I have waited in vain all these
years for your book on the Sandwich Islands.

I began one myself, you know. My first lectures were given on
the Sandwich Islands and, once having found such a rich vein, I
had every intention of mining it to death. In 1884 I began my
novel about the Islands—about the old kings and the old ways and
leprosy and idolatry, and shallow Christian missionaries and
strange pagan rituals, but by and by the story got shanghaied and
swallowed into a wilder tale that I called A Connecticut Yankee in
King Arthur's Court. But the Sandwich Islands tale is still around
here somewhere, and if these old bones and this old mind can
rouse themselves from their arthritic slumber, I shall dig it out by
and by and begin anew, as I did once on a long-laid-aside book
about a boy named Huckleberry. Perhaps I shall dictate the tale to
my daughter Jean, who lives with me now. Jean enjoys saying that
I never manage to shock her any longer.

Miss Stewart, I wander. What I meant to tell you, beyond the
repeated and sincere belated thank you for your sympathy and
kindness at the time of my loss this time last year, was how
pleasant the memories of our time together in those far-off isles
has become on this side of the ocean of memory.

While not the traveler that you have been, I have managed to
see a bit of this sad old world in my days since our days together,
and I must say that no alien land in all the world has had any

deep, strong charm for me but that one, no other land could so longingly and so beseechingly haunt me, sleeping and waking, through half a lifetime as that one has done. Other things leave me, but it abides; other things change, but it remains the same.

For me, Miss Stewart, its balmy airs are always blowing, its summer seas flashing in the sun, the pulsing of its surf-beat in my ear; I can see its garlanded crags, its leaping cascades, its plumy palms drowsing by the shore, its remote summits floating like islands above the cloud rack; I can feel the spirit of its woodland solitudes, I can hear the splash of its brooks; in my nostrils still lives the breath of flowers that perished almost forty years ago.

And in all these visions, Miss Stewart, I see your noble, indomitable visage. I hear your challenging laugh. I see both of us—young, innocent, uncorrupted and unbowed by time—and I wonder if, perhaps just if, that rather than a Christian heaven, our uhane might sensibly flee to the Sandwich Islands when liberated from these old and decrepit vessels.

For my part, I hope it is true. I do not believe it true, but I hope it true. For my part, I think that no prettier fleet of islands has ever set anchor anywhere else in this world, and I would welcome the opportunity to return there in different garb to introduce Livy to you and you to Livy. We would find us two hammocks for the first century or two and talk while we watched the sun sink down—that one intruder from other realms and persistent in suggestions of them—and allow ourselves to be tranced in luxury to sit in the perfumed air and forget that there was or ever had been any world but those enchanted islands.

Pray, do write, Miss Stewart. I know your prose style. I admire it. I look forward to further exposure to it.

Until that day, I remain—

Yr. Aging but Obedient Servant,

Samuel Langhorne Clemens